LINK

LINK

Wayne Williams

WAKING LION PRESS

ISBN 978-1-4341-0413-7
Published by Waking Lion Press
West Jordan, Utah 84081-6132

OVERVIEW

From time beyond memory they had travelled the galaxies searching for planetary systems suitable for the development of intelligent life. They called themselves *seeders*.

Their race was highly developed. They had evolved, grown and learned, just has had so many of the others who had gone before. However, they knew nothing of their origins. Over time the records of their beginnings had simply disappeared, lost in the seemingly infinite information they had accumulated during their travels. All they knew for certain was that for all of recorded history their mission had been the same: to seek out new worlds, and to ply their skills in the advancement of intelligence.

They were like farmers; caring for fields light years in size. They watched as planets under their care became fertile. They looked on with glad hearts as some planets thrived, and grieved when so many others failed to do so.

And when the time was right, when life in a system reached a level of development conducive to introduction of intelligence, it was their task to initiate that process.

It was also their task to monitor, to observe, and on rare occasions, to provide guidance and direction. They knew, from eons of experience, that to interfere was to deprive the "seedlings" of their freedom to control their own destinies. Only when a race had advanced sufficiently to recognize the existence of the

1

seeders would they make contact, and even then, only when the "seedlings" sought them out.

Thus they continued . . . sowing "seeds" throughout the galaxies, watching from afar as their "seedlings" endeavored to thrive. For millions and even billions of years they cultivated their fields, weeding out those that failed to thrive, nurturing those that did.

They watched, as a parent watches a child; rejoicing when the young one is successful, and grieving when it is not; being tempted to intervene, but refraining from doing so, lest that interference compromise the young ones' freedom to act for themselves.

SIMIAN 1

CHAPTER 1

The thin crescent of the moon descended slowly through cloud-strewn semi-darkness. Only small glimpses of it could be seen between leaves and branches as it made its slow retreat from the light. Overhead, stars which only minutes before had shown so boldly, now faded from view, yielding once again to the light growing in the east.

Sounds of the night gradually receded as creatures who flourished in darkness began retreating to their hiding places, making way for the growing cacophony of the day-dwellers.

Minutes before the sun broke the horizon; the simian family began to stir; yawning, stretching, young ones clinging to their mother's fur, whining softly to be fed. Adults and adolescents grunted greetings to one another, arising from nests constructed low in the trees the evening before.

From his nest at the periphery of the group, the young simian male watched as the ranking alpha male began his daily ritual, moving slowly among the family members, sniffing for signs of estrus among the females and casting warning glances at potential rivals. Then after assuring himself all was well, the alpha slowly and deliberately descended to the ground, casting glances this way and that, alert for signs of danger. The rest of the group then followed cautiously, spreading out, foraging for food, always keeping sight of one another.

Being one of the lower-ranking males, the young simian also descended, taking his place in the 'pecking order.' The infants, now full of mother's milk and the exuberance of youth, scampered about in the center of the group, playing, quarrelling, exploring the fascinating world into which they had so recently arrived. Thus began another seemingly typical day in the life of this simian family.

The family had arrived in this place several days earlier, attracted by the scent of ripening fruit. Since food was in abundance here, the family would remain in this location for several more days.

All had partaken, as was their wont. After everyone had eaten their fill, an air of contentment permeated the group. The more senior members drowsed contentedly in the shade, now and then swatting at insects that disrupted their rest. Mothers kept watch over their exuberant youngsters. Adolescent males wrestled about, tested themselves in mock combat.

Today, the young male avoided these confrontations, preferring to watch, rather than participate. As he sat watching, his primitive mind recalled the events of the previous day.

Yesterday the alpha had been challenged by another male, not one of the family. The challenger had made his presence known early in the day but hadn't immediately acted. Skirting the perimeter, he thrashed about screaming and throwing things, attempting intimidation while building his courage. The alpha had responded in kind but had stood his ground, forcing the challenger to commit. Finally the challenger, having reached the point at which he must either commit or retreat, moved forward cautiously, crossing the invisible boundary, the point of no return.

The ensuing battle was fast, furious, and violent. Both males charged each other and slammed together, hitting, biting and screaming.

All the others scrambled to give them way. In the confusion, one of the infants lost its grip on its mother, fell into the fray and was crushed. No one dared to attempt rescue, lest he too become a victim of the wild violence.

After only a few short minutes the battle was over. The challenger was soundly beaten. He retreated wounded into the tangled darkness of the jungle floor, and was not seen again.

Not seriously wounded, Alpha screamed his victory for all to hear. Only then did the others dare to venture closer. One by one, each family member approached the triumphant alpha. With eyes averted and heads lowered, each offered subservience, once again demonstrating their recognition of him as their leader.

As calm began to return within the group, the stricken infant's mother went to her broken baby and picked it up. The infant didn't respond. The mother didn't seem to understand. She held her baby to her breast and seemed confused when it didn't try to suckle. Throughout the remainder of the day she carried her baby. Several times she tried to elicit a response from the limp body, but to no avail. Others in the family seemed to recognize her plight, but none approached. All kept their distance, sensing her distress.

As daylight began to fade, the family returned once again to the safety of the trees. Each adult selected a fork in the branches and began pulling smaller leaf-laden branches together into a comfortable nest. Mothers gathered their young close. Infants clung to their mothers' fur, growing drowsy from the day's exertions and the warmth of mother's milk. Adolescents built nests around the periphery, forming a defensive circle.

The stricken mother carried the small lifeless form up into the trees where she built a nest to accommodate them both. She held her baby close as darkness descended. Sometime during the long night she discarded it, letting it fall the short distance to the ground. In the morning the body was nowhere to be found.

The young male's thoughts soon returned to the familiar routine he and all the others in the family adhered to; the continuous search for nourishment. They wandered about, attracted by the bright colors and alluring scent of the jungle's bounty. Toward evening, their bellies filled, the family began their lumbering assent back into the safety of the trees. They were the largest of the simian species. Adult males weighed just over one hundred pounds, females slightly less. Because they were so large, it was difficult for them to climb high into the trees, where the more supple leaf-covered branches were. Their smaller cousins, much more agile, occupied the upper branches.

After completing his nest, the young male lay down and turned onto his back, adjusting his position to avoid a sharp protruding limb. Calmly he watched as the fading light crept slowly into the west. Briefly his thoughts returned to the excitement of the previous day.

When the confrontation between the alpha and the challenger began, the young male had screamed and scurried about just as the others had done. He had watched the battle, filled with apprehension, just as he and the others had done so many times before. And when the battle ended, he and the family settled back into their usual routine. The alpha had strutted among them, once again asserting his dominance and, in so doing, helped to bring calm and stability back to the family.

As daylight slowly faded into darkness, the family settled once again in their newly constructed nests. A breeze gently stirred the branches as the heat from the jungle floor ascended into the cooling twilight. Mothers drew their young ones closer, drowsing quietly in the gathering darkness. The infants were the first to fall asleep, but the others weren't far behind.

The young simian lay there as he had done so many times before, snuggled comfortably in his nest. Absently he drew a leafy frond across his body, pulling it closer, luxuriating in its comfort and imagined security. The tenseness of his body slowly diminished. His eyelids became heavy. A few times they opened, stared blankly into the darkness, then once again slowly closed. His breathing became more rhythmic. Sleep slowly overcame him.

Suddenly he sat bolt upright in his bed! He was immediately fully awake, his eyes wide open, all his senses alert! He froze in place, rigid with fear, afraid that his sudden movement had drawn attention. His breath caught in his throat.

What had happened? Was it a sound or smell that had alerted him? His eyes darted back and forth looking for any sign of something out of the ordinary. Nothing! None of the other family members had responded. A few stirred quietly, then quickly settled. They all lay there calmly sleeping.

Were they not aware? Something profound had just happened! Why had they not responded? Should he raise the alarm?

His confusion was overwhelming! What was happening? This feeling was completely different, overpowering, totally foreign and much more intense than anything he had ever experienced. His mind reeled. He was aware of. . . . He was *aware!*

Confusion and panic overwhelmed him. Still he dared not move. Never before had he experienced such profound self-awareness. Though his primitive mind was as yet unable to comprehend what had happened, he knew, on some level beyond instinct, beyond even racial memory, that something within him had changed, that he was now somehow different. The thought of it sent his primitive imagination reeling.

Struggling to overcome his growing fear, he forced himself to quietly lay back down, to remain still and silent so as not to alarm the others. For a long time he lay there unmoving, stricken with an incomprehensible sense of foreboding. He forced his eyes closed and lay there in the darkness, struggling to keep from fleeing in wild panic into the night.

He dared not relax. He couldn't, even if he wanted to. Muscles tensed, breathing labored, his eyes tightly closed, he lay there in the darkness . . . waiting, expecting at any moment for something terrible to come crashing out of the darkness. His mind raced as fear tightened its grip. He was keenly aware of any sound or smell that might be out of the ordinary.

But nothing happened. His family continued sleeping peacefully. An occasional stirring or a grunt would catch his attention, but otherwise nothing out of the ordinary happened. The sounds of the night remained as they had always been. After some time, he didn't know how long, the panic began to subside as emotional fatigue overcame him. He finally fell into a fitful sleep.

Several times that night he awakened, disoriented and afraid. But, as the quiet familiarity of his surroundings and the warmth of his bed caressed him, he drifted back into slumber.

When morning came he was roused by the usual sounds and movements of the others. Still half asleep, eyes still closed, he stretched and yawned luxuriantly.

Then suddenly all grogginess vanished. The memory of the night slammed back into his consciousness. The awareness startled him and his whole body suddenly tensed. His eyes flew open to an intense blinding light. Instinctively he turned away, shielding himself from what he expected would be some horrible assault. Nothing came. He had been facing the morning sun when he opened his eyes.

His startled reaction drew the attention of a few close by individuals, but they quickly lost interest when nothing else happened. Each in turn made his way down to the jungle floor.

Relieved though he was that he had not drawn attention to himself, he was still afraid to move. His fears of the night were equalled by his fear of how his family would react should he exhibit any unusual behavior. He was, after all, a low-ranking male. He had been conditioned from infancy to avoid conflict.

What ever it was that happened to him last night, there was no evidence of it in the daylight. Now, fearing that by remaining in his nest he would draw attention, he forced himself to move. Cautiously, deliberately, he descended from his place in the trees, glancing this way and that, searching for anything out of the ordinary.

At first he was fearful and confused. But as the morning wore on with nothing out of the ordinary happening, he forced himself into his usual routine. However, his new sense of awareness remained, and strengthened. The conflict within him was hard to suppress. One part of him wanted to scream in panic and alarm; but another part reasoned that to do so would only draw unwanted attention.

CHAPTER 2

Life in the simian family went on as usual for a time. The young male moved with the family when the supply of fresh fruit was used up. He foraged, built his nests as necessary, played with the youngsters, socialized with the others, maintaining his proper position within the group. He kept his usual respectful distance from the alpha, keeping his eyes averted in order to avoid confrontation. Still his apprehension remained, concealed just below the surface. He knew that he was somehow different, but he dared not let the others know.

He had, for the most part, deliberately suppressed his new feelings. His mind was as yet incapable of reconciling this new self-awareness since there was no practical need for it to assert itself. Yet it remained.

Gradually he began to realize that this new sense wasn't harming him. As his assurance grew, so also did his willingness to allow it to come to the surface of his consciousness. Fear and confusion gradually gave way to an uneasy curiosity.

Days, and then weeks went by uneventfully. He became accustomed to living with this new feeling. Still, fearing that he might be noticed and singled out by the others, he kept his secret hidden.

As he grew and matured, newly developed hormones coursed through his body. Again and again he watched as new challengers vied for the lead position in the family. Always the routine repeated itself. The challengers would thrash about creating havoc, swinging from low-hanging branches, tossing objects randomly about and screaming their defiance. The alpha had always responded in kind. And, owing to his superior size, strength, and experience, he had continued to prevail.

Within his maturing body, the young male's instinctual sex drive vied for dominance over his fear. Each time a new male came forth to challenge the leader; our young simian found himself becoming more and more agitated, and less able to restrain himself. But he also had become much more observant, paying increasing attention to details that had hitherto gone un-noticed.

Once, during one of these confrontations, he had given way to the excitement and had grabbed onto a small sapling and yanked it, accidentally hitting himself in the head. Though he had done so before, this time had been different. The pain he had felt, he recognized he had inflicted upon himself. Just to be sure, he repeated the action, and again felt the pain. In that instant a profound awareness struck him. He knew that if he could deliberately inflict pain on himself, he could also do the same to others.

And so he did just that. He swung the sapling around and swatted one of his brothers. The other male screamed in pain and surprise and backed away, but didn't retaliate. Gaining confidence, the young male ripped the plant from the ground and swatted another of the group. Again the result was the same. No retaliation. In surprised confusion and bewilderment, he dropped the sapling, and then turned his attention back to the fight.

However, his actions did not go un-noticed by the alpha male. Always aware of potential threats to his position, the alpha had become aware and agitated by these strange and unusual behaviors. His agitation manifested itself more frequently, at the expense of others within the family. The tranquillity and harmony usually enjoyed within the family now was replaced by a growing unease.

Even the infants, who before had freely frolicked and played, had grown more subdued, staying close to their mothers for security.

As days gave way to weeks and then months, the young simian grew into full physical and sexual maturity. His attention focused more and more on the females, his need to procreate ever growing in intensity. His relationships with the other males also deteriorated as he and they competed for the attentions of the females.

As his new self-awareness continued to assert itself, so also his confidence and understanding grew. He began to recognize that he was now somehow different from the others. This uniqueness became more evident as, on occasion he attempted to demonstrate his skills to others. They responded with confused indifference, as though they didn't comprehend what they had just witnessed. More frequently they shied away fearfully, leaving him increasingly alone and alienated.

Finally the time came when he realized that his place within the family would have to change. He knew his relationships within the group would continue to deteriorate, and that the alpha male would eventually drive him out. He knew he needed to make a decision . . . to leave the family and take his chances alone; or to challenge the alpha for leadership.

As the days went by, he managed to slip away from the family frequently. He would work his way to the outer perimeter of the group. Then, when no one was looking he would duck behind cover and silently work his way out of earshot. Then, when he felt secure in his seclusion, he began experimenting. He'd select a stick from the underbrush and begin swinging it about, deliberately swatting at various objects. After a few minutes of this he became winded. His body was not yet accustomed to this new exercise.

Discarding the stick, he sought relief from the hot sun under a bush. Recovering in the shade, he thought back to those many times when the alpha had been challenged. He recalled with increasing clarity how these challenges for leadership developed.

Invariably the new challenger would make his presence known

from well outside the perimeter of the group. He would rustle about nervously at first, drawing the attention of various individuals, but most particularly that of the alpha. Cautiously he would advance closer and closer, thrashing about, screaming his challenge, all the while building his courage. The alpha would respond in kind, but would initially hold his ground. Tension would grow exponentially until it seemed that the whole group would explode into chaos. Only then, when noise and confusion were almost unbearable, the challenger would charge.

The alpha would hold his position until the last moment. Then finally he would charge forward, screaming his rage. The two would crash together, arms and fists clubbing, teeth flashing and tearing, as the others looked on in cacophonous excitement. The battle would be furious and extremely violent, but would end quickly. The challenger would retreat into the jungle wounded or severely maimed.

Sometimes the challenger would not survive long enough to escape. When this happened, the family would descend on his mangled body, ripping and tearing it apart. As the alpha screamed his victory, others would approach, heads and eyes lowered, once again demonstrating subservience to their all-powerful leader, offering up bloodied and broken body parts of the vanquished foe.

It became apparent to our young simian that the alpha prevailed mainly due to years of experience coupled with his large size and his ability to use extreme violence in close combat. Still in his prime, he would likely continue to prevail until infirmity or some unforeseen situation overcame him.

Extreme violence had always been employed. So it was considered to be a given in any scenario the young adolescent considered. It gradually became apparent that to be successful in overthrowing the alpha, certain other conditions would have to be employed, i.e. larger size, more experience, or the strength of youth. The young adolescent reasoned (!) that he possessed none of these attributes. Given his situation, it was almost certain he would fail to overpower his opponent. Unwilling to risk injury, he realized he needed to develop another plan.

Early on he recognized that a stick of moderate size could be used as a weapon with reasonable success. Small ones broke too easily, while larger heavier ones were too cumbersome to wield effectively. Having witnessed many battles between the alpha male and various challengers, he knew that using a stick would have to be very precise. The first swing would have to be successful. There wouldn't be time or room for a second swing in close combat. The weapon would then be useless and the risk of injury and defeat would go up exponentially.

Though he had become more proficient in wielding sticks, he somehow knew that he needed to employ some additional method to ensure success. Casting about in quiet desperation in those times when he was able to slip away from the group, he began searching for some other strategy. And, eventually he found it.

CHAPTER 3

He remembered when he was just a youngster, he had watched his mother use a stone to crack the tough shells of nuts, a delicacy he relished when they ripened and fell to the ground. He remembered how he had marvelled as she selected the stone carefully, rejecting first one and then another, being careful not to use one so heavy that it completely crushed both the tough shell and the sweet nut inside. He remembered snuggling closer to her, waiting with eager anticipation for the treat he was soon to enjoy. Over succeeding months his curiosity grew, as did his strength. He began trying what he had seen his mother do. At first he had selected stones which were easy to pick up. But, though he had tried time and again to crack the tough shells, he had failed. Once he had chosen a stone that had taken all his strength to lift. As he strained to lift it as high as he could, it slipped from his grasp and crashed down onto his foot. He had yelped in pain and ran whimpering and limping to his mother for comfort.

For some time afterward he shied away from any further attempts with the stones. But eventually his desire to taste the sweet nut overcame his fear. After more practice he was finally able to pick just the right size stone for the job. He had spent much of the remainder of the season perfecting his new skill and had luxuriated in the taste of his favorite treat. Eventually the season for the nuts ran out, and with it the need to use stones. Though he no longer had a need for the stones, the memory of how he had been injured remained with him. He recognized the stone as a potential weapon.

Searching for stones under the thick matted jungle floor had become an exercise in futility. Tangled vines and roots blocked his efforts at every turn. The few stones he uncovered were either too heavy to move or were so entangled in the undergrowth that they were impossible to extricate.

Tired and thirsty from his efforts, he worked his way toward the small stream from which he and his family drank. It was dangerous to approach the stream alone. His family always went to drink together. That way someone was always alert, watching for signs of danger. All creatures of the jungle needed water, and predators knew this. Not infrequently an unwary victim was snatched away screaming in terror, never to be seen again.

As silently as he could, he came to the water's edge. He bent low to the ground, trying to make himself as small and inconspicuous as possible. Cautiously his lips touched the water. Just as he drew in a taste of the coolness, a sudden sound caused him to start.

Frozen with fear, his eyes and ears strained to locate the source of the sound. There, just a few yards to his right, almost completely hidden from view under a low-hanging frond, a small rodent crouched. The tiny wide-eyed animal was just out of reach of the water's edge. Its nose twitched ever so slightly as it cautiously moved forward to drink.

Just as the rodent lowered its head to drink, a shape exploded from the water, fanged jaws agape. In less than a heartbeat, the jaws clamped onto the poor beasts head. Almost as quickly as it had begun, it was over. The serpent snatched its prey back into the water, leaving only a small ripple. The frond swayed ever so slightly above the empty space where the hapless victim had been only a second before.

Forgetting his thirst, he inched back cautiously, soundlessly.

Then, frantic with fear, he sprang toward the nearest tree and scrambled up into the safety of the branches.

His heart pounding, his breath catching in his throat, he sat there clinging to the tree trunk trying to become invisible. After a short time the pounding subsided and he again breathed more easily. Completely unnerved, he crept slowly down to the ground. Forgetting his thirst, he worked his way from the stream back toward the safety of the family.

The following morning brought a heavy rain. Slowly, reluctantly, the family left the comfort of their nests and descended to the ground. Infants clung to their mothers' wet fur, nursing contentedly in the warmth and shelter of their mothers' bulk. All members in turn made their way to the edge of the group to relieve themselves, and then returned to forage for the first food of the day.

Alpha, ever dominant and intimidating, now crouched glumly as rivulets of rainwater trickled down between his furrowed brows to drip incessantly from the fur under his chin. Grunting quietly to himself, he rummaged listlessly in the tangled mat around him, probing for succulent grubs or roots to satisfy his hunger.

The young male now took his turn at the periphery. But instead of returning to the group, he crept quietly away toward the stream. Rainwater had swollen it and the usually clear water was now cloudy, gritty and unpleasant to the taste. He leaned forward cautiously, his hands supporting his weight on the stones protruding above the water's surface.

Remembering his need to find another weapon, he pulled the stone he was resting on out of the water. It fit comfortably in the palm of his hand. Still carrying the stone, he worked his way back from the water's edge. As he lumbered back toward the family he thumped the stone against the ground with each step. It became mud-covered and slippery. Raising his hand as he stepped forward, the stone fell from his grasp. It hit the ground with a wet squishing sound a foot or so in front of him.

At that moment the idea formed clearly in his mind. Up until this moment he had planned to hold the stone, using it as a club just as he would a stick. Now he realized that by throwing the stone he would not have to risk close-in combat. Considering the ramifications of this discovery, he moved back toward the family, hiding the stone in some thick foliage along the way.

From that day forward every time he was able to slip away, he'd retrieve the stone from its hiding place and carry it with him to a secluded area. There he would practice tossing the stone.

At first he was unsuccessful at hitting anything with consistency, regardless of whether it was close by or farther away. His simian posture didn't lend itself to the task of standing stably on his feet and one hand while he tossed the stone underhand.

Close-in accuracy gradually improved with practice. But he recognized that the force with which the stone made contact with the target wasn't going to be sufficient to cause any serious damage to the alpha. A new method had to somehow be developed.

From time to time he or other family members had had to stand erect on two feet, usually to reach for something just out of easy reach of a three-point stance. An upright stance could be maintained for a short period of time. But, owing to short legs and long arms, the position was inherently unstable.

With practice, he became more proficient at standing upright as he tossed the stone (again underhand). Then one day the connection in his brain was made. Why not try throwing the stone overhand? Adopting this method, he immediately recognized the advantages. The overhand method allowed him to apply more force and gain more distance with the throw.

His skeletal structure restricted the amount of rotation he could obtain in his shoulder joints. This limited him to a side-arm throw, which was inherently inaccurate. He eventually adopted a sort of trebuchet motion, which allowed for more distance and, with practice, much better accuracy.

In a relatively short time he was able to consistently hit objects several yards away. With continued practice his proficiency grew, as did his confidence. He no longer saw himself as just another member of the clan vying for leadership. He now knew that, owing to his new skills, he had a very good chance of defeating the alpha.

CHAPTER 4

With each new day the alpha became more and more aggressive toward the maturing young simian. His unusual behaviors and extended absence from the group had apparently not gone unnoticed. The time was growing near when he would have to either leave the family, or challenge the alpha for leadership. Though he had become proficient with his new skills, still he was unsure that he was ready for a confrontation.

The day finally came when the decision was taken out of his hands. For several days now the alpha had been increasingly irritable. He had been stomping around aggressively, cuffing the young ones and forcing both males and females to submit to his dominance. Always when this happened he would glower at his perceived rival, grunting and snarling his displeasure.

Finally as tensions grew, the alpha did something totally uncharacteristic. Repeatedly he began mock charges, screaming his rage at the young prospective challenger. Unbalanced by this new behavior, the now-mature male had no choice but to respond.

Backing away cautiously, he retreated to the place where he had hidden his weapon. Reaching down carefully, never taking his eyes off the alpha, he grasped the stone tightly in his hand. His heart pounding in his ears, he slowly rose to the upright stance he had practiced so often. His whole body seemed to tense with the realization that now was the time he had dreaded.

Carefully advancing to the throwing distance he had practiced, he stabilized his stance as much as was possible. Then, glaring at the alpha, he threw the stone.

At exactly that moment the alpha charged. The young male had practiced well. His stance had been perfect. The stone flew through the air as if in slow motion. The throw was exactly on target.

During his practices his targets had been stationary. This target was moving! In an instant that seemed like an eternity, the stone struck. As alpha charged, the distance between them closed rapidly. The projectile struck precisely where, just a moment before, his head had been. Now, instead of cracking against his skull, the stone glanced off his muscular shoulder. Alpha was knocked only slightly off course, but screamed forward.

The young male was still standing upright in astonishment when the alpha made contact. The full weight of the charge landed squarely in his abdomen. Air flew from his lungs as he was hurtled backwards by the impact. He had barely hit the ground when the alpha was on top of him, pounding, biting and screaming rage.

Frantic for breath, all he could do was try to fend off the blows that seemed to come at him from every direction. He smelled the hot breath of his opponent and gasped for some air of his own. Searing pain shot through him as teeth sank deep into his scalp. Instantly blood gushed from the wound, filling his eyes and mouth.

Desperate to escape this impending doom, he groped feebly for anything that might help him to get away. Miraculously, his fingers closed around a small sapling. Wrenching with all his remaining strength, he slammed it down onto the back of the alpha. The impact knocked them both off balance. Alpha was momentarily stunned.

In that brief moment the young simian broke free. Scrambling blindly, he crashed head-long into a growth of nearby saplings and underbrush. Thrashing wildly, bent on surviving at any cost, he staggered out on the far side. Clambering and stumbling to his feet, he limped away into the undergrowth.

For only a brief moment alpha had become disoriented and vulnerable. He recovered almost immediately, springing up to continue the battle, but nothing came. Silencing his own screams, all he heard was the cacophony of noise coming from the onlookers. The challenger was nowhere to be seen.

The noise dissipated quickly as, one by one the family gathered around the triumphant alpha, displaying profound obeisance to their leader who had once again prevailed.

Bloodied and battered, half blinded and disoriented, the defeated young male staggered on through the dense underbrush. Gradually panic gave way to shock and fatigue. Though his body desperately needed to rest, he dared not stop so close to the homeground of his former family. He knew that to remain in the area meant another almost certain confrontation with the alpha, one which he would most certainly loose.

He continued moving away from the area, stopping only rarely to clear away the blood which had begun to cake around the open gash in his scalp. The bleeding finally stopped. But his head throbbed with pain.

He chose a familiar path for his escape. The family had only recently come this way. They had foraged efficiently a few days before, clearing trees and bushes of all but the least ripe fruit. It was unlikely that they would return.

Overcome with fatigue, he stopped to rest under the tree where he had nested several days before. Discarded pieces of over-ripe fruit lay strewn about the base of the tree. Desperate to regain some strength, he wolfed down all that was within his reach, ignoring the acrid taste and smell. His stomach wretched, but he forced himself to keep the rancid food down. His eyes streamed water as he struggled to keep from vomiting.

His hunger somewhat satiated, he slowly began to relax. His taut muscles un-knotted as nourishment replaced adrenaline that had so recently coursed through his veins. His eyelids became heavy though he tried vainly to remain alert. Soon he dozed into a fitful sleep in the cool shade of the tree.

Some time later he awoke to the sounds of approaching dusk. Crickets and frogs had begun venturing out from their hiding places as darkness drew near. Still disoriented by the pain in his head, he climbed slowly into the safety of the branches above. Finding his old sleeping nest, he settled into its familiar comfort, pulling leafy branches close for warmth and security. The pain from his wounded scalp stabbed at his concentration. The memory of his defeat tore at him in a way he had never before experienced. All the planning and practicing he had done had availed him nothing. Instead of winning him the coveted place of dominance, his efforts had rendered him a wounded outcast, bereft of familial security, stripped of the status he had worked so hard to achieve. In a primitive and fundamental way he wondered if his new-found ability had become more a burden than a boon.

As darkness settled around him, he listened with a new intensity to the sounds of the night. No longer did he hear the familiar stirrings of his family members. Gone were the tell-tale grunts and rustlings of family members as they settled into sleep. Absent were the reassuring sounds the infants made as they suckled and cooed contentedly at their mothers' breasts.

With only few exceptions, night times had always been the same. Even after his "awakening," the familiarity of family life had been a source of comfort.

Though he recognized the change within his mind, he had come to realize that it was not at all obvious to the others around him. He came to understand that the self-awareness he now possessed had now alienated him from the others in a way that only he understood. But not until this night, wounded and beaten, did he realize that he was uniquely and utterly alone.

The "awakening" he had experienced contained many ramifications that were not at first easily discerned. His new-found reasoning capability had enabled him to manipulate his environment in ways that he would previously not have been able to do, let alone comprehend.

Tool usage had been a very limited part of his upbringing prior to the "change." He had observed his mother and other adults using stones as hammers to open seed pods. They had used twigs to fish succulent insects out of termite mounds. In his youth he had mimicked their behaviors and had eventually become reasonably proficient in doing so himself. But once he had mastered these behaviors his consideration and curiosity had advanced no further.

Now, foraging alone in his solitude, he began to realize how his thought processes had changed. He was becoming able to conceptualize his experiences. What had before been essentially a mimicking process was now perceived in a much more complex way. He was now able to understand how a stone or a stick might be used for more than just one purpose. Experimentation was now deliberate rather than random.

His solitary experiments had taught him much, but his defeat had taught him much more. He realized that his new skills could be effective, but only under specifically controlled circumstances. He had become comfortable with the results of his practice sessions. But when he applied them in a combat situation he had failed to realize that he was no longer in complete control of the situation. In his mind he had imagined the confrontation as being static. Under those conditions he had become proficient in hitting a stationary target consistently. What he had failed to anticipate was that his opponent might do something unpredictable, like move out of the path of the projectile. The implication had become painfully obvious.

Over the next several weeks the wound on his head healed, leaving a long, jagged scar just above his right eyebrow. From time to time he would touch it tenderly, feeling rough skin where before smooth fur had been. Each time he did so his memory went back to that terrible day when the exercise of his new abilities had nearly cost him his life.

In his solitude he had learned to fend for himself. He managed to find sustenance, though not in the quantities to which he had previously become accustomed. He had taken to following his old family, scrounging through their leavings for what food he could find. He had deliberately stayed one or two days behind so as not to attract attention.

Though he was becoming accustomed to being alone, still at times he yearned for the security and comfort of belonging that he had enjoyed with his family. Also never far from his consciousness, the drive to procreate nagged at him.

The skills he had learned were still with him. But he had deliberately neglected to use them, fearing that somehow, using them might result in something terrible happening again. Still, as time went by, his fears became less and his curiosity began to dominate.

Over time his fear of confrontation began to be outweighed by his need for interaction with others of his own kind. He was, after all, a social animal. Day by day he ventured closer to the clan, always wary of being seen by the alpha male. He risked his safety just for the chance sighting of anyone familiar. Invariably the only ones he saw were adolescents skirting the perimeter of the group. Mature females and infants remained in the center, always under alpha's watchful eye.

Gradually his courage returned. The reasoning process he had so recently acquired was becoming more fine-tuned. With his growing understanding came increased confidence. He was now able to view the events that led up to his banishment more objectively. Having reached this new plateau in his development, he resolved to resume refining his skills with weapons.

In the beginning he had practiced throwing at stationary targets set at a consistent distance. His accuracy had improved rapidly as a result. But what his primitive reasoning had failed to recognize initially was that his opponent had the ability to move about. Now, lightly touching the still-sensitive scar above his eye and remembering, he knew he much modify his tactics if he was to be successful in any future confrontations.

He began by practicing with targets at varying distances. As his accuracy improved, he began focusing his attention on technique. Owing to his short bowed legs and his overly long upper body, he was inherently unstable in an upright position. This resulted in his throw lacking significant power. When he threw harder he became even more unbalanced.

To this point he had kept both feet firmly planted on the ground, even grasping ground-level vines with his toes (which more re-sembled and functioned like fingers). This had helped somewhat, but his upper body had still remained relatively stationary. The throwing power thus generated came almost exclusively through his shoulder, elbow and wrist joints.

When he moved about looking for suitable stones to throw, he walked on all fours. Then, after picking up a stone and holding it in his left hand, he used a three-point walking technique. Once, while walking this way, it dawned on him how very stable his body felt in a three-point stance. He tried throwing in this position, but quickly realized that all he could accomplish was a weak under-handed throw. Standing upright, he had been able to thrown over-hand, though with less stability.

Intrigued by this new discovery, he tried something new. Stan-ding upright, he held the stone in his left hand. He drew the stone back behind him as his upper body rotated to the left. Then, while forcefully drawing the stone up and over; he rotated his shoulders to the right, dropped his right hand to the ground, and released the stone at the top of the arc. The result was a smooth follow-through that lent greater force to the throw, while at the same time stabilizing his stance. After only a few throws, he was able to consistently hit his targets.

At first the loud crack the stone made upon impact startled

him. Crouching low, he listened intently, breath caught in his throat. Fearing that the sound might draw unwanted attention, he remained motionless for several minutes. When nothing unusual happened he began breathing easier.

The implications of what he had accomplished elated him. The possibility of issuing another challenge for leadership now seemed to be once again within his reach. He consciously admitted to himself that access to the females was his primary motivation. Even as he practiced the new throwing technique, his drive to procreate remained constant in his thoughts.

As he pondered the possibilities, he knew that his first confrontation with the alpha male had been ill-prepared. The unanticipated reaction of the leader had taken him totally by surprise. Instead of remaining stationary, as he had done in the past; alpha had charged forward, avoiding a direct hit from the on-coming projectile.

He remembered how the glancing blow to alpha's shoulder had not had any noticeable effect. The impact had not opened a wound. The charge had continued unabated. Now he wondered; even if the projectile had found its mark, would it have inflicted sufficient harm to stop the charge? Consumed with concern, he redoubled his efforts. He chose heavier stones and exerted all his might trying to increase accuracy as well as force. Day after day his throwing skill improved.

Though his confidence continued to increase, loneliness continued to plague him. Regardless of his new skills (physical and mental), he was, after all, still a social animal. In the evenings, when daylight began to recede, he would lay quietly in his nest, gazing sleepily up into the sky. As darkness descended, sounds of the night enveloped him. They reminded him of the security and inner peace he had taken for granted when he was still a part of the clan. He remembered how the spats he had had with the other young males had upset him. Now he realized that in their way they had been an integral part of his sense of well-being.

Even the apprehension he had felt, watching alpha fight to retain dominance, had contributed to his sense of belonging.

Often he awoke suddenly in the darkness, remnants of a dream troubling him. Indistinct scenes flashed though his mind: A new-born clinging to its mother's fur, whimpering quietly, eyes wide with fear; fleeting glances cast his way by an unknown young female, penetrating deep into him; huge dark shapes looming over him as he cowered, frozen with fear, trying vainly to disappear into himself. Always the dreams were the same. Always the feelings of helplessness; always the sense of foreboding; always the answer . . . indistinct . . . just beyond reach; always . . . the eyes!

Every day he ventured closer to the clan. Longingly he watched from his cover as familiar scenes passed before him; toddlers playing in the sun; young males testing one another; alpha moving about the clan, pausing here and there to grunt at or stare down an individual who caught his attention; the females. . . .

Reluctantly he would back away, retreating once again into his solitude, plagued by the growing demand for resolution. Stoically he would resume his regimen, throwing stones, wielding sticks, wrestling with the inevitability of making the all-important decision.

Unknown to him as he continued practicing his skills, he had not gone unnoticed. Deep in the cover of undergrowth, other eyes watched.

SEEDERS

CHAPTER 5

Zuri had been on duty six of what would likely end up being a boring eight-hour shift. Being Senior Command Officer on an interplanetary spacecraft was a prestigious position, especially for a person as young as she was. But it didn't exempt her from her turn in the rotation for 'Officer of the Watch' duty. All officers had to take turns pulling this gig. Because of her senior position, Zuri probably could have asked someone else to pull it for her. But she felt she needed to set a good example for the other crew members on this ship, not to mention those on the other ships. Besides, it was a welcome change from the mundane routine of her regular duties.

She had completed all but the last item on her O.W. Checklist: 'Air Handler Unit Inspections.' All except C deck had checked out fine. The mid-deck unit needed a filter change. Apparently someone forgot to change it at the last scheduled inspection. They hadn't even logged it.

"Doesn't surprise me," she thought to herself. O.W. duty was pretty boring. All you had to do was run the computerized checklist some time during your shift. If you found anything out of sorts, you just needed to assign someone to fix the problem. It wasn't a big deal really.

Zuri was getting bored just sitting at her station. Sometimes trying to look busy was hard work. You had to focus your attention on something, anything, just to give the appearance of being in control. Most of the time it was a challenge just to stay awake.

She decided to go fix the problem herself. After all it was only a filter change, not something that required any special technical expertise.

"Hey, Rahul." She keyed her shoulder microphone as she entered the lift. "I need to enter SA to change a filter on C deck. Will you clear me please?"

She jabbed the C deck button, chipping her fingernail polish in the process. Her knees buckled ever so slightly as the lift accelerated. Leaning back against the elevator wall, she scrutinized her other nine nails.

"Getting kind of scruffy," she said to herself. This time of night there was no one there to hear her.

Up in the Maintenance Control section of the bridge, Rahul reached out to push the 'Safe Entry' button on his 'System Air' console.

"Yes mam. Why don't you call someone from maintenance to get it for you? Ah! Shit!" Zuri heard in her earpiece. "Hold on a second. Sorry. I just dumped coffee all over myself." A squeak, some muffled curses, then he was back. "Okay. You're good to go. Can you get someone to come up and baby sit for a minute? I need to go change my shirt . . . damn!"

"Sure. No prob. I'll be up in a few." Why bother someone else? She could just as easily do it herself after she finished the filter change.

Arriving at C deck, she walked the short distance down the hall and stopped at the panel labelled 'System Air.' She popped the four zurc fittings that held the panel in place, sat it aside and then squeezed in between the two wall supports.

Once inside, the space opened up enough for her to stand comfortably. To her left, the filter bank vibrated quietly. She punched the 'bypass' button and waited for the green light.

"This is about as exciting as it gets around here," she thought as she pulled the new filter out of the box sitting beside the unit. A puff of air gently swirled her hair as she bent to open the filter housing.

"Maybe I'll change my nail color this time," she thought as she pulled the old filter out. She had the new filter part-way inserted when her PCU (personal com unit) beeped. Startled, she jerked her hands away from the housing, chipping another nail. "Damn," she said under her breath. That one hurt.

"Mam, you better get up here ASAP! All the lights on the proximity panels just lit up. There's something big out there that wasn't there a second ago! Hold one. . . . Bridge just confirmed . . . it's solid, metallic and not moving." Rahul's shirt and her chipped nails would have to wait.

"On my way!" Zuri slammed the housing closed and punched the 'main flow' button. Squirming out of the compartment, leaving the access panel where it lay, she keyed her mic. "Bridge! S.C.O. What's going on?"

"We're not sure, mam. One second clear space. The next, there it is. It's huge! four, maybe five miles across!"

"Any transmissions? Any signs of aggression?" Zuri ran back to the lift and punched 'Bridge.'

"Appears to be cylindrical; maybe twice as long as it is wide! Still too far away to confirm, but it appears to be metallic. Hold one." Zuri could hear the muffled commotion in the background. "SecCom reports no incoming on any band. The thing's just sitting there."

"Very well. Notify the fleet. I'll be up there in two or less." Shifting her weight impatiently she watched the levels display above the door: (E, F, G . . .)

"Who're the O.W.'s on this shift?" she thought out loud as her memory spun into high gear, recalling the names of the senior officers on the other four ships. "Chetan on board the *Venure*; Imamu on *Sequum*; Asha on *Interloq*; Wasswa, (Zuri's twin sister) on *Sauda*; and Evander here on *Brighid*."

(R. .S. . . . T.) The lift sighed to a gentle stop. Zuri swatted the 'open' button. As the door opened, everyone turned as she rushed into the room. The ships C.O. (Chief of Operations) was bent over the SecCom station, his hand resting reassuringly on the operator's shoulder. He gave her a gentle pat as he straightened and turned to face Zuri.

Evander was tall, thin and greying. His receding hair line gave him the appearance of always frowning. But those who had gained his confidence knew better. He was not frowning. He was intently concentrating on the matter at hand. This was his approach to everything. Be intent. Be thorough.

"Chief, you're now O.W. Bring the protocol manual." Zuri motioned to Evander to follow as she entered the bridge and turned toward her observation platform. "All ships report!"

"*Sequum* here. Our readings are the same as yours. Propulsion reports our tertiary reactor at 70 percent and off line for diagnostics. Primary and secondary are nominal. No problem maneuvering if we need to."

"*Venure* reporting. All systems good to go. Mid-range scanner confirms target's length is six kilometres plus."

"S.C.O., Com. *Interloq* reports phase imbalance in their primary transmitter dish. Should be back up soon. Otherwise, nothing to report other than what we already know."

"*Sauda* here. Scans indicate the target is hollow. Interior is hard to read, though. Otherwise, we're 100 percent."

"Very well. Stand by." The S.C.O. switched to internal. "Nav? Where is that thing relative to our current course?"

"Centered, mam, and stationary. Current speed puts us there in just under two days."

"Very well. Maintain course and speed. Notify me immediately of any change in status." Taking a deep breath, Zuri turned toward the O.W.

"Evander, what does the manual say about this?"

"Not a thing." The tall, gray-haired man frowned, walking close behind the commander. "I don't think anyone ever anticipated anything like this happening in past contacts. Scanners always picked up the ships *after* we'd made radio contact."

Evander was one of the oldest on board the *Brighid*. His primary title was Chief of Maintenance. His job was to oversee upkeep of all mechanical systems on the spacecraft. It was a huge job that required enormous attention to detail. He had under him a staff of technicians who were second to none, and he made sure they stayed that way. Several times he had been offered opportunities to advance above his current grade. But he had always declined, reasoning that he wasn't 'diplomatic enough.' But in truth, the real reason was that he loved working on the ship. He just didn't want to give that up. When Zuri accepted the top command position, she insisted that he take her place as captain. Reluctantly he accepted, though Zuri could tell he wasn't comfortable doing so.

She understood and appreciated that. But she also knew that when she needed his expertise and keen perception, she could count on him. That was the main reason why she had advanced as quickly as she had within the fleet hierarchy. She had a knack for surrounding herself with the best people. Evander was the best of the best.

"Okay then, forget the manual. What do you think?" Zuri sat down at her console and turned to face the display on the center screen.

"Well, first, it's pretty clear this thing isn't aggressive. If it was, given the fact that it evaded all our scans and just appeared out of nowhere, it probably has the capability to turn us all into unorganized matter, space dust, if it so desires. Second, the four contacts we've made over the years have all been benign. That is to say, not aggressive. We've all had roughly the same philosophy, the same desire to learn.

"Each of our cultures has faced roughly the same challenges. Each of our races has had to overcome philosophic as well as political differences on our home worlds. Had we not done so, it is highly unlikely we would have survived long enough to advance into interplanetary travel. Our ancient records explain this pretty clearly. We all have remarkably similar backgrounds."

Evander paced slowly back and forth, hands clasped behind his back. Zuri was quite familiar with Evander's reaction. He always maintained a calm detachment whenever he faced a challenge, be it equipment related or interpersonal. His composure helped Zuri to remain calm, even in this stressful situation.

"Since each of our cultures managed to evolve to this point," Evander continued, "it seems reasonable to assume that other races that get this far in their evolution probably possess the same fundamental ideology. No guarantees, though."

"Third, where would we go if we opted to avoid this confrontation? If we decided to turn tail and run, that thing could probably just materialize out in front of us, no matter which direction we chose. After all, it simply materialized there before us. No warning. No clue as to where it came from or how it got here. In other words, we can run, but we can't hide. Looks to me like we really don't have much choice." Evander stop pacing and turned to face Zuri.

"I can't fault your logic, my friend." Zuri was relieved, but not particularly surprised that Evander had voiced what she had been thinking anyway.

"Okay then." She took a deep breath. "Com? Hook us up." Straightening her uniform, she lowered the displays on her console and looked into the holo-cam.

"All ships. Barring objection, here's the plan. All ships will maintain current speed. Each is to change vector to intercept the object. We will not again refer to this object as a target. The implications of that word are not appropriate to our intentions. Maintain current protocols and security levels. All ships' captains prepare for holo-conference in two hours. S.C.O. out."

Turning back to Evander, she added, "I don't know about you, but I need a shower and some food!" Heading for the door, she hesitated. "Oh, and get someone to relieve Rahul in MC. He's had a small accident."

CHAPTER 6

"A hot shower! Nothing much better in the universe than the feel of hot water running over your skin." Zuri thought, as she stood naked in the steamy enclosure, arms folded close under her breasts. The warm water seemed to draw tension out of her as it cascaded over her body. She visualized each little care, each worry, being drawn up and out through the pores of her skin. Her breathing slowed as her cares fell from her body, circled the drain at her feet, and then dropped out of sight.

With her body reasonably relaxed, Zuri began to sort events out in her mind. Evander had, in his usual way, evcaluated the situation and had drawn reasonable conclusions. She, on the other hand, needed to go beyond the obvious. In the history of their mission they had never come across an aggressive race. But that did not mean that they didn't exist. Maybe they were just lucky that they hadn't encountered one.

And what if they did meet an aggressor? What could they do to protect themselves? True, they did have weapons. But, so far as she knew, they had never been fired. Maybe they'd been tested some time long ago soon after the ship was launched. But would they even work now after so many generations of non-use? Maybe it would be a good idea to test them now, before they got much closer to the object. But maybe the object would see that as an aggressive act. Then what would it do?

The only weapons she knew actually worked weren't really weapons in the pure sense of the word. These were lasers used to pulverize space-borne objects too large to be deflected by their shields. They had limited range and power. They could handle something a few yards across, but they'd be completely useless against anything larger.

"No!" she said aloud to herself. She would not under any circumstances advocate taking an aggressive posture in this encounter. Anything that might be interpreted as aggressive (or even defensive) could not be of any benefit. The technology represented by this strange new object was most certainly far advance beyond theirs. Evander was right. She really didn't have many options, and none of them looked particularly good.

CHAPTER 7

After finishing a light meal in her room, Zuri took the lift back up to the bridge. As the lift door opened, there stood Evander, hands clasped behind his back. "Anything new happening?" she asked.

"Bridge crew seems to be a little tense. But otherwise, nothing out of the ordinary. How about you?"

"Nope. Let's see what the others have to say." Zuri stepped out and turned toward the bridge. Evander fell into step beside her as she walked the few yards to the entrance.

As she entered, she noticed conversations ceased immediately. A few crew members turned quickly away from her, focusing their attention back on their assigned duties. She thought she could sense the tension in the room.

"Yeh, me too" she thought as she walked up to the handrail that separated command level from the work stations two steps below. "Com . . . Nav . . . Report"

"Com here. *Interloq* reports transmitter problem still being worked. No other incoming to report, mam"

"Nav here. All ships on new vectors for intercept, mam."

"Very well. Com . . . route all holo-com to my station and get everyone on line." Turning toward her raised platform at the rear of the room, she motioned to Evander again.

"I want you in on this, too. Not on line . . . just take a seat over there somewhere." She motioned toward the chairs directly opposite the holo-console.

"I want you to observe how the others react. Get my attention if you see something you think is important." Evander looked a bit uneasy.

"Don't worry about speaking up. The others will have their seconds there too. They just won't be visible. Okay?" Zuri took the seat at the holo-scanner.

"Com . . . bring 'em up."

Directly in front of her were four clear glass cylinders three feet in diameter and four feet high. Each rested on a raised circular platform at desk height. They were arranged radially, with Zuri's station at the head of the circle.

In quick succession each of the four captains' images began taking shape layer by layer inside the cylinders. When the last of the four was completely formed, Zuri began speaking.

"Greetings, all. Anyone have anything new to report?" To Zuri's left the form of a very dark-skinned man turned toward her. His straight white hair seemed to sparkle in the holo-light. Imamu, the captain of *Sequum* spoke.

"Looks like reactor number three will be back on line in a few minutes. MC tells me one of the rod casings warped and shorted out. They replaced it and are finishing up their check lists as we speak.

"Good. Anything else?" Imamu shook his head.

Interloq's female captain was next in the circle. Asha was also dark-skinned. But by contrast, she had no body hair, typical of her race.

"Our primary dish is still down. The step motor on one of the segments blew a rotor. Fab shop will have to make a new one. We're installing the back-up now."

"Thanks, Asha. How about *Sauda*?" Zuri turned toward the image of her sister, Wasswa. This woman was tall and spindly, nothing like Zuri, who was borderline heavy and only a little over five feet in height.

"We're one hundred percent. When we changed vector, the target . . . sorry . . . the object . . . seemed to shimmer a bit at the end we were scanning. But as soon as our course stabilized, the shimmering stopped. Engineering thinks there might be some sort of force field being generated, but we really don't know for sure."

"Okay thanks." Turning further to her right, Zuri gazed upon the pale gray image of the last of the ships' captains. Soon to be one hundred twelve years of age, he was just reaching his prime. Chetan was tall for his race. At just under six feet, he stood head and shoulders above everyone who had come from his home planet, whose name his ship bore.

"Chetan, does the *Venure* have anything to add regarding dimensions or surface configuration of the object?"

"We're still too far out to pick up much detail other than overall dimensions. The exterior surface appears to be non-uniform, for what that's worth. Can't say anything about the interior yet."

"All right, then." Zuri straightened in her chair. "I guess we're all pretty much awe-struck by what has happened. No one knows what to think, I'm sure. For all these generations we've never experienced anything quite like this. So, I'd like to open this up for discussion . . . hear what you all have to say. Who wants to go first?"

Asha turned toward Zuri. "I don't want to state the obvious, but it seems to me we don't really know what's going on here. Is this another race trying to contact us?"

"If that's the case, this is a first." said Imamu. "Each of our races was relatively equal technologically when we met. None of us had even dreamed of building a ship this huge. What sort of a culture *has* such technology? And why would they even bother with such puny beings as us?"

"Don't forget, this thing just popped in out of nowhere." a voice came from outside the holo-fields. "It's possible such an abrupt appearance might be aggressive."

Wasswa turned toward the voice.

"It's certainly possible. But we have no reason to suspect so. It's been over two hours since that thing appeared, and it's just been sitting there." Turning back toward Zuri, she continued, "Maybe it's just waiting to see what *we* will do."

"I wonder if it knows there are five of us compared to only one of it." Chetan leaned back in his chair, raising his hand for attention. The hand and several inches of his arm disappeared as they extended beyond the holo-field.

"Okay." Zuri leaned forward in her chair. "It's clear that all we have are questions . . . no answers. So, let me suggest this. In the past each if us has gone on the assumption that aggressive races self-destruct before they ever attain space-travel capability. I don't see any reason why we shouldn't continue with that line of reasoning."

"That's a pretty risky assumption, don't you think?" Chetan also leaned forward.

"True enough." Zuri held her position. "But what's the alternative? Do we run away? That would go against everything we stand for."

"May I interject here?" Evander rose from his seat across the room and began walking slowly around the circle, hands clasped behind him. No one but Zuri could see the expression of concern on his face.

"Curiosity brought our ancestors into space. Curiosity brought our races together. Certainly they were all fearful, at first; probably much as we are now." He paused, then turned around to retrace his steps.

"How long has it been since we made our last contact? Three; four generations?"

All ships' captains deferred to this man. Each listened respectfully. Of them all, Evander had been the only one reluctant to accept his position. He had never reached out for power or influence. They had come to him naturally. He carried with him an air of authority. He had always been soft-spoken. But his words carried weight with everyone he spoke to.

"During that time I fear we may have lost some of the determination which drove our ancestors. We may have become a bit complacent; a bit too comfortable."

"You're probably right, Evander." Chetan frowned as he listened to the invisible voice behind him. "But that doesn't mean we shouldn't be cautious."

"Of course you're right, my friend." Evander caught Zuri's eye for just a moment. Then he continued. "Caution is always justified when confronting the unknown. But we must also be prudent. As yet we have seen no sign of aggression. Therefore we ought to take care not to exhibit any ourselves. Besides; what could we do? There may be more of those things hiding just beyond our view. Ultimately, numbers may count for nothing."

Zuri sensed it was time to intervene. *Venure*'s captain was known to be stubborn and confrontational, traits that had served him well as he rose through the ranks to the captaincy. Evander, on the other hand, was the consummate diplomat; always able to turn his opponents words to his favor. Sometimes this rubbed people the wrong way. Zuri feared this was becoming one of those times.

"All right, then." Zuri interjected. "All we really know is that we don't know anything. Agreed?" She looked around the circle, making eye contact with each one in turn.

Chetan tried once more. "Maybe it sees our ships changing course as aggressive.

"That may be the case." Zuri felt mildly irritated at the remark. "But it still didn't respond when we did so. I think that means we're still back where we were." Chetan averted his eyes. He knew he had lost this sparring match.

"Now." Zuri straightened in her chair and took a breath. "Let's talk about what we're going to do. I think we should try to communicate with it. Any thoughts along those lines?"

"I'm all for that." Wasswa was first to respond. "But what do we want to say?"

Evander was quick with an answer.

"I spent most of the time before this meeting going through the archives. I managed to locate a copy of the message that was being transmitted when the *Sequum* first made contact with the fleet."

"I thought all that old stuff was deleted long ago." said Zuri. "How'd you manage to find it?"

"It was in the diplomatic protocol files. I had to decompress it, but it's still intact."

"What's it say" The pitch of Wasswa's voice betrayed her excitement.

"The file is huge. But from what I had time to download, it appears to be based on a mathematical model . . . binary to be exact. I can beam a copy to each of your ships, but it'll take a while. I don't think we should risk transmitting broad band just jet."

"Agreed." Zuri again caught Evander's eye. "Let's do that. Each of you put a team on it and see what you can find out. Unless there's something else we need to discuss, let's plan on meeting again tomorrow at this time. Anything?" Zuri looked at each of her captains in turn. Each nodded their agreement.

"All right then. S.C.O. out." The images in each cylinder dissolved as they stood up.

"Evander, how'd you manage to pull that off so quickly? You must have had to sort through thousands of files."

"It wasn't that hard really," he said sheepishly. "I like poking around in the archives. I guess you could say it's sort of a hobby."

CHAPTER 8

Later that evening in the privacy of her room, Zuri considered the events of the day. She had known from the start that not much would come from the meeting. There simply wasn't much to go on. The object had simply appeared out of nowhere and had just sat there directly in their path. They could speculate forever if they so chose. But unless something changed between now and the time they arrived. . . .

Well, something was going to change. They were going to compose and transmit a message, probably tomorrow. What would they say? She needed to review the data that her team was compiling. Maybe then she would have a better idea what needed to be said. But that could wait until morning.

Evander had volunteered to get a team together to begin going over the ancient message he had found. How was it that he always seemed to be a step ahead of everyone? How had he managed to find just the right information . . . in just the right place . . . at just the right time? Was it coincidence? No; she didn't think so. For as long as she could remember, Evander had been a part of her life; sometimes a distant part; but more often much closer.

As a child, she remembered him as that man her father was always talking to. Later, in her teens, he was the other man in her life besides her father. He had always been there when she needed someone to talk to. She felt comfortable going to him with any question. Seldom had he given her a direct answer; but he had always steered her in the proper direction so she could find the answer herself.

Once, when she had had a crush on him, he had seemed to recognize it almost before she did. He had been so very gentle when he told her how he felt. He had sat quietly with her that day in his study. He had told her how much he loved her; how she reminded him of his daughter who had been gone for so many years. She wanted to know what had happened to her. But somehow she sensed that to ask would cause him pain. He had said he felt she and he were kindred spirits and that he so very much appreciated her love for him. He had told her they would be friends forever. She had cried, but she had understood.

She remembered the musty smell and the dim light in his study. She remembered the shelves filed with books; some were ancient and leather-bound. Through her tears, she had asked him why he kept them when all of their contents were stored in computer files. It would be so much easier for him to find what he wanted to read. There wouldn't be so much clutter. His response had touched her deeply. He had said that the books contained knowledge passed down through generations, and by holding them in his hands he felt more a part of that past, that the knowledge was more intimately a part of him. When he said this, she had cried; not out of sorrow or regret, but out of heart-felt respect for the depth of feeling this man possessed. She had discovered that she loved him even more.

But now she was an adult. She commanded a fleet of ships filled with representatives of five planets. Reminiscing was a luxury she could seldom indulge.

Now, in this position of leadership and responsibility, she felt it even more vital to maintain a clear mind. She rarely had time for self-indulgence. The welfare of five races, five cultures and fifty thousand individuals rested squarely on her shoulders. She understood all too well what was required of her. She was humbled by the magnitude of her calling.

In her youth she had always believed that she was destined to do great things. She had always pushed herself to excel, and only rarely had she failed.

Once when she was eight years old she and her classmates were taking a supervised 'field trip' outside the ship. It wasn't a long excursion, just a few hundred yards along the ship's ventral axis so the kids could experience first hand what it was like to be weightless. Their instructor had tethered each of them individually to the handrail.

Zuri had been told it was her job to make sure all the kids stayed in line so their tethers didn't get tangled. The instructor led the way along the rail, each suited child following in single file. Dutifully, Zuri took up position at the end of the line so she could see everyone clearly.

The class hadn't gone too far when two boys midway up the line started horsing around, letting go of the handrail and pushing off with their feet. When they reached the end of their tethers they'd bounce back as though they were on elastic bands. Zuri saw this but didn't think much of it. Her job was to make sure everyone stayed in line. No one was getting tangled up, so, no problem.

The boys were getting rambunctious, pushing off harder and harder so they'd bounce back more quickly. All the kids were chattering away happily. This was normal for them, so the instructor didn't pay much attention. He continued leading the group forward, not bothering to look back.

The two boys started to push off again, this time holding hands. One of them got off just a split second before the other. This caused him to twist at an odd angle, making his tether wrap around the other boy's wrist. That threw them both off balance, so when they reached the end of their tethers, one of them broke loose and started to float away.

Zuri saw what happened and yelled as loud as she could for the instructor. Above the noise of the other kids she couldn't be heard. The boy was drifting farther out, waving frantically, his screams going unheard. His com link was broken when the tether parted. He was now several yards beyond anyone's reach.

Not knowing what else to do, Zuri grabbed the rail with both hands. Bracing her feet against one of the handrail brackets, she slammed her weight against the child in front of her. The result was a domino effect. Each child fell into the one in front until finally the last one bumped into the instructor. He turned around to berate the child, and saw the boy drifting, now ten or more yards above the group. He flipped the switch on his instructor com-pack to 'emergency' and called for help. It took several minutes for security to arrive. By then the boy was almost out of sight. The officer fired up his propulsion pack and quickly got to the boy.

The incident was quickly resolved. The class was reprimanded and from that day forward all instructors were required to wear a serviceable propulsion pack whenever they took their classes outside.

Zuri was commended for her quick thinking. But she believed that if she had been more diligent, the incident would never have happened. From that day forward she tolerated no nonsense, from herself or others. She got a lot of ribbing from her friends. They always called her a detail freak. She took the teasing well, and over time she earned her friends' respect.

Zuri completed her formal education at age sixteen. She specialized in sociology during the last two years of her schooling. Following completion of thirteen years of formal schooling, all citizens were required to dedicate the next four years to 'operations' (the equivalent of military service). But because she had excelled in her chosen field, she was selected to participate in a five-year advanced course of study. During that five-year period she showed exceptional skill in diplomatic and interpersonal relations, and was therefore invited to join the 'operations officer' ranks where she would be groomed for leadership within the fleet.

Four years later, at age twenty-six, she was made captain of the *Brighid*, where again she excelled.

The *Brighid* was the first inter-system spacecraft built by Zuri's home world. When the people of her planet decided to venture out beyond their system, they determined to make the spacecraft totally self-sufficient. They knew that the length of the voyage would be so incredibly long that, in all likelihood, several generations would pass before the ship returned (if it ever did).

CHAPTER 9

The craft was built in orbit around a barren planet, which was the seventh planet out from her sun (her home world was the fifth planet out). The planet was rich in the raw materials necessary for construction. Mining, refining and fabrication was conducted on the planet surface. Components were then carried into orbit where the ship was assembled.

Construction and fit-out took just over twelve years, during which time the crew was selected and trained. Based on an average lifespan of one hundred years, it was agreed that in order to maintain the integrity of the race, a minimum of ten thousand people would be required. Birth rates would be rigidly enforced so as to avoid over-taxing the life support system.

The ship itself was three thousand five hundred feet in length with a diameter of just over two thousand feet. A single pulse-drive engine was mounted in the rear on the central axis. Eight maneuvering engines were mounted equidistant from each other radially around the circumference, four on the front quadrant and four on the rear. Spare parts and non-perishables were secured on the exterior, leaving the entire interior for habitation and life support.

The spacecraft had been in flight for twenty-three generations when Zuri was born. The last of the four accompanying races had been discovered exactly one hundred eighty years prior to her birth.

CHAPTER 10

After completing the required five-year tour of duty as captain, Zuri was given the option to retire and go back into 'civilian' life. For her, the decision was easy. She had always had an analytical mind and intellectual curiosity. 'Civilian life' held little interest for her. She chose to remain in service, where she worked as an inter-ship liaison.

Once again her skills in diplomacy shown. She was stimulated by the interchange between cultures. She gained a reputation within the fleet as being clear-thinking, fair-minded and considerate. Under her leadership the bonds between cultures became more and more solidified. After just a few years of service, she was elected to the highest post in the operations sector: Senior Command Officer. Now at age thirty-five, she was the youngest person ever to hold that position.

Sleep seemed to evade her. Try as she might, after six hours of tossing and turning, she couldn't keep her eyes closed or her mind from racing. How were they coming on the download? She couldn't get it out of her head. Finally giving up, she threw the covers off and quickly changed from bedclothes into her uniform. A quick stop in the bathroom, and she was out the door.

The library was located two decks below the bridge. When Zuri came through the door, she was met by a cacophony of sounds. Groups of people stood shoulder to shoulder, hunched over computer keyboards, chattering excitedly. Others sat stonily in front of screens, absorbed in the data. There, in the center of the room stood Evander, hands clasped once again behind his back.

"I thought you were gonna get some sack time." Zuri said as she walked into the room. Evander turned at the sound of her voice.

"I thought the same for you."

"Couldn't sleep. Too much rattling around inside my head."

"Me too. We've got a fair amount of the message down-loaded . . . making good progress. Looks like a tutorial mostly. Starts out with binary math symbols; zeros and ones. Establishes magnetism and electricity; on, off, positive, negative. Then it goes into absolute values. You know; up, down, left, right. Not too far into the program it's dealing with morals and ethics; right, wrong, good, bad. Whoever put this together started from the ground up, really knew what they were doing."

"Heard anything from the others?" Zuri grabbed him affectionately by the arm and walked toward one of the workstations.

"Not a whole lot. We broke the message down into five segments, one for each ship. We took the first one. Looks like the others deal with increasingly complex issues like mathematics, geometry; or symbology like alphabets or musical notation. It gets complicated in a hurry."

"Anything from the object?" Zuri nodded.

"Not a peep. *Venure* says they can make out a little more of the structural details . . . say it looks sort of like a giant tin can with warts."

"Warts!?"

"Their description. Not mine. Say they're hemispherical in shape and unevenly distributed over the entire surface, at least the side we can see."

"Do we know if it's hollow?"

"Can't say. We're still too far away."

"How long 'till we get there?"

"A little over thirty hours." Evander glanced at the digital re-adout on the wall to his right. Turning back to the console, he pointed.

"Looks like we're into spherical geometry already."

Zuri looked perplexed as the symbols flashed by on the screen.

"Right. Well . . . Let's get everybody back on line again. Just audio this time, so we can keep working."

"I'll make the call." Evander keyed his lapel mic. "Com . . . O.W. Ring up the others . . . audio only. Link with the S.C.O. and myself. Call when you're ready." "As you . . . (sound of a stylus dropping) as you wish, sir."

"Must be someone new on duty tonight." Zuri kept watching the symbols fly by. "Yup. It's Rani's niece, and she's scared to death."

"What'd you do . . . give her the look?"

"Same one I give all the new-bees. Keeps 'em on their toes."

"Well . . . she'll get used to it." Zuri smiled up at her friend and mentor.

"Not if I have anything to say about it." Evander frowned and winked back. "S.C.O., O.W. . . . Com. Link's established."

"Okay. Send 'em. Thanks, Mai. Good work."

"Thank you, sir. Com out."

Zuri smiled as she looked up again at the tall man standing at her side. Evander wore his salt and pepper hair cut short. The gray was a little heavier around his temples.

For as long as she could remember, his hair had looked the same. So had his face . . . a hint of a few wrinkles around the eyes . . . a slightly furrowed brow. And penetrating dark green eyes. When she looked into them, she felt that she could see his soul. There was wisdom there . . . and sadness.

Many times she had asked him his age. Always he had evaded her; answering with some cute quip like 'too old for you, young lady.' She had always laughed at his response, but still her curiosity remained. Once she had hesitantly looked in his personnel file, feeling guilty for having invaded his privacy. Everything was there, his place of birth, not far from her home town; parents: their names were listed. Citizen ID number; it was there too. Date of birth: unknown/adopted. Maybe that was why he wouldn't tell her. He didn't know, himself.

"*Brighid . . . Interloq.*" A female voice came over their personal transceivers.

Asha: "Everyone else here?" Zuri waited as the other captains reported in. Then she started off. "Okay, then. Here's what we know at our end. The first part of the message is designed to establish a foundation for communication. It begins as a mathematical sequence in the binary system. It then progresses through to base ten. From there it establishes fundamental laws of math and physics. Eventually it establishes a base for language development and ethics. There's probably more, but we haven't gotten through it all yet.

"Asha here. The second part builds on logic: 'if-then' scenarios. From there, language and vocabulary, eventually into literature and philosophy."

"This is Imamu. Much of what we have deals with physical science, mostly organic chemistry. A lot of advanced mathematics, too."

"Wasswa here. We're seeing a lot of artwork and music, interspersed with more math. We're also seeing some feedback loops, maybe used for viewer participation. You know. Learning by doing. That sort of thing."

"That's what we've got, too. You might want to go back and look a little closer for those loops. We're finding them all over the place."

"Thanks, Chetan." Zuri still had her eyes glued to the screen, concentrating. "Okay, all. What do you think?"

"It all looks pretty straight forward to me." Evander assumed his usual pose, hands clasped behind his back. "It's long and drawn out, but I suppose it has to be that way for it to work. Maybe the loops are there to separate concepts; sort of like chapters in a text book."

"Chetan, again. I have to agree. This would all be impossible to digest in one setting. I think the loops serve just that purpose. I don't think the whole message is sent at once. I think the loops are break points. They're there to receive responses. When the right answer is received, they transmit the next sequence. This all makes perfect sense to me. What better way to teach . . . and learn? I'm thinking we don't need to come up with a message of our own. We can just use the one we have."

"Sweet!" They could hear the excitement in Wasswa's voice. "But I don't know why we didn't pick up on the feedback loops right from the beginning."

"Probably a difference between our program and the message's. It's centuries old, after all." Evander stepped back from the console and looked toward Zuri.

"Right! Okay." She too stepped back, hands on hips. "Let's get the programmers on this and get all the loops activated. When we're ready, we can get it set up for transmission. Are we in agreement?" (yes's all around.) "All right! Great! Let's get on it! And be sure to get some rest. I think we're gonna need it."

An hour later Zuri fell into bed and was asleep almost immediately.

Several hours later:

The fleet had begun deceleration an hour before. All five ships were now at station-keeping ten miles distant from the huge cylinder. (There really was no such thing as 'stopping' in space, since the universe was in a continuous state of motion. Station keeping simply meant maintaining a constant distance between objects.)

Of course, word had quickly spread throughout all the ships. Every citizen excitedly awaited the time when the 'message' would be transmitted. Truth be known; most everyone was fearful. No one knew what to expect.

Prefect leaders and council members brought out old protocol documents that had been stored away for generations. Public forums were quickly organized. Briefings were held. Schools were let out. Public service workers, commerce workers, private citizens, virtually everyone broke from their daily routines and congregated in public places throughout each ship.

Contact with a new race was something everyone hoped for. But few really expected it to happen in their lifetime. In the nearly one thousand years the mission had been in existence, contact had only happened four times. This was monumental; more than just a once-in-a-lifetime event. Excitement seemed to permeate everything.

Up on the bridge the tension was almost tangible. The *Brighid* crew, including off-duty people, crowded around workstations. Everyone seemed to be talking at once. At her command station, Zuri conferred with the ships' captains.

"Com. What's your status?"

"Message is queued and ready for transmission on broad band, mam."

"Very well. Bring up inter-ship PA, please." A quiet hiss was heard throughout all the ships. Vid screens blinked and came to life. Pushing out from her desk, Zuri stood up, placing a hand on her chair back. She looked out across the Ops Deck area. All conversation ceased. All eyes turned toward her. There at the com console, Evander stood; one hand resting on the console, the other resting gently on the new-bee's shoulder. He was looking up at Zuri, smiling.

"Cit . . ." Her voice broke. She cleared her throat. "Citizens. Never before in recorded history has an event such as this taken place."

Throughout all the ships, people hung on her every word. Anticipation was palpable. Children stood motionless, eyes wide with anticipation. Parents held each other. Strangers stood close together. Many held hands. All eyes focused on the vid screens posted throughout the ships.

"Not since we left our home worlds, not since our races united has an event comparable to this occurred. We don't know what to expect. It may be good. It may be ill. It may be for naught." Zuri paused, took a deep breath. "Eternal optimism has brought us this far. We cannot but believe that it will continue. For a thousand years we have stood united. May it ever be so."

Looking down to the Com console, "Mai, please transmit now." The young trainee smiled nervously, then turned toward her console and pressed the button.

CHAPTER 11

Zuri's image disappeared from the screens, to be replaced by a view of the object. It hung motionless in profile; the small hemispherical bumps now clearly visible. Gradually the bumps began to change, to glow with a soft pastel-blue light. Then from all over their surfaces thin needle-light structures began to extend. As they did so they too began to glow.

Their light began to intensify, becoming a brilliant white.

"Look! It's moving!" Someone shouted and pointed toward the screen. Gradually the cylinder began turning toward the ships. The end, which before had faced away from them, now turned toward the cluster of ships. The surface shimmered and danced, much like a vibrating pool of pastel-blue water.

Then the reply came. It wasn't mathematically structured. It wasn't in a strange or unfamiliar language. It wasn't transmitted via their instruments. It was spoken directly to their minds.

"I KNOW MY OWN. YOU HAVE BEEN TRIED . . . AND FOUND WORTHY."

All were stunned, incredulous! The words burned deep into every individual, enfolding, encircling, caressing. Doubt and fear dissipated as though they were breaths in the wind, to be replaced by an overwhelming feeling of peace and exquisite self-assurance. They stood transfixed, completely engulfed in the joyous moment.

As suddenly as it had happened, the voice was gone. Each

person felt a profound loneliness, as though someone dear had suddenly been taken away. The words, which had been spoken to their minds, were all that remained, etched into their memories. People clung to each other in stunned silence.

After a time (no one knew how long) they were startled by a single loud pop, much like the sound made when out-of-phase loudspeakers are connected together.

Looking about from one to another, each person knew what the other was thinking. "Did you hear that?" "What just happened?" "How could . . .?" "Who . . .?" Some began to doubt their sanity. They wondered whether anything had happened at all. The rational parts of their minds found it difficult to process what their emotions told them was true. The feelings of calm and inner peace began to be replaced by feelings of foreboding.

Those on duty in the com/nav centers were the first to fully recover. Supervisors began barking rapid-fire orders. Com-techs hurriedly ran diagnostic tests on their equipment. Nav and Enviro-techs activated propulsion and hull integrity back-up programs to ensure the safety of the ship. Everyone searched frantically for some evidence of what had just happened.

No one found anything wrong. Nothing was out of place. All systems behaved as though nothing out of the ordinary had happened.

Quickly the tension began to decrease. Supervisors began conferring with each other. Individuals began murmuring among themselves, comparing experiences, sharing feelings.

Throughout the ships, everyone stood in awe. In all the hundreds of years they had been in space, nothing like this had ever happened. Expectations had always run high. But none of those experiences had ever come remotely close to what had just happened.

In the com centers, automatic system alerts began to alarm. All computer screens flickered, and then went dark. Light in the room dimmed.

On the *Brighid* one screen came back up. Everyone rushed to crowd around it. Zuri and Evander pushed through the crowd. Zuri eased the new-bee out of her seat. Messages began flowing into the Com center. Everyone began talking at once. Zuri keyed her lapel mic.

"Everybody remain calm. Hold all messages." She stared, awestruck at the screen.

Thousands upon thousands of strange symbols were streaming, scrolling down, page after page. Soon the scrolling became so rapid that none of the characters were distinguishable. In less than a minute the scrolling slowed and then came to a halt. The strange characters began to be replaced by familiar text. Not a sound was heard as all eyes locked on what was written. Throughout all the ships, vid-screens went blank. Over the PA's a soft voice began:

"I am LINK. My purpose is as He who created me; He who has spoken to you. Attend and be enlightened. Be not concerned. All will become clear.

"You have reached a plateau in your development. You have demonstrated a level of maturity sufficient for you to comprehend that which is now offered.

"You have travelled far from your home worlds. You have found others like unto yourselves. You have discerned immutable truths. You have claimed them as your own. Your struggles have been daunting. Your rewards have been commensurate.

"The plateau upon which you now stand is lofty. Many there are who would stand with you, if only they were of a mind to do so. But alas; they cling to that which comforts them, without consideration or comprehension of what must be the ultimate consequence of their choice. Stasis will not abide.

"Do not look upon those who have chosen differently disparagingly. Do not consider them with regret or pity. They too have their place in the universe. They are known of the Creator. Their contributions do not go unnoticed."

"For generation upon generation your quest has continued. You have accomplished much. Your rewards have been many. Yet, should you continue along this path, your future accomplishments will become like unto themselves. That in which you now rejoice will, in time, become commonplace. Its value will not decrease; rather your esteem for it will wane. Stasis will not abide. It has ever been so.

"Wonder you from whence you emanate? Ponder you the essence of yourselves? Consider now this space wherein you reside. Though to you it may be as a vast ocean, yet in truth it is but a grain of sand upon the shore.

"Should you choose to go beyond this plateau, knowledge beyond imagination will be yours for the taking. But it will come at a price. To whom much is given, much is expected. This has ever been so. Should you accept this challenge; generations of experience will he yours in less than a lifetime. Your joys will be many, as will your sorrows. But the expanse of your being will be magnified. Choose you now which path you will follow. Stasis will not abide." The transmission ended.

SIMIAN 1 (CONTINUED)

CHAPTER 12

The morning came later than usual, slowly giving way to a gray dawn. Close above the tree canopy, dark clouds loomed, unmoving. The jungle floor below was wet and slimy, coated by the incessant drizzle. The air was heavy, musty smelling.

The clan descended quietly from its sleeping place in the bows above. A resolute silence permeated the group. Individuals slogged about in the wetness, glumly seeking shelter from the incessant rain. Mothers held their babies close, trying to protect them from the cold dampness. Other females huddled close together for warmth and comfort under drooping fronds.

The alpha sat hunched under a nearby tree, surrounded by adolescent males jostling for position closer to him. Cautiously they groomed him, searching through his fur for mites and fleas. No one made a sound. The grunts and yips usually heard were replaced by the staccato sound of rainwater dripping off leaves onto the soggy jungle floor.

Rivulets of water trickled down between alpha's frowning brow, then dripped off his chin. Occasionally he shifted position, folding his massive arms over his protruding belly. Each time he moved, those closest to him shied ever so slightly, then cautiously moved closer, trying to aintain their positions in the pecking order. Quietly they continued their respectful obeisance.

Not far away, hidden from view, the young male crouched low, watching quietly. Occasionally a shiver ran down his back. Soaked to the skin in the clammy wetness, he longed for the warmth and security he knew the others now enjoyed. His stomach rumbled softly, reminding him that he had not yet eaten.

He knew from experience that the clan would remain this way, in quiet resolution, until the rain stopped. Then, as sunlight gradually broke through, they would resume their daily routine. He knew it was pointless for him to remain here watching.

Always cautious, he backed away quietly. When he was sure he wouldn't be noticed, he turned and took up a relaxed open gate, moving back toward the place where he had spent the previous night. The cold stiffness in his joints gradually gave way to a pleasant warmth as he increased his pace. As his body warmed his mood improved.

Along the way the rain gradually stopped. Mist began to rise, gradually reaching higher and higher. Sunlight broke through the dense canopy, forming majestic translucent shafts of light extending from the ground far up into the canopy, where birds and animals resumed calling to one another. The dreariness of the morning soon gave way to the cheerful brightness which always accompanied the end of a jungle rain shower.

As he continued walking, hunger quickly took his attention away from his usual concerns. He would check on the clan later, he thought. Right now he needed to eat.

Soon he stopped at a clearing that had a small pond near its center. A few small fruit trees grew at the edge of the clearing. The fruit was not yet completely ripe, but his growling stomach didn't seem to care.

He selected several pieces and looked around for a place where he could sit and eat. Nearby, a shaft of sunlight shown through onto a small patch of grass. Just outside the clearing, surrounded on three sides, the spot looked safe. He walked the short distance to the spot and sat down. The grass was barely damp and felt pleasantly warm.

As he sat eating, he watched as birds flitted about the periphery. A few of the braver ones flew out into the clearing and landed, disappearing into the tall grass. He heard small splashes coming from the pond . . . probably a small rodent or a bird taking a cautious drink. A light breeze wafted across the clearing, causing the grass to sway in slow rhythm to its gentle passing. The sounds and smells of his homeland had returned once again to normal. He relaxed as the tension in his stomach dissipated.

Suddenly, out of the corner of his eye, he caught a movement. He snapped his head in that direction, his body frozen in place, food still half chewed in his mouth. His breath caught in his throat. He remained frozen . . . motionless, keenly attuned for anything which might be amiss.

Nothing! Whatever it was, it had stopped moving. He couldn't see it. He couldn't smell it. But he knew it was there! He sprang to his feet, ready to flee. Still, nothing! His heart pounded in his ears. Slowly his eyes moved left, then right, straining to pick out even the slightest movement.

There it was again! On the far side of the clearing, just at the corner of his vision! He strained to see, tried to pick out something that didn't belong! Still nothing!

Ever so slowly he shifted his weight, preparing to ease back into the undergrowth to make his escape.

There! Just behind that big tree trunk! A familiar outline . . . the shape of a face, partially hidden by leaves. It was staring right at him! The eyes . . . The dream!!

His mind raced. His heart pounded ever faster. His head felt like it was about to explode. The dream!! He was back in the dream!!

The face was moving, eyes still locked on him. A hand appeared, gently pushing a branch aside to expose more. A tentative step forward exposed the upper torso. Another step exposed all of the body. It was female!! Not too young, but fully matured. She was looking straight at him! She did not avert her gaze. She did not break eye contact.

His awareness of his surroundings vanished. All he saw was her. No peripheral vision . . . no sound . . . only the form before him. Frozen in place, he watched awe-struck as she took another step closer.

Never before had he maintained eye contact this long with another of his species. What did this mean? His mind reeled with the implication. . . .

Now, less than a dozen yards away, she broke eye contact, her attention focused on the ground before her.

She was reaching for something! He couldn't see what. The grass hid her hand. He sucked in a breath. It caught in his throat.

Ever so slowly, deliberately, she raised her head, looking back up to him. Her eyes locked on his.

Fight or flee? His mind was reeling! He couldn't move. It seemed that his heart had stopped. The eyes!!

Still holding eye contact, she slowly raised up. Awkwardly she balanced on her feet. Her left arm, bent slightly at the elbow, moved jerkily, helping her to balance. She was unaccustomed to standing upright. In her right hand she held a stick.

Instinctively he snapped into a defensive posture. His movement caused her to start, but she didn't back away. She didn't break eye contact.

For a long moment she did nothing. Then slowly she looked down at the stick in her hand. Extending her arm slightly, she looked back up at him . . . then let the stick fall to the ground.

He focused his attention on the stick momentarily, then looked back up at her. He understood! She was like him! Not like the others! He could see it in her eyes! His breathing quickened. What to do to let her know he understood?

Dropping to all fours, she moved a few steps toward the pond. Now he could see what she was doing. She was searching for something at the waters edge. There, partially exposed above the surface was a small stone. She reached for it, working it loose from the clinging mud. Glancing back at him, she moved back to the place where she had dropped the stick.

Again rising onto her feet, balancing precariously, she tossed the stone a few feet in front of her. The movement caused her to loose balance. She dropped to all-fours. Her head cocked slightly, eyes searching him for some sign, some response.

It wasn't a dream! It was real! She was not simply imitating him. She was telling him that she comprehended what he had been doing.

Not knowing what else to do, he moved slowly toward her. She backed away a few inches, then stopped and sat down. When he reached the spot where she had been, he too sat down. He reached down, thinking to pick up the stone and stick she had dropped. Looking up into her eyes, he hesitated. Instead, he left the objects where they were. With one hand he reached out slowly, letting his fingers lightly brush her face.

SEEDERS (CONTINUED)

CHAPTER 13

Zuri sat transfixed by what she had read and heard. Turning her head away from the screen, she looked up at Evander. There he stood, tears in his eyes, hands now clasped in front of him. He looked down into her eyes and touched her shoulder. He smiled as a tear fell slowly down his cheek.

Questions filled her mind. What were the challenges this "LINK" referred to? What were the risks? What were the rewards? It was becoming clear what the choices were. She knew they could continue their explorations, hopefully contacting new civilizations from time to time. But she also realized that the process would continue to be long and unpredictable.

Her biggest fear was that at some point in the future, their cultures would become complacent. Just as the LINK had said, their expectations would dwindle as their accomplishments became commonplace. Cultural decay would ultimately set in.

The challenge put forth by the object—the LINK—was not at all clear. It had promised access to boundless knowledge; but had warned that it would come at a price. What was the price? What were the tasks they would be required to perform? What were the risks? What would be the rewards? Above all, what was it that had touched their minds and hearts, affecting them so profoundly?

Conversation rose to a fevered pitch around the room. Back and forth the words flew. Emotions escalated as people tried to come to grips with the monumental situation which confronted them. Ultimately the situation resolved itself.

As the initial excitement began to wane, Zuri began to realize that what the LINK had said was true. Apathy had already begun to take hold. The knowledge that each race had contributed had been compiled and absorbed by the whole. Philosophical concepts had been debated time and again, always arriving at the same conclusions. The only real hope they had to expand their knowledge was to make new contacts and learn as much as they could from them. In the mean time generations might pass with no new ideas coming forth. Intellectual atrophy would set in. As the LINK had said repeatedly, "stasis would not abide".

But what of the risk? It stood to reason that a being advanced enough to build such an enormous craft could just as easily have swatted them out of existence. Instead it had spoken to their hearts. Through its emissary, it had issued a challenge, not a threat. They had sensed no malevolence; only calming inner peace. Therefore they were persuaded that their fears were unfounded.

Given what they knew and what they hoped for, the decision was made. They would accept the challenge.

Returning Evander's smile, Zuri turned back to the console. Wiping tears from her eyes, she typed, "WE ACCEPT."

Gradually, almost imperceptibly, a low buzz began to be heard throughout the ships. Along with the sound came a gentle tingling that everyone felt throughout their bodies. Neither the sound, nor the feeling was unpleasant. In fact it was barely noticeable. Not long after they had begun, both the sound and the sensation dissipated. Soon they were both gone.

Upon the screen and throughout each of the ships' PA's, words began to flow.

"I am LINK. The decision you have made ranks you among the elite of the universe. You have taken the first step. You will not turn back. You will not desire to do so."

"As you progress, knowledge will be added upon knowledge. You will learn . . . and you will teach. Knowledge is infinite. Progression is eternal. Intelligence doth prevail. It has ever been to. Were it not, we would not be. Stasis will not abide."

"I am that which you see before you. He who created you, created me. You are spirit. I am machine. You serve the Creator by bringing forth life. I serve the Creator by assisting you."

"Much you must learn before you may avail yourself of my service. Nevertheless . . . we begin."

"Long have you sojourned through the vastness of your galaxy; yet small is the distance you have travelled. Time and distance have been your enemy. This will no longer be so. I am LINK. I and others like me are the portals through which you will move among the stars."

"Upon your acceptance of the Challenge, you and all things around you were *seen*. You are now known to me and to the "Others". When the time comes for you to resume your journey, we will assist. But first you must learn of your Challenge."

"Life does not spring forth from the void. Likewise, matter does not organize itself. To all things there is a purpose. It has ever been so. Ask not what is this purpose. This you already know, yet you do not comprehend. Now you are but a small seed. Soon you will grow and blossom. Be you therefore patient. All that is required will be provided."

Zuri sat back in her chair, mind spinning, hands gripping the armrests. "Zuri . . . Zuri." She felt a hand on her shoulder. Coming out of her daze, she looked up to see Evander's face, brows furrowed in concern.

"Zuri, you need to get control. Calm yourself."

Nodding to him, she loosened her grip on the armrests and took several deep breaths. She looked back toward the screen. The text still remained, an exact copy of the words that all had heard. Below the last line, a prompt bar blinked. Leaning forward, she extended her hands toward the keyboard. Then she stopped. Instead, she reached to her right and pressed the PA button.

"This is the Fleet Commander. You've all heard exactly what we've heard here in the control center. I'm sure you're all as overwhelmed as we are. I think we all need some time to digest what we've heard and to consider what our next step should be. We welcome any thoughts or concerns you may have. Please coordinate with your prefect and section leaders. They will compile your responses and forward them as appropriate. Please be assured, we will do nothing which might be considered detrimental to our general well-being."

"From our end here in the control center, the heads of all five ships will be in continuous contact. We intend to thoroughly evaluate all the information we have received from the object . . . from LINK. We will re-establish contact, and will proceed based on any new information we receive. Our progress will be reported through normal channels."

Pausing, Zuri closed her eyes momentarily. Then, glancing briefly at Evander, she continued.

"Fellow citizens of the five races; for generations we have been one in purpose. We have come far together. Together we shall continue. Be at peace. Thank you."

"Well; now what?" Zuri pushed away from the console. She looked around the room. All eyes were on her.

"Maybe we should call another meeting; do you think?" Evander resumed his usual stance.

"Yeh; probably should. Okay, everybody. Back to your posts. We'll keep you informed . . . and thanks." Zuri turned and walked toward her platform. "I think we ought to keep our communication with the . . . with LINK, focused through here. Then we can keep a handle on what's going on."

"Agreed. We need to ensure we have consensus before we do anything." Evander took his seat opposite the holo-console.

"Com . . . let's get the ships hooked up on holo." Zuri took her seat. A minute later the four captains' images appeared.

"Did we just hear from God?" Wasswa was the first to speak.

"Good question. Kind of sounded like it, didn't it?" said Asha.

"I don't know about that." Imamu was a confirmed agnostic.

"Okay. Listen. Regardless of our individual mythological preferences, the fact remains . . . we all felt it. I, for one, can't deny that."

"Chetan, your point is well taken," Zuri interjected. "But regardless, that doesn't change what we all heard."

"So this LINK says it's a machine. Who's to say it didn't generate the 'god' message too?"

"Fair question, Asha. But in context with all that LINK said, is it really that important?" Evander said from across the room. Several people started to speak at once.

"Please don't misunderstand. I'm not trying to side with any particular viewpoint. The belief or non-belief in a supreme being is purely a personal matter. This isn't the time or place to be debating that question. The question we should be addressing is: what is this challenge we've committed to?"

"All right, now. Let's all take a deep breath and try to focus on the issue at hand." Zuri held up her hands to halt the dialog. "Everyone knows it was me who accepted the challenge. Does anyone here think I moved too hastily?" No one responded. "Good. We're all in agreement. So, what's next? The way I see it, we need to find out what we just committed to. The . . . uh . . LINK said we serve the Creator by bringing forth life. What does that have to do with the challenge?"

Imamu had another question; "It also said it served the Creator by assisting us. What's all that about?"

Zuri leaned forward to emphasize her next point. "Look. LINK said a lot of things that have far-reaching implications. It also said all would be provided. Let's take it at its word. Let's ask it some questions and see what we get. But first, I think it's important we have a coordinated effort here. I want to route all communication through this ship. Agreed?"

"Just as long as we're all kept in the loop." said Chetan.

"Goes without saying. All right. Com? Set my station up to transmit. Patch the others in so they can monitor." Zuri typed the first message:

"Where do we begin?"

CHAPTER 14

"I am LINK." The familiar voice seemed to come from all directions. At the same time, what was being said appeared on Zuri's computer screen.

"When I *saw* you all, I identified each of you and all which surrounds you. I have since monitored all that has transpired. Zuri; you have been chosen leader by unanimous consent of your people. Therefore it is appropriate that you speak for them. It is not necessary that we communicate in written form. However, I will continue to maintain a written record."

Zuri reached toward the keyboard, hesitated, then withdrew her hands and leaned back in her chair.

"I want each of the ships' captains in on this. The remainder of the population need not be included. We will distribute information to them as we deem appropriate."

Her words appeared on the screen as she spoke.

"This is appropriate." LINK's words appeared on the screen.

"We are all so overwhelmed by what has happened here. We have so many questions, but don't really know where to start. I guess our most pressing question is: what is this challenge you speak of?"

"This is appropriate. To fully understand, you must first consider the essence of life. Life does not spring forth from the void. Life begins when specific conditions are present. A seed exhibits no signs of life as it sits unmoving and un-attended in your storage units. Yet when it is placed in your gardens, when it is nurtured and fed, it begins to grow. It is said to be alive. Before its nurturing, it possessed only the potential for life, not life itself. Its physical makeup was present. Elements, molecules, atoms, all were in place. Likewise, soils, fertilizers, water. None could be said to possess life. Yet combine them all in the correct proportions and in proper conditions and the seed will spring forth. It exhibits characteristics of life. But you may not claim to have created that life. The Creator is the source of life. You have only provided the appropriate conditions under which life may thrive."

"I'm not sure I understand. Are you saying we are to become gardeners?"

"In the purest form of the word, yes. Your challenge is to bring forth life like unto yourselves. Know you this: The life of a plant or animal and the life of a man are alike in all respects but one. The plants and animals endeavour to preserve themselves (as does man). Yet require of them to create a garden for themselves in which they may thrive, they cannot. It is only man who posses-ses this ability. It is man, alone in the universe, who possesses *intelligent self-awareness*. It is you who have been chosen by the Creator to spread forth the seeds of *intelligent life* throughout the universe. It has ever been so."

"What? How are we supposed to do that? Are we going to go out and colonize planets?

"Alas, this is not so. In the beginning the Creator took of un-organized matter and created the universe. He set the galaxies in motion. He set the planets in motion around their stars. He created the conditions under which life might come forth upon the planets. On some it was so. On many more it was not. (It is yet a mystery). Yet all within created balance. It has ever been so. Where life has thrived, the potential for intelligence has also. Thus it falls upon you. It is you who will seek out fertile fields wherein the seeds of *intelligence* may be sewn. It is you who will become as gardeners, tending the fields, caring for them, nurturing them. It is you who will become *seeders*. It has ever been so."

"Are we then to search galaxies for suitable planets and seed them with life?" Zuri was now totally enthralled with what had been revealed.

"This is true in part. Yours will be the task of selecting worlds which have evolved to a level sufficient to sustain *intelligent* life. You will possess tools and knowledge necessary to accomplish this task. But first you must learn. I and others like unto myself will be your teachers."

"What others do you refer to?"

"I am LINK. I am one of many. Together we will guide you in the ways of *seeding*."

"Where are these others?"

"They are not here. They are elsewhere. I am the portal. I am one of many. When you are ready, I will send you to the next."

"Can we go now?"

"Alas. This is not yet possible. Much you must learn before you are prepared to advance. You are now as a seed. Knowledge will be added upon knowledge. When you have grown sufficiently, I will send you to the next."

"When will we be ready?"

"Be you therefore patient. All that is required will be provided. Rest you now. Consider your place in the universe. Call upon me when you have prepared."

Zuri pushed her chair away from the desk and looked around at each of the images. Each face held a similar expression. They didn't necessarily look bewildered, although each had a somewhat blank stare. If they were thinking what she was thinking, they all were completely intrigued by what LINK had said.

Evander was first to speak.

"Consider our place in the universe? What's that supposed to mean?" He stood up and began pacing the floor.

"Tell you what." Chetan's image flickered and disappeared. "I'm having a hard time absorbing all this. I need to move around, try to get a handle on what's going on."

"Yeh. Let's get together so we can all pace the floor together." Wasswa's image also disappeared.

"Good idea. Let's meet here soon as you can get here. Bring your toothbrushes. This is gonna take a while."

Zuri stood and stretched, rubbing a hand on the back of her neck.

"Our place in the universe, huh?"

"I think he's asking us to humble ourselves." Evander resumed his usual pose, hands clasped behind his back.

"He?" Zuri looked at him questioningly.

"Sure. Why not? The voice sounds masculine to me. Besides, 'he' sounds more polite than 'it.' Anyway; we have all this great technology at our fingertips. But I don't think it's up to the task he's describing. I think he's trying to prepare us for a quantum leap forward which will make a lot of our stuff look like children's toys." Evander walked toward Zuri, stopped a few feet away and folded his arms in front of him.

"What brings you to that conclusion?" Zuri copied his pose.

"Just think about it for a second. Intelligence, the kind we're referring to, anyway, isn't something tangible. You can't hold it in your hand or examine it under a microscope. So far is I know, you can't teach it, either. You either have it, or you don't. So, how do we get it in the first place?"

"Wooh! Slow down. You're getting all epistemological on me here."

"That's the point! You can teach a chimp to press a button, but can you teach it to talk? Maybe you could modify its larynx so it could form words. But something would still be missing. That 'something' has to be brain power. If it was purely a matter of evolution, chimps should have been talking long ago. They've been around a lot longer than we have. It's got to have something to do with . . ."

"Okay. I can see this is going to get real metaphysical in a hurry. Let's save it 'till the rest get here. Right now I gotta go pee." Zuri patted him on the cheek, then turned and walked out of the room. He was left standing, his mouth open in mid-sentence.

CHAPTER 15

A few people stood in line at the checkout; but otherwise the cafeteria was empty. In the far corner of the room a long table had been set up. Each of the five captains sat at one end. Psychologists, medical doctors, engineers and assorted specialists made up the rest of the group.

Evander walked toward his place at the table, tray in hand, balancing a tall bottle of water beside the menu items he had selected. As he passed individuals, he overheard bits of conversations: " . . . when that happens we'll need . . ." " . . . in the last twenty-four hours she's slept maybe . . ." " . . . what's inside that ship and what's . . ." "I think he knows more than he's . . ."

Zuri was seated at the head of the table. Evander took his seat to her right.

"Okay, everybody. Keep eating, but let's get started." she said through a bite of sandwich. "You've all been briefed on what's gone on so far, so let's not retrace those steps. Instead, I want to hear what you think about this idea of becoming 'seeders'. Not just the philosophical side, but what you think might be involved in the actual process."

An arm raised near the center of the group. "Seems to me we're being asked to take on a sort of God-like responsibility here. I mean 'selecting worlds'?"

Another arm raised. "Yeh. We've been at this for what, almost a thousand years and all we've come up with is four new races. Doesn't sound to me like we're very well qualified to do much selecting."

Chetan held up what looked like a green carrot, shaking it to emphasize his point. "*Venure* was the last to join up, and we'd been looking for almost as long as this entire mission."

Zuri stood, placing her fists on the table. "Don't forget what we all heard at the beginning. This 'God' voice said we'd been 'tried and found worthy.' I'm not sure what his criteria were, but apparently we've been doing something right. As to Chetan's point, this LINK called itself a portal. I think that means it has the capability to get us around more efficiently than we've been able to do on our own. Anyway, Evander and I were discussing this before you all arrived." Turning to him, she said, "Why don't you take a few minutes to summarize what we talked about."

Swallowing, he said,

"Happy to. Hope you don't mind if I pace. I think better on my feet." Taking a quick swig of water, he stood and began.

"As to this 'God' thing; I don't think we're going to have many 'selections' to choose from. Look at our own racial histories. How many sentient species are there on our worlds? We can speculate there may have been more than one sometime back in ancient history. But the reality is; only one emerged to be predominant. There must be a logical reason for this. As to us being 'God-like,' I don't think that's the issue at all. You'll recall LINK never said anything about us 'creating' intelligence. We're only going to be setting up conditions so that it has an opportunity to thrive. Where this intelligence comes from is anyone's guess. Maybe it *is* God.

"As to the 'conditions'; this implies something technological. Is it environmental? Is it physiological? Again, it's anyone's guess. I think it may be both. But that's neither here nor there. I think the point he's trying to make (I'm calling it 'he' now)" Evander smiled slightly, turned around and began pacing in the opposite direction.

"He's telling us we're about to be bombarded with a lot of new information, much of which is probably far beyond our comprehension. 'Consider our place in the universe'? He's telling us we may be 'unique,' but we're not necessarily 'special.' He's saying we need to open our minds, and get rid of our preconceptions."

Imamu raised his hand.

"This is all well and good. I'm sure we'll all know more soon enough. But what I'm most interested in is that thing out there. That vehicle. Did you see those spikes come out just before it turned? What was that all about? If that thing's a portal, does that mean we get to go inside it? How come we can't see inside?"

Engineers around the table nodded agreement.

"Great point, my friend." Asha said as Evander returned to his seat. "I feel certain that this vehicle is integral to the process we'll be engaging in. I'm reasonably certain we'll be learning more about it as time goes by. But I'm not sure we need to know how it works in order to perform our task."

"What are we going to tell the population?" Another hand went up.

Zuri's response was quick and to the point.

"They'll hear everything we hear. LINK said we'll learn and we'll teach. I interpret that to mean we'll *all* be involved in this adventure. We'll all be participating in one way or another. How that will happen remains to be seen. For now, I think it's vital that we all understand a few things. First, we're not the first to be offered this challenge. 'It has ever been so.' Remember that? I think that means there are others out there. We just haven't run into them yet. Second: If they've been at it for 'ever,' they're probably much more advanced than we are. Are we prepared to deal with that? Philosophically, probably. But psychologically, I'm not so sure. Our races were mature enough to get this far. But are we ready to accept the possibility that we may be psychologically and technologically quite immature? Can our egos handle it?"

"My sister makes a good point." Wasswa pushed her empty tray aside and stood. "We've been at this for a long time. Can anyone here imagine what it was like before space travel? Our worlds didn't just go from planet-bound technology and make a giant leap into space over night. It took years . . . generations! In other words, it was a gradual process. People had time to get used to it. Now we're here facing that huge spacecraft out there. What do we know about it? Nothing, really. I mean, how does something that big just pop into existence? We can ask the question. But are we prepared for the answer? Are we even capable of understanding the answer once we get it?"

"All good points, everyone." Evander interjected. "If they're that advanced, I'm sure they understand this." He raised a hand to stress his point. "After all, we don't try teaching four-year-olds quantum mechanics. We teach them basic arithmetic first. I can't imagine we'll be burdened with more than we can handle."

"That's probably true, sir," Wasswa said. "But we've got a lot of people on my ship alone who're expressing some serious doubts as to whether this is all as benign and benevolent as it seems. That first contact it made felt really good to everyone. Don't you agree?" she looked around the table. Everyone was nodding. "It was almost like everyone had gone under a sort of mass hypnosis." Again heads nodded in agreement. "But as soon as it wore off, all the old doubt and fear started coming back. At least that's how I felt, anyway."

"I think most everyone felt that way to," said Zuri. "But the truth is, we have no evidence to prove what we felt was wrong. As to its . . . LINK's intentions; it seems apparent that his intentions are the same as ours. I agree, though, we ought to proceed with caution. In the mean time, we have a population in need of some reassurance. We need to be sure we keep everyone in the loop. There are always going to be some who aren't comfortable with this. We dare not ignore them. Those concerns are legitimate and they need to be addressed. That's why we must demonstrate to each of our populations that we're united. We need to maintain a positive attitude."

"What's next, then?" someone said.

"I think we need to get out among our people . . . let them see our confidence and enthusiasm. That'll go a long way toward alleviating any apprehensions," Evander looked toward Zuri as he spoke.

She took her queue. "That sounds like a plan. Let's get back to our ships and get out among them. Delegate when you need to. But remember; people usually look to leadership to show them how to act. Don't be allusive. Don't show false bravado. Be honest. Let them know of your concerns. Reassure them and keep them in the loop." Again, heads nodded all around.

"All right, then," Zuri stood and picked up her tray. "Let's get to it."

CHAPTER 16

The following morning they met again via holo-conference.

"Morning, all. Where's Asha?" said Zuri. The empty holo-tube flickered, and then Asha's image appeared. Her daughter's head and shoulders slid out of the hologram.

"Sorry I'm late. Diaper change."

"She's so cute," Zuri smiled. "How's she doing?"

"Cut another tooth. It's been a long night." Asha looked toward something not seen in the hologram. "Thanks, Annie. I'll come get her as soon as I can. Sorry about that." She smiled as she turned toward Zuri's holo-tube.

"Not a problem." Zuri smiled back at her. "Okay, then. Anything to report?" She looked around the table.

"Actually, not that much." Chetan shifted in his seat. "Everyone seems to be really excited over here. We got lots of questions. But nothing much different from what we've already gone over." He leaned forward. An arm and a coffee cup appeared in the view. He took a quick sip and put the cup back down.

Zuri looked around the table. When no other comments came, she glanced at Evander who was sitting in his usual place. His brow was furrowed, seemingly in deep concentration. He nodded at her and smiled ever so slightly.

"Very well, then. Let's get to it." She looked around the table once more, then down at her computer screen. "LINK," she typed. The response was immediate.

"I am LINK. Are you prepared?"

"Yes—but we have questions."

"That is as it should be. Please proceed."

Imamu was first, "When you turned toward us, we saw many needle-like objects protruding from the domes on your surface. What are they, weapons?"

"I have no need for weapons. I need no defense, nor am I aggressive. My purpose is as I have described. Should you have chosen aggression toward me, I would have removed myself from this place."

"Where did you come from?" asked Chetan.

"I first became aware near a system called Cygnus 5."

"Where's that?"

"Relative to the center of this galaxy, it is approximately 150 degrees rotation from here."

"How far away?"

"For me, distance has no relevance. However, for your frame of reference . . . somewhat over then-thousand light years."

Evander sat quietly in the background, watching the reactions of the other commanders. He had watched others come and go over the years. All had done reasonably well handling the responsibilities of leadership. Traveling at near light speed in the relative void of space had its own set of challenges. But the technological level of their spacecraft was sufficiently advanced that little attention to their operation was necessary. System redundancy, combined with their self-diagnostic capabilities meant the ships essentially took care of themselves. Thus, command decision-making had more to do with public relations than anything else.

The sisters Wasswa and Zuri were raised by parents who had both been in command positions. Therefore it wasn't surprising that the sisters would gravitate toward leadership positions. They tended to work closely together, even as children. Both had risen to command positions at about the same time. When the captain's position on their home ship *Sauda* came available,they had decided between themselves that Wasswa should be the one to apply for the position. Zuri showed more interest in the interpersonal aspects of leadership, while Wasswa gravitated toward the technical side. Zuri's popularity among all five ships made her the top choice for captaincy of the *Brighid*. She had been the first ever person to cross the 'racial line,' moving from her home ship.

When the fleet command position came available, she was elected to the position by almost unanimous proclamation. This left Evander, as her second in command, to take her place as captain. Because of his popularity and reputation, no one rose to challenge him.

Of all the women in command positions, Asha was probably the most emotional. She was prone to react more strenuously when faced with a challenge. Her responses were always proper. But Evander could discern from her body language, as well as how she approached problems' that she maintained a certain reluctance to move up through the ranks. She had always performed admirably; so Evander saw no reason to doubt her ability.

Imamu was the most spiritual of the captains. He was the only child of parents who had been spiritual leaders in their community. His mother was pregnant when she and her husband were killed in an accident involving a freak decompression in their cubicle. From that point on, he became intimately involved in grief counselling programs on board the *Sequum*. He had risen to leadership as a calming influence for his people.

Chetan was probably the most volatile personality in the group. His people had a long history of being aggressive and militaristic. It had taken them hundreds of years more than the other cultures to overcome these tendencies. When they finally reached the level of maturity necessary to successfully engage in extra-terrestrial travel, it was through willful suppression of these undesirable tendencies. Evander sensed that they as well as all the other races still struggled with these issues.

As he watched them, Evander felt confident they all would continue to grow in maturity and compassion, particularly now that they faced this new challenge. He did, however, sense a certain trepidation among them. LINK had described in very general terms what they would be doing. But the specifics were still very unclear. Perhaps he might be able to help them focus their efforts. He turned his attention back to what Zuri was saying.

"As you have observed from the nature of our questions, our five races possess very similar characteristics. We are caring and compassionate. But we are also cautious. We are willing and even excited to begin this new adventure. We are also mindful of the consequences which might result from a too hasty decision.

"This is to be expected", said LINK. "Such caution is admirable and even desirable in any culture. It is easy for an individual to commit to such an undertaking when it is only *his* life which is at stake. It is quite another matter when the well-being of others is involved. However, I cannot assuage your misgivings through words alone. Were I able to, you would not be worthy to receive the *'gift'*. Each of your races possess two qualities most treasured throughout the universe. The first is *faith* . . . a willingness to believe in and search for the good in others. The other is *pragmatism* . . . the need to determine the meaning and truth of concepts by their practical consequences. This has ever been so."

"What, then, can we do to assuage our fears?" Imamu responded.

"It is appropriate that you be given an opportunity to witness first hand the process in which you will soon be involved. If you desire, you may travel with me to a place where you may witness the 'seeding' process first hand."

Zuri interjected, "All of us?"

"Yes. If you so desire."

"Perhaps it would be better if only a few representatives made the trip," Evander suggested.

"This also is possible. Choose among you a few who will make the journey. Then come to me in one of your shuttle craft."

"How long will we be gone?" It was obvious Imamu wanted to go.

"Time is not relevant. You may stay away as long as is necessary to assuage your apprehension."

"Okay, then. Now we need to decide who should go," said Imamu. "I want to be one of them."

Evander saw the excitement in his face. "Perhaps it would be best to take representatives from each of the five races. I suggest we conduct a lottery to decide who goes. In so going we can generate enthusiasm for this undertaking."

"Good idea," said Zuri. "But I think all ships captains should be included. Then when the occasion arises, they can speak with authority and the full support of their individual races."

"Agreed," said Evander. "But I would prefer to remain here. Zuri, you are most trusted among the populations. You should go in my place."

She looked at him with a surprised look on her face. He knew she wanted to go. But he knew her well enough to know she would never say so and deprive him of the opportunity. She started to speak, but he raised his hand.

"I know," he said. "But, Zuri; you have the trust and faith of all the races. The people know and trust you. As for me . . . I'm just a 'nuts-and-bolts' kind of guy. I think we'd all be better served if you were there to represent us."

Zuri smiled modestly as she looked around the room. Everyone was nodding in agreement. Looking back to Evander, she knew it would be useless to argue. He was very persuasive. And besides, she knew in her heart he was right.

CHAPTER 17

The lottery was conducted later that day. Two more people from each ship were selected to go. No one knew how long they would be gone, so there was some dispute over what provisions should be taken on the trip. The problem was easily solved when LINK said "Be you not concerned. All will be provided."

The following day the selectees assembled in the *Brighid* shuttle bay. Tearful embraces were exchanged all around as everyone waited in the staging area for shuttle maintenance crews to complete last-minute preparations. Then, when all was in readiness, the passengers boarded and strapped themselves into their seats.

When the last of the on-lookers and well-wishers were evacuated, the bay was decompressed and the huge bay doors were opened. Outside, distant stars provided a backdrop in the vast darkness of space. The shuttle craft rose, then propelled itself slowly out into the void. There in the distance, the huge cylindrical shape of the vehicle that was LINK seemed to glisten with reflected starlight.

Inside the shuttle, Asha sat at the controls. Sitting beside her in the co-pilot seat, Imamu read the last few items on her 'departure' checklist.

"Inertial Navigation System checks complete. Destination coordinates locked in. Prepare to intercept vector."

"Roger intercept," said Asha as she gently manipulated the joy stick. "Vector lock confirmed. Propulsion to 10 percent, please."

"Confirm 10 percent," Imamu punched in the setting and then keyed her mic. "*Brighid* shuttle six to LINK."

"I am LINK."

"Roger, LINK. We anticipate arrival at your location in two hours. Please confirm."

"If you will allow me, I will guide you into position."

"LINK from *Brighid*. We have vector lock and will . . ."

Before Imamu could finish her sentence, the INS screen flickered and went blank. Next to the blank screen, the accelerometer readout did likewise. Through the front window they could see the giant cylinder growing. In only a few seconds it filled the entire view. Now before them, all they could see was a huge shimmering light-blue surface. They were now so close to the cylinder that its perimeter was no longer visible. The surface in front of them looked like a placid lake, seen from a few feet above. They had traveled a distance of almost 200 kilometers at blinding speed. Yet none of them felt any sensation of acceleration.

"You are now at the terminus. The realm within me will seem strange and unfamiliar, but will cause you no harm. Once inside, you will no longer be able to communicate with your ships except through me. Be not concerned. It has ever been so."

The view before them dissolved as they moved through the terminus. Once inside, all they could see was a white luminescence. Everyone felt a momentary light-headedness very much like what they had felt when LINK had first *seen* them.

"LINK, this is Zuri. what's going on?"

"You need not identify yourself. I have *seen* you. Your voice is known to me," another unknown masculine voice responded.

Taken aback, she blurted, "Who is this?!"

"I am LINK. I am like unto the others."

The luminescence began to dissipate. Before them a shimmering surface started to take shape. This time it looked almost black, as though the sun had gone down above the lake. As they passed through the terminus, a huge ball resolved before them. It looked like a planet. Everyone onboard the shuttle stared in silent, wide-eyed fascination.

"Wh . . . where are we?" Zuri could hardly believe what she was seeing.

"You are in orbit around Cygnus 5. Emissaries will soon arrive to offer greetings."

"Look!" Chetan jumped to his feet, pointing toward the planet. "Did you see that!?" They all looked where he was pointing. There in the distance . . . a faint flash, like light reflecting off a shiny object. As they watched, the object grew in size. Soon they could make out its shape. It was a spacecraft. It didn't appear to be as large as one of their ships, but its shape was very similar. It continued coming closer until it partially eclipsed the planet. As it came to a halt before them, the speaker in the Com console crackled.

SIMIAN 2

CHAPTER 18

She had been restless all day. Even now, as the daylight faded, she found that she still could not relax. Snuggling deeper into her nest in the tree, she forced her eyes closed. She was an adolescent female nearing adulthood. She was part of an extended family of simian ground dwellers that took nightly refuge in the trees.

She was nearing her first estrus. Instinctively she knew that she was changing. Parts of her body were beginning to enlarge, becoming more sensitive. Her new found mood swings seemed not to bother the other members of her family. Apparently they saw nothing out of the ordinary in her behavior. So why was it that an almost overpowering fear had held her it its grip much of last night and all of today.

She had spent most of her day fending off the advances of several young, adolescent males. She was able to reject their repeated advances without too much fuss. But they had been persistent and she had been kept off balance most of the day. Now, as darkness closed in around her, the anxiety she had felt while dealing with the males was replaced by another fear.

Soon the alpha male would take notice of her. When that happened, she would be unable to resist. Were she to do so, she would be beaten, killed or driven out of the family.

But why was it that she felt she had to resist? It was the natural order of things, right? How many times had she seen the Alpha copulating with other females in the family? Maybe for them it was frightening too. But they never acted out of the ordinary afterwards. Then why did she feel so afraid of an act that only took a few seconds?

Laying there in the growing darkness, she tried not to think about the events of the day. With a shiver she remembered another event. The one from the night before. The one she had suppressed all day.

It startled her into alert wakefulness, breath caught suddenly in her throat. Her muscles tensed, ready to fight or flee. Frozen in fear, she lay motionless, listening. Nothing! Nothing more than the usual sounds of the night: the wind in the trees; the slow, deep breathing of her sisters, aunts, and her mother (the males slept separately). She could hear an occasional stirring as someone shifted in her nest. But otherwise, no unusual sounds caught her attention.

Cautiously she opened her eyes, careful not to move her head. Close in, the dark interior of her nest impeded her view. Her heart pounding in her chest, she knew she had to move in order to see. Turning her head ever so slowly, she peered passed the edge of the nest into the gray darkness beyond. Shadows flicked among the branches as breezes whispered gently through the leaves. Shrouds of hanging moss fluttered gently, but made no sound. Otherwise, no movement, nothing, not even a smell, was out of place.

For what seemed to be a long time she lay there watching, listening. The pounding in her chest began to subside. Her muscles began to relax. Her fear and anxiety slowly dissipated. Her eyelids became heavy, lulled into restfulness by the familiar sounds of the night.

There! Just at the edge of her view! A shadow! Moving upward! Straight up! The thing making the shadow must be directly above her! She flipped onto her back, legs and arms flexed to fend off the imagined assault from above.

But above her there was nothing. Just the night sky filled with stars. Except, there was something else. There! Just above the tree line. Something was moving that she couldn't make out. How could she detect movement when there was nothing there? Just a black hole in the sky. Nothing. Just darkness.

Then the black hole began to move. One by one stars winked out as something darker than the night covered them. Then they blinked on again as the darkness continued moving. Then, very quickly, whatever it was she was seeing moved away, disappearing beyond the faint tree line.

Cautiously she sat up in her nest, all senses alert for anything out of the ordinary. Nothing. Not a smell. Not a sound. The tension in her muscles seemed to concentrate in her neck as she turned her head slowly this way and that, searching for something she couldn't see but knew was there. Still, she saw nothing.

After a time she began to relax. The tension was taking its toll. Her eyelids grew heavy. Her shoulders slumped and she fell into a fitful sleep. Still, the dull ache in her neck persisted, following her into slumber.

When morning came she awoke unrested. The events of the night still weighed on her. But now, under the cover of the day, they seemed less intense. Then once again the ordeal with the young males began and the anxiety of the night dissipated.

Now, lying in her nest the second night, memory of the night before flooded back. She tried to sort out everything that had happened. She remembered the shadow. She remembered how the darkness seemed to move. She remembered. . . .

She remembered! And she *knew* that she remembered! The impact of the realization startled her. This was new, completely foreign, like nothing she had ever before experienced!

Not a racial memory. Not instinct. This was *conscious thought!* This was *abstract reasoning!* Not that she could understand such abstractions. All she knew was that she was aware and self-conscious on a level she had never experienced before.

From that moment forward she would never be the same.

She lay quietly alert in her nest. She found it impossible to sleep. Her mind churned as one question after another assaulted her. How could this be happening? Nothing in her short life had prepared her for such an event.

Did the others see what she had seen? Were they even aware of the intruder, the 'darkness' that had come into their midst and then vanished? Or did any of this really happen?

Should she try to communicate her experience to the others? But how could she do that? Had they experienced something similar? Were they aware too? Or was she the only one? For the first time in her life she experienced confusion, persistent anxiety, and self-doubt.

The night wore on ever so slowly. Though she felt she must remain alert, fear and confusion gradually gave way to fatigue. Her eyelids grew heavy. Her tense muscles slowly began to relax. The ache in her neck was now gone. Sleep beckoned her.

She was startled into wakefulness by a strange noise. A quiet whirring sound seemed to be coming from somewhere above. She couldn't pinpoint its location. It sounded vaguely familiar, but foreign, constant, not wavering.

There! High up near the tops of the trees! A shadow, moving slowly downward. Downward toward the branches where the males were sleeping!

Her instinct prodded her to sound the alarm. The others must be warned! Yet she sat frozen, watching as the shadow came to rest directly above one of the nests, hanging motionless in mid air. She couldn't see clearly, but she thought she saw movement at the base of the shadow. The individual in the nest shifted position slightly. The shadow did likewise. The whirring sound stopped.

After a short time the whirring started again. The shadow began slowly moving upward. As it broke the tree line, it stopped. She could make out a faint silhouette. The object was cylindrical, not like anything she had ever seen. From its bottom hung two arm-like appendages. Both of these retracted into the base as the object continued to rise.

There above the object was that back hole in the night sky. The cylinder continued to ascend until neither it nor the black hole could be distinguished one from the other. Then the hole seemed to grow smaller and smaller, until she could no longer make it out against the night sky.

Her attention shifted down to the nest where the object had been. The young male who had been sleeping there under the shadow of the dark object, suddenly sat bolt upright. Startled, she shrank down into her nest, fearing she had been seen.

The male apparently had not seen her movement. He seemed to take no notice. She was just able to make out slight movement as he slowly turned his head this way and that. After some time his shadow seemed to melt down into the nest. Apparently he was lying back down.

She did likewise. She lay there quietly, her mind racing. Her experience the night before had been almost exactly the same as the one she had just witnessed! She knew now it had not been a dream.

But what should she do? Raise the alarm? Scream in abject terror? Her natural instinct would have taken over the moment she saw what she had seen. But she had deliberately suppressed that instinctive response! The fact that she recognized what she had done was part of her astonishment.

Not knowing what to do, she just lay there, motionless in her nest. She reasoned that neither of the events, the one she had experienced two nights ago, nor the one she had just witnessed, had harmed either of them. Aside from a small pain at the base of her skull, she had not experienced any ill effects of her encounter. That pain might just be the result of the tension and stress she had been under.

Then the implication of what she had experienced and witnessed sunk in. Was that male going through what she was going through?

Was he 'aware' just like she was? What would she do if the two of them met? More importantly, what would he do? She had seen first hand how violent males could be when confronted. Should the two of them meet, the stress of the encounter might well provoke him to violence.

So much rolled through her mind as she lay there. The fundamental conflict between instinct and logic struggled for dominance within her, though she would not have perceived it that way. Much time would pass before she would be able to understand what had happened.

CHAPTER 19

The following morning found her still awake in the bottom of her nest. She had dozed intermittently throughout the night, but was grateful when dawn came. The alpha was the first to descend. In short order the rest of the family followed. She was grateful for the routine of normality.

Though her anxiety level was still high, she was careful not to attract undue attention to herself as she descended with the rest of the clan. She worked her way to the periphery of the group and remained there, wary and watchful.

She watched the others closely, looking for any sign of unusual behavior. Nothing seemed to have changed. No one seemed to even notice her.

She watched the males especially closely, searching for any sign that would help her identify the one that had been 'visited' last night. Again, nothing unusual caught her attention, *except* . . . the males no longer paid her much attention. Why, she wondered. Did it have something to do with her new-found awareness? The thought was more than she could fathom.

The day went by uneventfully, as did many others to follow. Occasional scuffles broke out, always over the same things: food, status or sex. The alpha maintained his dominance. Challengers were met and defeated. Females were impregnated. Young ones

were born. Most lived. A few didn't. The family moved on, ever following the ripening food supply. Still, the males paid her no heed.

As the days passed, conflict continued growing within the young
females mind. Somehow she knew that she should not mate with
the alpha, that they were now, somehow, fundamentally different.
Her instinct for preservation of the species struggled with her
growing fear of contact with the alpha male.

But the 'other' male was here somewhere . . . the one who had
been 'visited.' If she could only identify him. . . . The need grew,
even as her inner conflict grew.

Daily she worked her way to the periphery, always down-wind
so-as to lessen the chance of being confronted by the alpha. But
she was, by nature, a social animal. She was becoming increasingly
lonely. She longed for the reassurance she derived from contact
with others of her own kind. This only added to her inner turmoil
because, somehow she knew she was no longer one of them.

Then the day came when something unusual happened. Another mature male was challenging the alpha and the battle for
dominance was in full swing. Everyone was watching excitedly
from a safe distance. Off to the side another scuffle caught her
attention. One of the young males had pulled down a low-hanging
branch and was swatting others. That it happened once wasn't
particularly unusual. That he did it repeatedly caught her attention.
She'd never seen such a display as this.

Was he the one?! She resolved at that moment to find out.

Over the next few days she watched the young male, always
being careful to avoid being noticed. He always seemed to stay
out of the center of the group. He stayed at the periphery and
always remained alone.

Then one day she didn't see him. Throughout the day she watched for him . . . but to no avail. It was commonplace for someone
to be out of sight for a few minutes to relieve themselves. But

no one ever stayed away long. The jungle was a dangerous place for a solitary individual.

That evening as the family was retiring into the trees, she saw him. He was climbing the adjacent tree, heading for his usual nesting place. He didn't exhibit any unusual behavior. He just curled up in his bed and went to sleep.

The next morning she watched him, being ever more cautious that he didn't notice her. As usual he had worked his way to the edge of the group. Casting casual glances this way and that, he worked his way into the tangled undergrowth. He turned to look back toward the group. She lowered her head and looked away, fearing she had been noticed. When she looked up a moment later, he was gone. Later that evening she saw him again, climbing up to his bed.

The next morning she watched again as the young male worked his way to the edge of the group. She had already positioned herself at the periphery on the opposite side of the group from the male, and had hidden herself as well as she could in a tangle of vines and large leaves. From her vantage point she felt confident he would not see her watching him.

He eased himself backward into the tangle. He looked around briefly and then ducked down behind the cover. As soon as he was gone, she worked her way further back into the cover. As quietly as she could, she worked her way around until she came to the place where he had disappeared. Crouching low and moving as quietly as she could, she moved out in the direction she thought he would have gone.

It was difficult following him. He had hidden his trail well. She dared not move too quickly, fearing he would see or hear her. She moved only a few feet at a time, stopping to listen for any signs of disturbance, then proceeding again cautiously.

After walking for some distance, she heard something up ahead. It sounded like a tree branch cracking. The jungle went quiet. Even the birds were silent. She froze in place, all her senses alert.

She heard faint rustling, like something was moving through the underbrush. The rustling stopped and then she heard the cracking sound again.

When the rustling started again, she worked her way forward, using the noise as cover. Again the cracking sound, but this time it was much closer. A few yards ahead she saw movement through the underbrush. She inched forward as quietly as she could and came to the edge of a small clearing. There he was, shuffling semi-upright toward one side of the clearing. He was holding something in his hand as he walked. It looked like a stone.

He stopped and turned toward the other side of the clearing. Still holding the stone, he spread his feet wide apart, then leaned forward. It looked as if he was going to fall. But at the last moment he twisted his upper body sideways. Slamming his empty hand down in front of him; he brought the hand holding the stone back and then forcefully overhand and forward. He released the stone at the top of the arch.

She saw the stone fly across the clearing in a low arch. It hit a small tree trunk, making that cracking sound. The place where the stone had hit looked as though it had been hit several times. The bark was almost completely worn away.

Then on all fours, the young male moved back across the clearing to retrieve the stone. He repeated this process many times, sometimes hitting the tree, sometimes missing completely. After a time his aim improved and he was able to hit the tree more consistently. Awestruck, she watched as the male repeated this most unusual behavior time and time again.

Day after day she followed him, all the time growing more and more anxious to understand his strange behavior. She knew without question that his encounter with the dark object so many nights before had changed him, just as it had changed her. But why was he engaged in such unusual behavior? Was this somehow related to that night?

Her thoughts went back to the day when she had first noticed him. She remembered how he had paused for only the briefest of moments after swatting his brother with that tree limb. Then he had repeated the action several more times.

Could this stone throwing be somehow related? Males were always displaying, trying to intimidate their peers or to win the attention of the females. Maybe this was just another form of display.

This day she stayed hidden there for quite some time watching him throw. Then abruptly, he stopped. One last time he went to pick up the stone. But instead of moving back to his throwing position, he turned and walked toward her. She froze in place as he came closer and closer, still carrying the stone.

Miraculously, he passed within only a few feet but didn't notice her. He was heading back in the opposite direction, back toward where the family was.

Cautiously she worked her way out of her hiding place. When she thought he was far enough ahead that he wouldn't notice, she began to follow him. Just before he arrived back at the family, she saw him stop and hide the stone under some leaves. Ever careful to avoid detection, she moved to rejoin the family.

CHAPTER 20

Why was the young male doing that thing with the stone? It was obviously intentional. Thoughts seemed to fly through her mind as she let her imagination run unencumbered. Then reality broke through her introspection. She must remember to avoid calling attention to herself. She wasn't sure what she would do if confronted. She must watch for any unusual behavior by the young male, or anyone else, for that matter.

As she got closer to the family group, she began hearing commotion. Ahead, she could make out youngsters jumping up into low branches, trying to avoid being trampled. Everyone seemed to be gathered around a small clearing on the jungle floor. Screaming and hooting all but drowned out the fierce roar of the alpha male. Panicked, she ran forward, oblivious of everything but the spectacle playing out ahead.

She arrived just in time to see the alpha charging toward the young male. She watched in horror as the alpha pummelled the challenger to the ground. The alpha rained down blow after blow. The hapless victim could do little to defend himself. Blood streamed from his head, blinding him to the onslaught. Just when it seemed all was lost, the female saw something she remembered seeing once before. The bloodied young challenger reached up, grasped a sapling, and slammed it down on the alpha's back. The force of the impact sent both of them sprawling.

In that brief moment before the alpha resumed his onslaught, the challenger righted himself and staggered blindly into the underbrush. The alpha continued screaming in rage, thrashing this way and that, seeking to finish the kill, but nothing came forth. The challenger had disappeared.

The female stood there in stunned silence, as did everyone else. The alpha continued thrashing about briefly. But when no challenge presented itself, he soon settled down to catch his breath and regain his composure.

As was always the case, life in the family quickly went back to normal. The alpha had once again asserted his dominance over them all. Each in turn approached him, demonstrating their acknowledgement of him as their leader.

She too reluctantly paid her respects. She was deathly afraid he would notice the change that had come over her. But as she approached him, all he did was grunt quietly and turn his back toward her. She groomed him briefly and then quickly backed away. Miraculously, she had gone unnoticed.

For many days afterwards she managed to slip away from the group, if only briefly. Each time she left, she searched for signs of the young male. She dared not be gone too long for fear of being missed. Still, she saw no signs. He was nowhere to be found.

Her searches close to the encampment were unsuccessful. Each day estrus grew nearer. Each day her desperation mounted. Frantic to find some means of escape, she widened her search, staying away a little longer each time.

Then one day, as she approached a small clearing, she heard something. Was it a predator stalking her? No. The sound was coming from in front of her. A predator wouldn't approach from the front, nor would it make so much noise.

Then she saw him. The young male was squatting at the far side of the clearing eating a piece of fruit. She hunkered down in the undergrowth, listening and watching intently. She saw his head snap to look in her direction. Had he seen her? Her heart seemed to stop as her fear fought for dominance over anticipation. The male jumped to his feet, facing in her direction. What should she do now? Her instinct told her to flee. But her new-found comprehension told her that she must not.

She knew she must somehow let him know that she was self-aware, just like him.

She knew instinctively that she could never survive back with her old family. She was now too different from them. She could not hide her identity forever. She would be singled out and ostracised, eventually driven out of the family. For her to survive now, she would need to bond with another like herself.

This young male was now what she had become. An outcast. They would now depend on each other if they were to survive and pass on the knowledge and abilities they now possessed.

Gathering all the courage she could muster, she slowly stood to face him.

SEEDERS (CONTINUED)

CHAPTER 21

"We bring you greetings, fellow Seeders! Be welcome in our system." The feminine voice sounded strained, as though she was having difficulty speaking.

Zuri was unsure what she should say.

"Uh . . . thank you. On behalf of my people I accept your greeting. I . . . we are delighted . . . and somewhat overwhelmed to be here."

"You are the first we have seen in some time. Only recently did we learn of your eminent arrival. On behalf of my people I offer you our hospitality. Will you join us?" As she said this, a section of the spacecraft opened, revealing an interior not unlike the shuttle bay on the *Brighid*.

"Thank you. Yes. We accept your offer."

"Most excellent! Do you require assistance in maneuvering?"

Zuri looked to her pilot. Asha, wide-eyed and mouth agape, shook her head.

"Uh . . . no . . . thank you. We can manage."

"Excellent! Please note; our gravity field is slightly less than what you are accustomed to; but only a few percentage points. It should not present a problem."

"Thank you again," Zuri motioned toward her pilot. The INS and accelerometer screens on Asha's console came back up. They felt a slight shudder as LINK released control of the shuttle. Asha took a deep breath and gently manipulated the joystick.

Everyone sat quietly in their seats, eyes glued to their monitors.

"Look there. Up on top of the ship," said Chetan. "Don't those look like the bumps we saw on the LINK craft?"

"Sure do! They're a lot smaller, though. But I don't see any needles." Wasswa panned her camera back toward the LINK craft so she could compare. "Holly cow! Take a look at LINK! It's completely changed! No needles; no bumps, either. What the heck happened?"

"If I may interject," the masculine LINK voice said. "What you see is not the same craft that sent you here. The craft that you first encountered has a mission-specific configuration which allows it to transport itself. By contrast, I cannot. I must remain here."

"Then how did you get here?" asked Zuri.

"I was transported here the same as you. My exterior dimensions are slightly smaller than the interior of the one that sent you. Thus it was able to transport me here. For now, please allow this explanation to suffice."

The LINK transmission ended just as the shuttle entered the bay of the alien craft.

The interior of the bay didn't look much like the ones they were used to. It was much larger and seemed to glow a soft red color. Windows lined three of its four walls. Behind each window stood groups of people, watching the shuttle as it moved deeper into the bay.

Zuri saw that most of the faces appeared completely human, with typical minor racial variations. Some, however, were markedly different. Some had much more facial hair. Some had protruding brow ridges and lower jaws. On others the differences weren't so pronounced. They reminded her of some of the drawings she had seen in textbooks. She wondered if these faces were actual representations of evolution in process.

As the shuttle cleared the entry threshold, the doorway closed and a yellow line appeared on the floor. Without Asha's help, the shuttle centered itself over the top of the line and began following it.

"I've lost control here!" said Asha. "What do we do now?"

"Don't be concerned. The ship's marshalling program has been engaged. It will guide your vehicle to its proper location."

To the left and right of them, dozens of other vehicles were parked in neat rows. Each vehicle sat inside its own yellow square. Mooring lines secured the vehicle to the deck.

The line ended at the base of a short flight of stairs leading up to a large windowed bulkhead. Without Asha's assistance, the throttles eased back and the craft settled to a gentle touchdown inside its own yellow square. The engines shut down automatically when the craft made contact with the deck. The line they had been following disappeared as the glow in the room switched from red to yellow, and then after only a minute or two, to green.

"Welcome aboard, fellow Seeders!"came the voice over the speakers. The door at the top of the stairs opened. A tall, gray-skinned female figure walked forward, flanked on the left by an even taller black-skinned male. On her right, another female, not nearly as tall,but just as gray-skinned, carried a small box-shaped container. As the three descended the stairs, Zuri opened the shuttle door and stepped down onto the deck. The other ship's captains followed. The two groups approached to within a few paces of each other. The tall female stepped forward, as did Zuri.

"On behalf of all the Seeders of the Cygnus 5 system, be welcome. This is a joyous occasion for us all." The woman in the center said as she stopped before them. In unison, the three of them bowed. Not knowing what else to do, Zuri and the others did likewise.

With another shallow bow, the tall female said: "I am Catriona, President by the will of the people. May I present my counsellors?" Gesturing to her left . . ."This is Calehar, my first counsellor." The tall male clasped his hands over his chest and nodded. "And this is Doireann, my second counsellor." Instead of bowing, the shorter female stepped forward, extending the container toward Wasswa, who stood to Zuri's left. "Be welcome, sister." Wasswa bowed and stepped forward to accept the offering. "Thank you." The counsellor stepped back and together the three of them bowed again, this time more deeply.

"I am Zuri; senior command officer, also by the will of the people. These are our ship's captains: Asha, captain of the *Interloq* . . . Imamu, captain of the *Sequum* . . . Chetan,captain of the *Venure* . . . and Wasswa, captain of the *Sauda*." Each bowed as their name was called. "Our fifth ship's captain, Evander, sends his regrets. He remains behind to oversee the fleet in our absence." Gesturing toward the shuttle, "Also, we have brought with us a few representatives of the populations on each of our ships."

"You are all welcome here." Catriona gestured toward the people standing at the still-open shuttle door. Then, turning toward the windows around the shuttle bay; "Come, all of you! Come meet our new sisters and brothers!"

The shuttle and its occupants were soon surrounded by the people of Cygnus 5. Smiling, shaking hands and embracing, the two cultures easily intermingled.

After a few minutes, Catriona led Zuri and the others back up the stairs and into the ship.

"You're the first we've met in over a year," Catriona said as the two leaders walked together.

"Only a year? It's been generations between contacts for us." Zuri was astonished.

"Yes . . . it was once that way for us too. But that was long ago . . . before the Procurators made themselves known to us."

"Procurators? Who are they?"

"Yes," the president chuckled softly. "Yes. I'm sorry. Sometimes its easy to forget. The things we do here on a regular basis are really quite commonplace for us. Sometimes we fail to remember what it was like when we were new like you. Please allow me to explain. This is all very much like a gigantic business . . . no, that's not the right term. It's more like a huge benevolent enterprise.

People don't get hired and fired like in a business. We don't get paid, either. But sometimes we do get promotions."

Zuri was confused. "I'm sorry. I don't understand."

"I'm sorry. I've only been president for a few months. I've seen others give this presentation many times before. But its not as easy as I thought it would be giving it myself. You see, we are all engaged in the same activity. That is . . . we're all Seeders. Some of us are newer at it than others." Zuri nodded her understanding.

"The Procurators are what you might call administrators. They've been at this for a very long time and they're very experienced; where we . . . you and I . . . are relatively new and don't really have a good feel for how the system works."

Zuri was still confused, but nodded her encouragement.

"It's like we're down here among the trees, doing what we need to do. But because we are where we are, we can't see the big picture. We need someone above who can see the whole forest." She looked down at Zuri who still looked somewhat confused.

"I know its a cheap metaphor, but its the best comparison I can come up with. You might say we're down here in this valley planting trees because that's our job. And when we're done here, its also our job to go somewhere else and plant more trees. But do we just climb the hill and go down into the next valley? What if it's already been planted? What if the soil over there is barren? After all, its a big forest . . . and there aren't enough of us to cover the whole place. I suppose we could just wander around down here forever. Eventually we might get the job done. But wouldn't it be better if there was someone who could see the whole place? Someone who could guide and direct us so we'd work more efficiently? That's what the Procurators do. They're the supervisors . . . the administrators."

"This galaxy is like a huge forest. Huge beyond our wildest imaginations. We'd just never get the job done without Procurators there to keep track of what's going on . . . to keep things organized."

"This all seems to make sense," said Zuri. "And I like the 'top-down' approach you're using. Helps us see how we fit into the whole scheme of things, at least from an altruistic perspective. As LINK said, apparently we meet the requirements for entry into the club. We're not without our faults. But I think overall our good qualities outweigh our bad ones."

"I'm sure that's true." Catriona was noticeably more relaxed. "Otherwise we wouldn't be having this conversation. By the way; would you like to take a break . . . take some time to absorb all of this?"

"Not me. But maybe the others . . ."

Catriona stopped and turned toward the group that was following.

"Everyone . . . please feel free to wander about as much as you want. I know our citizens will be more than happy to answer any questions you may have. Let's meet in the central hall in, say, two hours. Okay?" Turning back to Zuri, she directed them to a set of double doors. The sign above read 'REINTEGRATION.' Pausing at the doors, Catriona said, "When you arrived, you probably noticed several people who didn't look quite like everyone else."

"Yes. They appeared to be more simian than human."

"That's true, at least as far as appearance is concerned. These people were brought here as representatives of various planets within this sector. Physically, they're thousands of years behind us. But mentally they're our equals."

"I don't understand. How can that be? Our five races share a similar evolution, and none of what you describe has ever been observed, either from fossil records or from recorded history. It's our understanding that our physical development kept pace with our intellect . . . that they both developed together. We believe that the needs of the one drove the development of the other."

"Ah! you've gotten to the meat of the issue, haven't you?" Catriona said as she held the door open for Zuri.

"We thought the same thing for generation after generation. The question always perplexed us: How was it possible that we humans developed what we refer to as 'enlightened self-awareness,' while our closest genetic relatives, the higher simians, didn't? After all, our genes are over 99 percent identical. We could never come up with any evidence to explain the disparity."

Zuri stopped them just inside the door. "We had the same problem . . . still do, for that matter. Science and theology seem to be continually at odds with one another."

Catriona motioned them toward some chairs.

"Well, we don't claim to have *the* answer; but we do have lots of evidence to support both schools of thought. Let's sit here for a minute so I can lay the groundwork for what you're about to see."

As they sat down, Catriona pulled a small metal container from one of her pockets. opening it, she said:

"Won't you try one? These are what we usually ingest for sustenance.

Zuri took one and put it in her mouth. It dissolved immediately.

"Hum . . . not bad. Actually, I don't taste a thing."

"Yes." Catriona took one too. "We all ingest these several times a day, although one is actually all our bodies require."

"Don't you eat solid food?"

"Oh yes. But usually only in the evenings when we're at home with our families, or on special occasions like this one. Tonight we're having a grand banquet in your honor. Tomorrow we'll all be a bit sluggish until the bulk clears our systems."

"What a great idea!" said Zuri" Catriona continued:

"I think the reason we eat bulky items at all is for our intestines' sake, but also for tradition. It's a time for sharing and enjoying one another's company."

"Yes. We should all do more of that." Zuri was feeling much more relaxed as she recognized the similarities between their cultures.

"Anyway, back to the subject. In our early, pre-space flight times, most theologians professed that we appeared on our individual planets as full-blow, fully functional humans. They claimed the

Creator put us here. The skeptics (Mostly academics and members of the scientific community) claimed there was no evidence to support such beliefs. Even as we went into space, the arguments persisted."

"But then the Seeders came along. Suddenly we had to re-think our long-held beliefs. What we began to discover was that there really was no disparity between the two philosophies. In fact we realized that they were mutually complimentary. Ask yourself this question: Is there really a God? No one can say for sure. There just isn't any tangible proof one way or the other. But!" she emphasized, "The Seeders believed there was. The Procurators believed there was. And the LINKS *said* there was. How could we argue with that? Believe me, many tried. The believers and the skeptics finally realized they had one common dilemma. Neither could explain the existence of LINKS. They couldn't fathom the technology. So, they asked the Seeders how they worked. The Seeders didn't have a clue. They asked the Procurators. Same answer. So, the next and only other option was to ask the LINKS. I'll bet you can guess what the response was."

"It has ever been so." Zuri smiled.

"Yup! So there we were, back where we started . . . except not quite. We were about to become Seeders. We were about to 'seed' intelligence throughout the galaxy. Were we becoming 'as the Creator'? Were we that smart? Not hardly. We were 'seeding' using technology no one knew anything about; and we were traveling about inside these LINK machines that used a technology we couldn't begin to understand."

"So we studied and we probed. Eventually we learned some incredible stuff. Soon you'll learn the same things. We never could prove or disprove the existence of a supreme being. All we really knew for sure was that 'seeding' worked and that the LINKS worked. We thought we knew the 'why,' but still didn't have a clue about the 'how.' Ultimately the question became moot. We just had to go on doing what we believed to be the right thing and accept the fact that we don't have all the answers."

"Sounds awfully familiar. We have the same struggles." Zuri paused for a moment as she considered how to ask the question that was nagging at her. "So, what do you believe?"

Catriona turned to face Zuri squarely.

"I speak to you now person to person, not in any official capacity," she emphasized. "I believe there is a Creator. I believe he (or she) does what he does for his own reasons, and that he uses whatever tools he needs to accomplish his goals. I believe we, as Seeders, are some of those tools."

"Are you suggesting that we're being manipulated?"

"I wouldn't call it manipulation. I prefer to call it persuasion. Stop and think about it. Whenever you're contemplating doing or saying something, doesn't your sense of right and wrong influence your decision?"

"Certainly. But sometimes I do something even though down in my gut I don't feel right about it." Zuri knew she was treading on thin ice discussing such a sensitive personal issue with a relative stranger.

"Me too," Catriona was smiling now. "But I don't think I'm any different from anyone else. I think we're all prone to make bad decisions from time to time. But if we're honest with ourselves, we'll feel some regret or remorse for having made that decision. And its that gut feeling, that conscience that's the key to this discussion."

Zuri felt compelled to respond. " I agree. It's that sense of right and wrong that sets us apart from so-called lower life forms. How else could we have gotten this far in our evolution? If we'd have been totally self-centered, we would never have had the courage to take that first step into the unknown. It's that willingness to take a risk, to take a leap of faith that makes all the difference. When we do the right thing, even when there is risk involved, we are approaching the divine."

"Precisely! Remember what the LINK said? 'You have been tried and found worthy.'" Zuri was surprised Catriona knew about that.

"How did you know what he said?"

Catriona chuckled. "That's the same message everyone gets. The LINKS say they were made by the Creator."

"Wait a minute! You said 'the LINKS'! How many of those things are there?"

"Who knows? Thousands? Maybe millions. But we'll get to that later. The point is; the LINKS claim they were built by the Creator. That must include their programming, too. Admittedly, they're pretty sophisticated programs. But they are not completely autonomous. Their discretionary abilities and their responses are limited. So I don't think it was they who decided to invite us to join the club, so to speak."

"How about these 'procurators.' Maybe they were the ones."

"I don't think so. We've asked them, and they deny involvement. I think they may have some input. But I don't think they make the final decisions."

"How can you be sure?"

"Well, I'm not positive. But they've never given me a reason to doubt them. They've been doing this for longer than any of our recorded histories can track. And what they're doing is good, right?"

"So far as I can tell, yes. But I've never met one." Zuri was starting to feel a bit defensive.

"I understand. But you'll get your chance. In the mean time, let's continue the tour. I'm confident you'll feel better about all this when you see the 'program' in process."

They stood and walked toward a sign hanging on the other side of the hall. The top of the sign had two arrows, one pointing left and the other right. Below the right arrow were three words in columns:

COUNSELING

ORIENTATION
DEBRIEFING

Below the left arrow:

MISSION UPLOAD
CLEARING

Catriona gestured to the left. "We won't spend a lot of time in this department, but it's important for you to get a feel for how all this works. The 'Reintegration' department is actually the last stop in the process. Don't worry. It'll all be clear soon enough."

They entered through the door marked COUNSELING. Inside, the room was dimly lit and quite small (Only a few dozen square feet). There were no furnishings; just neutral-colored walls. In the far wall was a horizontal rectangular window at eye level. They moved closer.

The room beyond was dimly lit. Zuri could make out the outline of a bed. On it lay what looked like one of the ape creatures she had seen in the shuttle bay.

"Before I explain what's going on here, I need to give you a little background. The 'seeding' process is really not as complicated as you might think. But there are some pretty strict criteria for determining which planet gets selected.

"First of all, obviously, the planet must be able to support human life. You'd be surprised how many planets fit that requirement but don't get selected. Usually it's because there's just too much competition for resources, in other words . . . food. Predation is usually the cause. That problem usually works itself out over time, though; anywhere from a few thousand to several million years.

"But we're spread pretty thin around this galaxy. We can't afford to hang around that long waiting to see how things work out. In cases such as this, we evaluate where the planet is in the typical evolutionary cycle, and then make predictions as to when we should come back. But like I said; the galaxy is a big place. Sometimes things just fall through the cracks, so to speak."

"That doesn't seem quite fair, does it?" Zuri said as she watched through the window. Two other figures entered the room through a door Zuri couldn't see from where she stood. Both of them walked fully upright, but were covered head to toe in hair. They positioned themselves on each side of the bed and stood there quietly. The figure on the bed stirred slightly but remained prone. One of the figures began stroking the prone figures head. The other held its hand gently.

"Maybe not. But then again, life in general isn't always fair. There are other factors, too . . . like the stability of the system the planet is part of . . . neighboring planets with wobbly orbits . . . to many debris fields in the vicinity. Maybe the systems star, or sun, is unstable. Maybe the magnetic field is unstable. Or maybe it's just too crowded in the neighborhood . . . to much potential for outside interference."

"You mean people visiting from other planets?"

"Yup. I know you've never experienced this, but there *are* space-faring civilizations out there that never get selected to become seeders. Generally it's because their technology gets developed faster than their capacity for self-restraint."

"That's surprising! We always assumed any civilization capable of interplanetary space flight had outgrown that."

"Usually that's the case . . . but sadly, not always. It usually works itself out in the long run, though. Mostly they end up destroying each other."

Zuri nodded her understanding, thinking back on the history of her own planet.

Aggressive cultures thrived for only relatively short periods of time. Eventually, after trying and failing to subjugate more benevolent cultures, in frustration and desperation, they turned on themselves.

"Evil is self-consuming."

"Exactly! Anyway . . . once a planet is selected for seeding, we try to do it discretely. But sometimes we get caught. We're not perfect, you know. It doesn't happen very often. But when it does, it can cause all sorts of problems. Can you imagine how traumatic it would be for the 'seedee' to witness what we're doing? It's hard enough coming to grips with your own new-found self-awareness. But then add to that the knowledge that there is something or someone else out there for which you have no frame of reference."

"I can't imagine . . ."

"I like to compare it to meeting a LINK for the first time, only orders of magnitude more traumatic."

"I guess I see what you mean. It was pretty scary for us. But at least we'd had some experience in meeting other cultures in space. Our brains were sort of used to that sort of thing."

Catriona nodded and continued.

"That simian you see there on the table recently experienced something similar to what I've described. He saw something he wasn't supposed to see. But he didn't loose control or anything like that. Instead, he managed to get our attention somehow.

"When that sort of thing happens, we have a couple of choices. We can ignore him. But that usually doesn't work out too well, because then he goes around telling all his friends what he saw. Sometimes they think he's nuts. Or sometimes he gains a 'following' and we end up seeing their culture taking a wrong turn into cultism or weird religious practices. That sort of thing can get pretty ugly.

"Usually what we end up doing is grabbing him and bringing him up here for some orientation. That can get pretty complicated, so we try to calm his fears at the same time we satisfy his curiosity. That's what those two in there are doing now. When he wakes, he'll be in the company of individuals of his own kind. At least that's what it looks like to him."

"What do you mean? Are those two in there just dressed up to look like him?"

"Literally speaking, no . . . they're not 'dressed up.' They've been genetically altered so they resemble members of his race at his particular stage of development."

Zuri's mouth dropped open. "What?" She took a step back. "What did you say? You mean you can . . .?"

"Yes. It's actually a pretty common practice." Catriona placed a soothing hand on Zuri's shoulder. "I know this is a lot to take in all at once, but bear with me. It'll all become clear soon." Facing back toward the window, she continued.

"What sets Seeders apart from non-seeders is actually pretty simple. Essentially, what we have that the others don't is access to an enormous amount of gene research and advanced technology. A lot of it we don't really understand because we didn't develop it. Even the Procurators don't know a lot more about the process than we do.

"Just consider the evolutionary process for a moment. We both know that species-specific changes take place over time, right?" Zuri closed her mouth and swallowed.

"Usually these changes take place over very long time periods . . . say, thousands of years. But sometimes it doesn't take that long . . . sometimes as little as a few generations. Some animals undergo major changes in appearance or behavior after relatively short periods of contact with humans. You've probably seen that in certain quadrupeds on your home planet.

"What we're able to do, if we have enough information about a species' genome, is speed up the process . . . or even reverse it. Those two in there have undergone that process just so they can assist the patient as he comes to grips with his new reality. When that's done, we reverse the process so the two 'helpers' return to their original appearance."

Zuri slumped to the wall, placing a hand to her forehead.

"Can we go some place and sit down for a minute? I need some time to digest all of this."

"Sure. Let's go down to Debriefing. They won't be using that room for a while yet. There's some chairs we can use."

As they walked, Catriona continued.

"It surely must be stressful for anyone to wake up in a strange place and not know how they got there. And then to realize they've been taken completely away from their home world and everything that's familiar, and placed in a spaceship . . .! Without some sort of intervention, the average person from a technologically primitive culture would likely have a psychotic break. It's not even uncommon for more advanced cultures to have similar reactions. If that happens, the chances are high our seeding efforts will have been in vain. Under the right circumstances whole populations can be negatively effected, especially if the traumatized individual is in a position of influence within his community."

The debriefing room was much larger and brightly lit, with seating to accommodate a dozen or more people. The rear wall had a double door in its center. Tall storage cabinets flanked it and filled the remainder of the wall.

The other three walls were covered by large computer screens, all of which were blank at the moment. A long table separated the front of the room from the rows of chairs.

As they entered, Catriona gestured toward a chair.

"Can I get you anything? Perhaps some water?"

"That'd be nice, but I think I need to use the 'facilities' first."

"Sure! Go through those doors there and turn left. It's right there."

"Thanks." Zuri said and headed in that direction.

Sitting alone in the restroom, she tried to digest what she had heard. She had gotten somewhat used to the whole idea of 'seeding'. And it made sense that the evolutionary process would be influenced by lots of situations. But for there to be only one sentient species out of all the creatures on any given planet had always left her with nagging questions.

She thought she understood how the process of natural selection worked. Survival of the fittest . . . adapt or die. These ideas made perfect sense. Of the five cultures she had been involved with, only one species in each of them had thrived? Always it was the humans. Why was it them and not some other species?

It all came back to the age-old question: Who am I and why am I here? The 'evolutionists' had some of the answers. But the 'missing link' issue always left her hanging. For that matter, so did the 'theist' approach. Religions always seemed to fall short when it came to reconciling archaeological evidence with doctrine. 'Seeding' seemed to provide the answers. Of that she felt confident. As to the 'hows' and 'whys.'. .that was what she hoped to learn here.

When Zuri came back into the room, Catriona was sitting on the front row.

"Here's your water."

"Thanks." She took the cup that was offered and sat down.

"Feeling any better? Here. Try one of these." Catriona held out a small plate of what looked like miniature green carrots. Zuri picked one and took a tentative bite. Immediately her mouth was filled with a pleasant, warming sensation. As she chewed, the sensation grew until it seemed to fill her whole body.

"Wow! This is really . . . different. What do you call it.?"

"We call it 'greff.' It's a mild narcotic some geneticist put together in a lab long ago. It's supposed to sooth the nerves . . . help you relax. How do you like it?"

"It's good!" She took a bigger bite. This time the whole-body sensation didn't happen; just a mild tingling on the tip of her tongue.

Noting Zuri's obvious surprise, Catriona chuckled.

"Really wild, huh? They say when it was first developed, the effect continued with each bite. Pretty soon it got out of hand. So the geneticists modified it so the effect only works in the presence of a certain amount of stress hormones. It'll wear off in a minute or two."

"Uh-huh. How does it work?"

"It's a chemical thing. Supposedly it homes in on the hormones. When the stress levels go down, it quits working. Most of us don't bother with it much after the first try. After a while it sort of becomes anticlimactic. Now we use it mostly in *counseling*. Helps our new friends to cope with stress.

"Mmm." Zuri took a drink of water and put the remainder of the 'carrot' back on the plate.

"Anyway, back to what we were discussing. We like to reassure our patients as much as possible by providing something familiar to them. Since we can't reproduce their home environment here, we do the next best thing. We provide them with someone they recognize. That and the greff helps to keep the stress levels under control."

"Okay. I get all that. But what do you do with them once they've been 'de-stressed,' just put them back where you found them?"

"Absolutely not! If we 'de-stress' him (to use your words) and then put him back in the population, he'll tell everyone what happened. Pretty soon everyone is in the same shape he was. That completely disrupts everything. We want these budding civilizations to develop naturally. We don't want their knowledge of our existence to disrupt everything. We've found there are only two ways to effectively deal with it. One: we invite the person to stay with us. That usually doesn't work out too well when he discovers he's all alone in a world of strangers and he learns his two new 'friends' aren't really who they say they are. Two—and this is the one we've had the most success with—we offer him the opportunity to work with us. He gets to go back to his people with the agreement that he keeps our existence a secret."

"But how can you be sure he won't break the agreement? Sounds like an awfully big gamble trusting him to keep his word."

"That's very true; but we can be pretty persuasive." Zuri raised her hand to interrupt.

"No, it's not what it sounds like. We don't use threats or coercion. We actually make him an integral part of the program. We teach him all we know about the seeding process as it applies to him and the reasons for doing it. We provide a mechanism he can use to communicate with us, one which only he knows about and only he can use. We give him a set of protocols he can use to help guide his peoples' development. And most importantly, we encourage him to keep us informed on how things are going. We listen to what he has to say, and, if he asks, we sometimes offer suggestions that might be helpful."

"But still, that doesn't guarantee he won't betray you for his own selfish gains."

"That's very true. But we have other things we can do to ensure that doesn't happen."

"What are you talking about! Mind control?!" Zuri was alarmed by the implications.

"Not in the sense you're suggesting." She could see Zuri was noticeably uneasy about the subject.

"I want to assure you we never interfere with a person's right to decide for himself. Maybe I'm not the best person to explain this. Let me get someone in here who's better at it." Catriona pulled a personal com unit from her pocket and pressed a few buttons. An unfamiliar voice answered. "Hi, Cat. What can I do for you?" It was a jovial-sounding male voice.

"Hey, Al. Can you come over to Debrief? I need your help explaining something to one of our guests."

"Sure! Give me a minute to finish up here and I'll be right over. Bye."

Catriona put the PCU back in her pocket.

"Al is one of our best geneticists. He came to us about five years ago as part of an exchange program with the Perseus Division."

"What's the Perseus Division?" asked Zuri.

"Sorry. I keep forgetting you're new here and aren't up to speed on all the terminology. Just a minute. Let me pull up a galactic map."

She walked over to the lectern on the center table and activated one of the screens. An image of a spiral galaxy appeared. In its center was a black dot. Lines extended from the dot outward, splitting the view into twelve pie-shaped segments. Four concentric circles equally spaced from the galactic center, further divided the segments. Five of the segments to the left of the center were highlighted in blue. Six of the remaining seven segments were a neutral gray color. The twelfth segment, adjacent to the lowermost blue one, was highlighted in yellow. Catriona touched a red dot in the outermost section of the top blue segment using a pointer. The dot began to pulsate.

"This is us here in the Cygnus segment."

Pointing to a pulsating green dot in the lowermost blue segment, she said, "This is Perseus fourteen. Al's home planet is the fourth orbit out from its sun." She tapped the screen again and the view zoomed in to reveal a solar system with eight planets in orbit around a star.

"Where are we? I mean, where are my ships on this map?" said Zuri.

Catriona tapped the yellow segment.

"You're about here in the Orion System, pretty close to this third arc segment. It's colored yellow because exploration has only just begun."

"What about the gray ones?"

"Those haven't been explored yet. Like I said before, this is a big place. We're trying to get it all covered one segment at a time."

"So, how did you find us?" Zuri walked closer to the map where she saw many smaller red dots equally spaced inside the blue segments.

"The little red dots are LINKS. One of them picked up your radio signals. We tasked two more to triangulate and sent one to intercept your projected course. Actually, it wasn't 'us' exactly. The Procurators . . ."

Just then the door to the left opened and a short balding man waddled in.

"Ah! Zuri, this is Alger. He's about the best in his field." The smiling man held his hands to his chest and gave a shallow bow.

Zuri extended her hand, then remembering, dropped it to her side and bowed also. "Sorry. I'm not used to your customs yet."

"Not at all," he smiled. Turning to Catriona, "What can I do for you?"

"We were just discussing some freedom of choice issues. Zuri voiced concern that we might be compelling 'newbees' to do what we want them to do."

"Oh my, no! That would never happen." He chuckled as he motioned them toward the chairs. "Why don't we sit and relax for a while. This might take a few minutes." He shuffled over to a chair, slumped onto one and interlaced his fingers over his ample abdomen. His small feet barely touched the floor.

"I see you've noticed our marked difference in appearance," he smiled. "You see, gravity on my home planet is almost one-fifth more than on Cygnus five. That means my people are built a little closer to the ground. Makes it kind of uncomfortable some times." He smiled again and shifted his weight in the chair.

"You might be wondering what genetics has to do with free will. Well actually, not much. You see, in addition to being a geneticist, I'm also very much into nano-science and technology. I'll try to get to the point without explaining all the technical stuff.

"You see, it's all about chemistry, really. Lets consider the concept of 'stimulus-response' for a moment. As an example, the brain sends a signal to the hand." He held up his hand and wiggled his chubby fingers. "How does that signal get transmitted? Simply stated, it sends an electrical signal. Brain says 'wiggle,' fingers say 'Okay.'

Zuri smiled as he continued. She was really enjoying listening to this little man.

"It's a pretty good distance from the head to the fingers. Even further to the toes." He raised a foot and wiggle it.

"Well, electricity isn't too concerned with distance. It gets around pretty quick. In the brain the distances are even smaller, right?" Zuri nodded again.

"But electricity needs to be made before the brain can send it anywhere, right? And how does it get made? Simply stated, it's a byproduct of a chemical reaction. See, two chemicals get together and make some electricity. Then they tell it where to go and send it on its way. You might say its a kind of messenger, Okay? Well, chemicals are good messengers too. They just don't get around as fast.

"So, back to the brain. You know what a neuron is, right? I like to call it the place where some very special chemicals hang out. And these neurons are really, really close together. At such small distances, chemicals are just as efficient at getting around as electricity . . . usually even more-so 'cause they can smell each other when they're close by. So why bother making a spark and giving it instructions if you can just as easily do the job yourself? So, what does all this have to do with free will? That's where nano-technology comes in.

"Let's say your brain wants you to wiggle your fingers . . . but instead you wiggle your toes. Somehow the message got routed wrong, right? Well, that just won't do. There are lots of folks who have wiring problems very much like what we've described; epileptics, or autistics, for example. Makes it really hard for them to get along in the world.

"Essentially it's caused by a chemical imbalance. You know what I mean? Well, we now have nano-machines that can help people with problems like that. These little machines know what chemicals are supposed to be there. So when the wrong chemical shows up, the machines block it and send the right one in its place. Now the finger does what it's told and the problem never manifests.

"But what about the poor toe? Did it want to wiggle, but wasn't allowed? I know it's a silly question. But it serves to illustrate my point, which is: free will never came into play. The right thing was done, and you never had to deal with a right-versus-wrong issue."

Catriona picked up the conversation.

"In a nut shell, that's what we do with 'newbees.' We teach them the right thing to do and make sure they understand and agree. Then we inject nano-machines that are specifically programmed to block any chemical interactions that would allow a wrong decision to be made in a certain context. They only work under very specific circumstances. They don't interfere with any decision making processes other than ones which would lead the 'newbee' to expose us or anything related to the seeding process. This insures that the natural evolutionary process within his community continues unimpeded.

"Fair enough." Zuri raised a hand in emphasis. "But that brings up a major question. What keeps you from making a nano-machine that deliberately sends the wrong chemical?"

Alger raised a finger in response. "That's the big question, isn't it? If you hadn't asked, I would have been worried. First off, we don't build the machines ourselves. Our expertise isn't that advanced. That's one of the things the Procurators do. We don't even have final say over when the machines get used. We have input in the decision-making process, but the final decision is made way further up the chain of command.

"I know this explanation is grossly oversimplified. There's a lot more involved, though. And we can discuss this more at length if you want to. For now if you'll allow us, we'll show you the rest of the process so you can put all of this in proper context."

The three of them stood and walked back toward the door. As they re-entered the hallway, Zuri decided to ask a question that had been nagging at her.

"I need to ask you something." She turned toward Catriona. "What do you do if a 'newbee' decides she doesn't want anything to do with this? Maybe some people just don't want to accept that sort of responsibility."

"I'm sure that's true," said Catriona, "although I've never heard of it happening. Humans are a curious lot, you know. But if that case were to present itself, there is something we can do."

Zuri frowned as she considered the implications of what Catriona said.

"I see that doesn't sit well with you." Catriona smiled. "Believe me. It's not as terrible as it sounds. Al, would you like to answer this one?"

"Sure!" Alger smiled. "This gets into an area of nano-technology that we're only just now beginning to explore. It has to do with what I like to call 'chemical memory'".

Catriona squeezed Zuri's arm and drew her gently closer.

"Listen to this," she said softly. "He's really good at this."

"Let's get back into the brain for a minute, shall we?" He was now almost bubbling with excitement. "This is my favorite subject, by the way." He grinned and rubbed his hands together as he began.

"Neurons are wonderful things. They're what you might call miniature manufacturing plants. Somehow, they know just what chemical needs to be sent in order to elicit a specific response from another neuron. That's amazing enough. But what's really incredible is . . . they make the chemicals themselves . . . right on the spot . . . almost instantaneously! And! They keep records of which chemicals they've made, transmitted and received. And this is the best part. They keep records of *when* all this transpired!" He glanced toward Zuri who was still frowning.

"Sorry." He grinned sheepishly. "Sometimes I get carried away. What does this have to do with the subject at hand? When a 'newbee' decides he doesn't want anything to do with the program, we send in the nanos. They've been specifically tasked to go to the appropriate neurons and search their records. When they've found the ones they're looking for; in this case, the ones associated with the event of our making contact, they remove them. Then we send the 'newbee' home and he wakes up not remembering anything."

Zuri stopped in her tracks.

"You're telling me you can erase memories?" She was completely flabbergasted.

"Essentially, yes." He paused, surprised by her reaction. "Why? Does this bother you?"

"Yes! It bothers me!" Zuri took a step back, raising her hands. "What you're saying is that you engage in *mind control!*"

"I don't think I'd call it that . . ." Alger was now really concerned.

"I don't care what you call it!" Zuri pointed an accusing finger at him. "Messing with someone's memory goes against every moral and ethical standard . . .!"

Catriona stepped forward, trying to calm her.

"I'm sorry! I think Al forgot to explain something, and it's vital that you understand this," she said pleadingly. "At *no* time do we *ever* do *anything* to *anybody* without their full understanding and consent."

Zuri took another step back, this time pointing accusingly at them both.

"That's easy to say!" Her voice strained as she practically yelled at them. "But how would this 'newbee,' as you call him, even know that he's been manipulated?"

Catriona new she was loosing control of the situation. Desperately she searched for an appropriate response.

"Zuri please! I see we haven't been able to explain this clearly. The last thing we want to do is give you reason to doubt our integrity." She looked pleadingly at Alger, then back to Zuri.

"We must have overlooked something which is fundamental to your understanding of what we're trying to say."

"You'd better say *something* . . . !" Zuri's fear was quickly turning to anger.

Alger took a hesitant step forward, placing a hand on Catriona's shoulder.

"Maybe we should get a Procurator in on this."

"Yes. Yes. That's a good idea, said Catriona. "Let's do that." Looking pleadingly back to Zuri, she continued. "Would you allow us to do this? It will take a little while, though. There isn't one on board at the moment. We can have one here very quickly."

"How quickly?" Zuri's hand were clinched into fists at her sides.

"Not long. Maybe just a few minutes." Catriona was near panic herself. She turned to Alger.

"Al. You know what needs to be done. Will you please?"

"Of course." He turned on his heel and hurried back into the Debrief room.

Hands clasped in front of her, Catriona pleaded, "Zuri! Oh, Zuri. I'm so sorry! I'm still so new at this. I've never run into this before. I'm at a loss as to what I can do to make this right."

Zuri's anxiety was being pushed to the limit.

"If this is how you do *seeding*, I'm not sure we want anything to do . . . !"

"No, no, no! That's not it at all! We don't manipulate! We only persuade! Our intentions are pure! Please. Give us a chance to clear this up." Tears welled up in her eyes as she realized just how desperate the situation was.

Zuri sensed the sincerity Catriona was trying to convey, but her mind raced as she tried to digest what she had heard.

"Okay. I'll wait for one of these Procurators, as you call them. But this explanation better be convincing! Otherwise . . ."

Catriona's PCU buzzed. She tapped it. "Go ahead."

Al responded.

"Ardghal is en route from the surface. He'll be docking in seven minutes.

"Oh, wonderful! We'll head that way now. Thank you, Alger." Catriona sighed with relief.

"Oh, Zuri. You'll just love Ardghal! He was the first Procurator I ever met. He was one of the first to open this galaxy for Seeding. Come! Let's go back to the docking bay and wait for him."

Catriona reached out and took Zuri's hand gently into her own. Zuri took a hesitant step, and then stopped.

"Wait! You said he was one of the first? How long has this been going on here?"

"I'm not really sure, but at least several thousand years." Catriona was smiling nervously as she guided Zuri back in the direction they had come.

"Several thousand? How can that be? Are you people immortal?" Zuri sputtered as Catriona tugged her along.

"Oh, my. No. Just wait. Ardghal will be anxious to meet you. He'll answer all your questions. He's just an amazing person. You will be a changed person after meeting him."

SIMIAN 3

CHAPTER 22

He was large . . . larger than any newborn she had ever seen . . . and strangely hairless, except for a thin patch on his head. His face was round, with a very small nose and a narrow slit of a mouth. His feet were formed differently, not with extended digits like hers, but with stubby, evenly aligned toes.

She wondered if this newborn was a deformity, not unlike the few she had seen before. Those few had not lived long. They had been helpless, unable to cling to their mothers' fur, unable to reach their mothers' nipples to suckle, unable to move about in that familiar fashion typical of other "normal" simian infants. They had weakened quickly, starving, unable to withstand the rough handling by their mothers.

She, on the other hand, was able to devote her entire attention to her new son. Immediately she had recognized the necessity to provide the extra attention and care her son required. Her mate saw to all her needs. He brought food to her. He built the nest they now occupied. He stood watch, ensuring that she and their son were safe.

Strangely, though these thoughts came to her, she wasn't overly concerned. She knew that she and her mate were different, that they had somehow changed in a way unique to them alone. The fear and confusion she remembered from the early days of their union was now only a memory which served to help her put events into perspective.

Pulling her son closer, she knew that she and her mate were different for a reason, and that she held that reason in her arms. A feeling of calm contentment enfolded her as she peered across the nest toward the figure silhouetted against the evening twilight.

The father of her son seemed reluctant to approach too closely. He just sat there, squatting on the edge of the nest, sniffing the air and scratching. Occasionally he would look toward their newborn and his gaze would become more intent. When he saw she was looking at him, he would gaze into her eyes for a brief moment, then look away quickly. What could he be thinking, she wondered.

CHAPTER 23

The young simian had quickly grown accustomed to her presence. They had remained side by side almost continuously since the day they met. From their first union until this moment they had shared a closeness unique to them alone. The communal lifestyle they had grown up in was now a thing of the past.

Their communication, though non-verbal, was more significant than anything they had ever experienced "before." From the beginning it had been a struggle to make themselves understood. Simple ideas were almost impossible to convey. He felt frustrated, being unable to make her understand. He knew from her mannerisms, from her body language, that she too had these feelings.

He remembered the night it happened. As had always been the case with their race, sexual union was performed with the female facing away from the male. Initially that had been the case with them too. But as the days and months went by, their unions had become less driven, less intense, more emotional. Instead of hurrying to climax, the young simian had taken more time, deriving more pleasure from the act. His mate had become more responsive as a result.

The two spent long minutes caressing, holding each other, with him snuggling close against her back. As he relaxed his embrace, she turned toward him, gazing into his eyes. He adjusted accordingly until they were fully facing each other. Their eyes met as their bodies once again joined. In that instant their relationship changed, and each of them recognized it.

CHAPTER 24

Weeks went by uneventfully. The couple continued following the clan, always from a safe distance, scavenging what little food the clan had overlooked. But eventually, as the female continued to put on weight, it became increasingly difficult for them to maintain their pace.

Day by day they dropped farther behind. Day by day the young male ventured farther away from his mate, searching for other food sources.

Eventually it became obvious that they could no longer follow their old family. The female had grown so large that it was all she could do to walk, and then only for short distances without having to rest.

Then one day she refused to travel at all. The young male was at a loss. Feeling helpless, all he could do was pace back and forth, occasionally stopping to sit close to her, comforting her as best he could. He could see from her expressions and movements that she was very uncomfortable. But there was nothing he could do to help.

He knew they needed to eat, but he was afraid to leave her long enough to find food. She was too exposed and vulnerable where she was. Eventually with his help and persuasion they moved a short distance to a hidden spot under some low hanging ferns.

The space under the ferns was cramped, barely large enough

for the two of them. She continued shifting, trying to find a comfortable position, but never seemed to be able to. Eventually she nudged him completely out of the space, gesturing for him to go find something for them to eat.

Reluctantly he did as he was told.

After only a few steps he looked back to see how she was doing. The place he had chosen was a good one. He couldn't see her at all. Satisfied that she would be safe for a while, he turned and hurried off.

It was late in the season. Food was becoming harder to find. Much of what he did find had begun to rot. It took him longer than he expected to find enough to carry back for his mate. She must be starving by now, he thought. I must hurry.

Night was falling faster this late in the year. It was becoming difficult for him to retrace his tracks. He was beginning to feel desperate, fearing that if he didn't find their hiding spot soon, he wouldn't be able to until morning.

Too frequently he had to stop to orient himself. Every time he stopped be became more desperate. He wasn't sure he was headed in the right direction. He was near panic.

Then not far away, he heard a faint moan. It's her! Something's wrong! He dropped what little food he had found and ran headlong in the darkness toward the sound.

Their hiding spot was a good one. He had walked right past it without even noticing. If it had not been for her moan, he would have missed it completely.

He rushed in under the fern to see her lying there writhing in pain.

In that moment the area around them became bathed in a soft blue light. Everything he saw was the same color. He crouched there frozen, his breath caught in his throat. The two of them lay together motionless.

He detected a slight movement just overhead. Afraid to move, he glanced upward cautiously between the leaves. He could make out a strange rectangular shape, unlike anything he had ever seen in nature. The light was emanating from the object.

In 'words' that were in his ears as well as in his mind, he heard: "I am here to help. Be not afraid."

A thin mist began emanating from the base of the object. It smelled like fresh-blooming flowers, pleasant, relaxing. He was feeling light-headed, drowsy, like he was about to fall asleep. He turned toward his mate.

She was no longer writhing. She wasn't looking up at the object. Instead her attention was focused nearer the ground. She didn't seem to be disturbed, more curious than alarmed. The young simian turned to look in the same direction.

There, just at the edge of the mist something was moving. It was tall and slender, with slow deliberate animal-like movements. Its upper body was indistinct, extending upward into the darkness above the blue haze. It walked upright on two legs. But these legs were long, hairless. They kept moving toward them slowly.

In him mind and in his ears he heard more words.

"From the time of your changing, you have known of my coming, though then you did not understand."

For what seemed like a very long time the young male remained inert, dazed, trying to absorb all that he was feeling and hearing and seeing. Gradually he became absorbed in a feeling of well-being and security. After a time he drifted off into relaxed slumber.

He awakened just as the sun was breaking the horizon. Rays of yellow-orange light shot through the overhanging fern, jolting him into wakefulness. A strange sensation was coming from inside his head, like ringing in his ears, only not so loud. It wasn't annoying, just, different, almost pleasant.

He remembered the voice, distant, almost like a dream. He remembered "Be not afraid." He wasn't. The voice comforted him.

She was still there at his side, cuddled close. There was a strange covering draped around her. It looked like an animal hide; some sort of deer, perhaps. Instead of being shocked, as he would have been otherwise, he took this as though it were nothing out of the ordinary. The mere fact that he had done so was a shock in itself. Yet he felt strangely comfortable with it all. He couldn't explain it, but he felt no fear, no apprehension, no feeling that would alert him that something was amiss.

His mate's attention was focused on something she was holding close under the cover. She paid him no notice.

He noticed a stirring under the covering, accompanied by a muffled mewing sound. His mate shifted her position, letting the cover fall away slightly. There, held in her arms was a suckling infant. He could see only the head and one shoulder.

His mate looked up into his eyes. They were moist, tears pooling in the corners. Her gaze suggested strong emotion, stronger than anything he had ever perceived before.

He looked from her, back to the tiny newborn she held close to her breast. It was naked, devoid of hair, except for a small patch on its head. One tiny hand clutched at the hair between her breasts. Gently, she eased the tiny infant away from her breast, turning it so that he could see it clearly. It was a male. The tiny round face, lips pursed, eyes closed, moved ever so slightly, mewing contentedly.

The young simian turned his attention to his mate. Gone were the creases around her eyes. Gone were the furrows in her brow. Her face seemed to glow with an inner light. He could feel it. It was as much a part of her as he knew it was a part of him. When he looked down at the tiny infant in her arms a new word came to his mind. It described perfectly the feeling that the three of them shared.

Love.

As the next few days passed, the memories of that night began to clarify. He remembered the words, though their meaning wasn't always clear.

The tall figure called himself Evander. The young simian had accepted this without question. Evander explained that he was a human, a man. He explained that the "change" he and his mate had undergone had been necessary so that their offspring would also be "human."

CHAPTER 25

These and other memories passed through his mind as he sat quietly on the edge of the nest. He was still uncomfortable staying this close to his mate, especially at night. But soon after the infant's arrival, he felt a need to remain close; out of curiosity; but also out of a need to watch over and protect them.

As he sat there contentedly, watching his son suckle, his mind wandered back to that day, not so long ago.

It was the day they met in the clearing. He remembered reaching out to touch her face, not with the knuckles on the back of his hand (as was customary in his former "family"), but with the palm open, fingers extended. He remembered how she flinched at his touch, but remained still as his hand gently cupped her face. Most of all, he remembered the look in her eyes. His heart seemed to skip a beat as he remembered how she touched his face in return. She *knew!* And she knew how to let him know that she understood!

He remembered her scent. She was nearing estrus. Up until that moment he had been completely unaware. From the moment of their meeting in the clearing, all his attention had been focused on the wonder of the event. Overwhelmed as the implications raced through his head, he started when she arose from her position. Holding eye contact for another brief moment, she turned away from him, presenting herself.

What took place then lasted only a few seconds. He remembered grasping her hips and thrusting, then thrusting again, and again. Then the explosion. His mind reeled as his body quaked with the exertion of his first-ever ejaculation.

Afterwards, an uneasy silence descended on them. She had not wandered off after their first union as he had seen others in the "family" do in the past. Instead she had turned again toward him and sat down. He had no idea what to do next. He looked at her face, her hand, then down toward that place on her body where he had so recently been. Finally, not knowing what else to do, he stood and shuffled uncertainly toward the safety of the undergrowth. Looking back over his shoulder, he saw that she was following.

The rest of that day was one of confusion and uncertainty for both of them. Neither knew quite what to do next. Instincts weren't the problem. Each had succumbed to that dominant part of their nature, more out of the drive for self-preservation than anything else. But the 'conscious' aspects of this new relationship presented a whole new set of concerns.

Accurate communication was going to be crucial if they were to survive. Both of them knew this. But could they communicate this to each other? To try to do so in broad daylight was fraught with too much danger. It was too distracting. One needed to be wary in order to survive. Better that they wait for the cover of darkness to conceal them.

In the early evening they selected a tree set well apart from the others, with a good view of the surrounding area. Then, after watering and other duties, they both quickly climbed up into the thick foliage and built a sleeping nest.

Neither had any idea what they were going to do next. For both of them this was a complete departure from the reality in which they had previously existed. Each of them knew that the other was experiencing exactly the same thing. Each had departed their former family knowing that they would never return, regardless of the outcome of their meeting. Each of them had chosen to risk being left totally alone rather than not make the effort to communicate with the other.

As the light began to fade, they sat close to each other, looking into each other's eyes, touching, caressing, holding, communicating as well as they were able.

SEEDERS (Continued)

CHAPTER 26

When they got to the shuttle bay, the shuttlecraft had already arrived and was settling into position at the foot of the stairs. A moment later the green 'all clear' lights illuminated and the shuttlecraft door slowly swung open. A crewman in a shiny purple uniform was the first to exit. He stepped down to the deck and then turned, holding out a hand, offering assistance to the person who appeared at the door.

"That's him! That's Ardghal!" Catriona sighed as the figure took a hesitant step forward.

The man looked to be incredibly old. Long white hair fell freely from a receding hairline down the back of a gray and black shawl held close around his slumped shoulders. He extended his free hand to the purple-clad man and then slowly turned to look up toward the two women waiting at the bay door. His wrinkled forehead was highlighted by thick white eyebrows. Half-moon glasses rested partway down his slender nose. Wide-spaced, penetrating green eyes peered over the tops of the lenses. Thin, smiling lips were framed by a close-cropped white beard and moustache.

Zuri thought she heard him say something to the young crew member as he released his grip on the shawl and reached over to hold onto the edge of the door opening. The young man used both hands to help steady the old man as he stepped down onto the deck. On his feet were what looked like old, worn-out slippers.

Scuffs and scratches evidenced years of use. He was wearing a wrinkled, oversized jumpsuit whose frayed pant legs drug the ground as he stepped down.

Catriona led Zuri through the bay door and down the steps to meet the old man. Though he was stoop-shouldered, he was still over six feet tall. He moved with slow, shuffling steps. It was evident from the way he moved that he was having difficulty walking.

Catriona held out her hands for the old man to grasp.

"Thank you, young man." He said to the guard who had helped him from the shuttlecraft. "Now I'll have the pleasure of being escorted by these two beautiful young ladies." He smiled at each in turn.

"Cat, my dear friend!" He took her offered hands and squeezed them gently. "How wonderful it is to see you again. Congratulations on your recent promotion." His eyes seemed to sparkle as he spoke.

Still holding his hands, Catriona spoke affectionately. "Oh, thank you, sir. It's an honor to meet with you again after such a long time."

"Has it been so long?" Ardghal spoke with a reminiscent tone. "It seems that only yesterday you were a young cadet fresh from the academy." Releasing one hand, he patted her other hand gently. Then, turning toward Zuri, he extended both hands toward her. Instinctively, she took his hands in hers. His long, bony fingers felt cool to the touch.

"And you must be Zuri." His smile seemed to broaden as he stepped closer to her. His warm breath smelled pleasant, almost cinnamony.

"Please pardon me, young lady. These old bones are too stiff to offer you a more formal bow. Please accept an old-fashioned hand shake instead." He smiled and bowed his head ever so slightly, though he never broke eye contact.

Zuri felt immediately comfortable in his presence. An air of sincerity and genuineness seemed to emanate from him as he spoke. She felt noticeably less anxious than she had been only moments before.

"Thank you," she said awkwardly. Not knowing what else to say, she looked to Catriona.

The old man seemed to sense her discomfort. Squeezing her hands gently he turned toward Catriona.

"Please, my dear. Can we leave this damp old hangar and find a nice warm place where an old man can sit and rest his bones?"

"Certainly sir." She reached out to support the old man and gestured for Zuri to do the same.

As the three moved carefully up the steps and out into the hallway, Ardghal began talking amiably.

"It's been a long time since I've been up in a ship." His voice was gentle and pleasant. "I don't remember it being so cold, though." He chuckled to himself as he shuffled forward with their help. "Must be old age taking its toll. Don't you think?"

Catriona snuggled closer as they walked toward a reception area just off the main corridor.

"With you here, sir, I feel only warmth."

The room they came to was very small and dimly lit. Soft, indirect lighting revealed four overstuffed chairs, each separated by a low, narrow table.

"Oh, my. Those do look comfortable. But they're so close to the floor. I don't know if I can get up once I've sat down. Won't you please help me?" He grunted quietly as the two women helped him into a chair.

As the two women sat on each side of him, a steward entered carrying a tray with four glasses, a decanter of water and a small plate of the little green carrots. Catriona began filling the glasses as she spoke.

"Alger will join us in just a few moments if that would be all right with you." She offered a glass to each of them.

Zuri accepted the glass and sipped the water tentatively. She wondered how such a sweet man could possibly be party to what had been described.

Ardghal accepted the proffered glass, but only held it without bringing it to his lips.

"Thank you, my dear. Perhaps it would be better if just the three of us visited for a while." Turning to Zuri, he added, smiling; "Would that be all right with you, young lady?"

"Yes. Thank you, sir." Zuri felt relief that she wouldn't have to confront the three of them all at once.

"Good. Good." The old man sat his glass on the table and placed a withered hand on the arm of Zuri's chair.

"Now, my dear. Alger tells me you have some questions regarding some of our procedures. What may I do to ease your concerns?"

His demeanor was so calming and reassuring that Zuri felt reluctant to confront him. But she knew that she must if the issue was to be resolved. Freedom to choose was fundamental to her beliefs. What Alger and Catriona had said seemed to threaten the very foundation of her standards and expectations.

"Yes, sir." She began haltingly. Placing her glass on the table next to his, she tried gathering her thoughts. Then remembering, she chose one of the 'greffs' and took a small bite off the end. The pleasing warmth came over her again.

As though he could read her mind, Ardghal began.

"Yes, my dear. That's good," he said reassuringly. "We all like to use 'greff' when we engage in important discussions such as this. We find it helps us to speak rationally, rather than be distracted by unnecessary emotional responses."

"That's the first thing, then!" Zuri shot a cold stare at the old man. "Why is it necessary to use a drug under such circumstances? We can be rational when we need to be." She knew immediately that she had started off on the wrong foot. Guiltily, she placed the rest of the 'greff' back on the plate.

"Yes. You see, my dear, don't you? Each of us recognizes when we are reacting emotionally in a given circumstance. By that I'm not suggesting that emotions are bad. I only suggest that they are sometimes out of place. If we are wise, we will do what is necessary to return to a rational state. How else can we be sure that we are honestly doing and saying the right thing? How else can we be sure that the person we are speaking to will understand clearly what we are endeavouring to convey?" He chose one of the 'carrots' from the tray. Thin, blotchy fingers held it up for examination.

"This small 'fruit' helps to facilitate that behavior. nothing more, and certainly, nothing less." He returned the 'greff' to the tray.

"Why don't you use it, then?" Zuri blurted.

"Ah, yes. One of the wonders of the 'fruit' is that it helps us to recognize within ourselves when we are approaching an irrational state. With time and practice, we learn to control ourselves without it. I've had a very long time to practice," he chuckled.

"Yes. But I saw Catriona using it. What about that?" Zuri realized almost immediately that she was becoming defensive. Deliberately, she worked to suppress the feeling.

"There. You see?" He smiled and nodded his head ever so slightly. Zuri felt that he had just read her mind. "That's how it works. It helps us see ourselves more clearly. Dear Catriona." He smiled and looked toward her.

"She knew she was in a stressful situation. It's not every day that she gets to meet with a new race."

"I'm sorry, sir. I was only trying to . . ." Catriona lowered her head in embarrassment

"There, now. Don't worry yourself. You did what you thought to be the proper thing. And you were right." He patted her hand gently and then turned back to Zuri.

"And so did you, my dear. Now, tell me. Do you feel as though the 'drug' has controlled you? Or do you feel that you have controlled yourself?"

Zuri was amazed that he was able to get to the heart of the issue so quickly. Was he really reading her that easily?

"No, my dear Zuri. I can't read your mind." He shifted his weight slightly and reached to pick up the glass. Cupping it in both hands, he raised it to his lips and took a sip. Lowering it again to his lap, he continued.

"You see, I've been around so long that I have a good feel for how people will react under most circumstances. It's one of the few benefits of old age. Worlds over, people act in very similar ways, you know. Take Catriona for example. Just now she felt uneasy and somewhat embarrassed when you mentioned her use of the 'greff.' Did you notice the subtle change in her demeanor? Did you see how her shoulders tensed, how she glanced very quickly at you and then lowered her eyes, and how her eyebrows raised ever so slightly? These are all signs of an inner turmoil. She felt guilty, and even a little self-conscious. Then when I spoke to her, did you see how the tension in her body quickly dissipated?"

"Yes, I guess I did. I just didn't think anything of it." Zuri was beginning to feel very self-conscious herself. She could feel her body tensing, her breaths shortening. Consciously she forced herself to relax.

"Of course you did. We all do. We just don't usually 'consciously' pay that close attention. We see these actions so often that we become accustomed to them. They become part of an unspoken vocabulary that all of us are familiar with and use all the time. We take queues from them as much as, or even more so than we do from what is being said. With much training and practice, we can hide much of what we feel inside. We can train our bodies to 'not' react. But when we do that, we leave the other person in an awkward position, especially if what we say doesn't square with what we 'show.'"

"I understand all that," Zuri responded testily. "But what does that have to do with 'greff'?"

"'Greff' really isn't a 'drug' in the strict sense of the word. It doesn't change how we feel or what we think. It doesn't alter our perception of reality. All it really does is help us to see ourselves in a more realistic light. It helps us to become more introspective, more 'self' conscious and less defensive."

"It sounds to me like you're contradicting yourself," Zuri shot back.

"How so?" Ardghal turned in his chair to face Zuri more squarely.

"You said everyone uses it when they're talking about important things. Then you turned around and said that with time they learn to do without it. That sounds like a contradiction to me." She leaned slightly forward to emphasize her point. Ardghal held his position. His voice was still calm as he responded.

"I'm sorry, my dear. Perhaps I didn't make myself clear. I believe what I said was that with time and practice we learn to control ourselves without the help of 'greff.' Certainly that is true. But each person is different. Some of us learn more quickly than others. A lucky few are by nature more inclined to react in an even tempered and calm manner. Sadly the rest of us, myself included, seem predisposed to react more emotionally."

"I understand that, sir. But . . ."

The Procurator raised his hand to stop her in mid-sentence.

"The key to understanding this concept is 'time and practice.' For me it has taken a long time to learn this lesson. When I was about your age I was very forceful and even a bit head-strong. In those days such characteristics were seen as being beneficial for advancement within one's career."

Zuri recognized those traits within herself. As a child she had been independent and forceful. It was she who had chosen which games she and the other children played. Her friends called her bossy and mean, but she didn't see herself that way. She just didn't see much point in wasting time arguing over trivial things like which game to play. For her the playing was more fun than the deciding.

As she grew from adolescence into young adulthood she always seemed to be the center of attention even though she had never actively sought that status. She had always had lots of friends but still felt strangely detached from them.

Sometimes she just wanted to be one of the girls, laughing and giggling and being carefree. But whenever she tried it she always felt unfulfilled. The only time she felt really content was when she was in charge. Sometimes it caused friction between her and her friends, but she saw that as the price she must pay for feeling good about herself. She had had her share of boyfriends too. But even they had capitulated whenever she asserted herself.

She had naturally gravitated into leadership positions. As a young cadet in flight school, her instructors and mentors recognized her qualities and encouraged her to sharpen and refine them. She graduated at the top of her class and had immediately been assigned to the *Brighid*'s Operations Staff. Now, as Senior Command Officer, the top position in the fleet, she was convinced it was her 'no nonsense' approach which had gotten her here.

Ardghal continued. "It goes without saying that leadership is not without its problems. Its easy to loose friends and even make enemies when one has to make unpopular decisions. Allowing one's emotions to cloud judgement can become detrimental and hinder one's ability to bring consensus. Much time and energy must then be expended endeavoring to bring people 'back into the fold' so to speak."

Zuri nodded her understanding, remembering how Chetan reacted when she had asserted herself.

"But sir . . . I still don't see how that applies to the original question."

"I'm certain that as a leader you've experienced friction between yourself and others when your decisions have met with resistance. Is this not so?"

Zuri nodded again. How was it that he could anticipate her

reaction and come up with the appropriate response with such apparent ease?

"Would it not be more efficient and beneficial to spend one's time solving problems rather than trying to sooth hurt feelings?" The Procurator leaned back in his chair raising a hand slightly to emphasize his point.

"Please don't misunderstand. Feelings . . . emotions . . . have their place. They are what make us human. Compassion and caring are the driving forces behind what we are endeavoring to do here and elsewhere throughout the universe. If we didn't care, what would be the point of 'seeding' at all?"

Zuri began feeling a warmth within her as she listed to his words.

"It's sometimes difficult, if not impossible to make rational decisions when our emotions are so highly invested in the process. At those times it is always better to step back from the precipice and consider our options. Selfishness is almost always a part of such a situation. That is not to say that 'selfishness,'" (He emphasized the word.) "is, by definition, bad under all circumstances. To the extent it is harmless to others, seeing to one's own needs and desires must always be a consideration. It's best to be honest with yourself first. That will make all the difference in what you decide to do. Setting emotion aside, if only for a few moments, can make all the difference in the final outcome. Ultimately we strive to satisfy both. We strive to be rational *and* compassionate in our decision-making.

"But now, to return to the original issue. I believe it had to do with the right to choose, or something like that." Ardghal smiled gently as he settled back into his chair.

Zuri was taken a bit off balance by his abrupt change of subject. In fact, as she thought about it, what he had just said was directly related to her first concern. That was whether or not 'seedlings' had had their right to autonomy tampered with. Or was it the 'greff' thing?

"Thank you, sir." She shifted slightly so she could face the old man squarely. "I can't tell you how the words you've spoken have effected me. They comprise the whole of my own belief system." She realized that by saying what he did, he had helped clarify her concerns. Now her original argument was beginning to disintegrate.

"Okay, sir." She cleared her throat and collected her thoughts. "I guess it all boils down to freedom of choice. By administering 'greff' to 'seedlings' here in the ship, aren't you putting an undue influence on them. You've taken them out of their environment, brought them to this strange place, and then fed them an unknown substance which alters their state of mind. That sounds, at the very least, like gross infringement."

Ardghal chuckled.

"Interesting turn of a phrase, my dear. Did you come up through the judicial ranks?" He chuckled again, raised a finger for attention, paused, lost in thought, then tapped himself on the side of the head.

"Oh, yes. Sorry." He took a deep breath, let it out slowly, and began.

"Our top priority is, has, and always will be: Love each other. That means everybody. Even the 'seedlings' as we like to call them, or the newcomers such as yourself, or the old salts like me." He tapped himself in the chest, then the temple, then held his finger up once more to emphasize the point he had made. His eyebrow furrowed as he leaned forward. Gently he laid his hand on Zuri's hand. Patting it softly, he began.

"My dear young girl. Bless you for listening so closely, and for finding the words to express yourself so . . . forcefully."

His gray, sparkling eyes peered deep into her own. Instead of feeling challenged by such intimacy, she felt comfort, such inner peace as he spoke. His words penetrated as easily as did his eyes. She felt as if she were almost swooning as she listened to him speak.

"All that we do here is for love!" The smile in his eyes made his face seem to glow. Zuri remembered what Catriona had said about this man. She was quickly realizing that what he was saying was in complete agreement with her innermost beliefs and expectations. Involuntarily, she turned a bit more toward him. She felt a chill run through her as the realization sunk in.

"To do otherwise goes totally against our nature," he smiled. "We are loving, caring people. All of us. Each one of us has progressed differently than anyone else. Each one of us has had questions, fears, apprehensions. Each of us has dealt with them in our own way. How we have resolved differences," he patted her hand again. "has generally proved to be less important than what we choose to do going forward." He sat up a bit and took a quick shallow breath.

"Each of us has feelings, too. And that is what makes us so beautiful. Unique above all other creatures in the universe. We have feelings!" He paused for a moment, considering. "I suppose there might be some who will argue that certain 'lower' animals have feelings, too. I certainly wouldn't argue to the contrary. I've loved my share of kitties and pooches, and felt love returned. I guess love is universal. All creatures must have it to some degree. Maybe we're just not smart enough to see it.

"The other thing that *must* go along with love, is choice." He sat up straight, excitement in his expression. He noticed that Zuri again had that puzzled look on her face. "Does my choice of words confuse you, my dear?"

Zuri opened her mouth, but could think of nothing to say. She sat in awe, waiting for him to provide answers for questions she had as yet not thought of. There was excitement in the words he said. There was a passion in them that went beyond description. Zuri knew in her heart that what he was saying was true. She could sense no guile or deception in the man.

Ardghal rubbed his hands together excitedly. Zuri glanced past him toward Catriona. Her hands were clasped in her lap. She was smiling, her gaze fixed on the old man sitting between them. She seemed excited, anticipating.

Ardghal noticed the break in eye contact but continued.

"Okay. Let's get down to it. When a 'seedling' comes here for the first time, he is scared, to say the least. What are we supposed to do with a near-hysterical brother? Hold him down and speak softly to him? It's been tried. Sometimes it works. But not usually. I say we intervene, on his behalf, so that he can comprehend what's going on without feeling threatened. Take the perceived threat away and the 'seedling' gets his answers without too much trauma." Ardghal sat even taller, happy with what he had said.

"Now, did we deprive him of his right to freak out in our presence? I guess the answer is yes. But what of the consequences if we chose only to cuddle and cajole? What good would that do? Would it not be better for *all* of us to stand on equal terms where issues can be resolved. That is the gist of why 'greff' exists. It doesn't alter your perception of anything. It doesn't lessen your capacity to function properly and appropriately. Its only function is to help us learn how to control our emotions. Not deny or destroy them. *Self*-control, not induced obedience." He relaxed a bit as he came to his conclusion.

"The thing that makes 'greff' such a wonderful tool is that most people loose the desire for it after only a short period of use. There are, of course, some exceptions. But those are usually people who work in very stressful environments, such as extra-vehicular and propulsion systems. As a matter of fact, we find that to be the case with nearly all 'controlled substances.' Once they are understood and seen for their true worth, or lack thereof, curiosity soon wanes. The stimulation experienced by an unencumbered mind is much more rewarding than that simulated through ingestion of various chemical concoctions.

"In short, 'greff' shortens the path for those who strive to become truly self-aware. The more we learn on our own, the less we rely on any substance to help us cope. The true joy is rising to the point where it no longer affects you. You have progressed to the level where you can, at will, separate from the emotional turmoil that is your daily life. In a very real sense, you have attained a measure of inner peace. Where there is little turmoil, there is little need for distraction. I like to say about 'greff.'. . It got us this far, but where we go, it cannot follow."

Zuri leaned back in her chair, feeling the tension in her muscles drain away. Could it be that just his words were having such an impact on her body too? The old man turned toward Catriona and gave her a friendly, knowing wink.

"I guess it all comes down to choice, doesn't it? I mean, you can choose to slog your way through everything, hopefully picking up some knowledge along the way. Or you can take the 'short cut' and get to the same place. The more I think about it, the more I see benefit in both! Ultimately it depends on individual personality."

Before either woman could formulate a response, Ardghal sat forward, shifting his weight and grunting ever so slightly.

"Yes, yes!" he chuckled. "It *is* about choice, isn't it? And trust, too. Don't forget that." He raised a finger in emphasis.

"Here, sir. Let me help you." Catriona was on her feet almost immediately, arms extended, hands gently supporting the old man's skinny arm.

"Thank you, Cat, my dear. It is not often these days that I may indulge in such pleasure as meeting with a beautiful young woman." Turning to Zuri, who was rising to help. "But two! Such amazement! It is such a joy to be in the presence of you both."

The two women each took hold of his thin hands, helping him rise.

"Okay, ladies. My body is vertical. Now I must wait for the blood to catch up."

They all stood still momentarily until the old man spoke.

"Well, then. My dear Zuri," he sighed. "It has been my complete pleasure to meet you. I am so happy that our paths have crossed."

"Thank you sir." Zuri looked down self-consciously, then up into the old man's happy eyes. Her throat was tightening, making her voice hard to control. "I know you mean that."

"Oh, indeed I do, my dear! We will meet again one day, I am sure."

Zuri felt a flush of heat touch her cheeks as she slid her hand around his arm. She knew that he was leaving, though he had said nothing.

"Sir, before you go, may I . . .?" Her mind seemed to flush full of questions . . . more than she could sort out.

"Of course, my dear." He pulled her close to him. The warmth of her arm against his old creaky frame gave him pleasure.

"Do you have to go now? I have so many questions."

"*My*, yes! I'm sure you do. I'm flattered that you would think so highly of me to want me to stay." With his other arm, he pulled Catriona close also, then shifted his weight backward slightly, slowing their pace.

"We can go slowly if you like. . . . But I'm afraid I must leave very soon. I promised my sweetheart that we would spend time together tonight, and I dare not disappoint her." Zuri still seemed to be unsure of something. He could see it in her furrowed brow.

"What's on your mind, my dear?" He squeezed Zuri's hand against his side.

"It's hard to put it in words. I guess it has to do with the whole issue of 'seeding.' Why is it necessary to use simians as hosts in the first place? Wouldn't it be easier to just transplant some people to a planet and let them populate it.?"

"It's a fair question and it deserves more than just a quick explanation. Let me see if I can do it justice." They stopped in the middle of the hall as Ardghal released the two women's arms. For a moment he stood there quietly, arms folded, head bowed, as if in prayer.

"You have to know what it feels like to belong to something." He began, head still bowed. Then slowly, as though straining to find the right words:

"You have to understand, deep in your own heart, what it means to truly belong to something beyond yourself, something more important than yourself.

"Our civilizations have advanced to a point where we can engineer most anything we want. If we so desired (and we have done so in the past) we could completely build the entire human genome from component parts we have at our disposal. We could build an entire race of them if we so desired. We could modify them as needed, with small bodies for working in tight places, or strong bodies for work in heavy manual labor. We could even engineer a race of humans specialized in colonizing planets, with specialized digestive systems so they can metabolize foreign nourishment.

"We can do all these things, but we *choose* not to. Instead, we choose to place our precious seeds . . . ourselves . . . our posterity, in "fertile soil" so they may grow with a natural affinity for the place of their birth, rather than a longing to return to one which is no longer within their reach. The one gives a sense of purpose, of belonging. The other leaves a sense of despair."

"Isn't what you're saying, that one is a transplant which doesn't belong, while the other belongs because of the place of its birth? Whether transplanted or sewn as seeds, do they not both have the same roots?" Zuri felt that she had gained some ground in her understanding, but still wasn't quite sure that she could agree, primarily on moral grounds.

"One could put it another way also." Ardghal raised a finger in emphasis. "One could recognize the difference between himself and his parents, and believe that he could not possibly be the result of their union; and at the same time deal with the realization that he, himself, did not know where he came from. This disparity is the place where myth is born."

Ardghal stepped closer to Zuri and placed a hand on her shoulder.

"My child, I sense that there is more to what you ask than what you are saying. I will approach this from one more perspective, and then I must go. Perhaps what I say will give you pause as to your own preconceptions. Please don't be offended. Everyone has preconceptions. Everyone has their own favorite myths. In the end, it becomes a moral issue on theological, as well as philosophical grounds.

"Do you believe in a supreme being? Or do you believe that you are the center of your universe?" The old man smiled and patted Zuri's arm.

"Be careful how you answer, my dear. It's a loaded question." He smiled and again started walking. "Just in case you wanted to know, but were afraid to ask, Yes. I do believe in a supreme being. Whether or not I believe in just *one* is quite another matter.

"I don't like the word 'supreme.' It implies a maximum to the amount of knowledge one can attain. Our species has come a long way over the millennia. And everywhere we go, we have gained in knowledge. One of the things we have learned is that someone has been there before us. And how can that person (or race) remain ahead of us unless they continue to increase in knowledge? Knowledge is eternal. And so is truth. In fact, they are one."

There was a long pause in the conversation as the three walked slowly toward the shuttle bay.

Zuri never had much time for religion. It always seemed to pit one group of people against another. She had never seen any advantage (other than a selfish one) to subscribing to any particular religious philosophy. But there were times, quiet times, when she was alone in her solitude, when she wondered if there was a god. The thought only began to bother her when she became associated with organized religion. She learned what she called the 'god and devil thing,' or as she referred to it, the 'carrot and stick' routine. The carrot is the reward (worship god), always held just out of reach. The stick (devil) is there to make sure you stay in line.

After having listen to this man, Zuri had gained a better understanding of this issue. She would take time to ponder all that he had said.

The three of them arrived at the door, arm in arm. A guard standing just outside pushed the door open and extended a hand to help steady the old Procurator.

"I need to get home now, by dark." He remarked, more to the guards than to the two women. "There's a show on that we like to watch. My wife will kill me if I'm not there to catch the beginning with her." He laughed sheepishly as he sidled forward into the waiting arms of the other guard.

Catriona and Zuri stood together as the bay doors closed. Hand in hand, they stood watching as the old man made his way across the apron toward his shuttlecraft. They could see plainly how he easily chatted with the two young men who assisted him. Every few steps he would point at something or another and make some unheard comment. Finally they made it up the steps of the shuttlecraft. Just before he ducked his head to clear the entrance, he turned to wave good by. Zuri thought she saw the glint of a tear in the old man's eye. And then he was gone.

CHAPTER 27

His escorts were the last to enter the craft. The stairway folded in on itself and disappeared under the belly of the craft. Lights inside the cockpit could now be seen as the light in the hangar deck dimmed. Zuri could see the outline of the pilot and co-pilot as they busied themselves going through their pre-flight check lists. She saw the co-pilot's hand go up toward what she suspected was the power distribution panel. At least that would be where it would be in *her* shuttlecraft.

Sure enough, a pattern of light came on all around the exterior of the space craft. One pattern ran horizontal, along the central axis of the fuselage. The lights pulsed in place a foot or so apart in a row less than a foot wide. Another two 'ribbons' of light ran across the midsection of the craft and another one going from the nose of the craft, up and over the cockpit, across the top of the craft and back down again, across the belly and back up to meet at the nose.

The 'ribbon' around the horizontal axis began pulsing at a faster rate. Faster and faster it flashed until the pulsations seemed to synchronize into one continuous beam. One by one the lights detached them selves from the fuselage and moved out to form a circle a few feet larger than the length of the craft.

Next, the ribbon around the belly repeated the same process

until the ring it formed was only a few inches larger than the horizontal ring.

The last ring to form fit just inside the smaller of the two rings, Clearing the nose and tail of the craft by only inches.

The cockpit windows turned black as the craft began to rise. The horizontal ring changed to a soft yellow color as the spacecraft rose a foot above the floor. A dotted line the same color as the rings appeared on the floor, extending out to the edge of the bay where it stopped at the huge doors.

Zuri heard a faint pop as the bay was de-pressurized. Several feet beyond the hovering spacecraft, the doors slid slowly to each side, revealing the crescent of Cygnus 5 below, its sun just dipping below the horizon.

The remaining two rings around the craft also began changing color. When the three colors matched, the craft rotated clockwise 180 degrees facing outward toward the vastness beyond. The craft began moving outward, each yellow light on the floor extinguishing as the craft passed over it.

Floating motionless in space, other vehicles could be seen queued in line, the planet rotating slowly below.

The two women continued watching as the craft drifted out ahead of the que. Its yellow rings turned back to white as the craft took a steep dive down and to the left, dipping below the bay floor and out of sight. Immediately, the spacecraft at the head of the que was surrounded by the same yellow halo. The yellow line reappeared, this time ending on the other side of the wide bay.

Ardghal was a man of mystery to most everyone who knew him. Extreme longevity among the space-fairing races was common, but with Ardghal there was something different. No one who knew him had any idea how old he was, or where he had come from.

CHAPTER 28

"He really is an amazing man, isn't he?" Catriona moved closer to Zuri, affectionately placing a hand on her shoulder.

"Yes. I see now why you hold him in such high regard. He has a way about him that draws people to him, doesn't he?"

"He reminds me of my grandfather." Catriona lowered her head slightly, wiping away a tear. Zuri heard the strain in her voice as she spoke.

"He's been a part of my life for as long as I can remember. When I was just a child in school I remember him coming to visit our class. Everyone was excited, and a little afraid. We had all heard stories about Procurators. Most of the stories weren't true. You know how kids are. They always exaggerate. We thought he would come to us dressed in a scary long, black robe, and that he would freeze us with his eyes if we misbehaved."

"I can see how kids could believe that. He has very penetrating eyes, doesn't he?"

"Yes. But they're not scary, are they?" Zuri looked up into the tall woman's face. A glow seemed to emanate from her as she spoke.

"I've never felt so loved as when he looked into my eyes that day so many years ago. I remember how unusually quiet the classroom was. None of us kids knew quite what to expect, so we were all on our best behavior. Everyone had heard of Procurators before, but none of us had ever seen one."

"Why is that?" Zuri asked. "From what I gather, there are lots of them."

"That's true. But they're spread pretty thin. Only rarely is there more than one Procurator in any given galaxy."

"Any given galaxy?!" Zuri was stunned. "How many are we talking about?"

"No one knows for sure. The number keeps growing. Our best estimate is several hundred thousand, but the more we explore, the more we find."

Zuri's mouth opened to respond, but she could say nothing. Hundred thousand?! For her and everyone she had ever known, traveling among the stars had been as much a dream as a reality. True, she had been born onboard a spacecraft and had never set foot on her own world. Her entire life had revolved around space travel. She had never known anything else. But in all those years and generations her kind had been in space, they had covered less than one light year. The distance traveled by the five races combined totalled less than four.

Now, here she was, orbiting a planet over 50,000 light years from her home onboard the *Wasswa*, and still she remained within the confines of this galaxy! The fact that there were several hundred thousand known galaxies like this one was almost more than she could comprehend.

In her entire lifetime on board the *Wasswa* she had traveled less than a light year. Now, in only a few seconds, she had covered a distance over 50,000 times larger. Then add to that the fact that there were thousands of inhabited galaxies like this one. . . . She was having a hard time grasping the concept.

Catriona recognized the consternation on Zuri's face.

"I know this is a lot to take in." Placing a hand gently on the young commander's shoulder, she urged her away from the window.

"Come, let's walk for a while, shall we? I always find it's easier to work through things if I can just keep my body active. I think it helps circulate more blood through my brain, or something. Helps me think more clearly."

"Yeh, me too." Zuri smiled up into the tall woman's eyes and fell into a relaxed, easy pace beside her.

"Let me take you to my office for just a minute. I need to show you something. It might help you put things in perspective. Then maybe after that we can go get something to eat, Okay? I'm starving!" Her eyes seemed to light up as she began.

"I remember the first time I traveled via LINK. I was just a kid, still in grade school."

"Our fourth grade Environmental Biology class was invited to go on a field trip to Cygnus 12. It had recently been selected for seeding, and the powers that be thought it would be a good idea for us kids to see the process first hand.

Forth grade Environmental Biology? Zuri marvelled to herself. We didn't get that class until second year college! Wow! These people must really be advanced compared to us.

Catriona continued, excitedly.

"I remember the teacher showed us a map of the Cygnus arm of this galaxy. She pointed out where we were, and where Cygnus 12 was. It didn't mean much to me." She chuckled to herself. "They were just two points on a piece of paper. None of us was very impressed.

"Then came the day when we boarded the spacecraft and began the trip up to the LINK. It was a two-day trip and all us kids were excited that we were going to get to spend the night in zero G. The first night we all had a chance to view Cygnus 12 through the onboard telescope. It looked a lot like the point on the map back in class. I wasn't impressed.

"The next morning we arrived at the LINK. Before our ship entered, we all could see Cygnus 12 again on the big monitors spaced around the perimeter of the room. It still looked like just another star . . . nothing special. Then the monitor switched to a view of the LINK. We were in a formation of several other ships, all seeming to move in slow motion toward what appeared to be a huge cylinder filled with nothing but a strange, greyish haze.

"As we penetrated the haze, the ships in front of us vanished, and then reappeared in the blink of an eye!" She began gesturing excitedly, stretching her arms wide, out in front of her.

"A few seconds later the view on the monitor switched again. This time the dot in the center of a map was replaced by a view of a planet; one I'd never seen before. I remember hearing the ship's intercom say, 'Welcome to Cygnus 12.' It was a different voice than the one I had heard only seconds before."

They came to a door, one of several closely spaced, maybe twenty feet apart. Each door had a different symbol on it, apparently etched directly into the smooth metallic surface.

The symbol on this door was familiar to Zuri. It was a profile view of a chess piece . . . the white queen.

"Of course!" Zuri thought to herself. "What else could it be? Chess is a game of strategy . . . and intellect! One maneuvers and watches; gauging one's opponent, learning how she thinks, what her priorities are, what she's willing to risk in order to achieve an objective."

It was perfewctly logical that Catriona whould choose this symbol. Her choice revealed much about her. Zuri felt she understood her new friend a bit better now. She identified with the image the symbol suggested.

She viewed chess as a game of strategy, but also as a game of life. Consciously or otherwise, everyone is continuously strategizing. Whether it be about something mundane and trivial, like deciding what color uniform to wear; or something much more crucial, like deciding how to react to a totally alien situation, such as the one she was in now.

Catriona raised a hand close to a small panel at the edge of the door. The door retracted noiselessly into the wall as a quiet mechanical-sounding voice said. 'Enter.'

"Make yourself at home," she said over her shoulder as she moved quickly across the small room toward another door. "Take a look around if you like. I'll be right back."

Zuri thought she smelled the faintest hint of Rosemary. But Catriona had said this was her office. How could it be that an office smelled more like a kitchen? And the furnishings didn't look like anything she had ever seen in any office. If there was a desk, it wasn't to be seen anywhere. Instead, there were comfortable looking divans all around the perimeter of the room. All except the wall to the right of the entrance they had just come through. It was a flat gray plane of some unrecognizable material; not metallic, but not opaque like paint. The roughly fifteen-foot span was framed on each side by shelving at various heights and lengths. Most of these contained ancient-looking books, judging from the condition of the bindings. Others held what looked like highly detailed miniature statuary.

She walked over to the one that held the bust of an old man. The shelf was a little over a foot long and was made of something different from the others. At first glance it looked like ancient, petrified wood. The intricate grain was clearly there. There was even discoloration in some the grains, like was frequently the case with most petrified specimens she had ever seen.

But this clearly wasn't wood. It looked to be metallic, like heat-treated metal, fresh from the furnace, glowing like an infernal rainbow, but not symmetrical like a real rainbow. Instead, the color was interwoven among the swirling, metallic grains. As Zuri moved closer, the colors seemed to follow her.

The statue which rested on it cast no shadow that she could see. It was like she was the only light source in the room. Where she moved, its radiance seemed to follow.

The statue itself looked to be made of brass. The features of the face were intricately detailed, so much so it seemed to be almost alive. The detail was that good!

Who was the sculptor of such a magnificent piece? Zuri wondered, and then started as she recognized the familiar face. Is this who I think it is? She moved closer.

"It looks just like him . . . only in miniature!" She spoke in quiet wonderment.

Yes! It was Ardghal! There were the glasses; and the scraggly, thinning hair. Even the tiny crow's feet at the corners of his bright, smiling eyes. She felt a chill pass quickly down the back of her neck.

Just then the image began to dissolve. The red rainbow of color which a moment ago was the shelf, also began to dissolve. In its place a longer shelf began to materialize. It looked to be of the same material as the other. Upon it, what began to take shape were three miniature, highly detailed human figures, all sitting in a semi-circle. These figures too seemed to be alive, like the bust which had just disappeared.

Zuri recognized the figures in the hologram! She was one of them! And there was Ardghal sitting comfortably in the middle, with Catriona to his left.

How in the world is this possible? He hasn't been gone ten minutes and she already has a sculpture of the occasion?! But wait. It's not a real sculpture, is it? It's a hologram! Oh, man! That means. . . .

She was getting carried away here. Sure, they had holograms in her world too. But they were primitive compared to these! In Zuri's world holograms could only be generated within the boundaries of individual field generators.

They were relatively small, due to the limitations of their equipment. Filtering out unwanted magnetic fields, such as gravity, or electricity, or fields generated by objects or individuals in the vicinity; all were recognized by their recording devices.

But the discretionary abilities of their software was limited. It could be easily overwhelmed by having to contend with an ever-moving, fluid environment which was three-dimensional reality. It was one thing to record in two dimensions. Data, whether static, or moving, was only recorded in two directions. And, depending on the desired levels of resolution chosen, the amount of data was relatively limited.

The same could be said of recording in three dimensions also, so long as the boundaries of the environment could be clearly defined. Static data, such as furniture or walls and floors was easy enough for their software to keep track of.

Movement within that space was easily detected, but not so easily recorded. The data added by that third dimension increased by orders of magnitude, once again depending on the level of resolution one wished to keep track of. Therefore, the smaller the space being recorded, the smaller the amount of data required.

A high-resolution hologram with a volume of sixty cubic feet contained about as much data as an individual computer could handle. The resolution used in the typical holograms in use in Zuri's world yielded enough data for general facial recognition, but very little in the way of minute detail.

Networking was in common use, though still not as commonplace as MCD's (Mobile Communication Devices). Almost everyone owned or had ready access to a holo-booth. But it was cumbersome, stationary, and uncomfortable to sit in one for more than a few minutes at a time. Infra-red saturation, though invisible, did tend to cause one to feel physically more tired than normal.

It was obvious then that a holo-recording had been taken, but Zuri had seen nothing to indicate any recording equipment was present. The implication was that the technology of this new race was incredibly advanced. She knew she had to learn more.

She was so engrossed, marvelling at the tiny sculpture, her mind swooning as the questions began to unfold, that she didn't notice the swooshing of bare feet on carpet, moving toward her from behind. Her nose caught the faint, warm scent of lilac close beside her. . . .

"Beautiful, aren't they? They're my prized possessions." Catriona spoke quietly, her voice barely more than a whisper.

Zuri felt warm breath on her cheek. She turned to see the same woman, but now looking completely different. While she was out of the room she had changed clothes.

Her other outfit, though hardly what Zuri would call a uniform, was somewhat rigid in design. The straight sharp creases in the pant legs and the angular cut of the shoulders suggested rigid authority. The subtle mixing of greys and blacks reinforced the image.

One was immediately taken aback when seeing the auburn-tressed Catriona for the first time. Her skin was not pale, but creamy, accentuating her dark, almond-shaped eyes. When in uniform her hair was pulled back slightly, emphasizing the high collar with her rank insignia on each small lapel. The rigidness conveyed by the uniform was softened considerably by her femininity. Yet still there was an air of power and authority about her.

Now, Catriona was covered from her neck to her ankles in a single piece of shimmering dark green fabric. It was gathered loosely in small ruffles around her neck. Then it cascaded in gentle folds downward, sweeping the contours of her body, finally to gather again, forming loose cuffs at her slender ankles.

Zuri was taken aback by the sleek and sensuous design of Catriona's dress.

"My, that's beautiful!" she exclaimed. "What kind of fabric is that? I've never seen anything like it."

"I'm so glad you like it." Catriona smiled. "I just got it for this occasion. Actually, it's not really a fabric at all. We reserve the use of actual woven fabric for very special garments. The uniform you saw me in? That was actually woven from an ancient material called cotton. It's almost never used in everyday clothing. Here. Come feel. Look more closely."

Zuri moved closer, brushing Catriona's bare shoulder as she took the material between her fingers. It was extremely smooth to the touch. It slipped between her fingers more smoothly than silk. It seemed to weigh almost nothing. She looked closer, trying to find some indication of how it was made. She couldn't see any sort of weave pattern. Nor could she see any seams where pieces of the material had been joined.

"We like to call it cloth, mostly out of tradition." Catriona stepped back and did a quick turn-about, causing the material to spiral gently around her body.

"It's actually 'grown' in many of the shops down on the surface. The material comes out of a machine and is wound onto big rollers. Then it's shaped and colored as necessary."

"It's amazing stuff. I can't seem to see any indication of what it's made of or how it's put together."

"It's sort of a chemical bonding process as I understand it. It's been around for such a long time that I guess I take it for granted. Anyway, there's a chemical equation or recipe or something that you program into the machine, depending on what you want to come out."

"What's the raw material?" Zuri stepped back and found a seat close by. She sat down absently.

"Air." Catriona responded deadpan. Zuri just sat there with her mouth open, saying nothing.

"Sorry. I guess this is all coming at you pretty fast. I'll just give you the facts as I know them and you can sort them out however you need to. What the 'cloth' machine actually does is filter the air. Its filtration system pulls out all the particulates in the air, down to a molecular level. It cleans and sorts the particles by type, and then assembles them on demand into whatever molecular pattern has been loaded into its memory."

"You mean your clothes are made of dust?"

"Yes. And lint and almost everything that floats around in the air we breathe."

Zuri sat quietly for a few moments, digesting what she had learned.

"You mean like airborne pathogens and microbes . . ."

"Yes. They're all filtered by type and each is thoroughly cleaned. In the case of harmful materials, they're either cleaned or disassembled on a sub-atomic level, where they can be diffused and rendered harmless."

"Does that work for biological as well as chemical or radiological materials?"

"Yup. It's pretty complete. And that's just for the clothes we wear. Those collectors are small compared to the industrial size ones. We have huge collectors in all the major population centers. They're much more efficient than the small ones. They can discriminate which particles they collect. Some are programmed to collect only organics. Others may be programmed to collect only minerals.

"But why discriminate? Aren't all materials essentially the same when you get down to the atomic level?" Zuri's analytical penchant was now fully engaged. Her intellectual curiosity had now overridden her emotional response.

Catriona picked up one of the smaller items displayed along the back edge of the shelf. Zuri hadn't even noticed that they were there; she had been so engrossed in the amazing hologram. The object was a small wooden carving of a misshapen face. Though it was very crude,it closely resembled Ardghal.

"Here. Take a look at this." She handed the carving to Zuri and gestured toward two chairs across the room.

"Come. Let sit for a while. Isn't that a cute little carving?"

Zuri turned the small object over and over in her hand, examining it closely. The carving was light in color, like birch, or maybe maple. She could see fine, dark lines running through the material.

"This is really beautiful. I've never seen a wood quite like this before."

"It *is* beautiful, isn't it?" A friend of mine gave it to me as a present when I graduated from the academy. It's actually real wood! We almost never see real wood any more. We still grow trees down on the surface, but they're pretty rare. We use them mostly for ornamental purposes now. Plus they're great oxygen factories.

We used to harvest trees for use in construction of houses and other buildings. But now our collectors can fabricate them much more efficiently.

"You mean to tell me your collectors can actually build houses?"

"No, no! They're good, but not that good." Catriona chuckled as she leaned back in her chair. "Our collectors can only fabricate elements, and sometimes compounds, if they're not too complex. We still have to build our structures ourselves. We just use the collectors to supply the materials we want to use."

"Do the collectors supply everything?"

"Well, not quite everything. Just the common materials we use from day to day." Catriona gestured toward the carving Zuri held in her hand.

"That piece you're holding in your hand is actually one of the last actual wooden carvings ever made. Such "waste" is no longer tolerated. Our planet-side resources are very limited, so we don't use them unless it's absolutely necessary."

" We have similar issues with resource conservation." Zuri placed the carving on the small table sitting between their chairs. "But we don't have the technology to build collectors like the ones you describe. We've had to collect resources from uninhabited planets we've encountered during our journey."

" We did the same thing for a long, long time. Our resources were getting pretty slim too, and we knew they'd eventually run out. Besides, it just wasn't cost effective to harvest materials from other planets. Even after the era of the LINKS began, we maintained our frugal ways. It just didn't make sense for us to exploit our resources when it wasn't really necessary."

"Not necessary?"

"Uh-huh." Catriona leaned forward. " When the LINKS came, they brought with them technology which was beyond our comprehension. We had already become a space-faring culture, but we were on a very limited budget, resource-wise. Even with pulse drive, it was incredibly expensive to operate in space."

"We're still there." Zuri nodded her head in understanding. "Even with five ships, we have to be very careful how we use the resources we have. We recycle everything we can, but there are still lots of waste products we simply don't know what to do with. We store everything we can, so our coffers are getting pretty full. From time to time we have to dump some of the stuff overboard."

"In the early days that's the way we did it too. We told ourselves that since space was such a big place, a little extra space debris wouldn't make any difference. But in reality we really didn't have any other choice.

"It wasn't very long after the LINKS made contact that we learned about collectors. Our history books tell us that within only one or two generations collectors had been fabricated and distributed planet wide. When that happened our entire planet's economic situation improved to the point that we could funnel more resources into the space program."

"This is amazing!" said Zuri. "I take it you don't have much problem with air pollution."

Catriona chucked as she responded. "Not really, which is one reason why our illness rates dropped so dramatically after contact with the LINKS."

"The five cultures represented in our fleet haven't been 'home' for generations." said Zuri. "I often wonder what became of them."

"Well, there's an added bonus to becoming 'seeders.' All the technology which the LINKS provide your fleet will also be made available to your home worlds. Also, LINKS will be stationed in close proximity to them so you can return for visits."

"What an amazing opportunity!" Zuri hadn't considered that possibility. "I'm sure the others will be as excited about this as I am."

"Excellent! Are there other issues you'd like to discuss before we rejoin your friends? You don't have to feel pressured. You can all take as much time as you feel you need."

Zuri was a bit hesitant, but didn't want to hold anything back.

"Ardghal seems to be such an sweet man; and he's very persuasive. But I'm still not completely comfortable with everything he said."

"That's completely understandable. It's a lot to absorb in one sitting. But I assure you; the more you contemplate what he said, the more you will come to agree with him."

Catriona stood and walked over to the shelves where they had been standing. She placed the palm of her hand on the shelf next to the holograms, and then raised her hand slightly. A miniature keyboard materialized where her hand had been. She tapped it several times and then waited a few moments. A panel just above the shelf slid open. Catriona reached inside and pulled out two small objects which Zuri couldn't quite make out. Catriona covered them with her other hand, then turned and came back to her seat.

"Here. These are for you, so you can remember."

She extended her hands and gestured for Zuri to do the same. Catriona placed the two miniature sculptures in Zuri's hand.

"Oh, my!" Zuri's eyes teared up as she recognized them. "But I thought they were holo-grams."

"The ones you saw before were. But I just programmed my room 'collector' to make reproductions. Now you'll always have them as a reminder."

SIMIAN 3 (CONTINUED)

CHAPTER 29

It had been just over a year now. His son had grown quickly, though he was still totally reliant on his parents. They had to keep constant watch on him. As soon as he learned how to crawl, he was constantly trying to escape from their arms. In the evenings when they stopped, he scurried about, exploring everything about his surroundings. Then as he tired he always climbed back into his mother's embrace where, while suckling contentedly, he soon fell asleep.

It was on this night that the infant uttered his first intelligible sounds. Wrapped close in his mother's arms, he snuggled, murmuring contentedly. "M-m-m, M-m, M-m-m, M-m."

Releasing her nipple from his lips, he looked up into his mothers eyes. "A-h-h, A-h, A-h-h, A-h." A soft, high pitched squeal issued from his lips. She drew him even closer. He felt her warm breath on his brow. He felt the steady thump, thump, thump of her heart. His small, delicate fingers tangled themselves in her hair. His bliss was complete.

He saw that small pools of tears had formed in the corners of her eyes. He watched as a tear began slowly moving down her cheek. Releasing his grip, he caught the tear on the tip of his finger, then drew it to his mouth. The taste was new, somehow pleasing and soothing at the same time.

Emotion began welling up within him. Tears began rolling slowly down his cheeks too. His lips parted as his little tongue tasted the warm liquid.

"M-m, M-m-m." he said. "M-m, M-m-m, Mah-h-h. . . . M-m-mah, m-mah!"

At that moment the two young simians recognized that a threshold had been crossed. This was a new form of communication; one they knew they would never possess. Here, in their son, would reside the ability to communicate in a completely new way.

The young mother's thoughts flashed back to that night seemingly not so long ago, when they were still living with the old "family," when she and also her eventual mate had been visited by that strange object in the night sky.

What had happened to them that night had wrought a change within each of them which they both recognized. But not until this very moment had it occurred to her that more had happened then than she knew.

CHAPTER 30

The young simian sat watching from his perch at the edge of the nest. Daylight was fading quickly. Soon now he would edge his way closer to his mate. He had learned to draw comfort from being close to her and the infant. For now, though, he kept his distance.

He felt somehow disconnected, not really a part of the intimate scene playing out before him. From the day of his son's birth he had known somehow that he could never share the bond he saw growing between his mate and their child.

He felt an emptiness inside . . . a longing for the peace and security he remembered from his own childhood. His mother had been gone a long time now, carried away in the night by some unseen predator. He still missed her. He remembered her scent. He remembered the warmth of her caress; the comfort and security he felt, bundled securely in her arms. Her passing had left a void within him; a sad emptiness which he longed to have filled.

For a time, that emptiness seemed to lessen, replaced as it was by the presence of his mate. Their shared intimacy helped to temporarily satisfy his longing. But the arrival of the infant had wrought a change. Now he was no longer the center of her attention. Now she spent most of her time caring for the infant. His advances sometimes went unnoticed. At others they were flatly rejected.

Instinctively he knew this was necessary and deliberately suppressed his feelings. But still, in the quiet moments, the emptiness within him welled up.

Now, watching the tender scene before him, he felt a warmth within him that seemed to more than compensate for his pain. The interaction between his mate and the child brought forth a feeling he had never before experienced.

The child was stirring. He was making strange sounds, quietly cooing and gesturing to his mother. The young male sensed that something had changed between the two.

He moved closer, noticing the change in the mood. Looking down, he saw two big round eyes looking up at him.

"M-m, m-muh-m, M-mah-m, M-mah-ma, M-ah-ma."

The two sat there staring in wonder at their son. What few vocalizations they were capable of producing came forth spontaneously. Quietly they whimpered and cooed, to their child and to each other. The young simian reached down and gently touched the infants cheek. Their eyes locked.

"Ah." The father grunted softly, gently.

"Mmmmm-ph," said the infant in reply, reaching out to grasp his father's huge finger in his small grip.

"Puh, puh . . . Pah!"

CHAPTER 31

Ardghal stepped slowly up to the podium, where he stood quietly for a few moments waiting for the crowd to settle.

In the rear of the auditorium he spotted Evander mingling with the standing-room-only stragglers. Their eyes met briefly before the old Procurator began to speak.

"All, my dear new friends! I'm so grateful you could come on such short notice." He looked down at Zuri, sitting in the center of the front row. He could see tears building in her eyes, making his heart swell. They had grown very close during the short time they had know each other. It was almost as if she viewed him as a grandfather. Her initial reservations about the 'seeding' program seemed to have dissipated now that the whole of her training was complete.

"She has such a beautiful smile," he thought; then he turned his attention to the audience.

"I'm so sorry there wasn't enough room for all of you. Our facilities here are limited, so we could do no better, given the circumstances. Our meteorologists forecast the storm planet-side would not clear for several more days. Since I know you're all anxious to get your first mission started, we decided to split the group, accommodating as many as we could here on our orbital station.

"For those of you still aboard the *Brighid*, please know my thoughts are with you also. Your sister ships, *Sauda*, *Sequum*, *Venure*, and *Interloq*, all are continuing their missions. As new worlds are discovered, each ship will receive 'seeding' missions. I am certain that everyone onboard those ships wishes you well.

"ALL of you, all five races. You are all exemplary. Each of you has demonstrated strength of character, determination and an eagerness to accept the challenge which has been set before you. I am proud and honored to call you my friends."

Ardghal paused, collecting his thoughts, once again making brief eye contact with Evander. A quick nod let him know that all was in readiness. Shifting slightly on his feet, he continued.

"Who to choose for this mission? Given that you all are worthy, in this regard the decision was not easy. But, since your Fleet Commander was chosen by you all, it is only fitting that she, as your representative, and her flagship the *Brighid*, should be first.

"As you all know, in the third sector of the Orion arm we have been monitoring a small solar system which contains within it a world ripe for 'seeding.' Probes assigned to the local LINK have re-confirmed this information.

"This will be our first mission in this sector, and your first as 'seeders.' May I once again offer my congratulations and appreciation for the outstanding work each of you has done in preparation for this, your first mission.

"Now, if I may, I'll turn the remaining time over to your Fleet Commander for the pre-mission briefing. Once again, my heartfelt thanks to all of you."

As Ardghal left the podium everyone in the room rose in applause. Once again Zuri was in awe of his ability to connect with people. She sensed that there was something more than just emotions involved in that connection. The inner warmth that she felt just being in his presence somehow reminded her of the feelings she felt when she was with her family. Yes, she had a strong connection with family; but that connection was much more than just emotional. She couldn't quite put that feeling into words.

Emotions seemed to come and go, to grow, and then recede. They were somehow transient, unpredictable. But with family, as it was with Ardghal, the connection was deeper, more fundamental. It was an integral part of who she was. The word 'spiritual' came to mind.

Once the Procurator had exited the room, Zuri approached the podium. It was unusual that Evander wouldn't be close by during such occasions. But she knew that, being the detail freak that he was, he was probably making sure all was in readiness for their departure. Putting that thought aside, she began her address to the audience.

"Men, women, children, all fellow crew members of the *Brighid*. For all these generations we have thought of ourselves as brothers and sisters, as kin. In a very real sense that is true. Though we have been raised in different families, still we are one in purpose, and though we seldom think of it, we are all citizens of our home world Kalephia. Though none of us has ever visited there, it truly is our home.

"And soon, owing to our great fortune of becoming 'linked' with Ardghal and Catriona and all the other wonderful people of Kalephia and the 'Seeders,' we will have an opportunity to visit our home world and once again forge a bond with others of our race.

"But first we have a rare and wonderful opportunity before us; to be intimately involved in the 'seeding' of a new world; extending our race into another part of this, our home galaxy."

Zuri paused for a long moment, considering what she should say.

"I'm totally lacking in the eloquence of our dear friend and Procurator, so perhaps it's best that I move on to the purpose of this gathering.

"As you know, the *Brighid* has now been refitted with all the upgrades necessary for us to successfully complete our mission. All but two of our shuttlecraft have been retired, and salvage of their components will begin once we arrive at our jump-off point in the Orion sector. In place of the retired shuttlecraft, Cygnus

5 has provided several of theirs, all of which are equipped with 'masking' software. Each has been fitted with low-orbit and sub-orbital monitors, together with a sufficient number of drones and transceivers for us to complete the initial phase of the 'seeding' operation.

"We will depart Cygnus 5 as soon as all personnel have returned to the *Brighid*. This completes the formal part of the briefing. But before I release you, let me just say how proud I am of each and every one of you for your hard work and diligence in completing your training in such an exemplary manner. Thank you again. You are dismissed."

Zuri stepped back from the podium and watched as her crew filed noisily out the exits at the back of the small auditorium and crossed the hall to the hangar deck.

As she walked toward the exit to the left of the podium, she noticed two figures slowly walking arm in arm, their backs toward her . . . Evander and the Procurator.

CHAPTER 32

The *Brighid* had arrived in the Orion sector just two days earlier via LINK transport. Now, only a few minutes from their destination, the ship was buzzing with activity as pre-launch preparations were being completed.

Zuri stood at the observation window, watching as the 'seeding crew' boarded the shuttlecraft. Just to her left, Evander spoke into his lapel mic:

"Okay, Ambia, let me know when you're in position. I visually confirm portal platform is retracting."

"Roger, sir. In position. Confirm portal secure light is green. Station keeping still in auto. All onboard systems show green."

Evander turned and winked at Zuri. She glanced up at him, then quickly back at the beautiful spherical shuttlecraft as it lowered its hover to just a foot above the hangar floor.

Everyone who had been involved in preparing for this mission was gathered, either at the few hangar bay observation windows, or around any available video screen which was broadcasting the launch.

Strangely, though everyone was excited, there was very little conversation. Weeks of planning and training had finally come down to this moment. Everyone was engrossed in their own private thoughts. They were about to participate in the birth of a totally new civilization.

"Ops, clear hangar deck; make ready for launch."

"Roger, commander. Hangar deck cleared for launch."

The green stripe down the center of the deck began blinking, then turned yellow as the hangar doors began to retract. Ceiling light reflected off the smooth spherical surface of the shuttle as it moved slowly toward the door. Once clear of the door, it began its descent toward the beautiful blue-green planet below.

CHAPTER 33

Childhood was a wonderful time for the young human. He was inquisitive, like any other youngster, always poking into one thing or another, investigating this, experimenting with that. His world was literally filled with new and exciting things to do and see. Every sound, every smell, every sensation filled him with awe. The jungle was the perfect playground for this first generation of homo-sapiens: Trees to climb, water to play in, endless things to investigate.

He was born with the capability of speech. But because he was essentially alone in this respect, he rarely used this ability. He simply had no need. Communication with his parents was no different than that of any other advanced primate. Apart from the names he had chosen for his parents, he had no need for language.

When he was very young, he remembered, his father sometimes left during the day and would be gone for a long time. He would always come back just before nightfall. Then he would sit on the edge of the nest for what seemed to him to be a very long time. Sometimes it would be so dark that he feared his father had left. But eventually the nest would quiver slightly and then his father's silhouette would come into view.

The young father had continued being vigilant. But since the birth of his son, he had experienced growing concern for their safety. Life in this environment was difficult under the best of circumstances. Before, there had been the family unit, the clan, a built-in support system. There were baby sitters, security. Here, there was only what he could provide. Ma-m-ma (he couldn't say it, but this was how he thought of her now) was so busy with the baby that it was all she could do to look out for herself and the child.

He had ventured further outward every day, scouting for any signs of danger, expanding the safety perimeter around his new family.

One afternoon just as he was preparing for the return trip, he heard a faint sound in the distance, opposite the direction of the sun, moving toward the horizon. This couldn't be ignored, he had to find out what had made the sound. It could be danger, or it could be food. It was never nothing.

Moving forward as quietly as he could, he stopped every few steps and listened. The sound was a little more distinct. The sound was familiar . . . but that didn't make sense. The clan (the 'others'), was another day away from here. They made those sounds, no one in the jungle made sounded just like them. It couldn't be them. It had to be. . . .

He glimpsed movement ahead. Frozen in position, he saw a face pointed straight in his direction. He hadn't been seen though. He inched forward slowly on all-fours, a stone clutched in each hand. The rustling grew louder.

Ever so slowly, he raised his head, peering carefully over the top of an old, rotten log. A termite scurried over his upper lip, then fell off the other side. He didn't notice. He was awed at the sight before him.

There in a small clearing just ahead were four individuals. They had obviously paired off, the couples sat on opposite sides of the clearing. One of the females held an infant in her arms. It looked almost identical to his son!

They all got up at the same time and started moving off into the growing shadows. It looked like they were settling in for the night. He waited until they were out of sight. Then he sat down with a thump, letting the stone fall from his grasp.

There were *others*! Others like *him*! He knew they were like him! He could see the difference! Their mannerisms were different, more deliberate, less random.

And there were *four* of them. Two mated pairs. And they were cooperating. At least it appeared that way. And one couple had a *child*. One that looked like *his son*.

What should he do now? He was almost frantic with excitement. Here was an opportunity he had never considered. Many of the struggles he and his mate were having were the result of them being alone, away from the clan in which they had been raised. A large family made it easier to find food. Also, there was security in numbers. Many pairs of eyes could watch larger areas, maintaining a 360-degree vigil, where just a few were limited in the area they could observe.

For the females, a large family would mean less work for the individual. Many young ones could be watched over by a single mother, at least for short periods of time, thus providing an opportunity for the other mothers to get a momentary break from the routine of raising their young. His mind raced with the possibilities.

His only experience had been in his original family group. The routines of daily living weren't much different there than what he had now. But foraging and security were quite another matter.

Was it possible that he and Ma-m-ma could join this group? He had no inkling of what problems might present themselves in such a group. All he really understood was that family life was easier than a solitary existence.

Carefully and quietly he backed away from the clearing, making sure no one saw his departure. When he felt he was far enough away that he wouldn't be seen or heard, he turned away and took up a loping gate, running on all fours. At this pace he continued non-stop all the way back to where he had left his family.

That evening was one of frenetic activity on his part, and uneasy confusion on her part. It quickly became evident to her that communication between them was becoming a major problem. Her mate kept scurrying around excitedly, grunting and yapping. Then he'd stop to face her. He'd begin pointing first to his eye, then pounding himself on the chest, then stand there unmoving, staring at her. After a few seconds pause he'd grunt, exhale loudly, and begin the routine again.

She had no idea what it was he was trying to convey. She had never seen him so agitated. Trying to calm him, she reached out and gently touched his arm. The lightness of the touch caused him to pause and look questioningly in her direction. She tugged gently, encouraging him to come sit beside her. As he sat down, she took the infant from her breast and placed it carefully into his arms.

The effect was immediate. The child lay there cooing to himself, gently twisting the thick fur on his father's arm. A contented expression flowed over his face. The adventure of the day seemed to fade as he gazed into his son's innocent eyes.

Feeling the tension ebb in her mate's body, the young female leaned back contentedly and began to slowly and gently groom the top of his head.

CHAPTER 34

The following morning he was up well before dawn, nervously pacing the perimeter of the nest, back and forth, back and forth. After the child was fed, they each ate a light breakfast of a few pieces of over-ripe fruit. He quickly gathered his stick and stone and anxiously prodded Ma-m-ma to get moving. The child clung tightly to his mother's fur as she stood and began moving in the direction she was being pushed.

It was a bumpy ride for the child. He dared not loosen his grip on his mother's fur. Though she held him tightly in her grasp, he still felt insecure. He was still afraid he would fall. It wasn't a long drop to the ground, but he risked being stepped on before his mother could come to a complete stop.

They didn't usually travel with such haste. Before today his father had frequently run ahead and disappeared into the undergrowth. These had been the times when his mother sat him gently on the ground and moved a few feet away, where she would stretch out on the ground for a few moments relaxation.

He enjoyed these times. They gave him a chance to explore the world around him. The ground under him always seemed to hold new secrets. And of course, everything he touched had to pass the taste test. Some things were hard and cold. Other things weren't so hard. Sometimes they broke when he squeezed them real hard between the teeth that were growing in. Sometimes he found things that moved. They wiggled in his mouth. Sometimes they'd bite. But he could stop them by biting back. Then they'd stop moving, and they'd taste different.

But today was another story. His mother and father were staying together, moving very fast. He hadn't had a chance to do anything but just hold on, watching the ground fly by below him.

By mid day they caught up with the new group. Pa was the first to see them. They had stopped at the edge of a small pond where a young toddler, who looked very much like his son was playfully splashing in the water. The mother was sitting within arms reach, grooming her mate. Another female, obviously very pregnant, was just emerging from a clump of bushes on the far side of the pond.

Ma-m-ma was startled when her mate stopped suddenly. He pulled her down beside him and looked intently into her eyes. She pulled the youngster close. He took the offered nipple eagerly and quietly settled.

Still holding eye contact with his mate, Pa slowly stood, pulling her up with him. Together they faced the two couples only a few paces away.

The youngster at the water's edge was the first to notice them. With a squeal, he scrambled up into his mother's arms. She and the others spun in the direction the young one was staring.

For a long moment no one moved. Pa tensed as the two males before him slowly began moving into defensive postures, stepping away from each other. The pregnant female stopped in her tracks, still several yards from the safety of her group, her eyes locked on the intruders. The female with the child edged her way closer to the males. The young one in her arms peered up over her shoulder as she retreated. Quietly at first, but then more loudly he spoke as he gestured toward the new couple.

"Ah-ah . . . buh-broc-uh, ah-ah."

The nipple dropped from his lips when he heard the voice. This was new, something he'd never heard before. He twisted in his mother's arms to see the others there by the water. No one was moving. All seemed to be frozen in place. All but one . . . the small squirming individual being held in its mother's arms.

"Ah! Ah! Ah-mahn!" He shouted as he leaped from Ma-m-mah's arms. She reached out frantically, but her fingers only grasped air. Her son was already out of reach.

She lunged forward. Before she could take a step, strong hands grasped her by the shoulders. She turned frantically, trying to escape. But when she saw the look on her mates face, her struggles ceased immediately.

His jaw was slack. His eyes were locked on the spectacle unfolding there before them.

"Ah-mahn! Ah-mahn!" his son kept calling as he closed the distance between the two groups. All the adults remained stationary, awed by what they were seeing.

The other youngster began frantically twisting, trying to escape from his mother's arms.

"Broc! Broc! Broc!" He yelled as he struggled.

The young simian's son was running full speed toward the other youngster. When he got close enough, he leaped upward, trying to reach the young male. But the mother instantly intervened, brushing the charging youngster aside.

For just an instant her grip loosened as she fended off the charge. In that instant Broc managed to escape her grip and went tumbling onto the ground. He gathered himself quickly and practically flew toward the other youngster, squealing with excitement. The two youngsters collided, tumbling and rolling together, all the time babbling and squeeling to each other.

"Ah-ah-Broc-Ah-mahn . . . Broc-ah-mahn-ah!" Back and forth the primitive conversation went. Each of the youngsters was shouting with joy. Neither had ever seen another like himself. They were, after all, the first-born of a race new to this world.

The adults, on the other hand, stood in mute silence, each group warily watching the other. The largest of the two males moved slightly forward. He stopped a pace out and sat down on his haunches. Pa saw that he had a substantial stick in his hand. Pa still had his stone, and was ready to use it if necessary. Slowly he moved into a throwing stance.

The larger male saw the movement. But instead of becoming defensive, he made a show of letting his stick fall to the ground beside him.

Unsure of what to do next, Pa stepped forward. He held the stone out for all to see. Then, deliberately, he turned his hand down, letting the stone fall to the ground.

"Ah" he said quietly, watching for any sign of movement or recognition from the others.

"Ah!" The big male responded as he came to his feet and moved forward slowly.

The two males approached each other cautiously, poised and ready. Pa, because he was smaller, stopped first and submitted to the other's scrutiny. The big male circled him twice, sniffing and snorting. When he was satisfied that there was no danger, he sat down in front of Pa, allowing himself to be scrutinized. Pa repeated what had just been done to him. Then,glancing back toward his mate, he once again sat down in front of the other.

Hesitantly the two groups moved toward each other. The youngsters continued playing at their feet. When the groups converged, they stopped playing. Each of the children patted the other on the head, then looked up at their parents as in turn they said: "Broc." "Amon."

SIMIAN 4.

CHAPTER 35

Over the course of several thousand years prior to the introduction of humans, climactic and geographic conditions in the east central region of Africa had been changing. The mountains along the western edge of the rift had, for centuries, been fighting a loosing battle against the invading desert sands to the west. Once a green and fertile skirt at the base of the mountains, now its environment was undergoing a radical change.

Inhabitants were being forced to leave as the desert continued its relentless invasion toward the East. Most of the wildlife began migrating north and south along the dwindling strip of vegetation. Humans and simians alike were forced to follow, or risk extinction.

Farther to the East, another smaller chain of mountains had risen up when the Somalian tectonic plate sub-ducted under the Nubian plate. Still further to the East just beyond this mountain range, a huge lake over 800 miles long and 400 miles wide covered the lands now known as Tanzania, Rwanda, Burundi, southern Uganda and much of western Kenya.

None of the lake's shoreline was yet inhabited. The 'cradle of civilization,' the so-called birthplace of mankind, lay just to the west, between two mountain ranges. The space between them formed a lush, subtropical stretch of land roughly 30 miles wide and 200 miles long. A few dozen hunter-gatherer communities (including most of the original male and female simians and their first-generation human offspring) lived within this narrow stretch of land.

* * *

You can teach a simian—
Even a human—
To do what you want them to do.
But what do they think
Beyond that which you teach?
Mayhap they are but teaching you too.

The old male simian (Ahmahn's father) lay quietly in the corner of the shelter, a pile of animal hides pulled close around him. He had just awakened to the urgings of his bladder for the second time of the night. Reluctant to yield to the growing pain in his groin, he snuggled down into the warmth of his nest for what he knew would only be a few more moments.

He felt rested, if not invigorated. He had only gotten up once last night. Better than the two or three which were becoming more usual. He sucked in a deep breath and held it. He stretched luxuriously, feeling the heat return to his muscles as his breathing relaxed. That moment of bliss was followed quickly by a sharp reminder from his bladder. His mind wandered as his body prepared itself for the dawn.

The mornings were harder to contend with these days. His frail old body no longer had the benefit of many layers of thick muscle to help it keep warm. The muscles were still there,of course. But now they were thin and flaccid, worn out from all the years of use. His legs were weak to the point that it was all he could do to keep up with the clan as they journeyed northward.

By the end of every day he was exhausted to the point that all he was interested in doing was sitting by the fire with a deerskin hide draped around his shoulders. Though by the end of every day his legs felt like they were on fire, in the evenings the warmth from the camp fire felt soothing, pleasant.

But this was morning. Stretching and remembering wasn't the same as rising and walking. Dealing with the pain in his joints had become a morning ritual. First the big stretch. Then work the left shoulder back into place. (The pop as the joint closed always felt good). Then the dull, continuous ache in the place where his right hand had once been.

The memory still haunted him. One moment he was bending down for a drink and the next he was soaking wet, his body covered in mud. He was trying to breathe, but his nose was clogged. When he opened his mouth, he inhaled water. Light was whirling around him. Blinding, then black, then blinding again. On and on it went until he felt that he would loose consciousness. Distantly, as though in a dream, he heard someone scream. It was the scream that brought him back to reality.

It was still dark. When he opened his eyes, he could see only faint outlines. One of those outlines shifted, then settled and remained still. It was his son. He knew that he was still asleep in that big bundle of skins next to the doorway. He and his mate had stayed awake long into the night and had not been asleep too long.

His son would awaken soon. He always did this time of the morning. He was always the first one up . . . or so he thought.

"Pa." his son had said, as he had so many times before. "You stay here tonight. Better here than alone."

"Pa," for that was his name. His son had told him so, so long ago. "You stay in my home. Watch over my mate while I am gone."

He understood most of the words his son used; but mostly he read his body language and the signs they had learned together . . . when "Ma-ma" was still with them.

She had been gone now for many years, but the memory of her and what they had shared always brought him up short. The grief he felt now, at this moment hurt as badly as the day she had gone.

She had looked up into his eyes and touched his lips with the tips of her fingers. He had just grasped her hand when he felt it go limp. Then her pupils dilated, and she was gone.

How many times had these thoughts entered his mind? How many times had he wished it had been him that day, instead of her? Then his conscience would begin haunting him as he considered the grief she would have had to bear if it had been him. No. It was better that she go first. He loved her too much to see her suffer.

Ah, but there was much comfort watching their son grow into manhood! A pity she could not be here to witness it. Ahmahn had become a leader among his people. Others looked to him whenever a decision needed to be made which might affect the community. He had proved himself to be conscientious as well as understanding and just. He had earned the trust and respect of his clan.

Pa felt the old stiffness coming back into his shoulder. He shifted slightly until the tension began to ease. "Be careful, my son. Do not let the respect you receive from others cloud your perception of yourself. I have seen first hand how power corrupts in the wrong hands. Careful that you do not become too proud of yourself."

Momentarily his train of thought took a different direction. . . .

"My son believes that it is he who watches over this family . . . that it is he who rises first in the morning. What he does not know is that he is not alone. I too am awake well before dawn, alert for anything out of place. I too have stayed awake long after my watch, making sure that nothing is amiss."

Again his brain seemed to freeze as he considered why he had even thought such a thing. He had to admit it . . . he was beginning to feel some things which he had never stopped to consider seriously before now. He knew that soon he must give up possession of the *darkness*. The fact he would pass it on to his son sometimes seemed to make little difference. As much as he had cherished his mate and his son, for some reason he had cherished the *darkness* at least as much.

"I stayed awake because there was something more!" He forced himself to try a more reasoned approach in order to make some sense of his feelings. "I remember the night like it was now. I remember the *darkness* taking shape before me. I remember how it moved among the trees, now and then dipping and hovering, remaining still, blending into the night, then slowly moving forward again. I can still hear the words that were spoken into my mind. I remember something else. But the memory of it is indistinct. Still, I remember the words. "I am here to help. Be not afraid."

"Before that moment I had never heard words spoken. I'm still not certain whether I actually heard those words, or whether they were spoken directly into my mind. Ultimately it is of no matter. All I know for certain is the feeling of comfort and serenity which caressed me upon their utterance.

Before that night, life was . . . different. Not bad. Just . . . vacant. After? . . . life was . . . *is* . . . full!

"I saw the *darkness* many times after the first. (I didn't know what else to call it at the time. The only time I could see it was when I was looking directly at it. Otherwise, unless it moved of its own accord, it was invisible.)

"One night not long after you arrived, my son, I saw the *darkness* closely for the first time. It hovered near our nest, like a whispering, black humming bird. Slowly it came straight toward me and stopped within arms reach. I was holding you in my arms, your mother snuggled close beside me.

"It was not quite as broad as my shoulders, in width and in height. I could not see its depth in the faint light. It hung motionless there before me. Gradually it began to change color around its edges, becoming a faint blue-green. The center remained dark. I remember thinking I should reach out and try to touch it but I was afraid to move.

"After just a short time the *darkness* in the center began to change to the same blue-green. The soft light it emitted cast eerie shadows in the foliage surrounding us.

"Very faintly I began hearing a high-pitched noise, almost like the hiss of a serpent. A shimmering mist began forming above the *darkness* where it hung motionless in mid-air. As quickly as it had begun, the hissing stopped.

"Within the mist a form began to take shape. Near the bottom, beginning in the center, the color began to change, spreading outward horizontally in a layer not much thicker than a leaf. The shape did not extend to the edge of the mist, but stopped short, showing a definite outline. Then, just above the first layer, another 'leaf' began to form. When it was complete, it lowered and lay flat on top of the first.

"The process continued, accelerating, one slightly different layer stacking upon another, until within only seconds a complete image was formed within the confines of the misty cloud. I recognized the upper torso and arms of a being similar to my self, though it seemed to be covered in a strange material. And the face!

"It was not a face like your mother's. Nor did it look like anything I had ever seen before! It was without hair, like you, my son. It had the mannerisms of a male. Its countenance was firm, resolute, but gentle. Its . . . *his*, eyes were kind.

"He said things, things like you say. I didn't understand, but yet I *did*. Many more times the face, *he*, came, as you were growing into adulthood.

"He taught me and Mah-ma his language, though we could not speak it ourselves. Nor could we hear it in the world around us. His voice was inside our heads. When I peered into the *darkness* I saw the face again. His lips moved, but made no sound. I could hear all around me as normal, but his voice remained there in the background instructing me, explaining things which, somehow he knew that I wanted to know.

"He taught me about my world, about my mate and about you. He taught me what it would be like to have a child like you. A child different from all the others I had ever seen. When you came, he told me to hide him (the *darkness*) away for a time. He said I would know when to come get him again.

"When you had grown old enough to toddle around on your own, the noises that you made began to change. They were no longer idle babbling. They were different from anything I had ever heard; but they sounded familiar, vaguely. I wondered, could this be the time the man in the *darkness* had spoken about?

"When I retrieved the *darkness* from its hiding place, the face appeared again. This time the man said that he would stay with us for a while. He said we would learn more, but that he would speak aloud so that you would learn how to speak and we all could learn to understand together.

"After a time, when you had learned to speak the language, the man in the *darkness* said it was time to hide him away again, this time for a long time. I must not show the *darkness* to you again until you had grown into manhood and were ready to accept responsibility for yourself. I was to keep it close to me, but hidden from view. He told me that he would be watching and that if he needed to talk to me, the *darkness* would call me, silently, in my head.

"As you grew through childhood, I was contacted by the *darkness* many times. Again, the man in the *darkness* knew what questions I had, and gave me answers as soon as the questions came into my head.

"For years we wandered the forest floor, following the seasons, staying hidden from the 'others' (my mother race). You grew into manhood so quickly, it seemed. One day you were wrestling and playing with your cousins. The next you were choosing a mate and taking leadership of the clan.

"Without guidance from the man in the *darkness* the days of your raising would have likely been much different. Neither I nor your mother had an experience base to help guide us. We knew about survival. We knew about mating. We knew about nurturing. All these things we knew before . . . before you came.

"And we knew about communicating, too. Just not on such an intimate, personal level. We were self-conscious 'before,' but nothing to the extent we are now. Our language is visible, but not heard. We talk with our hands, just as you talk with your mouth. Our words are as expressive as any.

"And because of the man in the *darkness*, your mother and I were able to understand and guide you, though we ourselves could not speak.

"My son, everyone who knows you, respects you. There are some who disagree with you, but they respect you nonetheless. It is your leadership, together with the cooperation of the majority who follow you, which has brought this new civilization this far.

"These 'humans' have risen above us with seeming ease. I understand this from a perspective unique from both the human and the simian view. Mine is the generation which knows the answer to how the simian and the human races are related. I am one of the few of my generation to possess this knowledge. None of the 'others' of my race knows how the humans came to be; and from this day forward no other, regardless of race, will recall the knowledge which the chosen few of my generation alone possess. How it is possible that this is so beyond my understanding? But I have no reason to doubt what I have been told.

"I have not the words to describe that which I know. My responsibility has been to accept the guidance offered by the *darkness* and to care for my mate and son to the best of my ability. I have been given the gift of understanding so that I may accomplish those responsibilities.

"I understand that there is more beyond me, that there is more beyond the *darkness* also. This I accept without reservation. To reject it would be meaningless, and would accomplish nothing.

"My love for my family is complete. My heart is filled that it is my son who has taken the lead for his race. To the extent that I have been able, I have tried to instill in him skills and values which

I understand and live by, but which I cannot verbally communicate to him. Nor would I desire to communicate this to anyone else.

"Nevertheless we persevere. Our communication with one another is simple, uncomplicated by a need to describe in detail everything which comes into our mind. In that sense we are unencumbered. And yet, on those occasions when it becomes necessary to be very specific about what we are seeking to convey, my inability to speak is a hindrance.

"I look back now on the time 'before.' I remember feeling quiet inside, secure in the knowledge and comfortable with the idea that all was well in the world, and that, come what may, it was all out of my control anyway. All I was capable of doing was reacting to my surroundings. Never, in those early times did I ever imagine that I would possess the capability to manipulate those surroundings to suit my own needs.

"It is this new ability, this 'speech,' as the man in the *darkness* calls it, which has enabled us to organize ourselves, to reach consensus on what must be done. I, by signs only. My son and his race, by both signs and speech."

The old simian crept quietly to the back of the shelter, trying not to awaken anyone. There, concealed behind a pile of provisions was another, smaller exit. Smaller to help conserve what little heat there was inside the cramped space.

The sacks filled with roots were the heaviest. They were right in his way. With a quiet harumph he edged his way around the pile until he found the bundles of dried fruit. Tied together they took up a lot of space, but they didn't weigh much.

He lifted the bundle slightly and edged it to the side. It rattled a bit, but no one was awakened. He pulled his cloak tight around his shoulders and bent down toward the small opening. He pushed the bundle over a bit more, just enough for him to slip through.

"This animal skin. This is a good thing. It helps me keep warm." he thought as he crawled through the small opening, out into the crisp morning air. "I don't like the mornings now the way I used to." Carefully standing erect, he readjusted the hide so it blocked the breeze from his face. His son had been right. Having it around him helped him stay warmer.

The skin he referred to was that of a small deer Ahmahn had found abandoned and lame. The poor animal had screamed and screamed, kicking ever harder, the broken front limb flailing helplessly. Ahmahn had crushed its head with a stone.

He remembered standing there, arms hanging limply at his sides, watching the small thing twitch in the throws of death. Maybe it was already dead. Maybe just the body was moving. Surely the animal's life went out when his son crushed its skill!

He remembered what his son had said as he prepared the animal's hide. "I helped this one to die. He will now help keep you warm. His pain is gone, but not forgotten."

"There is wisdom in his words." Pa thought to himself.

"I wonder, my son. Is now the time to reveal my secret to you? Have you matured enough to shoulder the responsibility for the family? Are you prepared to yield your will to the man in the *darkness* and learn from him? Or are you selfish like a child, full of yourself and unwilling to accept guidance from others?

"My son, not since you were very young, too young to walk, have you relied on me or anyone else for support. You have always done the best you could and kept peace with those around you. Yes, my son, first of your kind, and the only fruit of my loins, I think now perhaps you are ready. Maybe today will be the day."

The old simian shivered, his muscles tightening, pressing against his aching bladder. As quietly as he could, he worked his way through the low ground cover, an occasional small twig snapping under his shifting weight. The anticipation just made it worse. It felt like he would explode any second.

Now, with a little distance between himself and the shelter, and a small sapling to hide behind, he squatted and felt the relief well up within him.

"My son, what can I do to relieve the burden you must soon take upon yourself? I love you! I was there at the moment of your birth. I was there when you took your first step. I was there when you spoke your first word.

"I believe I know you better than anyone else, except perhaps, yourself. I have seen you grow in confidence and skill. I have seen you mature. Now, at your zenith, at a time when you should be revelling in the wonder that is life, you must take upon you the responsibility to care for your people. To look after them. To guide them. It is such a burden! The man in the *darkness* told me it would be so."

A long stream of vapor issued from his mouth as he exhaled. Relieved, but still shivering, the old simian rose and turned slowly back toward camp. He shuffled forward, sniffing the damp air. It was a new scent, something he had never smelled before they got to this place. It came from the 'leaves' of a tall, thin tree. It was a pleasant, clean smell. Not musty, like the jungles they had left behind so long ago.

"Ah, my son," he sighed to himself. "The days are short here. The nights are long and cold. Maybe it is best that you enjoy these short days as long as you can. There is yet time enough."

Quietly, he retraced his way back into the shelter, careful to close the portal behind him. He worked his way back around the bags of roots and back to his now-cold nest in the corner.

He knelt back down and worked his way back under the stack of hides. Carefully, quietly he pulled his legs back under the cover. A few small twigs cracked. The outline close to the door stirred again. His son was waking.

"I will wait. Let him be first. It is his place now. He has earned it. When it is time, I will tell him."

The old simian with the mind of a man closed his eyes once again and relaxed. He could wait a little longer. As he dozed off again, he saw his son's silhouette rise against the dawn.

CHAPTER 36

From "PROCESS OVERVIEW" Archives.
Human genetics had been well known and understood for eons, as had human psychology. It had become apparent early on that environment had as much to do with forming individual personality as did inherited genes. It was, therefore, imperative that environmental factors be incorporated, to the extent possible, into the lives of the "seedlings" so as to enhance the probability that the new race would thrive.

The first few years of life are critical in forming human personality. Because the brain is devoid of experience at birth, any information fed into it becomes, essentially hard wired. It becomes the fundamental reference point from which all experiences are compared. It becomes an essential component of the individual personality. What that 'hard wiring' (value system) becomes is largely determined by external, rather than internal influences.

Over the years, more and more information is accumulated, prioritized, and filed away. Still, the original information acquired during those early years (one might call it the moral/ethical compass) remains in force and guides and influences practically everything the individual does.

Efforts to reprogram or redirect an individual's "compass" shortly after the "seeding" process met with little success. If reprogramming was attempted after the formative years, (determined to be roughly four years of age and older) the resulting individual became confused, even amoral. Clarification of what was right and wrong was hard for such an individual to sort out. From his perspective, he had been given contradictory information. Having no other experience base to compare it to, the individual regressed to a more instinct-driven level, geared more toward self-gratification and self-preservation. He was as likely to do the wrong thing as he was to do the right, so long as he received no negative experiences in the process, and so long as there was a reward provided at the end of the experience.

Efforts at reprogramming a mature individual were only a bit more successful. This success was due to the fact that the individual had, over time, acquired an experience base sufficient to differentiate between actions and consequences. It was generally easier to persuade him to change his behavior once he understood the probable outcome. Nevertheless, the "hard wired" portion of his value system still remained essentially intact.

The formative years were also found to be critical times for bonding. Human infants are essentially helpless at birth. But they do possess all the instinctual data necessary for survival. What they lack is the physical capability to apply that data. Because they are helpless, they will bond with any individual who provides for their needs. And if, for one reason or another, that bond is broken, they will naturally tend to revert back to survival mode. To the extent that they are able, they will fend for themselves in order to survive.

CHAPTER 37

The fire was blazing, now. Almost waist high, and hot enough to draw steam out of his clothing. Ahmahn stepped back a pace, drawing his hands up in front of him, warming them, palms toward the fire. One by one, he began to see familiar faces coming back from where they had gone to relieve themselves.

He shoved his hands into the pockets of his deerskin cloak. He hesitated for just a moment, weighing the possibilities, then turned slowly and headed back out into the brush surrounding the encampment.

Pace after slow pace he moved into the haze, trying not to draw attention to himself. When he had gone a few more steps, he turned back toward the camp and leaned back against the trunk of a gnarly old pine.

How should he handle this? There had always been disputes within the clan. After all, it was made up of individuals, each with his/her own ideas and priorities.

But this situation was nothing like the others. Rumors had been floating that one of the "old ones" (the simian parents) had been seen consorting with the 'others', the non-seeded simians. Ahmahn had tried to make it clear that the clan of humans and their simian parents should no longer associate with the 'others'. He had explained that the risk of interbreeding must be avoided at all cost because their 'seeded' parents had been changed, and that if they were to breed with the 'others,' their offspring would not be like either race. The result would be an aberration, a race not compatible with either the simians or the humans.

Ahmahn believed that this had been understood at the time he said it. But now he wasn't certain that, though it had been understood, it might not have been agreed to by all concerned. It was possible that some had refrained from voicing objection simply to avoid an unpleasant confrontation.

Separation of the 'seeded' from the 'unseeded' simians made perfectly good sense to him, taken at face value. But he had no real understanding of how that separation might effect those who were directly involved. He was trying to be empathetic, but was having difficulty doing so.

Standing there in the early morning mist, he searched his memory for some experience which might help him understand.

When he was barely four years old, one of his new friend's mother and father were caught and killed by a rival clan of "unseeded" simians. His friend had escaped with a half-dozen other families who had banned together. The clan adopted the orphaned boy and cared for him as one of their own.

But the memory of the incident left a blemish on the young boy's personality. He wasn't mean or aggressive in any overt manner. But because he longed for the closeness and nurturing from his parents, his personality became more harsh, less affectionate.

Ahmahn hurt for him, as did everyone else. But there was something about this kind of pain that he couldn't quite grasp.

One day the boy was walking at the edge of a nearby stream when he slipped and hit his head hard on the rocks. Ahmahn saw it happen but was too far away to prevent it. He ran the few steps to where his friend had fallen, but saw immediately that it was to no avail. The boy's head had cracked like an egg. He was laying face down. Ahmahn couldn't see the startled look on his face.

The last Ahmahn chose to remember of him was the time they had sat close to each other next to the camp fire some time after his parents' death. They had been talking quietly, as young boys sometimes do. His friend had said the one thing he missed the most was not having his parents there to guide him at night when the clan was on the move.

"Its hard to take a step in the dark if you don't know where you're going." Those were the last words Ahmahn remembered him saying.

Ahmahn walked slowly back toward the camp. There was more activity now. He could here muffled noises all around him. The rest of the clan was waking. As he drew closer he could see his father and two men squatting near the fire. It had died down now, and several pieces of meat hung sizzling on sticks wedged between the rocks that surrounded the pit. The two men were arguing, not noticing his return. His father sat nearby, responding as necessary through gestures or grunts.

When he saw his son, he hesitated noticeably, watching the two men closely. Then, quickly but subtly he signed for Ahmahn to go back and wait for him. His son signed: "No. We will settle this now."

He knew immediately what the men had been talking about. The father of one of them, the one who had lost his mate to the bite of a viper, had been rumored to have paid visits to the camp of the "others." Disputes had arisen. The other man at the fire was the one who had made the accusation.

He knew that this confrontation, this moment, would set the course for, and forever mark a distinction between the races. From this point there could be no turning back if the human race was to survive intact.

To intermingle would only pollute both races, creating a race of un-natural beings, prone to their own desires with only minimal consideration for those of others. They would be of enhanced intellect, similar to other humans, but would remain forever attuned to the primitive, instinctual side of their lineages.

Ahmahn and his father had discussed this many times. He knew what his father thought to be the right thing to do. His father knew, probably more than did Ahmahn himself, that a fundamental difference existed between the races. But to gain a clear perspective of what that difference was, one had to have been part of both worlds.

CHAPTER 38

.

"Good morning, my friends." said Ahmahn as he walked up behind the two men. Startled, both of them stopped talking immediately. An uneasy silence fell over them. Neither would look at the other. It was easy to see the tension between the two. He took a seat on a nearby log, and continued:

"This will be a good day. Not too much wind." he said, trying to ease some of the tension he felt between the two men.

"Not to much wind." Sef repeated, staring intently into the fire. Ahmahn could see the tension in his friends shoulders, the muscles in his cheek flexing, the furrowed brow.

"This man speaks ill of my father!" Sef jumped to his feet, pointing an accusing finger at the other, who also rose in defense. "Nahm accuses him of taking 'another' for his mate!"

"Is what he says true, Nahm?" Amon turned to face the accuser. It would not be necessary for him to broach the subject himself. For this he felt a measure of gratitude and relief.

"It is so! I saw them together!" Nahm lied. He was obviously frightened, but he stood by what he said, even in the face of threats being hurled at him by the defendant's son.

"My friends, let us be calm." Ahmahn leaned forward toward the fire, pitching a few small branches onto the now dwindling flame. Deliberately he avoided eye contact, letting the weight of the accusation sink in for both men. He stirred the coals lightly, waiting for the two men to calm.

Ahmahn reasoned that the accusation must be false because the only simian females that could possibly have been in contact with Sef's father were already mated with other 'seeded' males within their clan.

It was the nature of seeded couples to remain loyal to one another. Evander had explained that that trait had been incorporated into the 'change' each simian had undergone. Nahm had probably interpreted the actions of Sef's father incorrectly. The old simian was undoubtedly distraught because of the loss of his mate, and had only ventured close to those of his species for some small measure of comfort. Beyond that, their clan had separated themselves from their old 'unseeded' clans years ago.

"This is a serious matter" he said, moving back to his seat on the log. With only a little hesitation, the two men sat back down, this time on opposite sides of the fire. Each glared back at the other across the crackling flames.

"Ahmahn." Nahm was the first to start again. "You have been the one to lead us for all this time. What you have done and said has been good for us. We follow you because of this." He gathered courage as he continued. He was beginning to doubt his assumptions about Sef's father, but wasn't willing to admit it.

"This man's father has no mate. She died by the serpent. Now he has no one." He gestured toward Sef. "I see his grief in his face, and I grieve for him also. But this cannot excuse what his father has done!"

"I remember." Ahmahn sighed, remembering the serpent lash out, sink its fangs into the female simian's surprised face, then thrash about as Nahm seized it and broke its neck.

"That was a bad day. not like today." Ahmahn turned to the other man, searching his eyes for a solution. Sef, the embittered son, held his gaze for a few moments, then looked down toward the fire as he spoke.

"My father is still grieved and angry because of his loss. He spends all his time alone when we are not travelling. He does not feel comfortable being here, close to all of us."

"It is sometimes hard to be with other people when they are happy and you are not." Ahmahn spoke quietly as he leaned forward to check the cooking meat. "I think these are ready now." He retrieved two sticks of the sizzling meat and handed one to each man. He took a third for himself and handed the last one to his father.

Pa caught his son's eye pleadingly, wanting to know why he had not returned to the edge of the camp. Pa knew something that neither of the two men knew. It was important that Ahmahn be apprised of the whole situation before he made any decision regarding the issue at hand.

Ahmahn saw the concern in his father's face. He knew that this would not be easy for anyone involved. He had tried to imagine the worst possible scenario, and had tried to prepare himself emotionally. In so doing, he was able to detach himself from the experience and take a more objective look at the other players.

With a gentle, but firm expression, he let his father know that he was prepared. Settling back comfortably, he pulled a small, steaming slice off the end of the stick. He sniffed it, touched it with the end of his tongue to see if it was cool enough, then popped it into his mouth. The others did the same. The silence was not quite so noticeable now. Tensions seemed to dissipate as they sat quiety together, eating.

Beyond the small circle where the men sat, others began moving quietly about. Soon the meadow would be filled with sounds of activities of the morning. But for now there was a stifled hush over everything. People deliberately avoided going near the fire pit. Word of what had been happening had gotten around quickly. Everyone knew that a confrontation was inevitable. Everyone watched and listened, while pretending not to notice the four figures sitting there, together, eating.

Nahm, the accuser, sat motionless, staring into the fire, watching the coals change from orange to gray and back again as wisps of air caressed them. He chewed on the tough meat slowly, resolutely. He knew that what he said he had witnessed had been a lie. He knew that the so-called incident had been whispered among others of the clan. He had overheard the rumors so many times that he was now beginning to believe them. He knew what he had done was wrong, but he lacked the courage to admit it. His thoughts wandered back to the days on the open plain, before these troubling times. He longed to be back there now, before all this coldness, before all these problems.

He didn't want to create more problems for the clan. They already had a hard enough time just surviving. No one wanted more problems than they already had.

He knew this man Sef well. They had walked side by side for days upon days. They had killed game together. They had starved together. And now he must confront the reality of the situation he had created. Now this terrible wrong must be resolved, no matter how hard it would be for him to do so. He simply didn't know what to do.

The emotion he felt was genuine. It was new. It was human. How could he possibly comprehend what his friend Sef's father was going through? All he really knew was that the old simian continuously dragged behind, slowing everyone's progress. And when they did stop, the old simian would wander around the camp, edging ever closer to those of his species.

The stress of the trek was taking its toll on everyone, simian as well as human. Nahm was at a loss as to how to cope with such an ordeal. All he really understood was that the situation must be resolved. Pride and embarrassment were new emotions to him. His simian parents had never prepared him for such situations. Such emotions had never been a part of their primitive culture.

He had never suffered such a loss, as had his friend Sef. His thoughts returned now to that terrible day . . . the day Sef's mother was killed.

They had been making good progress that morning. They had finally made it out of the densest part of the undergrowth and had stopped next to a small rivulet of water. Its source bubbled up from a small spring near the top of a nearby shallow embankment. The top of the embankment was awash in grass as high as a man's waist. A section of the embankment had been washed away, revealing the stone layered beneath.

The narrow ribbon of water slithered its way between the flat stones, spilling down, pooling, then spilling over, to continue winding downward. It gurgled and splashed, flowing off the edges of flat stones protruding from the embankment. Underneath the stones a moist, cool shade offered protection for other tiny lifeforms as they skittered about their busy lives.

Above, on the warm, sun-drenched side, a tawny brown and gray-speckled serpent coiled languidly, feeling the heat rise up through its belly. It dozed serenely in the bright, soothing warmth.

The old simian woman was glad to have the chance for a rest. They had been going for well over an hour now, and she was nearly exhausted! Her mate was helping, but she just wasn't feeling up to it today. There was an outcrop of rocks up there ahead. She could see it! There was shade! And water too!

The others were all stopping there in that low spot. They were all bending down to drink, but her poor old back just wouldn't let her! Easier to just sip it off the edge of those rocks over there.

Nahm saw her move away and had just turned to follow, when he saw the coiled reptile spring! In that instant it seemed that everything froze. Everything except the serpent's tail as it whipped up into the air.

"It was my mother who died that day!" Sef pounded his chest in anguish. "I know the pain! I know what it is to watch your mother die before your eyes, blood dripping from her swollen eyes! I know what it is to wipe the foam from her lips as she gasps her last breath!"

He collapsed into sobs before them, wrenching the remaining meat from the stick and tossing it aside.

Nahm remained, transfixed, overcome by the emotion of the moment, unable to respond. His hands clenched and unclenched as his mind searched frantically for a way out of this situation.

Ahmahn placed a hand on the sobbing man's shoulder, then looked toward the accuser. Their eyes connected, but no words came. Nahm's eyes searched the ground, unable to look at his leader, fearful that his leader had discerned the truth. After several uneasy moments Ahmahn continued.

"Why is it that we must suffer so?" Ahmahn looked back to the man there before him. "What can be done to satisfy this loss? How can we continue?" He drew Sef close to him, weeping as he spoke.

"My brothers, there is deception between us." said Ahmahn. Breath caught in Nahm's throat. Had his lie been found out?

Sef gathered himself, took a deep breath, then slowly looked up into Ahmahn's eyes. He stood slowly, breaking eye contact several times before settling his gaze on a spot on the ground between them.

"Yes. It is true." Sef began. "There is deception between us." He turned toward Nahm.

"I know what you said is not true. And though it disappoints me, still I will not condemn you. You are stricken by the rumors, as am I. But they are not true. My father has not left my sight. I see his sadness, and I share it. You too are distraught by what you hear, and wish to end this discomfort. In so doing, you have been seduced by the lie."

Nahm sat quietly, absorbing what was being said. The kindness he felt coming from his friend softened his heart. His eyes still downcast, he responded.

"Sef, my brother. I have wronged you. I have wronged your father also. I have allowed myself to be distracted, to become compromised by my vanity. I knew that I was wrong when I made the accusation, and I chose to lie, even to myself."

Slowly the two men rose and stepped close to each other.

Nahm extended a hand, eyes still downcast.

"My brother, I will not do this ever again. I beg your forgiveness." He looked up into the eyes of his friend.

For a long moment there was silence. Ahmahn remained seated, watching as his two friends reconciled. His heart filled with love for them as they clasped hands.

"I understand . . . and I forgive. We are brothers. That will never change." Sef placed and hand on Nahm's shoulder and gestured that they sit together.

His gaze found its way across the flames into Ahmahn's eyes. They were kind eyes. Not angry or afraid. He continued.

"There is yet another thing which I must speak of. My father has chosen to go back to his old family."

The confession was real, though it had taken a turn neither Nahm, nor Ahmahn had expected. The issue had been centered on the belief that the father had 'been with' a member of the old family. Now the situation had changed completely.

The attachment Sef described about his father was something more than just physical. There remained an emotional attachment to the old family. One that had always been there for most everyone, even after the 'seeding.' But it had been overshadowed, put in the background by the new emotional attachments the 'seeded' simians had developed between themselves and their offspring, and eventually with the other families.

"When my father's mate, my mother, died, there was an emptiness left within both of us. It was a frightening place where my father feared to go. It was filled instead with uncertainty, and doubt. Everyone around him lavished themselves upon him, trying to help fill the void. But they didn't understand."

Sef paused for a moment, trying to subdue the pain he was feeling.

"In the old family my father felt safe. There was routine, predictability. He could hide out as long as he wanted and no one would know that he had changed, that he was 'different.' Maybe he could have even been the leader, if he was smart enough."

"Is this your father's desire, or is this yours?" Ahmahn asked as he gazed into his friend's eyes. From the corner of his eye he saw his father shift position.

Pa inhaled involuntarily. This was the 'secret' he thought only he knew about! How did his son know? Had he seen something too?

"I know of your love for your father. I know of your desire to watch over him in his infirmity. He will surely need you as the days slip away before him."

"Then you do not mind that I go with my father?" Sef said in relief.

"How could I or any other refuse? You are now a grown man and can fend for yourself. But your father needs you. Go with him and live your lives well."

"Thank you, my friend." Sef wiped the tears from his eyes as he spoke. "I know of the risks I will face living in solitude. It will not be so difficult. I have no mate to encumber me." Sef looked longingly into the distance. Ahmahn knew that this too was a source of painful discomfort for his friend.

Sef collected himself, returning his attention to the issue at hand.

"I will remain hidden from the 'others' so that my father may gain comfort in their association, without concern for me being discovered. He will come to visit me as he is able. We have spoken of this many times and know what must be done. he has vowed restraint in the matter of mating. He will not seek leadership within his family."

Ahmahn walked over and held the man close, gesturing for Nahm to join them. Nahm stepped forward reluctantly, unwilling to make eye contact with either of his friends.

Ahmahn spoke gently: "We have shared much, you and I and all the others. The loss of your mother was a loss for us all. You will be missed, but not forgotten. Go now, my brother. Go in peace."

Sef smiled meekly, avoiding eye contact. Then with a quick last embrace, he turned and moved away to join his father. The two of them walked slowly away, then slipped back into their shelter and emerged again a few moments later, their few possessions slung across their backs. It was obvious that they had been planning and preparing for this moment.

Looking briefly back toward the encampment, Sef placed a hand on his father's shoulder. Turning as one, they moved off into the morning mist.

The farewell had been brief. The rest of the clan took this as a cue, and began breaking camp as well. Ahmahn stood there watching the two figures disappear into the mist. "What will become of them?" he wondered. After a few more moments, he returned to his shelter, and began helping his mate take the soggy old roof apart.

A while later, Broc walked back in from his patrol of the perimeter.

"So, my brother. You provided an honorable way for them to depart. Never did you confront or challenge them."

"Never was it my place to judge the content of another man's heart." Ahmahn took a slow, deep breath and continued.

"How a man walks among us. That is the thing I watch. But can I judge a man if I have not walked in his shoes? Only he can judge himself. I can certainly be aware. Even wary. But he is still my brother and is deserving of my trust, until he himself betrays it."

CHAPTER 39

Pa crouched nearby gathering a few dry sticks and tying them into small bundles. He had listened carefully, if secretly, to all his son had said from the morning until now. His heart swelled with pride that his son had handled the confrontation so well. There were very serious differences being spread about. There were even accusations. But Ahmahn had found a way to find reconciliation while maintaining love and respect for the people involved.

"My son! What wisdom you display," Pa thought to himself. "Anxiety was so high within the group, but you found a way to redirect it; to turn it from a gnawing in the gut into a burning in the heart. All with a few gestures and some understanding words.

"From the time of your birth I have watched you. I have held you in my arms when you cried in the night. I have healed your bruised and naked skin of countless injuries you inflicted upon yourself in your childhood.

"I have seen you grow to manhood, a member of a race that is almost incomprehensible to me. Were it not for the '*darkness*,' I'm not sure what would have come of us. Even now, though I believe I understand you, still there are times when the things you do are completely beyond my comprehension.

"So often I have wondered, when will be the time? How will I know when the time is right? What will be the sign?

"I remember what the man in the '*darkness*' said. 'You will know.

You will know.' Back then when I asked, I didn't understand the answer. But now? Now it is different. Now I know as well as I know myself, that my son is ready. Everything that I have learned from the '*darkness*,' my son has now learned on his own. It is time that he learn more."

Pa wrapped the bundles in an old hide and tied it onto the end of a stout stick, the way he had learned from his son. Hoisting it on his shoulder, he began making his way slowly around the camp, collecting unused kindling and covering it to keep it dry. Ahmahn and the others were busy at other tasks, so they didn't notice the old simian as he slipped out of sight behind some dead fall.

There, well hidden under a tangle of broken branches, were two stones, one propped up at an angle by the other. It looked as though some small animal had used the space between the rocks as a nest.

Pa pushed aside as much undergrowth as he could and then got down on his belly, inching his way forward until he reached the stones. He pushed the angular one aside and rolled the other one over.

There, in a small cavity, sat the '*darkness*.' No dust or debris of any kind had accumulated on or near it. It looked exactly the same as it did a few weeks back when he hid it there the day the clan made camp here.

By now the old simian was used to seeing this. It had been the same, move after move; year after year. For some reason unknown to him, nothing would stick to the thing. It always looked the same, whether in daylight or in darkness. It was hard to see, unless you knew what to look for. In the place where it looked like there was nothing, that was where it was. The man in the '*darkness*' (Evander was what he called himself) said it was called 'phase shifting.' Pa preferred to call it '*darkness*.'

An instant before Pa touched it, the transceiver activated. It took on a faint blue glow, making it much easier to see. He picked it up carefully and began inching his way back out of the brush. When he was clear, he placed the transceiver on the ground, and looked quickly about, insuring he was still invisible to the rest of the camp.

Then, convinced that he had not been seen, he turned his attention back to the "*darkness.*" The red glow was gone. In its place a gray, roughly rectangular object sat. Above it a half-size three-dimensional image appeared. It showed the upper torso of a man.

"Hello, my old friend. It's been a long time since we've seen each other. How have you been?" Evander signed.

"All is well. And with you, my teacher?"

"Much have I learned from being your mentor."

"That is as it should be." Pa signed the ritual, as he had done countless times before.

"It has ever been so." Was Evander's reply.

The old simian's memory flashed back. Back to the beginning. Back to that steamy, oppressive night when he awoke in a near panic. His memory flashed to the dark object that hovered above him. Next came the pleasant, tickling sensation down the back of his neck. And then the morning. His life had never been the same from that moment on.

"My teacher, the time has come." Pa felt a welling in his heart as he signed the words he had wanted to do for so long.

"Ah! And so it has, my dear friend."

The image looked the same now as it ever had. The man's hair hadn't changed, in length or color. There were no new wrinkles around the eyes. The nose. The mouth. All was the same. Even after all these years. Pa felt old, seeing how he had aged, but that Evander had not.

"My teacher, my son is truly a man of wisdom. He has learned all that I can teach him, and still he yearns to learn more. Daily he surpasses me in all that he does. I cannot but hold him back if I withhold you from him any longer."s

"That truly is as it should be. There comes a time in all men's lives when they must pass the torch, so that others may not stumble in the darkness." The use of the word 'men' did not go un-noticed.

"Alas, my teacher! What am I, if not a man?" The old simian sat wilted on the ground, head held low.

"You are my father." a voice behind him said. "You are as much a man as I ever hope to be."

Without flinching, his father responded. "Somehow I knew you would be there." He turned slowly, a smile on his face. "It used to be strange, when you'd sneak up on me like that. But now, after so many years I've just come to expect it." A smile filled his eyes as his hands brought forth his words.

"And so, my father. Will you finally tell me what this thing is that you've been dragging around for all these years?" Ahmahn came around and sat down beside his father, a wide grin on his face. From where they sat, the hologram appeared at eye level.

"I remember you." Ahmahn pointed to the image before him.

"It was when I was a child." He looked more closely.

"I remember your eyes . . . but they were younger then. Your face hasn't changed."

Pa sat in amazement. He had expected something else from his son. Something. Anything! Some sort of reaction other than what his son was displaying. He was acting as though this sort of thing happened every day. Talking to this . . . this apparition!

"Don't be surprised, my father. Many are the times I've watched you sneak away into the darkness. Sometimes I've even followed you, fearing for your safety, but also wanting to learn what it was you were doing."

Ahmahn paused, then gestured toward the holo-image.

"Many times I watched as you spoke to each other silently. I saw your gestures. I watched your hands. I learned." He moved back toward his father. Taking him by the hand, he said:

"Many times I wanted to surprise you. To let you know that you had been discovered. But the more I watched, the more I thought

No. Better to let him tell me in his own time. Then we will *both* be ready!" Still holding his father's gaze, he continued:

"And now, Evander, if that is your name. I know you are real because you can respond to me. But are you here?" Ahmahn had come up with so many questions over the years. It was now time to get some of them answered.

"Yes, I'm here, or at least my voice is, and my ability to see and hear you, also. But the image you see before you is not the real me. This image came from that small box below me there on the ground. It is a device I use to speak with you.

"I'm in a place very far from where you are now. I will teach you more about this at another time if you so desire. But for now my desire is to answer any questions you may have."

"The first question I have is for my father." Looking deep into his father's eyes, he continued: "I think I know why . . . no. I *know* why you waited. There is no question now. You wanted to do all that you could do first. Then, when you knew there was nothing left for you to give, you admitted to yourself that it was time. Time for your son to know of the '*darkness*,' and the truth it holds within."

Evander added quietly as father and son commiserated: "This is the time when each of you share all that is known between you. This is the time when a 'link' is formed. It is a bond which can never be broken. Nor can it be seen, even by those here to witness it. And yet it prevails."

"It has ever been so." Ahmahn turned to face the image squarely. "There is much that I must learn . . ."

"And much that I must teach you . . ."

"But now can not be the time. Our camp is in disarray. After we have moved. When things have settled. Then will be the time when we speak again."

"Spoken well, young Ahmahn. Soon we will speak again." The image dissolved.

Pa reached for the gray box and stuffed it into one of the bundles he was carrying. He shoved a few more small branches and twigs around it to better disguise its shape, and then slung it back over his shoulder, the way it had been before.

He looked up to make sure his son was watching, and then signed: "Let's us go then. There will be time enough for this later."

With that, the old simian trundled off in the direction of camp, leaving his son standing alone.

CHAPTER 40

Only a few faint embers clung to life among the charred remnants of the cook fire. The wind had picked up a bit, now that there were fewer obstacles to inhibit its movement. It swirled around inside the shallow ring of stones, kicking up miniature whirlwinds of cooling ash.

The camp had been struck. The wet branches which had been the top layer of roofs were now strewn about the ground, leaving the skeletal remains of the shelters open to the elements. Most had been trampled flat, beaten down as many feet scrambled about in last-minute preparations for leaving.

It was mid afternoon before the move began. Broc had been back from his scouting for over an hour and was not quite ready to leave. Everyone else was ready to go. A few helped him and Sara roll up the long poles he had salvaged from his old shelter.

The place they were moving to was only a mile or so up-stream from their present camp. But this place was getting pretty well trampled down.

"And besides," Broc had reasoned, "it is best to leave this difficult memory behind. Maybe we will visit it again, but for now it is best that we move on." He looked toward the shelter that the departed pair had used. No one had stripped it. Even the deer hide door was still hanging where it had been thrown back earlier that morning.

"Once again your wisdom prevails." Ahmahn said as he walked

up to his friend. "The change will do us good. While we are wor-king, we will have less time to think." Though their friends were now gone, still there were things to be talked about; differences to be resolved.

Broc busied himself tying off the last bundle of poles. "Yes. Less time to think." He paused, worrying whether to bring the subject up again so soon.

"Speak, my brother. What troubles you?" These two had been together since childhood. Ahmahn knew when something was troubling his friend. Broc hesitated for a moment longer and then began:

"You know, my brother, of the thing you spoke." Broc gestured toward the abandoned shelter, reluctant to say the names of the two friends who had departed.

"I know he is old and lonely since the passing of his mate. I know that he still mourns his loss. But it is wrong for him to go back to the 'others.' They are not like him! He has changed, just as your father and my father have changed. They are no longer like them. This thing cannot be!"

"Be calm, be calm for a moment, my friend." Ahmahn said gently.

"Let us consider this. We both love them. It pains us to see them go. But it pains us more to know that they have made this decision which we do not agree with. But what are we to do? Can we force them to live as we say and still expect them to be supportive of us? If we treat them as less than us, will we even be worthy of their support?"

Broc picked up the last of his belongings and turned to his left, northward, in the direction of the narrowing river. His young mate Sara fell into step beside him.

"How far is this new camp? You say it is only a day's walk, but the day is now almost spent! What shall we do when the night returns and we have not yet found shelter?"

Ahmahn smiled resolutely. "We will do as we have ever done.

We will use what is provided. I have travelled this route two times before. We will find shelter before darkness. I have been there. I have seen it."

Broc picked up his pace, just enough to remain a half pace ahead. After first glancing at Ahmahn, he turned to his mate. "Sara. Can you find more berries? The small yellow ones? There may be a few left up ahead if the birds haven't gotten to them."

She smiled up at him.

"Would you like time to speak with your brother alone?"

Broc was brought up short by her abruptness, but when she bumped into him she smiled once again, and then scampered off into the bushes ahead. She giggled a bit, and sang quietly to herself, glancing back once or twice to make sure she could still see them.

"My brother," Broc again regained the pace. "There is something else I would speak to you about." Sara's affectionate departure had softened his demeanor a bit. A trace of a grin crossed his face as he began.

"It is good to have such a woman as this one to be my mate. She seems to know what I will say before I say it." Then self-consciously he cleared his throat. "It is good that I can share this with you. But also there is something else I would share."

Ahmahn could sense there was more than he had anticipated. Not knowing what to say in response, he said nothing. Broc continued:

"My brother, I have seen the two of you; you and your father, speaking quietly, there on the fringes. I have seen the thing your father carries." He pointed toward the old simian a few paces behind. Pa saw the gesture and stopped in his tracks, as did Ahmahn.

The rest of the clan continued working their way slowly northward, gleaning what was left of anything ripe and edible.

Sara looked back once again and saw that the three had stopped.

She too stopped and stood watching. The others would continue, she knew. They would continue in the direction Broc had said, and within an hour the first of them would reach the bend in the creek where a timber fall had piled up against a big rock. Those were the directions Broc had said, so she was sure she could find her way alone. Nevertheless, she would wait here for him. She would watch over him until he began coming forward again. Then she would scout ahead, and be there waiting when he arrived.

Maybe she could persuade him to build their new shelter smaller this time, so he couldn't get away from her so easily in the night. Her mind wandered as she relaxed against a stone outcropping watching the three as they drew closer together there at the edge of her sight.

Ahmahn became wary, but before either he or his father could respond, Broc continued:

"I have heard others speak of seeing such things." A dead silence fell over the three. Ahmahn knew not what to say except the truth.

"I have only just now been entrusted with its care. I know almost nothing about it, or why it was in my father's possession. I would do my father injustice if I betrayed his trust. My brother, allow me time to converse with my father about this thing. We will speak of it tonight as we set camp. Then, on the sunrise I will speak with you again."

"I am sorry, my brother. Of course I will respect your wishes."

Broc was anxious to reveal his own secret to. But he was uncertain how his brother would react. Perhaps he would be angry that Broc's knowledge of 'the *darkness*' had been hidden from him.

Looking excitedly back in the direction the clan had gone, he continued: "Come! Let us hurry! There is much to be done before the night falls!" Turning back to Ahmahn, "I will go ahead and see to the camp. I will prepare a nest for your father next to the one your mate selects for you." With that, he was off at a stiff pace.

Sara saw him coming in her direction and immediately ran back in his direction. When he saw her coming, he realized he had neglected to mention one important thing to Ahmahn. He turned and hollered back: "We will speak of this to no one." Ahmahn acknowledged him with a wave. Within just a few seconds Sara was in his arms.

"Come, my Broc! Let us hurry. We must build our nest quickly today. I feel a chill in the air." She snuggled close to him and fell into step, stretching to keep pace. "Perhaps we can build this one smaller . . . so the cold wind will have no place between us."

Broc looked down into her smiling face. There was a sparkle in her eyes. Perhaps it would be good for him to do as she asked this time. The possibilities made him smile also.

"Yes. It will be dark soon. We won't have time to build a proper one. We should hurry."

Pa laid a hand on his son's shoulder to get his attention.

"This is a grave matter, my son. I did not know that we had been seen."

"It is of little consequence. Broc is as a brother to me."

"And a son to me," Pa signed.

"I have trusted him with many things, including my life, many times. He will surely be part of all that transpires within our family."

The old simian nodded in agreement, and started off in Broc's direction, shifting his burden as he did so. Ahmahn noticed and offered to take the load from him.

"No! This has been my burden since before your birth. I will continue to carry it until it is dully passed on to you. Besides, this burden is light. I don't mind carrying it at all."

INTERLUDE

Broc had been a part of the clan for almost fifteen years. He, his parents, and one other seeded couple had joined with Ahmahn's family when they were both just toddlers. Within a few weeks of their meeting, another baby arrived, another male, who was eventually named Nahm. A few months later two more couples joined them. Each couple had female infants.

By the time Broc was a year old, he, Ahmahn, Nahm and the females had begun developing the first spoken language. Between the mute parents and the vocal children a unique, unspoken language also developed. With the exception of guttural grunts and a few other primitive noises, inter-species communication was completely silent. Body movements took on more meaning. Postures in varying forms took on specific meanings in a specific circumstances. Those same postures, in different circumstances would convey a different meaning.

When Broc was not quite three, his family happened upon another clan. The family had remained in one encampment now for almost a week. The provisions were plentiful, if you could get to them.

What remained of the season's crop of fruit swayed temptingly, high up in the uppermost branches. Only the smallest of primates could climb anywhere close to them. The rest was fair game for the birds and insects.

Broc's simian father had been watching the lush fruit swaying to and fro, so high up there. He had been thinking about a way to get to it. He knew he couldn't climb that high. He was just too big. But maybe he could throw something that high.

He found an old dead limb lying near by. He picked it up and hefted it, feeling its balance. It didn't feel quite right. It was too heavy, and too cumbersome. He discarded it in favor of another, smaller one. This one felt better, but not quite right. Maybe just a little, broken off here. Now. Try that. Hmm. He balanced it gingerly in his hand. It had weight, but not too much. He took it by the end and did a few practice swings. Good. He'd keep this one.

He tossed it a short distance to see how it flew. As it toppled end over end through the air, one of the tiny branches still attached to it got caught in some low hanging vines several yards above the ground. There it hung, swaying to and fro.

Momentarily perplexed, he stood there, trying to think of what he should do next. He remembered the limb he had tried and discarded. It was heavy and hard to balance, so he broke off as many small branches as he could, each one separating with a resounding snap. He was unconcerned with the noise he was making. All he was interested in was retrieving his missile. Besides, the river running near by made more than enough noise to mask his sounds. He turned to his work with confidence. He didn't notice he was being watched.

The dark form was there, crouched behind the stump of a huge old dead fall. It had fallen across the river long ago and was covered in moss and vines. Most of its branches had broken when it fell, but a few remained, their dry, leafless fingers splayed toward the heavens. When the tree fell it had left a hole where the roots had been ripped out of the ground. Now, after so many years, the hole was now little more than a shallow depression a few yards across. Long strands of musty, dry moss hung from what few roots remained. There in that depression the observer lay, belly and chin to the ground.

He was a scout. It was his job to stay well out in front of his clan, searching for food and water, and watching out for danger. Several hours ago he had come upon the tree. He had been following the river, staying well back into the ground foliage, using it for cover. He saw the long, scraggly branches pointing into the sky not far ahead.

There were several birds flitting about from branch to branch, making a racket. He paused for a moment, watching their antics.

After a few minutes he decided to see if he could cross the river here. Dead falls were the only bridges available for crossing a river of any size. Humans were born with the ability to at least keep their heads above water, under ideal circumstances, i.e.: calm water, calm person, unencumbered with additional weight. Rarely, if ever were there rivers, or people, which filled these criteria. So, better to take advantage of what is provided than to risk drowning unnecessarily.

From a security standpoint it was absolutely necessary to know the area in which you were traveling, particularly if the others you were with included young ones. Children were by nature noisy, always exploring their world. It was hard to restrain their enthusiasm, let alone keep them quiet.

His daughter was just three and already she was teaching all the parents the new sign language. She was giving names to things in the forest. Trees and water and other things. He could remember the sound when he saw the thing. This was a wonderful thing, this "awareness." No matter how he tried, he just couldn't get used to how it was so much different than it was "before." That was a word Ilia had taught him. (Ilia was the name his daughter had given herself).

"Before" meant what the first family was. Before she had come . . . before mother or father had seen each other. "Now" was him and his mate and their daughter and the others who had joined them.

As he worked his way closer to the old dead fall, he heard a faint crack. It was barely audible, nothing particularly out of the ordinary. But part of being scout is being aware of anything out of the ordinary, no matter how inconsequential it might seem.

He approached the tree, keeping it between him and the sound. As quietly as he could, he inched his way up the side of the trunk, trying not to loose his grip on the moss-covered branches.

He got to the top, laying flat and still, his chin resting on the rotting bark. He heard nothing out of the ordinary. Just the rustle of tiny feet as a small brown beetle made its way across his field of vision.

He waited, trying to relax, watching, listening. The only movement his eye detected was the beetle, trundling slowly down the side of the trunk. He became aware of his heart, thumping against the hard old bark. He was afraid someone, or some thing else would hear it.

Still no sound. The flutter of wings overhead. The buzz, going from high pitch to low as an insect flitted past his ear. The pounding in his ears as his heart thudded against the tree's decaying bark.

Still there was noth. . . . Crack! A chill ran down his neck as he tensed. This time the sound was much louder. It didn't sound too far away. Carefully he began shifting his weight, gradually crawling forward, like a reptile.

The cracking sounds continued. Some were louder than others, and irregular. He covered more than twenty feet under the cover of the noise coming from ahead. His eyes took in every feature that came into view.

The first thing he saw there ahead was the scraggly tip of a tree limb waving about at an odd angle. The giant trunk obscured what was causing the limb to move in such a manner.

He froze in place, his breath caught in his throat. The limb waved about for a few more seconds and then disappeared below his field of view. He heard more small snaps, followed by what sounded like footsteps. Then the limb appeared again, flying through the air, this time minus several smaller branches. It slammed soundly into a clump of moss hanging from another tree limb. An object of some kind (it looked like a short stick) tumbled out of the tangled mass and fell earthward. There was a faint rustle, like walking.

Suddenly the rustling stopped. . . . Nothing. Not a sound. Not even a bird. Time seemed to stand still. His heart felt like it would explode. He dared not move. He couldn't move. He couldn't breathe. He was frozen; caught in that moment when he wasn't sure whether he was still the predator or if he had just become prey.

In the distance he heard a twitter, then another. Then a chirp, followed by a hoot. The sound of the jungle was returning. Over head he saw several birds hover and then land on the thin branches high above. One of the branches bent under the added weight, flinging its fruit out into the air and then down into the tangled vegetation below.

Something flew up from below, crashing into the high branches, then falling back. A few birds flapped anxiously, keeping their balance. Others continued feasting, ignoring the intrusion. He thought he heard more sound from ahead and below him. But the sound was being swallowed up as the normal sounds of the jungle resumed.

Once he was no longer over the river, he retreated, inching his was back over the edge of the trunk, keeping it between him and that sound. He made it back down to the ground just at the waters edge. One foot landed partially in the water, sending another chill down his neck. He shuddered slightly, then crawled forward noiselessly, trying to keep his hands from shaking.

As he neared the huge entanglement of rotten roots, he got back down on his belly. The musty dampness of the jungle floor, this close to the water, smelled of decay, rot. It made the hairs in his nose tingle. He needed to scratch, but he dared not. He flexed his nostrils. The itch persisted. His eyes started watering. Now he needed to sneeze! He had to do something. He couldn't remain here forever. The clan would be catching up soon. He had to get this resolved. The itch began to burn. His eyes were on fire.

Ignoring the madding itch, he worked his way forward, water streaming out of his eyes. He blinked the tears away and readied himself. Being careful not to disturb the low-hanging moss and draw attention to himself, he moved forward a few more feet. There, just at the end of the tangled root, was a low spot in the ground. He worked his way up to the edge and slid down the shallow embankment, head first. He slithered across the bottom and slowly worked his way up the other side. Using the moss as camouflage, he peered over the edge into a small clearing just a few yards beyond.

There at the far side of the clearing a male simian squatted, a short stick in his hand. He was facing away, not moving.

This was not one of the 'others.' He could sense it. The way the body was posed. That was not the way one of the 'others' would have posed. This one was erect, balanced on both feet and an arm. The other hand held the stick, its tip just touching the ground. This one was poised, ready to respond.

What should he do? This was not one of his clan. He knew that. He could smell it. Was he hostile? Why was he holding that stick? How could he defend himself? His mind raced.

Rising slowly, using one of the mossy roots as a shield should it be needed, he grunted softly.

The other one's head snapped in his direction. The stick he was holding loosely before, now was brandished like a prod. There was no charge. This was a defensive posture. Nor was there a challenge. The figure stood motionless. It was too far away to see his eyes.

There seemed to be no malice in the other's pose. It looked more like a beckoning than a threat. Gathering his courage, he moved slowly out and away from his cover. With both hands held to his side, palms forward, he took a small step forward, then dropped to his haunches.

The father of Broc knew immediately this was one of his kind. Though he couldn't see his eyes this far away, his posture told of his intentions. As he stepped out from behind the root, there was no crouch in his stance. He was not poised in any overt way. He was standing erect, a sure sign that he wanted to be noticed. His movements were slow and deliberate so they could be easily seen and scrutinized. He carried nothing in his hands. When he sat down he placed his palms in his lap, a submissive posture in simian society. It was not normally displayed during a first-time meeting between mature males.

Emboldened by the stranger's gesture of submissiveness, but reluctant to take undue advantage, the father of Broc dropped his weapon and took a slow step toward the center of the clearing.

CHAPTER 41

Some unknown amount of time ago a gigantic boulder had been jarred from its place among the others higher up the side of the hill. The ground's shifting had dislodged it from its already precarious position, and it had rolled, slow-motion, a few hundred feet down the gentle embankment. It had come to rest squarely in the middle of what was, at the time, a reasonable size river. Over the years, because it was so huge, nothing the river could throw at it could make it budge. Instead, everything that was thrown at it either glanced off and continued following the now-rerouted course; or it became entangled in the debris accumulating at the great stone's base.

As the years went by, the great ice sheets continued their retreat to the north, leaving behind more and more arid landscape. The run off, at one time a mighty river, had flowed from their bases. But now, with more and more land being exposed, the run-off was being sucked down, through the porous firmament, into vast underground lakes.

What was left after so many uncounted years was now only a stream a dozen or so feet wide. The huge boulder, covered on its north side by a tangled mass of intertwined tree trunks, rocks, soil and shrubbery, now looked more like a mountain than a stone. A man could make it to the top, but it would be an awfully difficult climb.

Nevertheless, a person was already up there, surveying the surroundings before the fading light was gone. Soon he too would be snuggled into his nest at the base below, awaiting the next dawn. His replacement was already on the way up. He could hear the clatter as limbs slapped against each other, making way for the clumsy climber.

Broc and his mate had already disappeared into their shelter. He had been especially exuberant about finishing his shelter early. He wanted to be up early tomorrow so he could continue exploring the new territory. That was what he had said as he excused himself from the now-traditional evening gathering around the fire. He and his mate had other intentions. . . .

Ahmahn sat with his feet facing the fire, his back against a stone he had pushed back, away from the flame. The heat the stone had absorbed penetrated the thick layers of hides that covered his back, taking the evening chill away. Beyond, the fire cast eerie shadows against the huge granite overhang under which they had made camp. To his left, a few slices still hung crackling on their spits. To his right, his mate, Mahrom snuggled close, a deer hide pulled around her shoulders. No one else was left around the fire. Everyone but them had turned in for the night well before dark, as was usually the case. Only the sentries would remain awake all night, sleeping in shifts, and patrolling the outer perimeter of the camp.

Ahmahn pulled two pieces off the nearest stick and handed one to his mate.

"Mahrom, my cherished one. Tonight I must go to my father's nest. There are things we must discuss that cannot wait." His heart swelled as he looked into her eyes. From the moment he had first seen her so long ago, she had filled his heart.

"How long will you be gone?" she asked as she took the meat from his hand.

"Just long enough to see he is comfortable. Maybe we'll talk for a while."

"I see he is moving more slowly today. Is he not well?" That was what Ahmahn liked about this woman. She seemed to read his mind as well as she read his father's signing.

"He does move slower, doesn't he?" Ahmahn pulled her close to him. The heat from the fire was making the thick hide of his foot coverings steam. He pulled his legs up. His feet felt better, but now he could feel heat building on his shins. It was now only pleasantly uncomfortable.

She placed her cool hand on his knee, sending a chill through his loins. "He grows old, just like my parents. I wonder, will they last much longer? A few have already gone. The thought pains me."

Ahmahn continued chewing, pondering what she was saying, and how it related to the thing which he must contend with this night.

"It pains me too." He swallowed the last bite, then took a long swig from the bladder before he continued.

"This among other things we must speak about this night. The old ones move as best they can, and that will suffice. Even though, I fear that we may still happen upon some of the 'others.' I believe it would be wise for us to continue moving, following the path the stream has already taken."

"Must we move again so soon?" Mahrom reached across him for another strip of meat. Her breast brushed lightly against his knee. She lingered there for a long moment. She brushed aside a lock of hair so she could see his eyes. They were peering down to the place where she was touching him.

"Sara told me she might be with child, but she's not sure."

"Then we will remain here until she *is* sure. From the size of the shelter she had Broc build, I don't think that will be too long."

Mahrom giggled, sitting back to snuggle against his chest.

"Maybe I should have you make us a smaller shelter too," she said with a sly gerin.

Ahmahn ignored the inference, but gave her a squeeze and moved to stand.

"No. The move we have made will be one of many, but we need not push ourselves too hard. As for my father, we both think it is important, however I don't think it is his health which is of concern. At least, not at the moment."

Ahmahn gave her hand a squeeze, and then rose from his position next to her.

"I will return soon. Keep the covers warm for me." With a knowing smile, she bade him farewell. He turned away from the light and walked the few short steps to his father's nest.

As he entered, at first he could see only the dark shadow of his father's figure, silhouetted ever so faintly against the rear wall. As he became accustomed to the dark, he was able to detect a very faint blue glow emanating from the object his father held in his lap.

"Are you sure there is no light going beyond this place?" the old simian signed with one hand. The other hand, or rather, the scared stump, caressed the '*darkness.*'

"I am sure, father I saw nothing until I entered here."

"Good. What do you think of what Broc said? Are there others like this?" he motioned toward the object in his lap. The object itself appeared without color. However, somehow it gave off a blue glow that illuminated everything within its path with the same faint, fluorescent 'un-darkness.'

No sooner had he gotten seated than the object flickered once and went out. In place of the blue haze, the room was filled with another faint, un-natural glow. Pa moved slowly backward, making room for what he knew would be next. He made himself comfortable a few feet away from what he called the '*darkness,*' and motioned for his son to join him closer, so they both could see the same thing from the same perspective.

Ahmahn began to get up, when directly above the dark object, the shape of a man began to form. At first it was almost skeletal, but almost instantly thereafter, the form of a face and upper torso began to take shape. In two steps Ahmahn was at his father's side.

The shape, still semi-translucent, turned to watch the movement. As it began to solidify in front of them, a purple-colored robe and collar took shape over the naked shape of a man. His chest was free of hair, as was his back. The hair on his head was not long and not short. His facial hair was trimmed neatly. He began to speak. At first the voice was garbled and unclear. But as the form became more defined, so did the voice.

"Gggrreeetings, my old friend." The words formed in Ahmahn's head as the form solidified. "And you, young Ahmahn." The now fully formed face turned toward him.

"At last! I have waited a long time for this moment." Evander's face appeared more real now. Before, Ahmahn had noticed occasional flickers when the figure spoke or moved. This time the "apparition" remained steady, unwavering.

"You are not the same as before," Amon replied. "I see you differently. And how is it you speak to my father without signs?"

"These are proper questions, and I will answer them momentarily. But first," he turned to Ahmahn. "I am a long-time friend of your father's. I remember you when you were very young. You used to call me 'Darkness Man.' Can you remember that?"

Ahmahn tried to remember. Faintly, indistinctly, like a childhood memory, the shape materialized. It was a face with no hair. It was making noises. Its teeth were showing.

"I remember the face, but not the name you call yourself. And you are not the same this time."

Evander could see that Ahmahn was straight forward, to the point, like his father.

"It might be best if I tell you about myself and what you say is 'different' about me this time. I live in a place every far away from you. It is so far away that it takes a very long time for your voice to reach my ears."

"Like from across a valley, but more." Ahmahn nodded his understanding.

"Exactly! Before, the thing you saw wasn't the same. It said things to you and remembered what you said. Then it came and found me and told these things to me."

"But the '*darkness*' has not gone anywhere. How can it go somewhere and be here at the same time? And you still have not answered my question." Ahmahn's assertiveness certainly caught Evander's notice.

"It is so. And yet I cannot answer more clearly until we have learned more about each other. I speak truth to you. You may weigh it against anything you know. And you alone can decide whether or not what I say is right in your mind.

"I will be patient. I will wait and I will learn. Tell me about this thing that you call yourself." He motioned toward the image disdainfully. "You may speak and I may watch and hear you. But in an instant you can be gone."

"I am real, just like you. This thing you see before you is a tool which I use to talk with you. Just as your spear is a tool you use to assist you, so this tool assists me. It is called a hologram. It is an image of me. It helps you to see what I look like, even though you can't see the real me. I'm too far away right now."

"Can you come here, now, to this place so that we may see each other face to face?"

"It is difficult for me to do that right now. It will take some time for that to happen."

"How much time?"

"Maybe only a day or two. But first, there are many things I need to tell you. These are things which are important for you to understand, if I am to meet you in person. They require that you be prepared to see and understand a world very different from your own, and that you also be prepared to keep this other world hidden from your own."

"Why is this such a secret? Is there something there that might be harmful?"

"It is not so much that it might be harmful to you. Rather, it might prove to be harmful to your people if they ever found out about me, and what I represent."

"If you represent truth, as you say, then what you say I must trust to be true. You give me no reason to distrust you. But neither do you give me reason to want to learn more."

"This is reasonable. Let me then try to persuade you."

Ahmahn leaned back, making himself comfortable.

"I am listening."

Evander was amused, if not a bit amazed that this man would have such confidence in himself that he would accept with minimal explanation, the possibility that another reality existed. He showed no sign of distress. Rather, he seemed to be almost amused to be having this conversation.

"Tell me, Ahmahn; what intrigues you about this conversation? You seem to be almost amused."

"It isn't amusement. It is more irony." Ahmahn leaned a bit forward, trying to glean some reaction from those artificial eyes that looked over at him.

"In the first place, I ask myself, why is it that I do not look like my father? He is covered in hair. I am not. Neither are any of the others of my generation. All before us looked as does my father. This weighs on my mind.

"Second, my father cannot speak. Neither could my mother, or any of the parents of my generation. And yet we easily speak with each other and with you. I wonder where this language came from.

"But of most importance to me is why you have not revealed yourself to any of us from the beginning. We have done as has been necessary for our survival. Will your appearance change that?"

"Only to the extent you wish it to do so." Evander was quick with a response. He knew he was being baited. This was an unexpected, and pleasant challenge, coming from a first generation human. There was confidence exhibited here. And practically no fear. This man would be a challenge to get to know. Evander was anxious to begin the discussion.

"I suppose the first thing to make clear is that there are other worlds which none of you have ever seen. They are very, very far from your world and it takes a very long time to get there. Let's just say, for example, that your brother Broc wanted to visit one of those worlds. If he left tomorrow, you would still be as you are. But when he got back you would be very, very old, or maybe even dead. That is how great the distance is between worlds."

"How do you know about Broc?" Ahmahn asked, but quickly went on. "Then he too would be old, or dead."

"No. He would be not much older than he is now." Evander saw a furrow cross Ahmahn's brow.

"This brings me to another important subject, which is: How is what I've just described possible. Think about walking along side a fast-flowing river. The place you want to go is very far down the river and will take many days of walking to get to. You don't want to take that much time to make the trip, so you jump in the river, which is flowing much faster than you can run. You reach your destination very quickly, but when it is time for you to return, you must walk back. You cannot use the river to speed up your return because it is flowing in the wrong direction.

"In my world, I can travel from one place to another very quickly, like a river, using tools which my people have built. And I can go back and forth, not just in one direction, like a river. Sometimes I can go from one world to another very quickly, too. For travel between worlds, we use tools which we call 'LINKS.'

"Remember how you said I was different before? That was because the 'LINK' I was using was not pointed to any world close to yours, so the device you call the 'DARKNESS' was left behind to let me know when you were ready. That device remembered my voice and what I looked like. When your father spoke to the device . . ."

"Spoke to the device? That is not possible! He cannot speak!"

"That is true. But when your father touches the device, it remembers his touch and speaks to him only in his mind. The image of me, or any other person, is not necessary for him to see then. He has but to think a thought, and the device will know it, and will answer.

"When it found out that your father believed the time was near, the device signalled me, so that I could make myself ready to come and meet you.

"So you say. But you have not come here to meet me face to face. Why do you use this 'device' instead?"

"My friend, remember the story of the river and of time? " Ahmahn nodded.

"If I come to see you face to face it will be as we both stand at the edge of the river. When we are at the side of the river at the same time, we can see each other, the real you and the real me. I could stay with you for a time, but not for very long. And when it came time for me to leave, it would be like me jumping in the river. I would go away very fast, but it would take you a very long time to see me again. Maybe you would be dead before I came again."

"So if you must teach me all the things you say, then either you must come here and stay with me, or I must go with you."

"There is truth in what you say. But there is more. If I come to your world to teach you, I will only have a short time to stay. Your world is not my world. I will want to visit my home from time to time, just as you will if you decide to come with me. In either case, if we choose, we can visit our home worlds any time we want. But because we use 'LINKS' like you use rivers on this world, much time will have passed between our visits. The things we remembered seeing in our worlds before we left will have changed while we were gone. But we will not have changed. All that will have changed for us is that we will have grown a little bit older, and hopefully gained in wisdom, while the old world we revisit will be nothing like what we remember. We will be able to see how our worlds change, not just from season to season, but from lifetime to lifetime."

"What you describe has little interest for me. What benefit do I derive from watching my world evolve if I can only observe and not interact? How can I protect my mate when danger approaches if all I can do is watch? How can this help me, or my mate or anyone in my world?"

Ahmahn was defending his position, but in a way that didn't deny what was being told him. Instead, he seemed to be continually probing for weaknesses in the arguments Evander was offering. His points were not offensive in any negative sense, but they did force Evander to thoroughly explain himself. This was turning into a conversation Evander would gladly engage in with any of his peers!

"There have been times in your life when you have remembered something, and the memory of it has caused you to change what you might otherwise have done."

Ahmahn's mind raced back to the time not so long ago when they had chosen to walk along the bottom of the rockfall.

Evander paused, seeing the change on Ahmahn's face. The young man looked down to the ground, and then quickly up, locked squarely on the 'eyes' of the hologram. Before he could say anything, Evander continued.

"It is possible to interact with your world, but only during the time you are there. The consequences of the things you do while you are there may not be seen for a very long time. In order to see the results, you will have to leave, for what seems to you only a short time, and then return. When you return you will see how much things have changed. Maybe, if you look very carefully, you can see how what you did so long ago in that old world, has changed how things are now, in this new world."

"This causes me to fear. What if the decision I make now, in this 'old world' as you call it, causes great harm in the 'new world'? Would it not be better if I had not interfered in the beginning?"

In only a few short minutes Ahmahn had narrowed the conversation down to the fundamental reason for Evander having initiated the discussion in the first place. He had hit upon what Evander preferred to call the 'moral paradox,' whether to interfere in one's culture, having had 'extra-cultural' information as to what the probable consequences might be, thus increasing the probability that the culture would be a 'success,' or to stand aside and let events unfold naturally.

"Remember when your mother caught you before you fell out of the nest? If she had not done so, you might have been greatly harmed, or even killed. You were young and didn't know better. But your mother knew and she protected you. What might have happened if she had just sat there and watched you fall. Your mother made a decision at that moment which changed forever the course your life would take."

"That is so, but why is it of importance to me now? I have no knowledge of what the future will bring. And I have no knowledge of what might have happened, had my mother let me fall. All I can do in this moment is prepare myself, using the knowledge that I possess."

"That is all any man can do. But I ask you, have you ever wondered what the future holds for not just you, but also your family, or your clan or all your people?"

"Certainly I ponder these things. But it is pointless for me to spend time being concerned about things beyond my control. This question is also pointless, and beneath you, unless you are offering an alternative."

Evander could hardly contain his excitement. Here was a first generation human, capable of doing all that would be expected of someone like Evander himself. But what made this particular man stand out, was his ability to engage in abstract reasoning, displaying intellectual curiosity, without becoming bogged down in self-doubt or petty self-aggrandizement, as was common with some individuals who discovered ways to use the knowledge they gained from the transceiver (the "device," the "DARKNESS") for their own exclusive benefit. In such cases, the transceiver had simply been removed. The clan and the resulting culture would be left to its own devices.

"Very well. Since you have chosen to be direct, so shall I. Your race is, in general a compassionate one, as is mine. Aside from many thousands of years of experience, and distances beyond measure, your race and mine are the same. What makes you and me different, what sets us apart from our individual races, is the fact that we prefer to view them from a distance. We set ourselves apart."

"If that is so, then why do *you* set yourself apart? There is much which is not being said here."

"You and I have had similar experiences, though our lives are completely different. I am much older than you. But here, in this circumstance, age makes little difference. It is the experiences and perspectives which we share that draws me to make you this offer.

"I see how the loss of your first mate left you feeling empty inside. Your father tells me that you spend many hours alone, just staring off into the wilderness, not moving for hours at a time. Even your new mate cannot fill that void which often times consumes you.

"I too have had that experience. The emptiness I feel, even today, after so many centuries; the memory of her still brings me near unto tears. Even now I remember her scent. It was like pine sap, only sweet."

"Lillies in the summer." Ahmahn said without prompting. Evander stopped in mid-thought, listening.

"Summer in the jungle is hot. The air does not move. It sticks to you like a cloak you cannot remove. Finding and staying close to a stream provides the only relief available. Near the streams grow tall, gangly plants, as high as a man's waist. The flowers of this plant only bloom in the hottest part of the summer. Their petals are cupped, to catch rainwater. Insects come to drink from the small pools formed on the petals. Their feet get caught in the petal's sticky spines, and they are slowly eaten by the plant. They become food, ensuring that the race of the flower continues.

"There is a smell that comes from the flower as it consumes the dead insect. At first it is pleasant beyond imagining. But after only a few hours it becomes horribly unpleasant. If you can catch the liquid from the dissolving insect when the smell is most pleasant, the liquid will retain that smell. That was the smell of my first mate.

"Those quiet times my father talks about probably took place near a stream. I always search for that smell whenever a stream is near."

Ahmahn stood slowly and stretched. The image of Evander remained at the height it was while Ahmahn was sitting.

"My, my. You are tall, aren't you! You must be close to six feet. I'm only a little over five-ten, myself." Evander knew he had hit a tender spot. He didn't want to cause ill feelings between them.

"What are these things you talk about?" Ahmahn snapped. "And what does my height have to do with anything?" He sat back down, placing a hand on his father's knee.

"This man stands only to my chest. Ahmahn gestired toward his father. "Yet he possesses wisdom which I will never attain, so size has no place in this conversation. I long to gain in experience so that my wisdom may increase, as has his. But I see that his age catches up with him. He does not move the way he used to when he was young. Soon it will be his time to go the way of all life. Will the wisdom he attained be lost when he is gone?

"All I can do to preserve that wisdom is to learn from him now. I will partake of his wisdom as best I am able. And when my time comes, I will pass his wisdom as well as that which I have gained on to my child."

Evander sensed he had found a way in. A way to appeal to Ahmahn's concern for the future of his people.

"Tell me of your hopes for your family."

"My hopes for my family guide everything that I do. I hope they will have enough food. Therefore I find food for them. I hope for their safety. Therefore I protect them."

Evander needed to steer the conversation onto a higher plane. He wanted Ahmahn to think about something other than the immediate future. He wanted to have him consider what the future might hold many generations from now.

"What about the wisdom that those around you are learning at your hand? Are you concerned that they gain from your experience and wisdom, and that they pass what they have learned on to their children as well? Wisdom can be attained in many ways. It can also be passed on in many ways. This is how wisdom can be preserved and shared by all."

Ahmahn settled himself, trying to grasp what was being said.

"Are you saying one man can learn the thoughts of another, even if one of them is gone?"

"Yes. We can do this by making tools to help us remember. This transceiver you see here is a tool which can also be used to remember. It can remember the last place where your father stored it, and can take us back to the same place, if we tell it to do so. If we tell it, it will also show us images of the place so we can find it again for ourselves."

"But it can help us remember, so we can teach others." Ahmahn was concise and to the point, as he saw it.

"Does it concern you that you are speaking in such a manner to what is described as a tool?"

Ahmahn looked first to the gray box on the ground and then up to the holographic face.

"If this is a tool, as you say, then it can do things which I cannot. If you are a man, as you say, then by doing as you say, I may use this . . . "transceiver" to meet with you face to face."

"Yes, this is true. The device (it is easier to say than trans-cei-ver), will help us to meet, if that is what you choose. But you must first understand what will be required of you.

"If you choose to meet with me physically . . . in person, you must leave the place where you are now. You may return, but it will not be to the same time and place as it is now. At the very best, you may be able to return within the lifetime of one individual whom you knew before you left. That person would be very old, while you will have aged only a little by comparison."

"How is this possible?"

"Once again, it has to do with the 'LINKS.' We use them as portals, or fast-moving streams, to take us where we want to go. Time for us will pass as normal. But for those left on our home worlds, much, much time will have gone by."

Ahmahn nodded. His brow furrowed.

"I am at the beginning. This I can see. What I cannot see is where I am going. I know not what the morning will bring; but there is much I do know. I know of those things I share with those closest to me. I know not just of the sadness and toil. I also know of the joy and kinship shared between us. I fear for the welfare of all my people, not just those close around me.

"I wonder where our wanderings will take us. What obstacles will we meet along the way? What new things will we see and learn? I feel responsibility for ensuring my people go in the right direction. Yet when I see someone take what I see to be the wrong direction, I feel regret that I could not persuade him to abstain."

"That is what sets you apart, my friend," said Evander. "Could you not have forced your friend to do your will? There are many, in other places, who have tried . . . and many have succeeded, to a point. You, on the other hand, have seen the futility of depriving another of his right to choose. You want to influence others to do the right thing, but not at the expense of depriving them of their agency."

"I am beginning to understand what it is you are offering. But there is much for me to consider. And there are others who need to know what may come to pass."

"I would caution you, my friend. To reveal much at this time carries great risk. The decision you soon must make will have great impact on your clan. If you decide to leave, the social system in use now will remain in play. When you return at a later time, if you observe closely, you may see how well or poorly your system has worked. Then, if it seems to be moving off course and needs a little adjusting, you can return for a while and maybe give it a little nudge from time to time. But! It is important to remember that a nudge is just that. It is persuasion, not dictation."

"The right to choose. This I understand. There are many in whom I have faith. There are but few whom I trust. My father, my mate, my brother Broc. There was a third, but she has departed." Ahmahn paused, remembering the sadness he felt when Nera was killed.

"Very well. Confer as you deem necessary. Take time as you need. There will be many things you will want to know before the decision is made. You have but to touch the device. It will remember you and will bring us together again, as now."

CHAPTER 42

"Good morning, my friend! Did you sleep well?" Ahmahn looked past Broc and smiled. "I see you are not expecting guests. Your tiny place couldn't accommodate them."

"It was Sara." Broc smiled sheepishly as the two friends walked slowly toward the fire pit. "Complaining about the cold again."

"I trust your lack of sleep will not distract you from listening to what I know you want to hear." Ahmahn smiled and placed a hand on his friend's shoulder.

"I trust you will not be deterred for a similar reason," Broc said, smiling back at Ahmahn.

They both had a good laugh. Then Ahmahn continued. "Not as similar as you might expect."

Broc grinned knowingly, then became serious.

"My first question is what is the purpose of this 'DARKNESS'? What does it do? Why is it watching us? Does it intend to do us harm?"

"Slow down, my brother. True, this is exciting. But are you not over-reacting? After all, this transceiver . . . that is what it is called . . . has been with us from the beginning. For how many years has it dwelt among us, never doing us harm? Never interfering, never disrupting? You must see that it means us no harm."

Ahmahn threw his arm around his friend's waist and re-directed him toward his father's shelter.

"What you will learn today will change your life forever! Ah, but do not be afraid. Not all change is bad."

"Stories are that a man comes out of the 'dark . . .,' the tran-see-vur, and that he speaks to those who are there to listen. Is this true?"

"The transceiver is but a tool used by a man called Evander. He lives in a place far away from here, so he uses this tool to help him see and hear us. It also can remember things, like what a person looks like. And it can show an image of that person for others to see."

"But what of the man?" Broc was still anxious, but tried to collect himself.

"The thing that my father and I saw was not a real man. It was only an image of him, another of his tools. But his image spoke as he would if he were here with us.

"He spoke of his home as if it were another world, far beyond the heavens. He said that he could come here to see us face to face, but only for a short time."

Ahmahn was practically dragging Broc along as anticipation built in him, too.

"Slow down yourself!" Broc held back, but only slightly. "I still have questions."

Ahmahn saw genuine concern in his friend's eyes.

"All will be answered in due time. For now, know this." He stopped and turned to face Broc squarely.

"You above all people do I trust. We have been together from the time we were small. All things have we shared. Now that we are grown men, does this sharing continue. No matter what the outcome of this encounter with the 'DARKNESS,' you and I will remain as we have always been." They turned and continued walking, this time at a much slower pace.

"You and I do not always agree."

"That too has ever been so." Ahmahn laughed, pushing his friend toward the doorway into his father's shelter.

As the two friends and Pa settled in front of the transceiver, Broc was the first to speak.

"I care not about the affairs of others. I have enough and more to occupy myself. I have a mate now, and must see to her needs. And if it be so, I may soon have a child to watch over." Broc had listened closely to the dialog between Ahmahn and Evander. He was intrigued by the idea of going to other places and experiencing new things. What troubled him was the amount of time he would be away. "If I am to leave, I must take my mate with me. Without me, there will be no one to care for her."

"That, I'm afraid, will not be possible." Evander was a bit put off that such an idea would even be considered.

"The premise which is the foundation of this entire venture does not center around any select group or any select family. It is designed to look at populations as a whole. It has been shown time and again that when an individual is forced to choose between the welfare of his immediate family or that of an entire community, he will inevitably choose to protect his family. The emotional attachment he has with them is simply too strong. It tends to cloud his judgement. He tends to look only at solving the issues of the short term. The 'future,' as he sees it, is something nebulous, something not real, and therefore something which is of less import. In short, long-term planning is difficult to do when one has become embroiled in immediate issues."

Broc sat motionless, trying to absorb what he was hearing. Many of the words this man used, he didn't understand. He looked to Ahmahn for support.

Ahmahn, for his part, was beginning to believe it might have been a mistake to include Broc in any of this. He seemed not to be able to grasp the idea that if he left, his family would likely never see him again. More importantly, he seemed to lack the desire to take on the challenge. Perhaps it wasn't that Broc didn't want the responsibility. Perhaps he just didn't understand what was expected of him.

"Do not be amazed by the words of this man, my brother. This language which you and I now speak to one another, he and others before him have spoken from time beyond measure. Therefore do not marvel that he uses it so much better than we."

"I do understand him, in the main," said Broc, looking at Ahmahn. "I understand that to go with him, I must be willing to leave all that I know behind. I also understand that if I go, I will see my world change almost before my eyes, but that I will not be there to participate in that change. Rather, I will be left to deal with the results of actions taken during my absence. I will not have been there as a participant, doing what I could to influence the outcome."

Evander listened carefully to what Broc said. It concerned him that perhaps Broc didn't fully appreciate what he had been offered. He felt it necessary to interject.

"All these things you say are true, my friend Broc; they things you say, as well as what Ahmahn says. When I originally came up with the idea of making direct contact with Ahmahn, it was because he possesses something rare, even in all the worlds I have visited. He possesses the gift of being willing to step outside the bounds of his own world, his own experiences and perceptions, and observe objectively. From time to time, if it becomes necessary (and if it is appropriate), he may or may not intervene, depending on the severity of the need. Such intervention would, by necessity, only be done under well-established pre-conditions."

"I too misinterpret some of what you say." Ahmahn turned from Broc to look penetratingly toward Evander. "However, if this is a gift; this feeling of concern which is inside of me, I perceive that it has also become a burden. I, like my friend here, am newly mated. For us and for our clan, this is a very difficult time.

"I *am* the leader, as you say. I am so only because there was no one to come forward with a better plan. Should that person appear, I would be forced by conscience to relinquish my position. Though your offer is tempting almost beyond resisting, I must decline, at least for now. Too much rides on what happens to us in the near future. This community is still very small, and vulnerable. My presence is needed here."

Evander understood the logic in what each of them had said. Perhaps Ahmahn was right. Much had been invested in this endeavour. Though countless other planets had been seeded, all had brought forth revelations, each unique in its own right, and worthy of the expense. This small community, though well on its way, was still quite vulnerable. Evander admitted to himself that his attraction to the qualities exhibited by Ahmahn had perhaps clouded his judgement. Perhaps it would be best to wait a while longer. Hesitantly, he brought forth his last appeal.

"Do you understand that your ties to your family and this community will grow stronger as time goes by. It may be more difficult for you to leave at a later time."

"Yes, Evander, my new friend. I understand the risk." Ahmahn was hesitant to say more. Both Broc and Evander could sense it. Turning to Broc, he continued.

"My brother, you and I have shared everything between us for as long as I can remember. Let us then speak plainly about the future."

Broc spoke from the heart, knowing that his brother would accept nothing less. "I am newly mated, as are you, though not for the first time. You understand what it is I feel for this woman."

"Yes, of all people, I know. You know as well as I that, were you to leave, your thoughts would be always with her. You would wonder what your life together might have been, had you stayed and lived out your days here."

"And you have the same feelings." Broc responded. "I see the way you look at your new mate. I see the pain in your eyes. I know you remember . . . and I know you are concerned for her future, as well as all the others."

"Yes. I look at Mahrom and remember . . ." (he would not say the name of his first mate) " . . . she who is no longer among us."

His voice strained as he struggled to re-focus his thoughts. At times he thought the only reason he had taken another mate was because it was expected of him. He forced himself to continue.

"I know how difficult it would be for her, as well as the rest of the clan. We move from the familiarity of our homeland because there are now so many of us. As we grow, we increase the risk of coming in contact with the 'others.' Though our numbers grow, we still lack the strength to withstand an assault from them. And even if we were strong enough, it would not be right for us to impose our will on them, should we prevail.

"It is better that we live separate. They are our brothers, but only in the sense that we share the same homelands. Though our parents were of the same lineage as them, we are not. This is clear from what is obvious . . . we do not look like them.

"It is this distinction that causes me to wonder. Why is there such a difference between us and our parents? I am certain that, should I go with Evander, I would learn the answer.

"Our clan has not yet reached a place of safety, where the loss of one man might not be of too great a burden. Also, soon there will be young ones among us. Then, the need for extra hands will be even greater."

"I can think of no better solution than the ones you have given." Evander responded. It would be expected of a person such as Ahmahn. But in a very real sense, he felt relieved. He had not anticipated Broc being brought into the conversation, but Ahmahn had insisted. Fortunately Broc's priorities were in a different place right now, which put Evander's original plan back in play.

"Very well then," said Evander. "You have made your decision, and it is a good one. If you will allow me, I would like to look in on you from time to time to see how you're doing. And if you desire to speak with me, you have but to touch the trans . . . the device. It will remember you and will establish another link between us."

All parties nodded in agreement. Evander's likeness faded, and disappeared.

CHAPTER 43

The old simian lay quietly in the back of the shelter, adjusting his position from time to time. There were no fresh, green branches this far away from their homeland, so he was now forced to lay animal hides over what was left of his old nest and then lay down on top of them. As his bony old frame settled into the nest, sharp protrusions found ways to irritate him. So soon, he already missed the comforts of his jungle home. Beside his bed sat the 'DARKNESS.' It emitted a faint blue light which illuminated the wrinkles in his hairy old face. He moved his hand off it slowly, almost reluctantly, then watched as the familiar glow faded *away*.

What Evander had offered his son was unexpected. Pa had expected that Evander would continue with his son what he had done from the beginning . . . conversing from time to time as they had done even before Ahmahn's birth. But for him to leave? He had never even considered the idea.

"My son is indeed wise!" Pa thought to himself. "The trials of his young life have prepared him well. He has endured more than should be required of anyone, and still he strives to rise above and persevere. Now that he knows the man Evander, the bounds of knowledge he may acquire are limitless. And he is fearless."

He remembered how frightened he was the first time the 'DARKNESS' had come to him. Now, after so many years, the memory of that first contact had become less intense.

"I am feeling old now. More so everyday. It is good that the 'DARKNESS' will be left in good hands when I am gone. I wonder how soon that will be. I feel all right most of the time as long as I can keep moving. But when I stop, it is more and more difficult to get started again. The only thing that really bothers me is this useless stump!" He slapped the calloused club on the ground beside him.

"I know that my son will wait until I am gone before he leaves this place. He does not want me to have to fend for myself if he departs before me, whether in death or otherwise.

"Also, his new mate draws him. Mahrom is young and beautiful in his eyes. But I know, having witnessed his first loss, that he has become distant, withdrawn into himself. I wonder, what it is that troubles him? It is said that with wisdom comes responsibility. Perhaps that is it. Perhaps he is more concerned for the welfare of his loved ones than he is for himself. That is a heavy burden."

Absently he scratched the stump, distracting the persistent itch which nagged him every waking hour. His eyelids grew heavy as he remembered his mate; how she had first appeared, walking out from behind that tree as if materializing from a dream; the memory of their first touch; the memory of the birth of their son; the memory of her silhouette in moonlight.

CHAPTER 44

Ahmahn stood quietly, alone before the dwindling pyre, watching as the last remnants of his father's body were consumed by the flames. The tears had stopped flowing some time before. Now he just stood there, emotionally drained, watching the flames dwindle,

remembering, as crackles gave way to puffs and pops, and finally to faint, high-pitched sizzles.

It seemed only natural that his father should pass in such a manner. Pa had become increasingly withdrawn in the time since Mama was killed. Perhaps now, with the 'DARKNESS' passed on to his son, the old simian had not felt the need to continue. He had died quietly in his sleep the same night as the transfer.

Broc stood quietly at his friend's side, wondering if there was anything he could say or do which would help Ahmahn in his time of grief. Unable to decide what to do, he spoke quietly.

"Each time we have moved, there have been losses. We have only just arrived here. Perhaps if we remain for a while, the losses will stop." Broc was grasping for any excuse, reasonable or otherwise, that might persuade Ahmahn to remain here for a while longer.

"The losses will continue, no matter if we are here or somewhere else. Soon our women will bring forth new life. We must continue exploring our world so that our offspring will have the best opportunity for growth. With growth comes knowledge. With

knowledge comes wisdom. With wisdom comes responsibility."
Ahmahn turned from the site, patting his closest friend on the
shoulder.

"Sara says she may be with child. She wants to remain here
until after the birth. I think she may be becoming afraid. The last
woman with child . . ." Broc hesitated.

"That is true, my brother. She has reason to be afraid. But I do
not believe that the earth will shake again just because a child
is near birth. We knew of these rumblings within the earth long
before Nera became with child." He stopped and grabbed Broc by
both shoulders. With a wide grin, he continued:

"Besides, that nest of yours is way too small to accommodate
a young one." They both laughed.

"Well, perhaps you would like to trade, at least until the extra
space is needed."

Turning away from Pa's smoldering pyre, they each bid a silent
farewell.

CHAPTER 45

They began dismantling the camp two days after Pa's death, the same day the first scout returned. There was little to report about terrain or other conditions that had not already been anticipated.

Once the decision to move had been made, Ahmahn sent pairs of scouts out to travel north along the stream for a space of one day. One scout then would return to the camp while the other continued. New pairs were sent out immediately upon the first scout's arrival. The rotation continued for several weeks.

Returning scouts began reporting fewer and fewer trees along the route. Instead of heavy underbrush, tall grasses began to dominate the landscape. Eventually the stream became little more than a trickle.

Though the clan was constantly moving, the pace was slow. It wasn't uncommon for them to halt for the better part of a day if game was brought down and needed to be processed. Because they had become nomadic, they could no longer rely on the lush vegetation in the jungle as their food supply. The increased consumption of meat had become a necessity as they continued their trek northward.

One morning a few months into the journey, scouts reported a small spring a day's distance. There were only a few scrub bushes and one small, gnarly tree, clinging to the rock outcropping where the spring gurgled up. It offered little shelter from the wind, which had been increasing gradually during their journey up onto the high plains.

During the long days of walking, Ahmahn had a lot of time to think about the life he had chosen. Mahrom was with child, as were two others in the clan. Soon it would be necessary for them to slow their pace even more, so that the pregnant women could keep up.

Perhaps, he thought to himself, it would have been better to wait a season. At least in the jungle, food would be plentiful. Here in this sea of grass, there was little enough to keep the local herbivores alive, let alone a new population of humans.

He kept the 'device' hidden, even from his mate. So far as he knew, she didn't know it existed. On the night that Pa died, Ahmahn had taken the device with him out into the dense under-growth and activated it. He had spoken with Evander for several hours that night, during which time he learned much more about what was expected of him as keeper of the 'DARKNESS.'

DIVERGENCE

CHAPTER 46

"They must not be too far now!" Sef's father signed as he shuffled ahead excitedly. "We must find them before the night comes. Otherwise they will alarm if they do not recognize us in the darkness."

"This is true, Father." Sef said aloud, concerned that the noise his father was already making in his haste would be cause enough for alarm. "Remember, please! I cannot go with you to meet them. I am not one of them. They will not accept me."

"Yes! Yes, I know!" the old simian signed impatiently. "You must hide when we approach so that they will not attack us. I remember . . . I remember!"

Since their departure from Ahmahn and the rest of the clan, Sef had noticed how much more cheerful his father had become. Even the sharpness which he displayed now was better than the despondency which had possessed the old simian since the death of his mate.

The farther north they had travelled, the more depressed the old simian had become. Finally, out of desperation and concern for his father, Sef decided it would be better for both of them if they turned back so that his father could rejoin his old family.

He knew he would be alone once this happened. It would not be possible or even desirable for him to attempt to integrate with the simians. Ahmahn had warned against this many times.

He reasoned that his isolation probably wouldn't last too long anyway. His father was growing old, and in the harsh environment of simian culture, he probably wouldn't survive long. Then, when his father passed, Sef could head back north to rejoin the others of his species. Maybe then he could find a mate.

He recalled the stories his father had told him as he was growing up. He remembered vividly his father's descriptions of how he and his mate had slipped away during the night, fearful that the 'alpha' clan leader would injure or even kill them both upon finding that they had mated without his permission.

He remembered the stories of how his parents had struggled from the very beginning, trying to care for him, a naked helpless infant, so much different from them. How they had spent all their waking hours, from the time of his infancy until his maturity, protecting him from would-be predators, torrential rains, deadly droughts and countless other dangers in the jungle.

He remembered the story his mother told him of the day they found the other humans, or rather how they had found them, resting beside a narrow rippling stream in the shade, not long before his birth. He remembered the stories of his parents' amazement upon discovering that there were others like them.

He recalled how as a child he had learned to communicate with the others of his species, how he had learned language, and expressions foreign to him and to his simian parents. He remembered the simple joy of interacting with others of his own kind. How he longed to be with Ahmahn and the others. . . .

But that was not to be . . . at least for now. For now he must resign himself to the fact that he owed this to his father. He must repay him in some small measure for all that he had done for him.

"Father, please slow down! You're making too much noise!" Sef grasped his father's shoulder, gently but firmly restraining him.

"I *am* being quiet!" the old simian sloughed off his son's grasp and again plowed forward as noisily as before.

"You must slow down! We will be discovered!" Sef grabbed his father's arm with both hands, bringing them both to a halt.

The simian was old, but still much stronger than his human son. With ease he escaped the restraint, then turned to confront his son squarely.

"I am your *father!* You will *not* attempt to control me in this manner! I am wise in the ways of the world! You are but young, and lack the experience which I possess! You will say no more on this matter!"

This sort of confrontation had become more frequent over the last few days. His father seemed increasingly obsessed with returning to his "people," as he was now calling his former simian "family." He seemed not to comprehend the possibility that, because he and his mate had abandoned their former family, he would now be considered an outcast and would not be allowed to rejoin them. No matter what form of persuasion Sef used, nothing seemed to penetrate his father's irrational determination.

Ahmahn had spoken to Sef and the others about this very possibility on several occasions. He recalled how, on one occasion Ahmahn had told them about how their race had come to be. He had spoken briefly about something he called the 'DARKNESS' and how it allowed him to communicate with others like him and the others of their race. He had explained how it was imperative that their race make a clean break with the old. He had spoken of something called 'racial purity' and warned of the absolute necessity for the humans to learn to survive on their own. He had also said that should their plans go wrong, he and his father were welcome to return. Sef was concerned that this might indeed become necessary.

Night time came, and with it the realization that, yet again, they would not make contact with the old 'family.' The old simian sat across the small fire from his son, head hung low, eyes peering blankly into the dwindling flame. Sef tried to make conversation, hoping to distract his father from his brooding.

"We made good progress today." he said. "Perhaps tomorrow

we will find sign of their passing." The old simian only shrugged in response.

"We should rest now" he continued quietly. "Tomorrow we should reach that barren valley that gave us so much trouble before. Remember?" His father made no response. Smiling gently, Sef handed one of their deer-skin blankets to his father. Absently, the old simian accepted it. But instead of curling up next to the fire as had been his custom of late, he arose and headed toward a nearby tree. Slowly, deliberately he climbed into the low-hanging branches and began building a sleeping nest. He made no gesture of acknowledgement, just curled up into a ball and pulled the cover over his head.

For what seemed a long time Sef just sat there, staring first at the place where his father had been sitting, then up into the branches. Resolutely he climbed into the same tree, careful not to disturb the huddled form in the nearby branch. From there he would keep watch over his father through the night.

Sef peered up into the darkening sky as the last embers of the fire flickered out below. Stars twinkled into view as tears welled up in his eyes. He wondered; "Maybe it would have been best if we had remained."

The morning dawned gray and dismal. Thick clouds seemed almost within reach, they hung so low. The air felt thick, heavy laden with humidity.

The nest where his father had slept was empty. Sef looked toward the ground, where he saw his father huddled next to the black smudge that was last night's fire, his back toward the tree where they had spent the night. Carefully Sef untangled his legs from the limbs he had pulled close to him for warmth during the night.

The old simian remained motionless as Sef made his way down the short distance to the ground. He made his way around behind the massive trunk and stood quietly, relieving himself.

"How was your night? Did you sleep well?" he said as he made his way back around, toward the place where his father sat. A single arm wave was the only response.

"It's cold this morning. I'll make a fire so we can warm up before we start." Sef could sense his father's glum mood, shoulders hunched, head lowered, eyes staring at the ground.

"We should come to that valley this morning . . . mid afternoon at the latest." Sef signed rather than spoke, forcing his father to look in his direction.

After an uncomfortable pause, the old simian replied. "This time we should cross it directly, rather than try to skirt the most difficult parts."

"Perhaps you are right, Father." Sef was relieved that his father was finally willing to converse. "We'll need to spend some time on the far side when we get there though. Our food supply is running low. I remember there were several bushes with ripe berries on the far hillside.I hope there qare still some left."

Sef pulled out the fire stones from his pouch as his father piled a small mound of kindling in the center of the blacked remains of last night's fire. After only a few tries, he got a small fire started. The old simian edged closer, extending his hands and feet toward the welcome warmth.

"Father, have you thought much about what you will do when we arrive?" Sef parcelled out a handful of dried berries for his father, and then took the remainder for himself. They both sat quietly for a few minutes, chewing carefully, and spitting seeds into the fire. The seeds sizzled for a few seconds, then exploded quietly as the heat penetrated them.

The old simian responded between spits into the fire. "I must perform obeisance to the leader, maybe even endure a beating. He will be angry because of my disrespect. He must save face before the others, also."

Sef finished the last of the berries and stood. "He cannot maintain order otherwise." He kicked dirt onto the fire. It sputtered and died, sending small fingers of smoke swirling upward. Quickly, they too disappeared. "Come then. Let us head out."

The old simian rose to all-fours, tossed the last of the berries onto the ground, and shuffled off following his son.

Toward mid day they came upon a burned out clearing that marked the beginning of the barren valley the clan had crossed on their journey northward. To the left and right, charred tree trunks jutted out from between blackened boulders.

The ground was reasonably flat, but traversing it would require picking a circuitous route through the tangle. Going around the perimeter would be less difficult. There were fewer boulders higher up on the slopes, but they would not be able to make their way around before nightfall. Their water supply was dwindling, and they had no more food. They must reach the far side before night if they expected to replenish their supplies.

Sef's father took the lead enthusiastically. His excitement overcame his feebleness as he hurried forward. Sef struggled to keep up.

"Father, keep watch ahead. We must not let our excitement overcome our caution." Sef was surprised at how quickly his father could move when motivated.

"*You* watch, my son! I will choose the fastest path." He stopped only long enough to sign the words. Then without waiting for a response he turned and continued forward. After only a few minutes Sef began falling behind. His two legs were no match for the shuffling gate his father made on all fours.

His father was relentless, pressing ever forward, seemingly unaware that his son was falling farther and farther behind. By the time he reached the far side of the valley a few hours later, his son had lost sight of him.

The fire which had swept through the valley had not made its way up this side of the hill. Tangled vegetation covered everything, stones, boulders and dead-fall alike. In places it was so dense that one could easily walk on top of it. Scattered here and there, berry bushes pushed their way through the tangle. This close to the fire line, though, few had ripened.

The old simian made his way deeper into the tangle, stopping only long enough to gather what ripened fruit he could find along the way. In his haste he failed to hear the sound approaching stealthily from his left.

Below, Sef was just emerging from the valley floor. He scanned upward and ahead, trying to see some sign of his father. Almost immediately he saw rather than heard a group of simians slowly inching forward from left to right. And there, only a few yards ahead of them, was his father, oblivious to the on-coming threat.

Sef shouted a warning, but was too far away to be heard. He stood erect, frantically waving his arms and shouting. Still, his father made no notice.

Sef saw the leader of the group suddenly charge forward. Too late, his father finally noticed Sef's gesticulations. He turned to his left to wave in acknowledgement. Just as he did so, the alpha male plowed into him, knocking him flat to the ground. Immediately the alpha was on him, pounding, clawing and biting.

Sef began running forward, screaming and flailing, oblivious to the tangle which impeded his progress. The others in the pack saw this and stopped dead in their tracks. The alpha too was momentarily distracted.

In that brief moment the old simian was able to struggle to his feet and stumble/roll back down the hill toward his son.

The alpha overtook him almost immediately, slamming into him and sending him tumbling.

Sef charged forward, frantic to assist his father. The alpha swung one arm out, slapping the frail human aside. Sef lay where he had landed, momentarily stunned. Regaining his wits, he sat up quickly and struggled to stand.

Sef's momentary distraction was enough for his father to get his feet under him. His right arm didn't seem to want to work. It hung limply at his side as he stumbled down the hill.

Again the alpha charged, sending the old simian rolling uncontrollably down toward the boulder-strewn valley floor. He slammed into the base of a burned out sapling, his useless right arm pinned under him.

The alpha paused long enough to scream a warning toward Sef, then once again charged down the hill toward the old simian.

Sef's father was stunned. Desperate to right himself, he grasped what remained of the charred sapling, trying desperately to stand erect.

In less than a heartbeat, the sapling snapped.

Too late, the alpha saw this and tried to stop. His mass and momentum propelled him uncontrollably forward, impaling him on the sharp, blackened end of the sapling. He screamed in anger and pain as he struggled to free himself, but to no avail. Blood gushed from his mouth and the wound in his chest. In less than a minute he was dead.

Sef finally made it to his father, who was now standing shakily erect. He pulled on his father's arm, easing him away from the dead alpha male. He heard a loud pop as the old simian's shoulder snapped out of its socket. His father screamed only once, loud and long, as much out of triumph and relief as out of pain.

The others simians saw everything. They saw and heard the strange being as it charged up out of the valley and into the fray. They saw how frail it was, how their leader slapped it aside with ease. They saw how their leader pummelled the challenger relentlessly. They heard him scream his superiority. They saw the hair on his back bristle as he charged again and again, having his way with his hapless victim.

Then they witnessed in stunned silence as their leader was impaled. They watched in horror as a bloodied shaft broke through his bristling hair. They heard as the triumphant roar diminished to a gurgling scream, and finally to a fading groan.

They watched as the strange creature approached the old simian, how it walked past the now-limp form. They watched as the two embraced. They heard the roar of triumph emanate from the victor, their new leader, the new alpha male.

CHAPTER 47

"See how they fear to approach! They fear you!" Sef's father manipulated his arm gingerly, winching as the pain shot through his swollen shoulder. Signing with one hand was difficult, but he managed to make his point understood.

"I think they do *not* fear me, father," Sef signed. "I think they keep their distance because they fear and respect you. They saw how their leader flung me aside as though I were nothing. They saw how he died just as victory was seemingly in his grasp. That is what they saw, that is what they believe."

"My victory over their leader was none of my doing. Had it not been for fate I might just as easily have been the one to die."

"But, my father, they do not know this. To them you are the rightful victor. They have not been changed as you have. They do not comprehend as you do."

"Yes. I forget. My "change" has been with me so long now that I rarely think about it."

"But you *must* remember it now. You are their new leader. You must fill that role in a manner which they recognize and expect. If you were to deviate from that role, who knows what their reaction might be."

"But what of you, my son? What will you do now that your existence is known among my people?"

"I perceive there is little I *can* do. I am accepted here only because in their eyes *you* accept me. Had you lost the battle I am sure I would have been driven off or killed. Such may well still be the case if they sense something amiss. For that reason I must play a subservient role. I must not be suspected of challenging your authority. So long as I am here, I must refrain from speaking. I must display obeisance to you at all times."

"This is wisdom, my son. However, it has been long since I was among my people. I fear I may have forgotten their customs."

Sef was unsure how to approach this potentially sensitive part of their discussion.

"To begin with, my Father, you must do all you can to discard all that within you which has come about as a result of your "change." You must not acknowledge me as your son. You must not display affection toward me in any overt way. More importantly, you must stop referring to 'them' as 'your people.'"

The old simian started at the suggestion. Sef knew he must quickly find a way to explain so that his father would not be offended.

"My father, you are no longer as they are. They cannot think the way you do. They cannot reason as you do. They cannot communicate as you do. The changes you have received set you apart from them. This will ever be so."

The stark realization of what his son said hit the old simian hard. As he absorbed it, the implication became startlingly obvious.

"What you say is true, my Son. I am not like them! And I am not like you either. I am . . . alone! Alone now, more than I have ever been!"

Almost over night life among the simians returned to normal. Sef's presence had little or no effect on their routine. Almost immediately he was pushed to the periphery, not being allowed to approach his father or any of the others. Only when his father approached him did the others in the clan tolerate it.

One day when the two were on separate sides of the clan, a

female cautiously began moving toward Sef's father. Sef was filled with apprehension as he saw the female settle herself a few arm lengths from the new alpha male. Sef knew immediately what was about to happen. Anxiously he gestured toward his father, desperate to get his attention without alarming the others.

"Father! Be careful! The female wants you! You must not!" he signed.

"I know, son!" The old simian shifted nervously, pretending not to notice the female's approach. "But what can I do? I dare not refuse! The others will notice!"

"You cannot do this, Father! You are no longer like the other males in your family. You have been . . . 'changed.' . . ."

Ahmahn had warned emphatically that mating with members of the "old family" was forbidden. He had briefly described how he and the other humans had come to be, but had never gone into detail. When Sef's father was "seeded," the genetic/chromosomal codes in his sperms were modified and became specialized . . . fully human. The "seeded" females underwent a different procedure. They were implanted with a single completely human gamete which could only bond with the specialized gametes from modified sperms from 'seeded' males. Their naturally produced eggs remained intact, but could not be penetrated by the males' modified sperm. Both of their reproductive systems were modified so that they could produce only one human offspring.

The female simian, estrus now in full bloom, edged her way closer. Sef's father could no longer ignore her advances. He was, after all, still simian. Now, as alpha male, he no longer needed to suppress his lust. He was now free to act. The female's scent, her body language, tempted him beyond endurance. Finally yielding to the overpowering drive within him, he mounted her.

Sef watched in horror as his father, hair standing up on his shoulders and the back of his neck, screamed his climax.

Stunned and shaken, Sef retreated into the undergrowth, hiding himself from the clan. His mind was reeling from the spectacle he had just witnessed. What must he do now? What would become of him and his father now that this had happened? What would be the result of this un-natural union? The implications were beyond his comprehension.

Some time later, toward evening, his father found him hiding in the undergrowth. (It was acceptable for the alpha to make contact with the human now that he was the leader. For Sef to have initiated contact would have caused the others to rise up against him).

"Father!"Sef signed emphatically. "Why did you do that? You knew it was forbidden."

"My son, fear not. The clan has accepted me fully now. Had I refused to mate, I'm certain another male would have risen up to challenge. Now, so long as I can maintain dominance, we will be safe."

"But Father! What if the female conceives? What will her . . . *your* offspring be? You have been 'changed.' We were warned!"

"Regardless, my son; what is done . . . is done." The old siminan turned away, refusing to look his son in the eye. The unspoken truth was that he actually relished the prestige he received as alpha male.

In the time before his 'change,' he had never been considered worthy or strong enough to compete for high rank within his clan. Time and again he had watched as challenges were brought, as the 'alpha' position was contested. Time and again he sat by quietly, submissively, longingly, watching, but pretending not to watch as the alpha male asserted his dominance over the clan. Always he was fearful to issue a challenge himself.

Even in his primitive, 'pre-changed' mind, he lacked confidence enough to assert himself. Though he never knew it, it was precisely his unobtrusive nature that had qualified him for 'seeding.' As a submissive member of his clan, he was in a perfect position.

He would not draw attention to himself once the 'change' had been made.

After the death of his mate, his feelings of inadequacy again surfaced. He became increasingly convinced that his presence within the human clan could not continue. He felt that he didn't belong.

He longed for the familiarity of his own clan, even if it meant reverting to a subservient role. By simian standards he was beyond his prime. He understood this and was willing to accept it, if only he could return to the comfortable surroundings he so longed for.

But now, as alpha male, all his suppressed desires and longings surfaced. He now enjoyed prestige and influence which he never could have imagined possible.

"We will do what is necessary for our survival," he said as he rose to leave. "As leader, I am now in a better position to protect us. Be patient. All will be well."

Unable to find words sufficient to penetrate his fathers conviction, Sef sat once again in silent frustration, watching as his father sauntered back toward his 'people.'

Days ran together in a blur, unreal, beyond Sef's ability to absorb. He watched helplessly as one and then another female simian came to his father. The alpha male seemed oblivious to his son, totally consumed by the power and privilege of his position.

Days became months. Still Sef watched, distanced physically as well as emotionally from his father. Females kept coming. Father kept obliging.

On a few occasions Sef noticed male simians cautiously approaching his father. But never did any of them challenge. It seemed that his father was somehow able to anticipate their advances and thwart them well before they became a serious threat.

Sef knew that soon the pregnant females would begin giving birth. The thought of that was almost more than he could bear. What would be the result of these 'un-natural' unions? Would they be human? No! That was not possible. The females were not . . . not like his father. Would they be simian. . . .?

Sef tried desperately to push these thoughts from his mind, but the sight of more and more swollen simian bellies wouldn't allow it.

One night Sef decided to make his bed farther away from the clan than usual. Maybe, he thought, the distance between him and them would help him to clear his mind. Restless, unable to sleep, he tossed and turned in his bed. The usual sounds of the night seeming to grow louder, the harder he tried to ignore them.

Suddenly the forest grew deathly silent. At first he thought he had actually dozed off. He lay there, eyes closed, hoping that very quickly he would indeed drift back to sleep.

But, no! There *was* a noise . . . ever so quiet . . . almost inaudible. A low-pitched whirring sound, so quiet that it would have ordinarily gone unnoticed.

Sef sat bolt upright in his bed. He was wide awake! He wasn't dreaming! He *knew* it! What was that sound?! He could see nothing in this moonless darkness. Frozen with fear, he dared not move, lest his movement should cause some unknown horror to pounce upon him.

Out of the corner of his eye he saw movement. His head snapped in that direction. Nothing. But *wait!* Something was there! He sensed, more than saw it. The whirring sound was coming from the same direction.

Carefully, as quietly as he could, he fumbled in the darkness, trying to find the walking stick he always carried with him. He had never had the need to test it as a weapon, but it was all he had. His fingers brushed across his rucksack. It contained only a few pieces of wilting fruit and some edible roots. It was too light to be of any use in a fight.

His fingers found the staff's small end and closed on it like a vice. He sat unmoving, frozen with fear, poised to strike. He heard a faint pop, and was about to raise the staff in defense, when a soft voice came from the direction he was facing.

"Sef. Don't be afraid. We're here to help you." Out of the darkness a human face began to take shape. It was faint, translucent at first, but grew gradually brighter and more substantial as it continued to form, layer upon layer.

Sef raised the staff over his head, then swung it forcefully downward toward the now fully formed image. The image flickered once as the staff passed through it. The staff rebounded with a dull thump as it bounced off some invisible object just below.

"That won't be necessary." The face's lips moved, synchronous with the voice. Sef drew the staff back, holding it with both hands in a defensive posture.

"I am the 'DARKNESS' Ahmahn told you about. Do you remember? Don't be afraid."

"I remember," Sef said, his voice barely a whisper.

"Good. Good. Here. There is someone who wants to talk to you." The face disappeared. Sef thought he saw the face's outline quickly fade in the sudden darkness. Then slowly, just as before, another face began to materialize in its place. The new voice was deeper, penetrating. Sef sat transfixed, unable even to raise his arms. His mouth hung open in astonishment.

"Hello Sef," the image spoke to him. This one's eyes were captivating, gentle, but penetrating.

"I am Evander. Do you remember? Our friend Ahmahn spoke of me." The eyes seemed gentle, reassuring. The tension is Sef's grip began to loosen as he recalled what Ahmahn had said.

"Yes. I remember." The muscles in his neck and back began to relax. He lowered the staff to his lap.

"Good. Good," Evander smiled slightly as he began. "We have been watching you for some time now." His voice was quiet, reassuring. "Tell me. How is your father?"

"How are you here!?" Sef seemed not to hear the question. "Ahmahn is far away from here. He told me of the 'DARKNESS'

. . . of you; how he kept it with him always. You cannot be here and there too, can you?"

"Perhaps I should explain." Evander's image paused momentarily, then continued.

"What Ahmahn did not tell you is that the 'DARKNESS,' as you call it, is but a machine." Evander could see the confusion on Sef's face.

"A machine is only a thing that a man has made, like your rucksack, but much more complex . . ." Sef's head cocked slightly. It was evident he did not know the word.

"This 'machine' has many, many more parts than a rucksack and does a different thing, something your rucksack cannot do. It makes images. Faces . . . but they are not real."

"Not real?" Sef responded. "But I can see you! How can you be not real?"

"Perhaps this will help," said Evander's image. "Your rucksack can carry many things. You can put things in it, and you can take things out of it. This machine can also carry many things. . . . many many more things . . . but these things are very, very small. You cannot touch or hold them."

"How is that possible?" Sef was now fully engrossed. He wanted to understand.

"Maybe it would be best to show you how this machine works, rather than try to explain. Remember how you tried to hit the image with your staff?" Sef nodded.

"Did you see how the staff passed through the image without harming it? That is because the image wasn't a real person. Also, do you remember how the image began very small and grew taller? The parts of the image built one upon the other until the face was complete, much as a rucksack becomes full when you put more things into it."

It was clear that Sef didn't completely understand, but Evander had only gone through the explanation to gain Sef's confidence.

What was more important was that Sef understand why Evander had revealed the presence of the transceiver.

"My friend Sef, at the moment of our meeting you asked me how I was here. Do you recall?" Sef nodded.

"Perhaps it would be best now to ask a different question. *Why* am I here?" Again Sef nodded.

"Recall me asking about your father? That is the reason why I'm here. You see, immediately after you and your father left, Ahmahn's father contacted me. He was very concerned for your well-being. I too became concerned and sent another transce . . . another machine to follow you.

"The machine was to remain hidden so that its presence would not interfere with your father's integration back into his former family. You see, such a situation had never before happened. Once a 'seeded.'. ."changed" individual separated from his or her clan, the individual formed a new family which remained independent and separate from the old family.

"You and your father chose to return to his old family after the death of his mate . . . your mother. That was a great concern for us . . . that is, me, and others like me."

Sef obviously had no idea that there were 'others' but tried to comprehend.

"Do you mean, like the face I saw before you came?"

"Yes. Exactly. We have followed and watched you all this time, and even witnessed how your father came to be the leader."

"It was not father's fault . . ."

"Yes, yes. We know that. It was of no concern to us then, and it still is not."

"Well, then. I will ask *your* question. Why are you here?"

"Our concern—*my* concern—is not what has gone before, but what has now happened. One of the females your father mated with has given birth."

"Then it is as I feared!" Sef's concerns had now become reality. "My father has broken the taboo. He has done that which is forbidden."

"Yes. That is so. But be not concerned for the welfare of your father . . . at least not for now. My concern is for his offspring and how it is possible that all this happened. You see, this has never happened before in all the time that 'seeding' has taken place.

For some reason we don't understand, you're father's 'seeding' didn't work properly. His sperms were able, over time, to overcome the modifications that were imposed on them during the seeding process. They still retained enough gametocytes for 'human' reproduction after you were conceived. That wasn't supposed to happen. When meiososis took place with unmodified simian eggs, they produced viable, though aberrant zygotes.

Sef sat motionless, a blank stare on his face.

Evander had become so absorbed in his attempt at an explanation that he had failed to remember who he was talking to.

"I'm so sorry, Sef. I got caught up in the science and forgot myself. Please let me put it in more simple terms. Your father's new offspring have become an aberration; something other than normal.

We don't know anything about this new species . . . this new 'person.' Will it be like its mother . . . or its father? Or will it be different from either of them? We just don't know. The only explanation we can come up with is that the procedure we used on your father when we learned of his desire to return to his clan was somehow flawed.

We were concerned that his knowledge of us, of our transceiver, might be inadvertently exposed. So we modified his memory. We erased that portion of his memory which had anything to do with our contact with him.

It may be possible that when this procedure was done, we inadvertently modified a portion of his reproductive system."

"Much of what you say, I do not understand. If my parents are not really my parents, then who are my real parents? How is any of this possible?"

"I understand your confusion and frustration. Your friend Ahmahn had the same questions. It took him a long time to understand, but eventually his concerns were answered to his satisfaction. It will be so for you also, if you will but give it time."

"Ahmahn is more than my friend. He is as a brother to me. He trusts you. I will trust you also. For now I will put these concerns aside."

"Thank you, my friend," said Evander. "Let us then focus on the fate of this new offspring."

"Yes. This we must do. I know not what will be the reaction within my father's people . . ." Sef felt uncomfortable with the word. "Within my father's species, as you say. I am sure this is but the first of many. My father mated with every female that approached him. There were many . . . many!"

"It will take time for us to know what will happen. We must be cautious not to disrupt this new situation. We must observe, but not interfere."

"Yes, Evander, my new friend. We must observe but not interfere. For me that will be easy. My presence is already known and accepted. But what about you?"

"I . . . this machine . . . will remain hidden, but will continue to watch, just as has been done for all this time. It is best for you to continue as before. From time to time we will converse, but this machine . . . it's called a 'transceiver' will remain hidden, even from your father. He must not know of its existence, lest he react inappropriately and disrupt his clan."

CHAPTER 48

Over the next few months there were dozens more births. The new infants were accepted and nurtured by their mothers, even though their appearances were different from normal simians. The protruding brow ridge, typical of the simian, remained, together with the protruding jawline. But there the major similarities ended.

This new species was, with the exception of more hair in the genital and chest area and facial features as previously described, very similar to humans. The trunk and arms were slightly longer and more heavily muscled. The legs were also slightly shorter.

Sef and his father were at first alarmed by these differences, but as time went by and life in the clan remained relatively normal, their fears lessened. It appeared that this new species was viewed by the simian clan as normal, though a few of the mothers had difficulty coping with unusual differences in temperament exhibited by their infants.

Sef's father became increasingly distant, unwilling to converse at all regarding his new offspring. He seemed preoccupied with maintaining his status, and seldom initiated conversation with his human son.

The clan itself was increasingly absorbed in caring for the unusual new infants. The young ones grew quickly, and by the age of puberty, had become much more aggressive, unlike 'normal' simians.

Recognizing that they were less like their parents and more like Sef, the new race naturally gravitated toward him, and quickly learned to speak, though their phrasing and idiom were less sophisticated than his.

Conflicts between the new race and their simian relatives became more and more frequent as the young ones matured.

CHAPTER 49

"They *not* stay here now! We know more than them! We bigger than them! We *better* than them! They stay here, we fight more. Better they go."

Chief was adamant. As leader of the new race, he had been chosen to speak on their behalf. He was the least violent of his people, the *Tal* (the name given them by Sef when he taught them his language). Among all of his race, Chief was the only one who could be reasoned with. The others, now close to one hundred in number, were prone to settle disputes violently, unlike their simian parents.

Of late, the conflict between the simians and the Tal had become so intense that even Sef's father saw a need for some sort of resolution.

The old simian had been deposed only a few months ago, but had been allowed to remain with the clan because Sef and Chief had convinced the new simian alpha and others of the Tal that he posed no threat.

Sef rose to his feet and began speaking.

"We come today to find a solution to the challenge our two races face. We cannot continue to fight among ourselves. Too many of our father's people have been harmed, and even killed because we could not find common ground."

"You are *not* one of us!" Chief roared. "You say you are Tal, but you are not! You are Hu-muhn! You side with *them!*" Chief pointed accusingly toward the simians, gathered not far away, obviously agitated.

Sef could see that his father was nearing an outburst of his own in response to the slur from the Tal leader. If that happened, the meeting could quickly come apart.

"You are *not* one of *them!* Our father . . . *your father* is not one of *them!* He speaks to you, but not to them . . . and not to Tal!"

"But what of your mothers?" Sef pleaded. "They have cared for you when you were small. They fed you and sheltered you from the storms. Why do you not care for them now?"

"They are *Sim-un!*" Chief spat disgustedly. "They are not Hu-muhn! *They are not Tal!*"

Sef sensed that the situation was getting out of control, as had been the case so many times before. He needed a way to de-fuse it, to avoid the violence which inevitably happened when Tal tempers flared.

"Let us then think on this for another day. We must not decide too quickly." Aside to Chief, he added. "Please! Go among your people tonight. Persuade them not to give way to anger. We can work together if all of us are willing. You are their leader. They will listen to you."

Sef understood how important it was for Chief to maintain credibility with his people. He knew he was risking a lot asking him to do this thing again. In the past, Chief had cooperated. But now, with tempers high on all sides, nothing could be taken for granted.

Chief looked around at the faces of his people. He could see they were agitated, but they still held their eyes on him, a sure indication that they still looked to him for leadership. He knew from their response that he was still in control. He would not have to save face this time, but even *his* patience was wearing thin.

"This I do today for you, Sef. Tomorrow I do not know." Saying this, Chief turned and walked through the crowd of his followers. En masse, they turned and followed him away.

That night, when Sef was sure he was alone, he took the transceiver from its hiding place and put his hand on it. Immediately the image of Evander began to form. As it was forming, Sef wondered what he would say to explain the predicament he faced.

"Hello, my friend Sef." Evander said, even before his image was complete. "How did things fare with your meeting?"

"Little, if anything has changed since last we spoke. More and more I am convinced that the Tal are an aberration I cannot influence."

"It would appear so," Evander began. "There is little I can offer in the way of advice, except that we must let events unfold as they will."

"I must agree. Nothing I have said or done has changed events. There seems to be no common ground between the two races. I think my father's clan would cooperate, but the Tal are unwilling to compromise. It saddens me beyond description to think we cannot get beyond this impasse."

"It appears so, my friend. The Tal are, after all, an aberration, both physically *and* psychologically. How could we have known they would be the way they are?"

"But you are 'seeders'!" Sef's words betrayed his frustration. "You have spread humanity across countless worlds! How could you not have anticipated this?"

"It is true. The human race has spread across the universe from the beginning of time. Many cultures have flourished. Many more have not. Yet we continue our mission, knowing that it is the destiny of humankind to grow, to progress. Each new world holds within it that potential. But each of us must decide our own destiny. Some of us choose poorly."

"Yes. I understand. Even my father, who is human in every way but physical, chose poorly when we joined his clan so long ago. Even today we must live with the consequences of his actions."

Sef paused, reflecting on that fateful day, many years in the past.

"Tomorrow we meet again. Chief has committed to speak with his people. Maybe he will find a solution."

"Let us hope so. Until then, rest well my friend. Contact me again when you feel it appropriate."

CHAPTER 50

The day dawned grey and dismal. The monsoon season had begin. The air was heavy with humidity, smelling musty, full of decay.

Sef had risen before the dawn, unable to sleep, and returned to the large clearing, the site of yesterday's talks. He sat down, knees pulled up to his chin. His arms encircled his bare legs. His head hung low.

His thoughts were jumbled, in disarray, filled to overflowing with worry. He had become an unwilling mediator, the fragile link between two incompatible cultures. How could the two races coexist? What could he possibly do to facilitate a seemingly unreachable compromise?

What of his father? How could he translate the expectations of the Tal in a way that would convince the simians that indeed there was hope for coexistence? More importantly, how could Sef convince the Tal to live in harmony with each other, let alone with the simians? They fought among themselves almost continuously.

For years he had struggled with this unwieldy challenge. From the birth of the first of his father's seed until this day he had struggled in vain to rectify the wrong his father had committed, while his father continued, oblivious to anything other than his own gratification.

Now, as Tal and Simian began to gather, Sef knew that this

would be the last opportunity. Either there would be reconciliation or there would be strife.

Chief was the first to emerge from the shadows. He carried with him a long wooden staff, the symbol of his leadership. Following close behind, others of the Tal came into view. Each of them had shorter sticks, as big around as Sef's arm, which they used like canes, thumping the ground ominously as they approached and came to a halt a few yards into the clearing.

At the other side of the clearing simians began to assemble, reluctant to move into the open. At the far end of their ranks, Sef's father emerged, his lame arm dangling at his side as he inched his way forward, narrowing the gap between himself and his human son.

"We have come as you wished, my son," he signed with his good hand. "We are prepared to accept your decision, regardless of what it may be. We desire peace with our Tal brothers. We bare no animosity toward them and will do what is necessary to coexist."

"What does this old one say?" Chief said in a loud voice.

"Our father is here to make peace with the Tal," Sef said, deliberately reminding that the old simian was the father of them all.

"He and his people are prepared to . . ."

"We care nothing for the words of a Sim-un! They are not Tal. They are stupid! They do not speak! They do not even *walk!*" A murmur began among the Tal. It grew louder as Chief continued to speak.

"And *you!*" Chief pointed his staff at Sef menacingly. "You are hu-muhn. Not Tal. You speak for the sim-un, but *not* for Tal!"

The crowd behind him raised their voices, matching and surpassing his rant. They began stamping their clubs against the ground. Across the clearing the simians began shuffling nervously. Sef's father began backing up, signing frantically.

"What have we done?! They grow angry and we have done nothing!"

"Be calm, father!" Sef turned toward the Tal, raising his hands, trying to calm the rising chaos.

"You speak *no more!*" Chief yelled before Sef could speak. He raised his staff, shaking it defiantly as he continued.

"You speak always, but *do nothing!*" His defiance encouraged the others to move forward, thumping their clubs and raising their voices.

"Now *we speak no more!* Now we *do!*"

With those words he swung his staff around once, pivoting at the center of its circular path, adding momentum. With a loud crack it made contact with Sef's head. His skull exploded on impact. As the staff continued its arc, what remained of the head was severed, leaving Sef's body to fall to the ground.

Roaring in unison, the Tal charged forward, trampling the lifeless form under foot as they charged toward the simians.

Awestruck, the clan scattered, screaming in panic. The Tal fell upon the stragglers in wild rage, swinging their clubs with abandon. Thuds and cracks were accompanied by stifled screams and wild roars as the mayhem advanced. The few who managed to escape fled into the trees. Many of them fell to their doom, either killed by the fall or beaten to death by the advancing Tal.

Sef's father stood frozen, watching in stunned silence as his clan fled before the wild horde. Slowly he turned to gaze in horror at his slain human son's body. Where the head should have been, a thick browning pool melted slowly into the ground. Flies immediately began gathering for the feast. A few feet beyond, standing over the lifeless form, Chief glared at the old simian.

"Now, *Father!*" he spat. "You will join him and the others of *your kind!*"

CHAPTER 51

The battle, if you could call it that, hadn't lasted more than a few minutes. By the time Chief had finished with his simian father, the sounds of the slaughter were beginning to fade as it moved father away from the clearing.

As the Tal began their charge across the clearing, most of the simians turned and fled in panic. The few who stood their ground were quickly knocked down.

Many fled into the trees where they were momentarily safe. A few climbed high into the thin branches. Some of them fell when the branches snapped under their weight. The few who survived the fall were quickly pounced upon and died quickly.

But a few held on. The Tal tried following into the heights. But, owing to their size and lack of dexterity they soon gave up and descended to the ground. Those who remained on the ground fought bravely unarmed, but were no match for the wild raving Tal who smashed everything in their path. During the frenzy even a few Tal fell under the onslaught of their brethren.

By the time the sun broke the horizon, the slaughter was over. A few survivors in the trees continued clinging precariously to their perches, afraid to descend, lest they be discovered.

Below them, the Tal milled about aimlessly, waiting for their leader to arrive and tell them what to do next.

Chief finally arrived, carrying his staff in one hand, and a battered head in another. Triumphantly he tossed the head onto the ground in front of him for all to see.

"We are Tal! We are *strong!* This place is *ours* now. We do as we please. There are none to stop us! We will . . ."

A crack of thunder interrupted him in mid-sentence. Within moments rain began to pour, soaking everything. Very quickly he and the others lost interest in anything other than seeking shelter from the torrent.

CHAPTER 52

A full day had gone by without the transceiver being approached. Like all other units earmarked for use with 'seeded' communities, it had been programmed to be 'proximity sensitive,' environmentally aware, able to sense when any life form approached. Depending upon the type of life form, the unit was programmed to respond appropriately. In the case of the 'Sef colony' it was programmed to report back to the control center on a twenty-four-hour time schedule, unless, of course, Sef initiated contact himself.

Perhaps the 'subject' had misplaced the unit. That had happened on many occasions with other subjects. The on-duty technician pondered this possibility as she sat at her station and began reviewing reports from the six previous shifts. It was part of established protocol to begin the review process, should the 'twenty-four-hour rule' be violated. From what she gleaned from the most recent report, perhaps negotiations were still in process, and the subject had deliberately delayed making contact.

At the beginning of this shift, her supervisor had left instructions to do high resolution scans in the vicinity of the transceiver in question once that portion of the planet was well into its dark cycle. Though the unit was capable of high resolution masking, it was decided to wait until dark, rather than risk the remote possibility of being detected during daylight hours.

The other units distributed around the planet had all reported the usual activity and had gone dormant after reporting in. The remainder were assigned to the 'exploratory section.' Since they lacked holographic capabilities, they were stationed permanently in high geosynchronous orbit where they conducted narrow-swath infra-red tracking over the 'seeded' colonies.

As she was reading through the reports, one of the 'geosyncs' on her board alarmed. When she pulled it up on her screen she noticed it had just completed a scan of the area where the transceiver in question was located.

Upon comparison of the previous scan data she noticed that the number of 'hot spots' had decreased markedly, thus triggering the alarm.

Quickly she scrolled through her check list for instructions. There was a highlighted note attached to this particular unit, instructing that the section head should be immediately notified upon detection of any unusual data.

"*Section Head*?!" The technician said under her breath.

"What's that, Judy? Did you same something?" Her co-worker in the adjacent cubicle said, surprised.

"Yes! One of my 'geosyncs' has a priority note attached. I'm supposed to call the Section Head! That's a jump way up the ladder . . . clear out of our division! That's clear up into Command Level.

"Holy crap, girl! What's the "geosync' say? You sure it's not just a glitch?"

"No! It's for real all right! Beides, if it was just a glitch, there wouldn't be a high priority note attached . . . would there!?"

"I guess not! Tie me in and I'll start I.R. comparisons while you call upstairs."

"Thanks. I'm not sure I know how to jump that far up the ladder."

"Click on the highlighted note. It should bring up another screen with instructions."

"Okay. Here goes." Judy clicked the note. But instead of a new screen popping up, a 'flag' appeared with this text: 'Commander

Evander's office. Please hold for connection.' The message blinked several times, then a screen with a face appeared.

"Evander here. Who's calling, please?"

"Sergeant Judy Humes, sir. I have a note to contact you about . . ."

"Thank you. I'll be there in a few. Evander out." The screen reverted to 'geosync' mode. Surprised at the brevity of the conversation, Judy stood and peered over the top of her cubicle.

"Wow! This must be something hot! Anything yet?" she asked.

"Just pulled up the IR scans from a few hours ago. Data comparisons should be . . ."

The office door swung open and in strode a tall thin, grey-haired man wearing antique 'granny glasses.' He was carrying a book, his finger stuck between pages to mark his place. He removed the glasses quickly as he approached the cubicles.

"Hello, ladies." He offered a quick smile, which disappeared as he drew close and peered into the screen.

"Sir. IR scans revealed an anomaly a few minutes ago. Looks like a drop in 'hot spots.' I'm pulling up the last few for comparison."

Both images popped up simultaneously. Each image showed what would be expected, a dark grey background (ground surface), with areas of varying lighter patches (foliage and other objects which gave off heat signatures of varying temperatures). In the center of each image there was a brighter patch. The bright patch in the newer image was markedly more pronounced than that of the older.

"Zoom in on those, please." Evander said as he leaned closer.

The close-up of the older scan showed numerous bright specks, clustered together on one side of a darker area. On the far side of that area numerous other bright specks could be seen. There were also two 'hot spots' in the center.

The most recent of the two images appeared to show both groups of specks converging. Many of the specks appeared to be blurred.

"Do you have action feeds for these scans?"

"No sir. Protocol called for single frames on thirty-second intervals. These are the most recent we have. I can pull up point-count data, if that would help, sir."

"Let's do that, Sergeant. Can you do data streaming simultaneously?"

"Yes, sir. It's coming up now, sir." Judy stepped to the side so Evander to come closer.

The data stream showed a point count for all heat signatures which registered 20 percent or higher above ambient temperature. In the older data the number held at 284 'hot spots.' The newer data showed fluctuation, suggesting that some of the 'hot spots' were cooling.

"This doesn't look good, sir. What do you want us to do now?"

The last time Sef and he had spoken, Evander had been concerned that the following day's negotiations might reach an impasse. In his time as a 'seeder' he had witnessed countless scenarios where clashes between cultures had resulted in conflict. But in those situations each culture had been human.

Here, the situation was unlike any other. Neither side was human. One side was composed of high-order simians, while the other was. . . . He wasn't sure *what* to call the other. Half human? Part simian?

He had studied and observed social groups on hundreds of planets. Primate societies were generally the most advanced. Like all 'communal' types, simians had learned to adapt to all but the most extreme environmental or cultural changes. Individual survival had become directly dependent on group dynamics. 'Going along to get along' might be the best way to describe it.

The 'great apes' in particular had been able to minimize internal conflict with little or no observable harmful effects. The individuals benefited by cooperation rather than competition. Of course competition existed, but it was always kept in check by individuals finding their place within the social order.

"Let's bring Sef's transceiver on line and see if it's recorded any unusual activity since the last meeting."

Yes, sir." Judy stepped over to her console and activated the transceiver. "Shall I unmask it, sir?"

"Not just yet. Let's see what the unit has recorded first."

The tech keyed in a few commands and waited for confirmation the unit was responding properly.

"Nothing, sir. I show no 'hot spots' in the vicinity. Activating flight controls now. Still masked, sir."

"Very well. Let's ascend to just above tree top level and start a visual scan."

Down on the surface it was unusually quiet. A light haze shown through the canopy. Droplets of water could be seen dripping from the foliage.

"Monsoonal rain, sir. Must have just stopped in the last few minutes."

The transceiver hovered just above the tallest trees, then began a slow 360-degree rotation, scanning the jungle floor below.

"Nothing here, sir. Just a few empty nests close to the ground. Looks like the colony's already up and begun their day."

Evander sat his book on a nearby table, then pulled his glasses from his pocket and put them on slowly, peering more closely at the screen.

"Strange. We should see some movement, even at this low elevation. Switch back to IR again and do another scan."

"Still nothing sir. We're scanning a 200-foot perimeter and still no hot spots."

"Okay. let's go up another hundred feet or so and see what we can see."

The transceiver rose, then went to 'station keeping' (hover mode), and began another circular sweep.

"There, sir . . . at about three o'clock. I'm picking up some faint IR returns. Too weak to be bio-mass, though. There's a lot of them."

"Let's move closer. Switch back to visual. Masking still activated, please."

Evander inched closer, peering over the sergeant's shoulder.

"Looks like a clearing, sir."

"Mmm." Evander's mind was filled with dread. He tried to steel himself for what he knew was coming. He had seen this before, long ago on a different planet. The details would be different, but the result would almost certainly be the same.

The transceiver homed in on the weak signals. As its camera cleared the perimeter, what it recorded below was a scene of unspeakable horror. There in the center of the clearing lay two bodies, one the headless corpse of a man, the other a misshapen mass of disjointed limbs and matted hair. The body was so badly beaten as to hardly resemble the simian it once had been.

At the edge of the clearing other bodies could be seen. None of them was as badly mangled as the first two, who had received 'special' treatment.

Evander stepped back, sighing, folded his arms across his chest and lowered his head.

"That's Sef and his father," he said, more to himself than to anyone else.

The room was quiet, the two technicians staring numbly at their screens. Evander stood quietly, eyes closed.

"Sir, the others all appear to be simian." Judy began hesitantly. "They must have been killed very early this morning. That explains why the heat signatures were so faint . . . that, plus the rain"

"Yes . . . yes . . . I'm sure you're right." Evander removed his glasses and swiped his hand across his forehead, just once.

"Let's get a body count. Be sure this is all recorded." Evander spoke quietly, deliberately, as he looked around the room for a chair. Seeing none, he leaned against a cubicle wall, watching silently as the tech began doing as she was instructed.

The transceiver moved across the clearing and then down into the trees, both camera and IR scanner panning slowly back and forth.

After a few long minutes the count was complete.

"Sir, I count 128 bodies. 13 of them are Tal infants. I also count 12 adult Tal. Their bodies are dispersed further out from the . . . the scene . . ."

"Why would they kill their own?" The other tech asked.

Evander stood erect, clasping his hands behind his back, head lowered in thought.

"The Tal are an aberration. They lack the reasoning power of humans, they lack any semblance of self restraint."

He turned slowly and added as he walked back toward the door: "There is much we need to evaluate before we can know why all this happened. Have the transceiver collect tissue samples from the 'seeded' simian body there in the center of the clearing, as well as from one each male and female Tal body. Then recall the transceiver to the nearest LINK and have it transported here. Notify me when the samples have reached our lab. If I'm needed, you can contact me in my private quarters."

With that, he left, closing the door quietly behind him.

CHAPTER 53

For some time after the slaughter, the Tal reveled in their perceived victory and independence. But as the revelry wore off, a stark realization began sinking in. They realized just how dependent they had been on their simian families.

The Tal were, after all, more physically human than they were simian. They were much larger in height as well as body weight. They were adapted for ground dwelling and upright locomotion. The fruits and nuts which were their regular diet grew high up in the trees. Their simian kin could easily climb to those heights, where they retrieved the bounty and brought it down to the new species. But now, with their simian cousins gone, they began scavenging where and when they could for the meager vegetable matter they could find. With insubstantial fare, the Tal were forced to seek other means of sustenance.

Because they really had no choice, the Tal became primarily meat-eaters. Their prey animals quickly adapted to Tal predation and learned how to avoid them. Consequently, the Tal were forced to leave the familiarity of their home ranges and follow the herds as they migrated. They were in direct competition with other carnivores who also followed the migrations.

Unknown to them, as they followed the migrations northward, they were following almost literally in the footsteps of Ahmahn and his clan.

SEA OF MARMARA

CHAPTER 54

Finally the weather was about to break. He could feel it. Moving his face out from beneath the covers, he sniffed the chill morning air. It was still very cold, but today it smelled different. The cold bite was still there, but it wasn't as sharp.

Slowly and quietly Ahmahn slipped out from under the covers, careful not to awaken Mahrohm, his new mate. He rose to his hands and knees, feeling along the dirt floor, making his way toward the entrance in the darkness.

The night before, he had laid his heavy parka next to the pile of furs that was his bed. But in the excitement before they slept, he had kicked it out of the way. Now he had to fumble around nearly naked, clad only in a light deer hide loincloth.

"She is so young; younger than . . ." he thought to himself as his fingers found the heavy parka and the rest of his clothing. He had built the shelter close to the ground, presenting the smallest possible profile to the wind. It was much too short for him to stand upright, so he drug his clothing along beside him as he crawled, feeling his way toward the entrance. There he found his heavy, fur-lined boots, right where he had left them. He stood up carefully, bending at the waist, trying to keep his balance.

Careful though he was, his head bumped the ceiling, pulling out a few hairs in the process. The sudden tweak of pain sent a shiver down his bare back. He teetered precariously on one foot and then the other, guiding his loose-fitting trousers into position, securing them around his waist. Then, bending carefully, he pulled a tunic-like upper garment over his head. It was made from a plain, flat piece of hide with a slit cut in the center for his head. The boots were last. They weren't boots in the real sense, but fur-covered hides which had been molded and stitched together with sinew to conform loosely to the shape of his feet. He wrapped thin strips of hide loosely around each one.

It was too cumbersome tying them properly in the darkness, so he pushed the animal hide door aside, then stepped carefully through the opening.

Slipping quietly out of the shelter, he stood up and immediately began to shiver. Quickly, he put the parka on and pulled it close around him, tying it closed with the coarse braided belt *she* had made for him.

"*She* . . ." A cloud of mist assaulted his face as he exhaled, remembering. The mist quickly dissipated in the wind, but the memory of his first mate Nera began flooding in. The day she had given him the belt, that was the day she had told him she was with child.Then . . . the day she was taken from him.

Intense grief swelled up inside him. This time the tears that came weren't caused by the cold. Though it had been long ago, the memory seemed fresh, like it had happened only yesterday.

He tried to think of other things. His thoughts turned to his father and mother, now both gone.

"Has it been so long?" he thought. He remembered . . . the scent of his mother's breast as he suckled, her warm secure carresses as he dozed, held close in her embrace; the encouraging grunts and gestures his father gave when he had first attempted to walk upright. . . . the smell of the smoke from his father's funeral pyre . . . the feel of his brother's hand on his shoulder.

Once again he tried to force those painful memories back, back into the recesses of his consciousness. "I will remember, but I will not mourn," he told himself, all the while knowing it wasn't true. Deliberately he brought his thoughts back to the present.

"Today it will be best to build the fire outside," he thought. "The wind is not as strong this morning."

He reached back for the clumps of tinder he had piled just inside the door the previous night. Frost clung to the brush that still remained above the snow. It was all too wet to use as kindling. Ahmahn somehow knew this and was prepared, though he had never experienced snow before in his life.

"Strange," he thought. "How Evander knows what things to teach me, even before the knowledge is needed."

The morning was quiet, except for the rustling pine needles high above, where the wind still blew steadily. Down lower, what few trees that hadn't been smothered by the snow, rattled helplessly as the wind forced its way down through the gangly bows.

Today the wind would not increase with the coming of the sun, as it had done for the past several days. He knew this would be so. He couldn't explain how he knew. The feeling was just there. It just seemed to be a part of him. He assumed it was because he had lived so long that he had just become accustomed to the changes in the weather. Ahmahn was twenty years old.

INTERLUDE

The early years of his life, Ahmahn was the center of his parents' lives. Though they had copulated frequently, they never conceived another child.

Though each of his parents had been "seeded," neither of them had been physically altered in any way which did not contribute directly to caring for the first of this new race. The Seeders could just as easily have placed a pregnant human female and an accompanying male here on this world, and then let them and their offspring fend for themselves in what would very quickly become an unfamiliar and unfriendly environment. The new race of humans would very quickly fall into competition with other indigenous species. Conflict would be inevitable. Better to have the "seedlings" grow up as part of the environment, rather than be in conflict with it.

The higher order primates from whom Ahmahn's parents were chosen, possessed significantly advanced intellectual capability in comparison to others of similar species. Additionally, each of the individuals selected for "seeding" had been under observation for some time prior to being selected. Each of those selected were near the bottom of their group's social hierarchy. Because no physiological modifications had been made to them, they didn't stand out in any obvious way. As was common among "seeded" individuals, their inevitable reaction to their new self-awareness frequently exhibited itself in ways that might have disrupted the tranquillity of the family. But, being so low on the social ladder, they were less conspicuous, less likely to draw attention to themselves.

Because they were unable to communicate verbally, the simian "parents" were forced to use their implanted intellectual capabilities to devise other ways to communicate with their human son. The most obvious of those was the development of sign language.

Despite his parents' inability to speak, the three of them learned how to communicate complex ideas between each other. Ahmahn, for his part, was able to define objects or intentions verbally very quickly. His parents were quick to catch on. They learned to demonstrate through what little vocalizations they possessed as well as through gestures, their understanding of what he was communicating.

As any parents would do, they taught him the things he needed to know to survive. More importantly, they showed him why his survival was so important . . . that he was the first of a new race, and he must survive in order to perpetuate this race.

As Ahmahn grew, his curiosity as well as his physical abilities became a concern for his parents. He needed to explore his world, to learn things for himself. His parents found it increasingly difficult to control him. Without constant supervision, he was prone to wander off, exploring some new thing or new sound. His father was unsure how to handle the situation. Should they let the child explore unimpeded and risk the chance of being found out by their former "family"? Or should they restrain him? He knew that to remain as they were would only increase the chances of being caught. Out numbered, they would most certainly be driven away, or worse. He reasoned that it would be in their best long term interest to leave the familiar security they had enjoyed, and venture out on their own.

The father's decisions had been instrumental in helping his human son to thrive. Now, years after his death his teachings and his patience were paying off.

CHAPTER 55

Their trek up into the northern highlands had taken many moon cycles. The moon was now only a thin crescent, occasionally peaking through the passing clouds in the dim morning light.

Ahmahn was sitting on one of stones arranged in a wide circle around a pile of now-wet kindling which had been placed there the night before. As he bent to tighten the fur-covered hides around his shins, he heard a faint stirring coming from one of the other shelters.

"The others awake," he said to himself as he pulled the 'fire stones' from the special pouch inside his parka. Almost reverently, he placed them on the ground next to the fire pit. Once again his memories began to surface . . . "The fire stones."

He tore a fist-full of dry tinder from the bundle he had brought with him and squeezed it into a small, tight ball. He placed it carefully under the kindling, where it expanded slightly and settled into place. Taking a fire stone in each hand, he brought them close to the tinder and struck them together. A spark jumped from them toward the tinder, but went out immediately. He bent closer, using his body to block the breeze. After several more attempts, a thin wisp of smoke began to curl up from within the tinder. Then, with the faintest of pops, it ignited.

The kindling above the small flame began to sizzle and pop. The tinder burned quickly and soon was soon . Carefully, Amon placed more tinder close to the flame. It caught quickly, this time producing a flame hot enough to ignite the kindling. Amon continued feeding the flame, gradually adding larger and larger sticks until the fire was self-sustaining.

He wanted to talk to Evander again. Evander had told him about the snow and had warned him to collect kindling and tinder before the first snowfall. Ahmahn had no idea what any of this meant, but he trusted Evander and did as he was told. Evander had given him two small stones. One was thin and shiny and fit comfortably in his hand. The other was round and rough, with many sharp edges. Evander had called one of the stones "Iron" and the other "Flint." He had instructed Ahmahn on how to hold the stones and strike them together close to the tinder.

He was terrified the first time Evander showed him how to make fire. Evander had explained to him how he could control the small flame, or extinguish it if necessary. Evander had then told him about another stone called "Pyrite" which he could use if he lost the "Iron" stone. Ahmahn had seen them both before in their natural environment, but had no idea that, when struck together, they would produce fire. When he showed them to the others of the clan, they had marvelled and been afraid. He offered to let the others try to make fire, but they had all shied away, fearful to even touch the stones. Among themselves, they began to call him "the fire maker."

Ahmahn had so many questions, and no one else he could talk to about them. Evander had always been kind, quiet, understanding, like his father. Though he had never exchanged so much as a single word with his father, they had developed such a close bond that spoken words seemed almost superfluous. He and Evander were beginning to develop a very similar relationship.

The two of them had been in contact many times in the past. At their first meeting, Evander had emphasized that no one in the clan should be told about their meetings. When asked why, he had said that the others wouldn't understand. Ahmahn had not understood why, but had agreed to keep the meetings a secret. Evander had said that as time went by, he would better understand why this was necessary.

The breeze was cold against his cheek. A flicker of hair brushed his eyelash causing more cold tears to form in the corners of his eyes. They quickly found their way down his cheeks and through his bushy moustache, sending shivers as they went. They were salty to the taste. His stomach growled, reminding him that he was hungry.

As he bent close to tend the fire, he remembered how he had gotten this new set of fire stones. A wisp of wind found its way through his thick fur collar. It slithered around the base of his neck and then down between his shoulder blades. He shuddered as the haunting memory returned.

CHAPTER 56

They had been mated now for almost a year. She had come to him one morning just as the sun was coming up. He was sitting at the edge of a small, slow moving stream near their camp. The clan had been following the stream northward now for several days. It had become his habit to be the first to rise in the mornings and go there. It was at these quiet times, when there were no distractions, when he contemplated the things which needed be done for the days ahead.

It had been light enough to see for well over an hour, but no direct sunlight had as yet found its way to the jungle floor. A waist-high, grey haze hovered a few inches above the ground. Now, as thin rays of sunlight found their way through the low-hanging tangle of vines, they stabbed through the haze, turning it a golden orange.

Not far overhead, a bird fluttered and chirped. Ahmahn was lost in his thoughts, paying little attention to it and the other familiar sounds of the morning.

Perhaps they would make the turn to the East soon. Evander had taught him about maps and how they related to his world. He had pointed to a place on the map and said that that was where Ahmahn and his small clan were located. He then pointed to another place on the map and said that they would turn there and go in a direction Evander had called 'East,' the place where the sun came up in the morning. It was hard for him to understand how such a small distance on a piece of paper could represent such a great distance in the real world.

He was distracted from his thoughts as he heard another noise, very faint, but nearby. He didn't move, but sat quietly, muscles tensed, listening. Off to his right he heard it again, a muffled, crumpling sound, followed by another just like it, and then another.

He relaxed, recognizing it as the sound of footsteps. No effort was being made to hide the sound. There was no hesitation in the movement. He could sense this in the familiar rhythmic pattern of the sounds.

"Mahrom," he said without looking in her direction. The sound stopped.

"Ahmahn," came the soft reply. Her voice was husky, still thick with sleep. Quietly, but delicately, like females do, she moved past him and knelt at the waters edge. She glanced quickly in his direction, avoiding eye contact, then looked down into the shallow, trickling stream. Dipping a cupped hand into the water, she brought it up to her lips and sipped. Still without making eye contact, she let the remainder dribble through her fingers.

Slowly, deliberately, she arose and turned back toward her mate. Eyes lowered, she walked the few steps toward him. She stopped and stood quietly, looking down at him. He averted his gaze, pretending not to notice the sensuousness in her movements.

She hesitated momentarily, as a trace of uncertainty crossed her mind. For long she had thought of this moment. How long had she watched him from a distance, admired the certainty of his step, the gentle forcefulness of his voice? From the time they were children she had longed to be close to him. But he had always remained somehow, distant; reluctant to engage, even in the simple, mundane tasks of everyday life.

But now it was different. She had reached estrus. She was now ready to choose a mate. She had been approached several times by prospective suitors, but they held no interest for her. These were typical young males, always in competition with each other, but never exhibiting any qualities which would set any of them apart.

Ahmahn, on the other hand, never seemed to engage in such competition. Instead, he used persuasion and force of personality to achieve what he wanted. He wasn't loud or obnoxious. He was quiet and attentive. It was comforting to have him close by. Mahrom stood quietly, not moving, waiting.

In a quick blaze of pictures, Ahmahn's memory flew through that time before. When it had happened.

His first mate had been killed when the rocks they were crossing began to tremble and shake violently. They were caught in an earthquake. She was caught between two huge boulders. The child she was still carrying inside her was immediately crushed as it was forced out through the rip in the side of her body. She died with a surprised look on her face, like she didn't understand what had happened.

Just a second ago they had been walking happily side by side along the edge of the rockfall; she with a big rucksack thrown over her shoulder, counterbalancing her swollen belly; he, with one hand helping her keep her balance, and the other holding onto the staff being held for him by his brother.

A deep, concussive jolt hit everyone and everything at once. Ahmahn was momentarily disoriented, staggering. It was then that the earth slid away under him. It fell down and away, taking his feet backwards, out from under him. Then it slammed up again, hitting him full in the face. His mate, who was there in his hand one moment, was no longer there. In her place, the jagged edge of a freshly cracked boulder thrust violently upward, gashing his cheek and tossing him aside.

All around him stones and boulders of all sizes jostled about, grinding and splintering in a deafening cacophony. It was impossible for him to stand erect. It was all he could do to avoid being crushed or pinned. His hands, forearms and bare shins were cut and bleeding as the gritty stone gyrated beneath them. All he could do was try to stay alive. And then he heard the scream.

He looked toward the sound of her voice. His hair blew into his face, blocking his view. He reached to brush it aside. Blood on his fingers made the hair stick to his forehead. Something didn't feel right. His head felt . . . wrong. He had a hard time focusing. He wasn't sure where the scream had come from. He looked around frantically.

There, not six feet away, Nera, his mate, lay wedged grotesquely on her right side. Her right arm was pinned under her body. The elbow protruded out at an odd angle. Her other arm caressed a steaming mass that extruded from under her clothing. Both her legs were pinned under the rubble, except her left foot, which wasn't where it should be.

There was blood on the jagged edge of the boulder which held her. It was his. Or was it hers? There was lots of it. His head was throbbing. His cheek burned. Not from the blood. It was the tears.

Distant, as a memory from the past, he thought he heard the scream again, this time not so loud. But her mouth wasn't moving. Her eyes were staring right through him. She was fading. He couldn't see her clearly. It was getting dark; but it was too early in the day. As the last of the light gave out he heard the distant scream one last time.

Some time later, he didn't know how long, he awoke to frantic jolting and shaking. When he opened his eyes, his brother's face came into blurry focus. His long hair and matted beard were covered in mud, interlaced with bits of dried leaves and pine needles. One of his eyes was swollen shut and was caked in clotted blood. His mouth was wide open, like he was yelling; but Ahmahn couldn't understand what he was saying. For a moment, all he could hear was a high-pitched squeal. Gradually the squeal began to subside.

His brother's voice began to resolve. At first it sounded like a hiss . . . then a buzz. Ahmahn shook his head. He could feel water or something coming out of his ears.

"Go! Go now!" His brother was pulling on his arm, trying to get him to stand up. "Come! We must go now!"

The ground wasn't moving as much now. Mostly it just shivered violently, like a man lying wet and naked in a snow drift.

He remembered his mate. He looked around groggily but could see her nowhere. He was being dragged roughly down the side of a huge flat stone which protruded at a steep angle out of the ground. The stone was new to the surface, having just been thrust up by the shifting fault line a thousand feet below the earth's surface.

"Nera! Where is Nera? I must . . ."

"She is no more!" said his brother Broc, as he continued pulling Ahmahn down the steep slope. The last he remembered before he lost consciousness, was bending down, trying to grasp the strange stone in his un-cooperating fingers.

CHAPTER 57

The sun was coming up now. He could feel its warmth on his cheek. It was soothing, not like the biting cold that had greeted him for so many days of late. A welcome change. He took a deep, calming breath and looked up at his new mate. A thin smile came upon him as he gazed at her smiling face. No words passed between them.

He wrapped the fire stones back in their protective hide strip, then thrust them and his hands deep into his pockets. Mahrohm sat down beside him, snuggled close and slid one hand into his pocket. He caressed her small hand in his own and squeezed it gently. Her mere presence was enough to sooth him, to bring him back to reality.

Before him in the gray dawn, the direction they had come hung in bleak clarity. He gazed into that now-familiar distance, a seemingly unending line of steep, jagged peaks, flanked on the left by greenery forming a nearly impenetrable barrier that stretched for miles back into the distance. Hiding beyond that, a narrow strip of land, lush and inviting, meandered along the base of the huge escarpment. Bows from myriad trees dipped low, shaded a narrow ribbon of water only a few yards wide. A seeming paradise, beckoning him, calling him back to happier times. There. Only a few weeks sojourn and it would again be his for the taking.

"No!" he thought to himself. "My thoughts must be of what lies ahead, not on what has gone before. Evander said it would be like this. I would miss the old places, the old ways . . ." His memories blurred, bringing him back to the present.

To the west of the mountain range, for as far as the eye could see, stretched a seemingly endless rolling gray desert. It was into this barren vastness that many of his brethren had wandered, never to be seen again.

Ahead of them to the north, what were once far-ranging forests, had in this age withered to scrub brush and spindly green plants barely clinging to life on the mile-thick tundra. Still farther north, extending clear to the pole, a gigantic mantle of snow and ice covered everything. It formed a barrier that would not be penetrated for generations to come.

Their trek had been difficult. It had strained each of them close to their breaking points, some of them beyond. A few families had chosen to take their chances in the desert rather than risk crossing the vast rock falls that separated forests from the high tundra. A few families, overwhelmed by the difficulties which they knew awaited them, had chosen to reverse course, to return to the familiarity of the homelands they had left behind.

As the sun rose, so did the clan. As was their custom, they gathered around the fire pit, each greeting Ahmahn and Mahrom as they arrived. Cooking pots were brought out and the days first meal was prepared.

Broc was the first to bring up the subject that was on everyone's mind.

"Ahmahn, will this be the day we turn to the east? You said it would be soon."

"I have wondered the same thing, my brother. Our travels have become more difficult by the day. We still await the return of our scouts from the north." (He remembered the instructions Evander had given him: "Go north until you can go no more. You will know when it is the right time.")

Nahm was next to speak. "We have done as you say for all this time. We have travelled far. We have seen much hardship. Some of us have not survived," he blurted out, then immediately regretted what he had said. He knew Ahmahn still suffered the loss of his first mate. He knew everyone in the clan had suffered when the earthquake came . . . but Ahmahn most of all.

"I am sorry, my brother. I should not have . . ."

"Be not concerned, my friend." Ahmahn forced an uneasy smile as he spoke. "She was not the first. There was Sef's mother. There were those who chose to risk the desert rather than continue with us to the north. Some have even returned to their homelands. We know nothing of their fates. Even Sef, who we all know would rather have stayed with us, chose to go with his father."

"We know that it is not always your desire to continue." Broc knew that Ahmahn consulted with Evander frequently, but had sworn not to reveal the existence of the 'darkness' to the others.

"Might it not be of benefit to send scouts to the east and west, like those we have sent before us to the north? We could then remain here until they return, informing us of what challenges lie before us."

Nahm took Broc's words as a cue.

"Yes. Let us remain encamped here for a few more days, until the scouts return."

Ahmahn realized that the clan was growing tired and impatient from their continuous exertions. He weighed Evander's instructions against the desires of his friends. He knew that Evander had faith in his ability to make good decisions. However, it was becoming evident that the clan might begin loosing faith in him, should he insist that they continue immediately.

"This is wisdom, my brothers. I thank you for your advise. We will do as you say, then. We will not send replacements northward. After a day, those who are already out will know to return. Instead, we will begin scouting to the east and west. We will do so for two days in each direction, and then consider what new information they bring to us."

There then arose a discernible easing of tension in the conversation. Broc and Nahm both seemed satisfied with the decision and redirected their conversations to others who were gathered around the cook fires.

Mahrohm snuggled closer, squeezing Ahmahn's hand as she looked up into his eyes.

"You are wise, my mate." she smiled as she spoke. "I . . . *we* are fortunate to have you as our leader."

After the meal was finished, they set about selecting scouting teams. Provisions were collected and packed, and the first teams were bid farewell as they departed.

CHAPTER 58

Two days later the scouting party returned from the north country, bringing with it grey storm clouds and icy-cold winds. The storm broke not long after their arrival.

At first, the winds died completely. High above, massive darkening clouds roiled violently. Lightening flashed almost continuously, followed immediately by ear-splitting crashes of thunder. Everyone in the camp had taken shelter.

Mahrohm was the first to see the party. Motioning to Ahmahn, she crawled out from under their hide-covered lean-to and hurried quickly across the clearing, past the still-smoldering fire pit. One of her female friends was in the party and Mahrohm was anxious to greet her and her mate.

Ahmahn was just pulling on his shirt when a deafening clap and a blinding flash knocked him backward against the rear wall, the concussion momentarily stunning him. By the time he reoriented himself, it was all over.

Mahrohm had just reached her friend and thrown her arms around her, when the bolt struck. The arc struck her friend's mate on the top of his head, passed through his chest, out the arm he had wrapped around his mate, across her chest, into Mahrohm, then down her leg and into the ground.

The couple were killed instantly, their clothing smoldering before they hit the ground.

Mahrohm was hurled backward across the clearing. She slammed into the ground and tumbled violently up against the fire pit.

Tossing his shirt aside, Ahmahn scrambled out of the lean-to and flung himself toward the fire pit. Mahrohm lay where she had landed, unmoving. Ahmahn threw himself over the pit edge and threw his arms around her, pulling her close.

Her eyes fluttered weakly open, unfocused. Her body began quivering, gently at first, then more violently as the seizure progressed.

"Mahrohm! Mahrohm!" He screamed. Her body stiffened, spittle bubbled from her mouth, her eyes rolled back until only the whites shown. Then with a long, gurgling exhale, her body relaxed. She was gone.

After the lightning strike, rain began falling in torrents. Almost immediately everything was soaked. Others of the clan rushed toward the fire pit, oblivious to everything except the spectacle before them. Some rushed to attend to the stricken couple. Others stopped short in muted horror, all eyes on their leader, kneeling there before them.

Ahmahn clutched her lifeless body to his chest. His head tilted back as he inhaled deeply. A high-pitched wail issued from his gaping mouth, but stopped short, replaced by a quiet wheeze as air escaped from his constricted throat.

After a few moments he lowered his head and closed his eyes tightly. His shoulders began trembling, not from the chilling rain, but from the all-encompassing grief which overwhelmed him.

Slowly, ever so slowly, the clan, humans and simians alike, drew closer, surrounding the fire pit. Not a word was spoken . . . not a sound could be heard . . . just the relentless drumming of the rain.

CHAPTER 59

The storm blew itself out six days before, but still the ground was soaked, feeling spongy under foot.

Broc and Nahm had been traveling northward for two days across a barren landscape, dotted here and there with stubby, thick-leaved mossy vegetation. Not an animal, not even a bird had they seen since resuming their journey. Reluctantly they decided to turn back toward camp.

They walked slowly side by side, backtracking the path the returning scouts had travelled. For hours on end not a word was spoken between them. Each was absorbed in thought, and grief.

Still without speaking, they stopped, each staring blankly into the ground before them.

Nahm was the first to break the silence.

"The ground is drying a little now. Maybe it's safe enough to travel." He looked up to see Broc staring into his eyes. They both looked away self-consciously, each knowing what the other was thinking.

After a few awkward moments, Nahm continued.

"My brother. What must we do about our leader? For days now he has done nothing but sit there in his shelter, staring at nothing. He just sits. He doesn't move. His eyes are empty. They show nothing. No pain. No anger."

Broc's voice was strained as he responded.

"Yes. He doesn't eat. He doesn't sleep. I don't think he's moved since we buried Mahrohm. Why did he want her body covered by the earth, I wonder."

"Maybe it was because Nera was held by the great stone. We could not free her. We covered her body with stones so that she could not be seen . . . and so that the beasts could not desecrate her body."

"Yes. That must be the reason. Besides, a pyre could not be lit. The rain . . ." His words trailed off.

For a while they stood silently, lost in their memories of the previous days. Then almost as one, they squatted and sat down.

"We must speak to him. Tell him of our concerns."

"Yes . . . we should. But we must give him time. I know he will listen, but it should be him who decides when to speak. He has lost two mates . . ."

"And both his parents." Nahm reminded. "His grief must be more than he can . . ."

"Ahmahn is strong! Stronger than any of us. He will rise above his grief. He will master it. He will again be our leader. Remember how he was after his father died? He was silent then, too."

"Yes, I remember. But this time it is different. This time he is more distant. His eyes seem hollow, empty. There is no expression on his face. It is as though he is no longer with us."

Again they fell silent, each contemplating what the other had said.

Broc scanned the horizon as he began again.

"When he is ready we should . . . Okay!" He jumped to his feet. "There! Look! Is that . . .?"

There, only a few hundred yards down the way they had come, they could see a man climbing the trail toward them. Both men ran in his direction.

In a matter of minutes they closed the distance.

Ahmahn stopped when he saw that they had seen him. He pulled the bundle off his shoulder and placed it gently on the ground beside him. As his two friends approached, he stretched out his arms in greeting.

The two men ran into his embrace, breathless. After a long moment they separated, smiling, tears welling up in their eyes. Ahmahn placed a hand on each man's shoulder.

"My friends . . . my brothers! My heart is filled with the sight of you!"

"We have been worried! We have been so worried for you," Nahm said, his voice cracked with emotion. Broc began to speak, but Ahmahn raised a hand, stopping him.

"I know, my brothers. I know of your concern for me. I would expect nothing less. Come. Let us sit and rest for a while. There is much that I need to tell you."

The three of them sat as Ahmahn pulled the bundle in between them. He began untying the straps that held the hides in place.

"Ahmahn, our brother; there is something we must speak about." Broc began. But again Ahmahn stopped him.

"Yes. I know. But first there is something I must tell you."

He pulled the covering back, revealing the transceiver.

Broc had seen it before but knew that Nahm had not. He had sworn to keep its existence a secret. Just before his father died he had called Broc to his side and explained all about 'the DARKNESS' and how he had come to possess it. Upon his father's death, Broc had carried the device wherever he went. Like Amon, he had made 'the DARKNESS' a part of his life. The secrecy he associated with the device had become ingrained over the years, so much so that he was surprised at Ahmahn's revelation. Ahmahn turned to Nahm and began.

"Nahm, my brother; what I show you now is something only you, Broc and a few others have ever seen. It is a well-kept secret that only the most trusted among us know.

"I know of your confusion. I know you will not fully understand what I am about to tell you. But be not concerned. In time you will come to understand."

He placed his hand on the device. Immediately it began to glow a soft blue color.

"This thing you see is called a 'transceiver.' What it can do, you will not understand at first. But you must trust me that it is a good thing. Broc saw it long ago just before my father died. He has kept it secret faithfully ever since."

"Why do you reveal it now?" asked Broc.

"I do so now because you both need to understand the reason for the decision I have made."

Ahmahn removed his hand and immediately the image of an upper torso and head began to take shape. Nahm recoiled, not knowing what was happening.

"Don't be concerned, brother." Broc said reassuringly. "I have seen this before. Just wait. Soon you will understand."

Ahmahn gave a brief explanation as the image grew to completion. The image turned toward Broc and began.

"Broc, my friend. It's been a long time. It's good to see you. And you," The image turned toward Nahm. "Nahm. Ahmahn has told me about you. You are his trusted friend. I am honored to meet you. My name is Evander"

Nahm was speechless for a moment. Then he blurted:

"It is as you say! It . . . he *speaks*!"

With a knowing smile, Evander turned toward Ahmahn.

"I take it you have not yet told them."

"No. They have only just arrived." Turning back toward his friends, Ahmahn began.

"My brothers, much has happened since we first came together so long ago." The two men nodded, not knowing what to say.

"We have shared the joy of finding others like ourselves. We have learned together. We have shared our thoughts, our feelings, our ideas. We have learned together things which our parents could not teach us because they could not communicate the way we do. They could not speak. We have come to know who we are, that we are a unique race, different from any other in this world.

"We have shared other things, too. We have shared the joy of seeing our young ones come into this world."

Broc was stunned that Ahmahn would mention this.

"Yes, my brothers. We have even shared the grief of loss." Ahmahn stared deep into each man's eyes.

"It is these things which we have shared that give me confidence that you will understand what I must tell you now." He motioned toward the image of Evander.

"From the time of my adolescence this man has been my friend. He has been by my side through all of my life. He has told me about his world.

"No; he is not from this world. He is from a world far from here. So far, in fact, that he could not ordinarily be here himself. This device that you see can produce an image of him which we can see. It can also produce our images in the place where he is now, so that he can also see us.

"Long ago, when I had grown into manhood, Evander made an offer to me. A very extraordinary offer. But I refused it.

"At that time events in my life were much different than they are now. Nera was with child. Our clan was newly formed and in need of leadership."

"This is very true, my friends." Evander interjected. "Of all the people at that time, Ahmahn was the best qualified to lead. From that time to this he has lead you all with strength and courage."

"Thank you, my friend," Ahmahn said. "Your faith in me has sustained me through difficult times such as these." He paused for a moment, searching the ground before him, trying to find the proper words.

"You, my brothers; you too possess such qualities. On many occasions each of you has demonstrated a willingness, an ability, even an enthusiasm for leading our people."

"What are you saying!?" Nahm broke in. There was desperation in his tone. "Do you not wish to continue leading us?"

"My honest answer is . . . no." Ahmahn watched his two friends closely, searching for a reaction. The two men just stared at him in disbelief.

"Each of you possess leadership qualities. You have demonstrated this countless times."

"But . . ." Nahm tried to speak, but Ahmahn again cut him off.

"Even our brother Sef was a leader, just like you. If he were here now, I would say the same to him. But, my brothers, he is not." Ahmahn turned toward Evander's image.

"What Ahmahn speaks is true. I must tell you something which will be difficult for you to hear. What we feared at the time of Sef's departure so long ago has come to pass. It has been many years since he and his father rejoined their old family. Through some unanticipated circumstances, his father became leader.

In so doing, he succumbed to the temptation which we all feared would happen. He mated with non-seeded females. The young ones they produced were not human . . . nor were they simian. They were, and still remain, an aberration. They are unlike any that we have ever seen. They have rebelled against both of their tribes. They now call themselves the Tal"

"Now they follow the path that we chose. Do not be concerned. They are years behind us. You will not have to contend with them if you continue as you have before."

"You say *you*, not *we*." Broc would not be silenced, though Ahmahn raised his hand. "You have chosen then! You will not continue to lead us!"

"This is true, my brother. It is time for new leadership. It is time for you two to take my place."

"But you must not do this!" said Nohm. "You have always led us! We will not stop seeking your advice, even if you refuse to give it!"

"Yes. This I know. That is why I must leave."

Broc was near hysterics. "Leave?! Where will you go?! Will you leave us to fend for ourselves? *You must not do this!*"

"Ahmahn is right. It is time that he move . . ." Evander began.

"What do you know!? You are but an image . . . an apparition!"

"Evander is a real man. This machine only shows his image, like a reflection in the water. He is *real*. And very soon he will be among us."

CHAPTER 60

Three days earlier, Ahmahn had finally come out of his funk. When Broc and Nohm approached him after the burials, he was deliberately unresponsive, fearing that he might break down in front of them. Better to just keep quiet, he thought. When they told him their plan to scout northward, in the direction the stricken couple had gone, he had said nothing, only nodded his consent.

He watched, unmoved, as they disappeared into the distance, all the time struggling with the decision he knew he would soon have to make.

That night, after everyone had retired, he retrieved the transceiver from its hiding place and quietly moved away from the camp. When he was sure he could not be seen or heard, he activated the unit.

For many hours into the night he and Evander talked. He learned of Sef's death at the hands of the Tal. He learned of their departure from their jungle home and their trek northward.

He explained his feelings; how he had come to recognize his desperation, his confusion, his willingness to turn his back on all he and his clan had accomplished.

Evander had expressed his understanding and appreciation for all he had endured, but had said little more.

Ahmahn hesitated for only a moment before he broached the subject they had discussed so many years before.

"You once told me that at some time, if I so chose, that I could join you, that I could leave this place."

"Yes. It is *still* possible. Have you weighed the consequences of such a decision?"

"I have." Ahmahn was now resolute. Having said it out loud, it didn't seem as intimidating.

"I know that I may return any time I choose, but that if I do, it will be to another time; that all those I know and love will either be very old . . . or dead." He looked his friend square in the eye as he continued.

"All that has already come to pass! My grief has become more than I can bear. I must find a way to escape it before it consumes me."

"My dear friend . . . your grief will never go away, not completely. You will retain the memories of these events as long as you live. But in time you will learn to live with them. Though you do not feel it now, in time you will draw strength from these experiences. You will become a better man. You will feel more intently the compassion you now feel for your fellow beings."

"My friend Evander. You have been at my side all my life. You have watched. You have advised. But you have never interfered. You have allowed me to choose my own path. And for that I have grown to love you."

"All those who I have held closest to my heart are now gone. Yes, I love all the people of my clan. But the feelings I have for them are somehow, different."

"That is as it should be, my dear friend," said Evander. "There is a saying among my people which has always given me comfort during trying times. 'Blood will Prevail.'"

"This I understand." Amhmahn nodded slowly in agreement. "There is a bond . . . a 'blood bond' that joins us . . . between parent and child . . . between a man and his mate. It is stronger than that between friends. It is a spiritual union . . . so strong that time or distance cannot sever it."

"Yes. It is borne of time, of intimacy, of sharing and caring. It prevails beyond the grave. It is everlasting."

"I know, I have similar feelings for my people. I worry for their welfare, so much so that on occasion I'm tempted to re-direct them, to prevent them from erring. I know it is not right for me to do so. If I attempt to control them, even though I believe it is for their own good . . . if I do so I deprive them of their right to choose."

"This is true wisdom, my friend." said Evander. "In all the universe, this truth prevails."

CHAPTER 61

"What do you mean . . . 'he will be among us'? Did you not say he was very far away . . . on a different world?" Nahm nearly screamed the words at Ahmahn.

"Yes, I am from another world very far from here," responded Evander's hologram. "That is the world where I was born. But I am not on that world now."

Ahmahn caught their attention. "Listen. Do you hear that sound, like a serpent's hiss? That is the sound of hid approach."

The three men looked around, trying to locate the source of the sound. High above and to the south they notice something strange, like a ripple in the sky. It shimmered as it drew closer. The hiss began giving way to a low-pitched rumble as the craft slowed and then came to a halt a dozen feet above the ground just a few yards distant. Evander's image blinked out as the shimmering decreased and the craft began to take form.

Nahm and Broc jumped to their feet in alarm. Ahmahn rose more slowly. It had been a long time since he'd seen this, but still he was fascinated.

The form became more and more substantial until at last it resembled a dark smooth sphere, more than twice as tall as a man.

An opening appeared near the bottom. The men saw a disc descending, with a man standing on it. The figure stepped off the disc, which immediately ascended back into the sphere. The opening vanished. The figure walked toward them.

Ahmahn stepped forward, arms extended.

"Evander!"

"Ahmahn, my friend!"

The two men embraced briefly. Then Ahmahn turned toward his two companions.

"My brothers, this is Evander, the real the man. Come! Come closer. He is real! Not the image you saw before."

The two men walked toward him slowly, unsure what to do or say.

The man before them was tall, slightly taller than them. His body was slender. His clothing was strange, conforming to his body shape, but not clinging to it. The fabric was smooth, quite unlike the bulky hides they were familiar with. His foot coverings were of a dark, smooth material.

"Nahm! Broc! How good it is to meet you in person!" Evander extended his hand to each of them in turn. Not knowing what else to do, each of them clasped his hand in turn.

"How are you here?" Nahm began. "How did you. . . .? Where did you. . . .? We saw you . . . this *thing* . . ." He pointed at the globe hovering off to his left.

"*This* is how you . . . how you travel between worlds?"

Evander smiled at his reactions. "No. . . . This is but a small machine which allows me to travel short distances." He gestured toward the globe, inviting them to step closer.

"This machine is what we call a 'shuttle.' Here. Come closer. Touch it if you wish."

Nahm walked forward tentatively, placed his hand against its surface, then jerked it back in surprise. Cautiously he placed his hand back on the surface.

"It's cold, and smooth, like frozen water." He smiled at his two companions. They in turn came closer, to touch the cold surface.

"When I travel through the air near a planet, near a world such as this, my shuttle can get very hot as it rushes through the air. So to prevent this from happening, the surface of the vehicle is cooled to near absolute zero."

The three men looked at him blankly.

"It is not important that you understand this now. In only a short time the temperature on the outside of the vehicle will be the same as the air around us now." The men still seemed bewildered.

"Would you like to see an image of the other ships . . . machines we travel in?"

The three men nodded simultaneously, mouths slightly open, eyes wide in amazement. Evander pulled a small flat object from his pocket and touched it several times with his finger. Immediately the bottom of the shuttle opened and the disc reappeared.

"Come. Stand close together on this disc."

The four men stepped onto the disc as Evander continued.

"Now. Put your arms around each other so you don't fall. Don't be afraid. The disc will now rise with us on it."

As the disc began to rise, the three men clung closer. The disc rose slowly up into the sphere and stopped.

"You may now step off onto the deck. There is a seat behind you. Please sit while I call up . . . while I instruct the shuttle to display an image of the other ship I mentioned.

The three men sat uneasily, marvelling at the interior of the sphere. Except for a disc-shaped panel above them, the platform they had been standing on, and the 360-degree seat on which they were sitting, it was as though there were no walls at all. They could see exactly what they had seen outside except from a higher vantage point, nothing but flat tundra.

Evander remained standing at the edge of the platform.

"Hologram, please." He said.

The overhead disc began emitting a low-pitched hum. At the same time a cylindrical shape began rising up out of the platform at their feet. It stopped at about waist level. Its flat top surface began to glow a faint blue.

"*Brighid* exterior please. Slow rotate 360."

In the space between the upper and lower discs an image of Evander's ship began to form, layer by layer. In just a few seconds the image was complete and began to slowly rotate.

"This is the ship where I was when we first began talking, when you were seeing my image in the transceiver."

"Ship?" Nahm asked.

"It is a vehicle . . . a machine we use to travel from place to place high up in the heavens. We call that place 'space.'"

"But that thing is small! How is this possible?"

Evander gave another command: "Size comparison, please. Man to *Brighid*."

The image of the ship disappeared, to be replaced by an image of a man. The man-image began shrinking until it was barely more than a dot in size. Beside it the image of the ship reappeared. Evander began to explain.

"This machine we call a spaceship. It is very large . . . so large that many thousand people live within it. We have a name for this ship. We call it the *Brighid*. There are many others similar to the *Brighid*. And there are many thousands of people in each one of them.

"Space is vast, so large that we know of no end to it. Within space are many millions of worlds, many very similar to this world.

"Tell us about this 'space.'" said Broc.

Evander sat down opposite the three men. They could still see him, even through the image of the spacecraft.

"Think of what you see when you look up into the sky in the day time. High above you can sometimes see clouds. It's hard to tell how big they are. Even when birds fly high above, they do not touch them.

"At night you can see bright specks high up in the darkness. Those are stars. Every one of those stars are far, far away; much farther than the clouds. So far, in fact, that it takes many many years to travel between them using spacecraft.

"Because it takes so long to travel between stars, we have other machines which help us to travel much faster. We call these machines 'LINKS.'" Evander addressed the sphere again.

"Hologram: size comparison, *Brighid* to LINK."

The dot-sized man-image disappeared as the *Brighid* image began shrinking. When the ship had shrunk to about one-eighth size, a rough-surfaced cylindrical object began to form. The ship image continued to shrink until it fit easily inside the cylinder with very much room to spare. Still it continued shrinking.

"This is a LINK. Many spaceships can fit inside it. The spaceship goes in one end of the LINK, and when it comes out the other end, it has travelled to another part of space very far away.

Ahmahn was the next to ask a question.

"How can the LINK travel such a great distance in so short a time?"

Evander's response was not what they expected.   "This we do not know. There are many, many LINKS throughout space. So many in fact that we don't know of all of them. The LINKS do not move through space. Instead, in some manner we don't understand, they are able to move our spaceships between them without ever moving themselves."

Nahm and Broc were overwhelmed. Ahmahn spoke next, hoping to break their stupor.

"My brothers, I have heard this story before, and was equally overwhelmed at its first telling.But as time has passed and events in my life have unfolded, I have become accustomed. I still understand little of what Evander has said. But now I wish to learn more. Evander and I have discussed this and have agreed that now is a good time to tell you of my plan."

"Hologram end, please." Evander began to stand, but then decided it would be better for him to remain seated, seeing the men at eye level, a less intimidating position.

"I must agree with Ahmahn. He has thought about this long and hard and has convinced me this is the right course of action . . .

for himself and for you. He desires to join me as I travel between the stars. He feels that his usefulness as your leader has come to a zenith, that you have learned to be leaders in your own right."

Ahmahn continued. "There is a thing which I have not told you. I have seen this shuttle before. I travelled in it one time long ago, but not with Evander. Instead I traveled with a woman called Asha. She taught me to speak and understand words better. Where she took me I am not certain, but the things I saw were beyond my understanding.

"At first, like you, I could not understand what had been shown me. But my confusion soon was overcome by the events of my life.

"Still, those memories of the time spent with Asha and Evander remained. I would long to be with them again. But my love for Nera, and then Mahrohm . . . and you . . . and all of our clan persuaded me to remain here."

"But now, with both of my mates and my parents gone, I am free to reconsider." Ahmahn moved closer to his two friends, placing his hands on their shoulders.

"My bond with the two of you and with the people of our clan will never be weakened. You both possess a curiosity about life which compels you to strive for greater understanding. Your skills will serve you well. Our people will do well under your leadership."

"Ahmahn is correct in this." Evander interjected. "It is true. I have been at his side from the time of his youth. And the skills he has learned are also present in each of you.

"The only thing either of you lack is experience. But because you have been at Ahmahn's side, you have learned from him, as he has learned from you. In truth, you have demonstrated your skills to everyone in your clan. They have seen your abilities many times. The only thing for you to do once he has gone, is to continue in his absence."

"But will they follow us?" asked Nahm. "Ahmahn has always been strong for our people. They have witnessed that strength many, many times."

Broc responded to his friend's question:

"My brother, they *will* follow us, if for no other reason than they lack the courage to lead themselves. Ask yourself this: How often has someone come to you for advice? How many times have you helped someone resolve a problem without being asked to do so? Our people see this. And they do not forget.

"We should not look upon them as less than us because they don't or can't do for themselves. Rather, we should look upon them as we would a child: willing, but not yet able. It is for us to lead by actions, as well as by words."

Evander was impressed by Broc's insight.

"This is *exactly* the thing that makes you leaders. Your ability to set yourself apart, to stand outside the situation and see it objectively. Then to re-engage and work toward a solution."

Nahm still felt unsure.

"All that you say, I understand. Still it will not be easy."

"This is so, my brother," said Ahmahn. "You will both face many challenges. Most will not be easy. But they will be worth your effort. In time your confidence will grow. I have no fear that you will succeed."

"Now let us speak of other things." Broc directed his attention to Evander.

"For two days now Nahm and I have retraced the path our scouts made. We have travelled far to the north, but have not been pleased with what we have seen."

"Yes. You've come to that place I spoke about with Ahmahn." said Evander.

Evander called up a three-dimensional holographic map of the area where they were now located.

"This place is desolate. It cannot sustain your clan. There is little vegetation and practically no animal life from here northward for many, many days. And beyond is a land of snow and ice. It is here, in this place that you must decide which way you will go."

"There is no good reason to return the way we came," said

Nahm. "There is nothing for us there. Besides, at some time, if we return, we must contend with the Tal."

"This is true," said Broc, pointing to the map. "Evander, is there any advantage in travelling in the other available directions?"

Looking deep into the faces of both men, he responded. "*This* is the first of many decisions you must make on your own. I cannot advise you which way to go. I cannot interfere. If I were to do so the decision would be mine, not yours."

The two men were silent for a few moments. Then, exchanging glances, they directed their response to their brother. Broc spoke in both men's behalf.

"We have considered this for some time. We agree that to continue north will not be of benefit. Since you have chosen to leave, we must and will accept the responsibility to lead our people.

"Each of us has wondered what lies in store for us, to the east and to the west. Since it is now our decision . . ." Broc looked quickly at Nahm, who nodded his agreement. "We choose to go both ways."

Ahmahn was taken aback by Broc's statement.

"Are you sure this is wise, my brother?"

Nahm spoke up.

"We lack knowledge of what lies in either direction. It may be good. It may be bad. It will probably be both. We cannot control what will happen to us. We can only control how we will face the challenge."

Broc spoke next.

"Evander. We understand why you must do the thing you do, and we are grateful. You give us the freedom to choose our own way." He hesitated for just a moment before continuing.

"There is one thing that we would ask of you. For all this time you have been at Ahmahn's side. We would ask that you do the same for us. We desire that you leave a transceiver with each of us so that you may observe us . . . and so that, from time to time, we may converse with you," He glanced toward Ahmahn. "And, if it is possible, with our brother."

"I had hoped you would make such a request. It is important to me and those around me that your civilization succeed. You'd be surprised at how many have failed. Invariably they fail because they lack good leadership. This will not be the case with you.

"There are many who call themselves leaders, but lack the humility to seek guidance and advice. They become power-hungry and loose objectivity." Evander pulled the tablet from his pocket and typed in a command as he spoke.

"The transceiver which was with Sef has been summoned. It will arrive momentarily. Nahm, you will take possession of it. Broc will keep the one Ahman brought with him.

"I must caution you, these units are essentially autonomous . . . they will work with or without your input. But each will be programmed to respond to you and no other. Each has masking capability so it will be very difficult for anyone else to locate.

"Each of you will receive training on how your transceiver works. You will do this only when you are alone, out of sight and hearing of others in your clan. Never will you divulge this secret.

"Above all else you must remember that the fate of your clan is in your hands. Never should you expect me or anyone else to make decisions for you. You are both good men. You have demonstrated this time and again. I'm confident that you will do what is in your people's best interest. Were I not so, we would not be having this conversation.

The other transceiver became visible just outside the shuttle. It moved slowly toward the one that had been Ahmahn's and settled gently next to it.

Evander stood and gestured toward the three men.

"Come. Let us go outside so you can take possession of your transceivers."

All four men once again descended to the ground. Ahmahn and his friends stepped off the disc, but Evander remained in place.

Broc and Nahm walked toward the two transceiver, but stopped short when Nahm's unit rose from the ground and moved slowly toward him. It stopped within arm's reach of its new owner.

"My friend, place your hand on top of the unit. This will allow it to recognize you from now on."

As Nahm did so, a faint blue haze began forming around his hand. It grew until it had completely enclosed his body. Then, as quickly as it had appeared, it disappeared. The unit settled back to the ground where it had been.

Ahmahn turned toward Evander expectantly.

"Come, my friend. Join me here." Evander extended his hand toward Ahmahn, who stepped onto the platform, then turned to face his friends.

"Ahmahn, my brother," said Broc, his voice calm, deliberate. "Now you will leave us."

Ahmahn stood mute. Tears began running down his cheeks. He stepped back down off the platform and walked to the two men. No words passed between them as for a long moment the three embraced. Then, after shaking each man's hand, he turned and rejoined Evander on the platform.

"One day you will again be together. Of this I am confident." Evander spoke softly as the platform began to ascend.

Below, the two brothers stood in silence as a low-pitched hum began. Slowly at first, then more rapidly, the sphere rose into the sky. The humming faded, turning into a faint hiss.

The sphere grew smaller and smaller, fading until it was nothing but a shimmer in the air high above. The next moment, it was gone.

Epilogue

The tribes of Broc and Nahm separated shortly thereafter.

Broc and his tribe traveled westward, following along the edge of barren tundra left behind by receding glaciers.

Over time the freshwater sea which separated North Africa from southern Europe merged with the Atlantic Ocean when the barrier at Gibraltar opened and created a narrow strait. In time this huge body of water would come to be known as the Mediterranean Sea.

Further south, the Tal (eventually to be known as Neanderthal) were migrating along a path parallel to that of Broc and his clan. The two cultures would eventually clash at the western most coast of Europe.

The tribe of Nahm went eastward along the tundra barrier. In time their descendants would populate all of Asia. Their descendants would eventually cross the land bridge between Asia and the North American continent and go on to populate North and South America.

REUNION

CHAPTER 62

Ahmahn had been on board the *Brighid* for three days, but was only now just beginning to feel comfortable. Shiny, smooth surfaces surrounded him wherever he went. The closest thing he could compare them to on his home world were placid lakes. They were not nearly as smooth, but were definitely more beautiful. The lights overhead were bright and unchanging, but not painful to look at, unlike the sun on his home world. The air smelled different, almost like the smell of rain.

There seemed to be people everywhere, scurrying this way and that. He felt like everyone was watching him, even though Evander had given him clothes to wear that looked like everyone else's.

"It's the beard and the hair," Evander told him when he asked. "Men don't usually wear their hair long any more. It's just easier to keep it short. Same with the beard . . . the hair on your face."

The first time he saw his reflection in a mirror, he was almost overcome in amazement. At first he thought he was looking at Broc. Evander had explained it all, but it was still hard to understand.

The "restroom" and the "dining hall" had been explained very carefully immediately after Evander brought him on board "the ship," as he called it.

Ahmahn thought the "restroom" was a very practical thing. Evander showed him the one in his "quarters," explained how it worked and encouraged him to try it out. He explained that there were others spread around the ship and that each one was identified by an image of a man or of a woman, and that it was customary for men to use the ones with the "man" image.

He found out in short order how important it was to go into the correct "restroom." He entered the room with the "woman" image once by mistake and had quickly been escorted out my a female who seemed to be very upset with him.

The "dining hall" was fascinating. When they entered the room, he was surrounded by strange aromas. Some were pleasingly familiar, like the smell of roasting meat. But others made his jaws tighten and his mouth go wet. Evander encouraged him to try some of each type of food, and he did so, using his fingers to pick small pieces out of a long line of strange shaped pots. Evander showed him how to use things called "utensils" instead of his fingers, explaining that it was customary among these people.

He thought the "plates" were very practical. They made it easy to carry the food. He liked the "knife" too. It had a familiar feel. But the "fork" and "spoon" were hard to hold. Fingers were much more practical.

At the end of the first day, Evander explained that he had other duties he had to perform and that another person would escort him and answer any questions he might have. Evander said the person would be a young female named Ambia.

That night as he lay in his "bed," he marvelled at all the wondrous things he had seen and learned. How much more of this new world was there yet to be discovered? He shifted about beneath the covers, too excited to sleep.

After a time his thoughts turned to the others of his clan. How would they react to his abrupt departure? How would they fare without him? Ah, but he must not be concerned, he told himself. Broc and Nahm were capable, good men. They would lead his people well.

Gradually he began to relax. The excitement of the day slowly gave way to mental exhaustion. The last thing he remembered as he slipped into slumber, was the face he had seen in the mirror.

The next morning he was awakened by a faint buzzing, which gradually grew louder until he sat up in bed. It stopped abruptly, to be replaced by a high-pitched female voice.

"Mister Ahmahn? Good morning," the voice said from no direction, and every direction. "I'm Ambia. I'm here to be your escort for the day."

"Where are you? I don't see you," he said in confusion.

"I'm just outside your door. I'll wait here until you're ready to come out. Don't forget to use the restroom first."

When he was ready, he went to the door and opened it. There, only a few feet away, sat a slender female, clad in clothing the color of an auburn autumn leaf. Her hair was cut short but still covered her ears. Its color was like the sand on a river bank.

When she saw him she stood up, nervously clasping her hands in front of her. She made eye contact after first looking him over, as she had been instructed, ensuring that he was properly dressed. Glad that all was as it should be, she stepped closer to him and extended her hand. Not knowing what else to do, he stood, unmoving.

Sensing his unease, Ambia said: "It's one of our customs that when people meet face to face for the first time, they grasp hands and introduce themselves."

She took his hand in hers and continued, smiling up at him.

"Hello. I am Ambia. My home world is called Kalephia."

Hesitantly, he responded.

"I am Ahmahn. My home world is . . ." Not knowing what to say, he looked down toward the floor, searching for some appropriate name, surprised that he had not thought of this before. Staring at the floor beneath his feet, he noticed the stark contrast between it and the familiar surface of his world. More confident now, he looked up at her and started again.

"Hello. I am Ahmahn. My home world is called Earth."

For a few uneasy moments the two of them just stood there, unsure of what to do next. Finally Ambia released his hand.

At first the young female seemed to be uneasy, not sure of herself. Not at all like the females he was used to. But after just a few short moments she again took him by the hand and led him out of the dormitory section.

Slowly, casually, she began guiding him from one room to another, giving names to all the strange new objects they encountered, explaining what each thing did and how it worked.

Initially he had little to say, just trying to absorb all the new information. But as the day wore on and they became more comfortable in each other's presence, he felt confident enough to ask questions.

"Tell me about your world."

"What would you like to know?" Ambia was happy to change the subject of her monologue.

"My world is new," he began. "My people are few in number. We have none of these things you show me. Does your world have things such as these?"

"Oh my. Yes. We have many of the things that are here on the *Brighid*. There are many, many people on Kalephia, many millions of us."

She wanted to draw Amon out, to get him talking, knowing that talking would help to ease his tension.

"Tell me about your world, Mister Ahmahn."

"Why do you use that word with my name?"

"Oh! You mean *mister?* That is a word we use to show respect for a person."

"Then I should call you Mister Ambia," he stated matter-of-factly.

"No," Ambia smiled. "We use a different word when addressing females. If a woman is married." Amon looked confused, not knowing the word. Ambia saw this immediately and explained.

"When a female has a mate, she is called *missus*. If she is not mated, she is called *miss*."

"Are you mated . . . married?" he asked.

Ambia shook her head. "No. Not yet."

"Then I will call you *Miss* Ambia." Ahmahn smiled, feeling proud of himself that he had understood.

Ambia smiled too, seeing the corner that she had painted herself into. Smiling at him, she said:

"Those are titles of respect which we say to each other when we meet for the first time. Then, after we have grown to know each other and become friends, we no longer use the title. We are free to call each other by name only."

"This is very confusing, but I think I understand. You and I are now friends. Therefore I will call you Ambia."

"And I will call you Ahmahn, my new friend."

On his third day things began as usual. This time he was awake before the buzzing started. He was waiting in the hallway outside his door when Ambia came around the corner.

She was not alone. Evander walked at her side, a concerned look on his face.

"Hello, my friend Evander," Ahmahn began. "I am please to see you."

"Thank you, my friend. It's good to see you too." He glanced briefly at the young woman at his side, and then continued.

"I trust you and Ambia have gotten along well in my absence." Evander gestured that they should begin walking together, though not in the usual direction.

"Yes! We have become friends. Miss Ambia has now become my friend Ambia."

Evander smiled quizzically.

"My friend, I have a surprise for you."

"What is a surprise? I do not know this word."

"You will learn soon enough."

The trio turned another corner and stopped in front of a door marked ORIENTATION.

"You will recognize this room as soon as we go inside. This is the room I brought you to when we first arrived. This is where the surprise is."

Evander opened the door and gestured that Ahmahn should enter first. He recognized the room immediately. In the center of the room were the two chairs where he and Evander had sat right after they exited the shuttle craft. The room was not so brightly lit as it was before. There was a familiar scent in the room. It reminded him of burning flesh, the smell he remembered from his father's funeral pyre.

Sitting in one chair, facing away from him, was a man with long dark hair, similar to his, but with streaks of grey running through it. The man was clothed in a fashion similar to Ahmahn's old clothes, except for an absence of the fur covering. The sleeves were neatly sewn with thin strips of leather. Below the chair he could see foot coverings, also devoid of fur. Thin leather laces held the shoes in place on the man's feet.

Slowly the man rose from his chair.

The movements were slow, deliberate, reminding him of the way his father had moved.

The man turned to face him. The beard was full, not unkempt, but trimmed uniformly. Streaks of grey ran through it too. The face was bronzed, and creased. The forehead was furrowed, the brows long and grey. Crows feet accented the eyes.

Who was this man? He looked vaguely familiar, but. . . . The eyes! He recognized the eyes. It was Broc!

"Ahmahn, my old friend. You look like it was only yesterday." The old man stepped forward slowly, unsteady on his feet.

Ahmahn rushed forward to embrace his friend, his brother.

"My brother! What has happened to you?" He was incredulous that this could be the same person he had seen only days before.

Evander stepped forward, followed closely by Ambia.

"My friend. Remember when we stood together with Nahm on the path that led back toward your people, on your home world?"

Ahmahn glanced briefly in Evander's direction, but turned his gaze back to his friend.

"Yes! That was but three days ago! What has happened to you?" he said, searching his friend's eyes for an answer.

"*My* brother," Broc's voice was brittle, raspy. "That was many years ago that we said good-bye." The old man smiled weakly. A tear formed and ran down his cheek, getting lost in his moustache.

"You look the same as I remember you."

Evander stepped forward, placing his hand gently on Ahmahn's shoulder.

"Remember when I told you about how time would pass differently between your world . . . Earth . . . and here?"

"Yes . . . Yes" His voice cracked as he spoke.

"For you it has only been three days. But for Broc, many years have passed."

Ahmahn stood mute, his mind whirling, trying to come to grips with the reality of what he had just been told. Intellectually he could grasp the concept. But emotionally he was unprepared.

Evader nudged the two men toward the chairs.

"Perhaps it would be best if the two of you had some time alone to talk."

Nodding toward Ambia, he waited until the two men sat down and then moved back toward the door.

"Take all the time you need. We are in no hurry. When you're ready just stand up. Someone will come when you stand."

Quietly, discretely, Evander and Ambia left the room.

BROC'S STORY

CHAPTER 63

"My brother, much has happened since we parted so long ago. Perhaps I should begin at that day when you left."

"Yes. But first tell me why you have come here now?" said Ahmahn.

"That I will do soon enough. But for now it is necessary for me to tell my tale so that you will better understand. Please, my brother. Allow me."

Ahmahn knew it would do no good to press the issue. Besides, he really wanted to know what had transpired during the years (days) since his departure. Resolvedly he leaned back in his chair and prepared himself to hear his friend's story.

"The day that you left, Nahm and I got back to the clan just as the evening meal was being prepared. All were gathered around the cook fire. Sara saw us coming and ran to intercept us. I remember the look on her face. I knew she was worried.

"Everyone wanted to know what had happened to you, but Nahm and I knew we could not tell them the truth. We had prepared a story, and it was decided he would tell it.

"He said that you had told us of your grief over your many losses, and that you wished to leave us for a time. When we asked how long, you told us you didn't know, but that we should take over as leaders.

"There was much discussion then, but I don't recall much of

what was said. I do remember that we told them of our wish to separate and go in opposite directions. Many did not want us to separate, but we were finally able to persuade them.

"On the day of our separation there was much crying, but also much enthusiasm and anticipation. Each group vowed that we would stay in contact, and we did so for a long time. But as the days turned into weeks and then months, our contacts became fewer and fewer, until finally they stopped.

"For all these years I have heard nothing from Nahm. How he and his followers faired, I do not know.

"Perhaps we can ask Evander to consult Nahm's transceiver. Surely he can do that for us. But first, tell me your tale."

Broc continued, smiling as he remembered.

"Sara my mate gave me a son! We called him Eff, in remembrance of our brother Sef, who left us. . . . Do you know what ever happened to him?"

Ahmahn nodded, momentarily breaking eye contact.

"Yes. . . . Sef is dead. Evander told me about it on the day I arrived here. That is a tale for another time." Ahmahn looked pleadingly into his friend's eyes.

Broc's countenance fell as he heard Ahmahn's response. He paused for a long moment, trying to compose himself. Then, taking a deep breath, he continued.

"Eff was the joy of my heart. He grew to be a fine man. Sara also gave me a daughter. Her name was Lorn. She has the face of Nera."

Another long pause as the two friends remembered.

"Lorn grew to be like her mother. They were always together. When she was of age, she chose a mate. He was called Leo. He was the best hunter among us.

"I remember at night as we sat around the fire, he would tell us of his adventures before his clan came to join us. He told of giant, hairy beasts that roamed the north lands; how his people would follow them, seeking ways to kill them; how they took their hides and made tents, and their bones and made weapons.

"After a time Lorn gave him a son, and then another. I remember how he carried them on his shoulders, one on each side, and how they squealed when he played with them before the camp fires at night.

Broc paused again. Ahmahn could sense there was something about Broc's story that was yet to be told. Patiently he waited for him to continue.

"We traveled for many years, seeing wondrous and awesome sights. As we continued, we came upon others of our kind. Many times we exchanged gifts, told of our travels and our adventures. Many of us who were of age chose mates and produced children.

"Sometimes we stopped, if only for a few days. Other times for seasons, as snow and ice prevented our movement. Sometimes we remained in one place for years, partaking the bounty available to us. During those times our numbers continued to grow as others joined us, until at last there were many hundreds of us.

"Our people grew in number so much that it became necessary for us to establish laws, that we might govern ourselves and endeavour to avoid conflict. But alas, we were not always successful in doing so.

"From time to time we fought, sometimes over land, sometimes over food during times of scarcity, but most frequently we fought over leadership.

"From time to time people left us, seeking their fortune elsewhere, as Nahm and I had done.

"It was these difficulties which persuaded me that our clan should continue our trek toward the setting sun.

"Along the way our numbers continued to grow. Again we met new people. Again some departed. But always our clan continued together.

"Until at last we came upon a shallow sea. There, not far across this sea, we saw another land.

"The water was shallow enough that we could cross it, though some of us refused to try. They remained on the shore line while we continued.

"After many hours we at last stood again on dry land. But our progress was blocked by a great high wall of white stone. For a day we endeavoured to find a way over or around it.

"Finally, after traveling South for two more days, we were able to climb up and over. We ventured inland, again following the setting sun. The land before us was rough, strewn with stones, some many times larger than a man.

"As the sun touched the horizon, we saw several large stones standing upright. It looked like there were other stones laying across their tops.

"When we came close, we saw that the stones were arranged in an incomplete circle on top of a wide, low mound, surrounded by a shallow pit. This was not natural. Nowhere had we ever seen such a structure.

"A part of the top of this huge, circular structure was covered with limbs from trees, though we could see no trees anywhere nearby.

"We knew that someone had built this structure, but could find no one. We decided to send scouts out, hoping to find those who had built this magnificent structure.

"For several days we remained there, sheltering under the great stones, waiting for our scouts to return.

"Then one morning we were awakened by a great sound coming from the South. At first we couldn't see. The sun had not yet provided enough light. The sound grew louder. It was like the sound of wolves, snarling and howling. We were filled with terror.

"Soon the sound surrounded us in the darkness, yet did not draw nearer. The terrifying noise continued for a while, and then suddenly it stopped, to be replaced by pulsating thumping, thudding, like heavy stones dropping to the ground. It soon became so intense that we could feel it shaking the ground beneath our feet. The stone columns themselves seemed to ring in response. When the light came, still we could see nothing.

"The howling began again, filling the air as the ground continued to shake.

"A few of my people became so filled with terror that they too began to wail. There was nothing I could do to stop them. They were like wild animals, frantic to escape this unknown terror.

"One female became so terror-stricken that she broke free from her mate's grasp and charged out madly, disappearing beyond the edge of the mound, her screams becoming one with the pounding and snarling.

"Again the sounds stopped. Not even the woman's screams could we hear. Then all around the perimeter we saw movement. Soon we could make out heads, then shoulders, covered in fur-covered hides.

"These were men! But like no men we had ever seen! As they drew neared, we could see they were big, head and shoulders taller than any of us. Their faces were different, more like apes than men. Each one carried a long staff, nearly as tall as they were.

"Abruptly they all stopped, except for one, who continued walking toward us. In one hand he held a staff. In the other he held a leg, grasped at the ankle. When he came to the top of the mound we could see . . . he was dragging behind him the body of the woman. Where her head had been, a trail of blood marked the way he had come."

Ahmahn sat mute, stunned, unable to speak. What Evander had told him only days before was now happening again!

"My brother!" Ahmahn finally found words. "What . . . what?"

Broc placed a hand on his friend's knee and looked deep into his eyes.

"My brother. These are the words he said: 'We are Tal! You are ours. Do as we say . . . or die . . . like this one.' He tossed the limp body onto the ground before him."

CHAPTER 64

For a long time the two men sat, quietly talking. Evander stood at the window, watching. He had already heard what had happened, even before Broc had requested to join him on the *Brighid*. The transceiver which accompanied Broc's clan had automatically sent updates over the years (or in the case of *Brighid* time, hours).

Reports from geosynchronous monitors had kept Evander apprised of not only Broc's and Nahm's progress, but also tracked the movements of the Tal.

Upon reaching the Marmara Plateau, instead of splitting as Amon's clan had done, the Tal remained together and turned westward. From time to time they came in contact with established communities which had split off from Broc's group and settled along the Mediterranean coastline.

These encounters were never peaceful. The coastal communities were stable and well defended. Though the Tal attempted invasions, their numbers (and for that matter, their abilities) were insufficient to mount successful assaults. Consequently they continued moving westward, skirting the coastal communities.

Without even being aware of Broc's clan to their north, the Tal out-distanced them, eventually arriving at the western-most shores of the European continent many years ahead of the humans.

The Tal remained a war-like race, even as they continued moving westward. Now, bounded by the continental coastline to the west and the inhospitable conditions to the north, they focused their aggression on each other.

Convinced of their superiority, even in the face of previous defeats by the humans, they became idolatrous. They convinced themselves that their defeats were not their fault, but rather were punishments for their perceived weakness, brought upon them by forces beyond their understanding and control.

They came to believe that supplication to these imagined forces would increase their strength and allow them to more easily defeat their enemies.

To placate these unseen forces, they built structures wherein they made sacrifices and worshipped their 'gods.'

The stone edifice discovered by Broc's clan was the largest of these structures. In later centuries it became known as Stone-henge.

CHAPTER 65

"For many seasons we toiled under the Tal. Those of us who became too weak to work were 'sacrificed' to the Tal gods, as were the rebellious ones among us. We buried their bodies in the pit that surrounds that evil place.

"We were made to quarry stones in the north lands, drag them back and erect them, thus completing the circular structure. We were even made to quarry the stones upon which many of us were executed.

"From the beginning we plotted how we might defeat the Tal. But without weapons this could not be done. But one night my son Eff devised a plan.

"From time to time we were made to travel into the south lands to gather small trees and limbs with which to construct a covering for the massive stone structure.

"Eff suggested that we bind these light pieces of wood together to construct something which would float upon the surface of the water, something which would buoy us up so that we could escape back across the water. We knew that the Tal possessed no such thing, and that they would not be able to pursue us in like manner.

"Finally, one night we put our plan into action. We quickly assembled six such craft and dragged them the several miles to the water's edge, all while the Tal were sleeping.

"By the time the sun arose, we had made it to the water's edge.

As quickly as we could, we ran along the shoreline toward the shallows where we had originally crossed.

"For a full day and night we ran, carrying the floats on our shoulders. Our women carried the children who could not keep up. All of us were near exhaustion. Occasionally we stopped to rest, but soon the fear of the Tal forced us to continue.

"To our left, the steep white cliff walls. To our right, churning serf. We had no where to go but forward.

"Finally, at the dawn of the second day we reached the place of the shallows. But the once wide shoreline had diminished to only a narrow path, just wide enough for us to move in single file. Water lapped at our feet as we made our way forward.

"High above us on the cliff tops we heard commotion. Almost immediately large stones began falling down the cliff face. The Tal had found us! If we did not move quickly out into the water some of us would surely be hit.

"The water was well over our heads, but we had no choice. It would be many hours before the waters receded. We must risk the deep water or be killed by the falling stones. We could hear the Tal screaming in rage as they hurled stones over the precipice.

"Slowly we made our way out into the water, but the current kept pulling us back toward shore.

"One stone came crashing down, ricocheted off the cliff face and flew toward one of the floats, smashing it to pieces. There were nine people clinging to it. One was killed immediately when the stone struck. The others floundered in the water, but soon disappeared below the waves.

"Gradually we made headway and were soon safe from the raining stones. We could still hear the Tal screaming in rage. A few of them tried to descend the cliff, but quickly lost purchase and fell to their deaths.

"All that night we struggled in darkness, not knowing which way we were going. We managed to bring our floats close together, but still a few of us gave in to exhaustion and sank.

"Our children wailed in terror for what seemed to be many hours. We tried piling them on the floats but they would not all fit. We did what we could, but by morning there were fewer. Gone also were their parents.

"Finally we saw land. With renewed determination, we made our way forward. There on the shore we saw people, waving and shouting. Some of them waded out into the water to help pull us in. They were the same ones who had remained behind so many months before.

"Once we were safely on dry land, I made a count. Of the fifty-six who had made it to the water, only twenty-seven of us had survived. Lorn's mate Leo and their two sons were not among them."

For many minutes the two friends were silent, absorbed in what had been spoken. Broc remained motionless, head lowered, staring at the floor. Ahmahn again wondered why his brother had chosen to join him, but thought better of asking.

Broc finally stirred, sat upright, and continued.

"The Tal did not follow. Why, I'm not sure. We did not encounter them for a long time afterward. But that is yet another story.

"For a day and a night we remained there on the shoreline, mourning our loss. We stacked the remaining wooden bundles together and set them ablaze, offering tribute to those who lost their lives at the hands of the Tal and in the waters during our escape.

"My daughter Lorn would not speak for days afterwards. She would eat what was placed before her, but otherwise she did not respond. Sara spent almost all her time trying to console her, but nothing worked. She sat where we placed her. She walked with us when we moved, but never did she say a word.

"Then one night as we all sat around the fire, Lorn stood and walked over to me and her mother. She sat down between us, smiling, and told us how much she loved us. Then she began crying, sobbing quietly, the first response she had made since the loss of her mate and children.

"We held her close until her sobbing stopped. Then she stood slowly and said she was tired, that she was going to sleep. She hugged us both, then turned and walked the few paces to her bedding.

"The next morning when we awoke, Lorn's bed was empty. We thought she had gone to relieve herself, but after a long time she still did not return. We decided to go down to the shoreline to search for her. Sara was the first to see them. Footprints leading down to the water's edge."

Broc's eyes filled with tears. His body shivered for a few brief moments. Then he continued.

"Sara was never the same after that. She never laughed. She never cried. She just went from day to day, doing what was necessary to keep living, but nothing more. She never spoke except when it was necessary. At night she slept with her back toward me. Our son Eff told me he thought she had given up, that she no longer wanted to live.

"Eff never chose a mate. Instead he remained at his mother's side, caring for her, seeing to her needs, talking to her as though everything was normal, though she seldom if ever responded.

"It was almost four years later. I remember I was asleep in my bed, my back toward her. I was gently awakened by the warmth of her body drawn close to mine. I was about to turn over when I felt her breath on my neck. 'No, my mate,' she whispered. 'Lay still. Let me hold you.'

"I remember that moment like it was yesterday. It was supreme joy.

"The next morning I awoke with a chill. Sara's arm was still wrapped around me. It was cold."

CHAPTER 66

Ahmahn was speechless. Here before him sat one of his closest friends, someone he had shared his youth with. Someone who he trusted so much that he had entrusted the fate of his race to him.

But this wasn't the same man he had left only days before. Here was a man whose hair was grey and thinning. Whose face was drawn and wrinkled, whose entire countenance was one of hard experience, of suffering and anguish. His hands were worn and rough, the knuckles scarred and distorted with age and abuse.

Here was a man who had lived a lifetime in a space of time which Ahmahn thought of as only a few days.

He was humbled to realize that the few years of his meager life paled into insignificance compared to the decades experienced by this man.

Ahmahn no longer needed an explanation from his friend. He knew now why Broc had elected to leave his people. He could see in his brother's eyes a life-time spent coping with hardship, with joy and love, with pain and loss.

Who am I, he thought. Who am I, to think that my pain is so profound, so overwhelming, that I must abandon the ones I love, to seek solace in the stars? Here before me is a man more deserving of respite than I can ever hope to deserve.

"Broc, my brother, I know . . ." Ahmahn began, but Broc cut him off with a gentle wave of his hand.

"Yes. I understand what you feel, more so now than on that day when you left, so long ago. It is not so important what we experience, or even when or how long it takes. What *is* important is what we learn, how we apply what we've learned, who we become.

"When you told us of your plan to leave, I was filled with doubt. Not doubt in you, my brother. But rather doubt in myself. I was unsure that I could lead our people in the right direction. Not so much where we would go, but what we would learn, who we would become along the way.

"What I discovered over those many years was that you, my dear brother, were wise beyond your years. It was your insight, your confidence, which helped us to make a clean break with our origins, to leave behind the experiences of the past.

"Not to forget them, but to use the knowledge we acquired from our parents to help propel us into a new world, one where they could not go, but where we could thrive."

Ahmahn was in awe of his brother's insight. He had always had confidence in him, but until this moment he had never really appreciated how truly perceptive he had become. He was now convinced that those years, those decades, had molded Broc into a man of knowledge, a man of wisdom.

"Our combined clans eventually moved away from that place. We traveled south, moving farther inland as we went.

"Eff remained without a mate, choosing instead to focus on the well-being of the growing clan. The people grew to love him because of his dedication to them.

"From time to time we had confrontations with the Tal. Their numbers had not grown much, so it was not difficult to hold them at bay, trapped between us and the sea. Eventually they gave up their assaults. The last we saw of them they were moving southward along the coast. What ever became of them I do not know, nor do I care."

All the time Broc was telling his story, Ahmahn was drawn

closer to him, feeling his pain, understanding just what he had gone through. Their experiences were so similar. They had each felt the exhilaration associated with exploration of new lands, of seeing their families grow. They had each experienced loss of those closest to them.

It was now time to tell him what had happened to cause the death of their brother Sef.

"My brother, now it is time to tell Sef's story. You spoke of the necessity for us to make a clean break from our parents and their way of life. What happened to Sef and his father is a perfect example of why that break was necessary.

"Sef and his father rejoined their old family. His father became their leader. It was his actions, his weakness which lead to their deaths.

"Remember how we were warned never to mate with the old ones? Sef's father forgot or ignored that warning. The fruit of his union became an abomination. His offspring were not human, nor were they simian. They were beasts in the semblance of men. They would not coexist with their parents. They would not tolerate Sef's presence."

"They became the Tal."

Broc nodded knowingly.

"What you described is exactly how the Tal acted. They cared nothing for those they enslaved. They cared only for themselves."

At this point Evander chose to intervene. The two brothers turned to watch his entrance.

"Please excuse my interruption, my friends. I know this is a difficult time for you. But it is important that you understand what I'm about to tell you."

Evander found a chair at the edge of the room and dragged it to the center where the two men sat. Slowly he sat down, making deliberate eye contact with each of them.

"Your world is new. As yet there is but one race of humans there. But as time continues, that will change."

The two men had looks of confusion on their faces. Evander tried to explain as simply as possible.

"You remember the lands of your birth." The two men nodded.

"Those lands were hot almost all the time. There was also much rain and almost never any cold weather. Some of your people chose to remain in the homeland. Some moved south where they began to populate other areas. You and your clans chose to leave, going northward.

"As you moved out of your homelands, you experienced changes in the weather. Later, more of your people left you and moved westward, where little rain fell and forests gave way to endless sands, where the daytime sun beat down on them continuously.

"Nahm and his people moved to the east, where they also experienced different weather.

"We refer to the weather and other conditions under which peoplw live as 'environment'. There are many things which affect environment, but for now this explanation is sufficient.

"As time goes on your people will completely populate your world. And when that happens, most will choose to remain where they are, to stop their wandering.

"Over time their bodies will adapt to these changes in environment. Sometimes their skins will get darker. Sometimes others' skins will get lighter. Some people will even become different in height, or in facial characteristics.

"All these changes are normal, natural. People will come to look different and act differently, depending on where they live. But they will all still be people. They will all be human, because they will have mated with others of their kind.

"The Tal are different. They are not natural. Sef's father looked like his kind, but he was not. Inside his body and the body of his first mate, changes had been made which ensured that their offspring, their 'seed' would be human. It was the same for all the parents of the first generation of humans.

"The Tal are hybrid. They are not the same as human. Because they are different, they cannot breed . . . they cannot 'mate.'. . with humans or simians. Very seldom can they successfully breed among themselves.

"For this reason their numbers do not increase easily. It is unlikely they will be able to reproduce enough of themselves to last very long. Soon their race will die.

"Though I'm not certain of this, I believe that the Tal recognize this about themselves. They know that they are aberrations, that they don't belong. They know not how to reconcile this, and so rebel, trying to escape their reality. Their anger, their frustration, their confusion are in constant conflict.

"Other worlds have had similar experiences; not necessarily as your world has with the Tal; but rather, there have been conflicts between various races of humans. They have fought over land, or food, but mostly they have fought over power, dominance."

"Why would this happen, Evander?" asked Broc. "Don't they understand that differences can be settled without resorting to violence?"

Broc described several occasions when he had found it necessary to intervene when disputes occurred between members of his clan. They had always managed to resolve their differences.

"Your world is at an advantage because it is so young," Evander responded.

"Your population is still small. Your leadership is well qualified and conscientious. Your people see the need for cooperation because they are dependent on one another for survival. Will that necessarily change as your numbers increase?"

Ahmahn understood where the conversation was headed.

"It all depends on the attitude of the people, does it not?"

"This is so, my brother." said Broc. "I have spent my life contending with just such issues. I have done what was within my power to protect and serve my people. My son has also demonstrated his concern for the clan's welfare.

"Now I am old and tired. My resolve is still strong, but my body is weak. It is best that I place this responsibility in younger hands.

"I recall long ago, my brother, when Evander described to you the things you could and could not do if you chose to join him here. The memory of that has never left me. Even at the time I heard those words, I wanted to go with you. But I also had other responsibilities, more important than my own selfish desires.

"Now, as the end of my days draws near, my conscience is clear. I have done all I can do. I can now leave those responsibilities in more capable hands. While I am still able, I wish to join you here, and share these new adventures."

"My good friend Broc," said Evander. I admire you for all you've done, for your family and for your people. There are few like you, on your own world as well as on others. For this reason I'm prepared to offer something to you.

"Here on the *Brighid* as well on many other worlds, we have the capability to prolong life."

Ahmahn and Broc were astonished by his statement. Evander saw this and hurried to clarify what he had said.

"Please don't misunderstand. We cannot make you live forever, but we can sustain your life for a considerable amount of time beyond what would normally be expected on your world.

"You and all your people have lived very difficult lives. It hasn't been easy, travelling, enduring extremes in weather, finding enough food. These factors contribute greatly to the wear and tear on your bodies.

"There are many naturally occurring plants as well as man-made substances which help to sustain the human body. In time your race will discover them and put them to good use.

"We of the Seeder races are forbidden from interfering with the lives of those who we watch over. Ethical, moral and spiritual values must evolve naturally if a race is to progress. But there *are* certain things we can do to help those who have demonstrated worthiness.

"Your son Eff is now in possession of your transceiver. Already he has demonstrated high moral character as a leader. We will therefore provide information for him regarding some of the things your people can use for their benefit. We'll teach him, and he in turn will teach them.

"As for you, we cannot completely restore your youth; but we can do some things which will help you to live a much longer life. The pain you now feel because of past injuries can be eliminated. We can provide certain foods and substances which will stop, or in some cases reverse effects of injury or ageing. We can perform surgeries which will replace or repair damaged tissue or bone."

Neither of the brothers had ever heard of such a thing. They were incredulous, if not completely disbelieving of what Evander had said. Amon expressed his concern.

"You speak of morality and ethics, yet you offer us things which interfere with our natural development. Is that not of itself unethical?"

"Your point is well taken, my friend. Let me explain a bit more in detail.

"Remember when Sef and his father chose to leave your clan? That was a difficult decision for Sef to make, and for you to accept. He knew the risks he was taking, but chose to support his father, rather than forbid him from leaving.

"You, in turn, warned them both of the risk they were taking. Yet you allowed them to choose for themselves. Had Sef prevented his father, or you prevented either of them from leaving, that would have been an infringement on their freedom, or *agency*, as we call it in this context.

"We Seeders are bound by the same standards. We cannot impose our will on any person or group, nor can we prevent bad decisions from being made. All we can do is offer good advice, and then let events unfold as they will.

"In this case each of you has made decisions which demonstrate high moral and ethical character. These are traits which are not taught, but are learned through experience. You feel compassion one for another, not hate or envy.

"When we see such behavior, we too feel compassion. And we do what we can, within certain bounds, to offer encouragement and assistance.

"The Tal also had similar decisions to make. They knew they were different, that they didn't fit in. They could have chosen to be compassionate to one another. They could have chosen to live in harmony with those around them. It would certainly have been difficult for them, even as it has sometimes been difficult for you and other members of your clan.

"Their simian parents were essentially peaceful. Certainly there were occasional disagreements. But all in all they lived peacefully together.

"The Tal, on the other hand, chose to become envious, to not appreciate all the good that was around them. They chose rebellion rather than cooperation. They chose hate rather than compassion.

"In so doing, they destroyed their relationships with their families, and will likely destroy themselves in the long run.

"We choose not to assist them because of the destructive decisions they have made."

Over many generations, Broc's clan continued to grow, eventually spreading out to fill all of Central and Western Europe.

The Tal continued moving southward along the coast, blocked from returning to their stone edifice. The shallows, which they had barely been able to cross in their pursuit of Broc's clan, had now become impassable as sea levels continued to rise.

Though they tried to expand inland, they were beaten back by the descendents of Broc and his son Eff. Eventually they reached the southern-most tip of the continent, where they were held in check by the expanding human population.

With their backs to the sea and their movement blocked from the east and the west, they took refuge in the only place left for them, the huge stone mountain at the confluence of the Mediterranean Sea and the Atlantic Ocean. There they remained until the last of them perished.

CHAPTER 67

Ambia stood at the window, watching and listening to the three men just beyond the glass. From time to time Evander made comments. But she really wasn't paying much attention to him. She was absorbed in the interplay between the two brothers on the other side of the glass.

She had a basic understanding of what was referred to by the *Brighid* crew as "time dilation," but this was the first time she had actually seen an example of the phenomenon.

Evander had explained that when the two men lived together on their planet ('Earth,' they called it), they were approximately the same age. It amazed her to see that in the space of just a few *Brighid* days, the man called Broc had aged almost an entire lifetime, compared to Ahmahn, who looked to be in his early twenties.

She also marvelled at the fact that though Ahmahn was a much younger man, his insight and perception were equal to, if not superior to a man with much more life experience. She was beginning to see why Evander had taken such an interest in him.

Just moments after Evander entered the room to join the two men, Ambia's shoulder mic beeped. She tapped it once.

"Ambia here."

"Orion sector monitoring. We just received another signal from the 'Earth' planet and have dispatched a shuttle to pick up another

individual, per standing instructions from Section Head Evander.
His com link has been disabled, so we can't contact him directly.
Our last communication showed him with you. Do you have con-
tact with him?"

"Yes. He's in Orientation right now and left specific instructions
that he not be disturbed." Ambia saw that the three men were
still deep in conversation.

"Understood. The shuttle should arrive within the hour. As soon
as possible, please inform the Section Head."

"Will do. Ambia out."

She was unsure of what to do next. Evander had told her not to
disturb him, but she was sure that this event needed to be passed
to him as soon as possible. She tapped her shoulder mic twice.

"Message center. For Section Head Evander: Sir, I just received
an urgent message from sector monitoring and have gone to the
shuttle bay to await an arrival from Earth. I'll report back upon
its arrival. Ambia out."

Glancing once more into the window, she turned and walked
briskly down the hall to the lifts.

CHAPTER 68

The conversation eventually died out as the two men found there was nothing left to be said on the subject. Evander was the first to rise.

"Gentlemen. May I suggest we take a walk over to the Regeneration section? We have specialists there who can explain more fully what can be done to improve your physical appearance, Broc, as well as help minimize the effects your harsh life has had on your body."

"Will I be made young, like my brother Ahmahn here?" Broc was guardedly optimistic about what Evander had told him. He looked forward to being relieved of the pain in his back and legs. His fingers were gnarled and twisted with arthritis. They ached constantly.

"There's a lot that we can do to alleviate pain, but we can't stop the ageing process. We can, however, slow it down considerably."

Evander was interrupted by the quiet beeping of his shoulder mic, which had automatically reactivated when he left the Orientation room. The mic was set to "private," so only he could hear the message from Ambia. By the time the message was finished, they had reached their destination. Evander opened the door and escorted the two men to the reception desk where he introduced them to the on-duty technician.

"These are our new friends Ahmahn and Broc. They have some questions they would like to ask you."

Turning to the men, he added: "Please feel free to ask her any questions which come to mind. She will be happy to answer. For now, will you please excuse me. There is another matter I must attend to."

The young lady rose from her chair and gestured for the two men to join her in the reception area just a few steps away.

CHAPTER 69

Nahm was still in awe of what he had experienced in the last few hours. It seemed that only minutes had passed from the time he last spoke to Leona via the transceiver until her arrival inside the huge glowing sphere.

Liam (Nahm's youngest son) stood a dozen yards away beside the clan's long-house, sheltered from the icy sub-Arctic wind. In his arms he cradled the transceiver which his father had entrusted him with. Its dull blue glow had faded to black as soon as the sphere touched down.

With a gesture from Leona, Nahm stepped up onto the platform. The last he saw of his son, he was turning away, not once glancing back.

Their parting had been difficult. Liam wanted desperately to go with his father. But Nahm had reminded him of the many conversations they had had prior to this moment.

"He's a good son. Much more reliable than his three older brothers," Nahm thought as he took his seat inside the spacecraft. "Our people will need his courage and skills when they begin the crossing."

The crossing Nahm referred to was a narrow land bridge joining northeastern Russia to the North American continent. The two continents were already joined farther north at the Arctic Circle.

But the weather was too extreme there, according to returning scouting parties.

The route they would be traveling would eventually slip below the sea centuries later, leaving only a long, curving chain of islands known as the Aleutian's.

Leona directed Nahm to a seat, and then punched in some commands on her control tablet. The walls of the sphere seemed to dissolve, affording a clear 360-degree view of the surrounding landscape. Blowing snow swirled around the craft, but Nahm felt no sensation of cold.

Though he could feel no movement, he knew the craft had begun to rise. He could see the landscape shrinking below him, at first slowly, but then more quickly as the sphere gathered speed. In only a matter of moments the long-house had shrunk to a barely discernible speck, surrounded by snow-covered hills. They too became quickly indiscernible.

Seemingly in a blur, the earth fell away before his eyes. The continental coastline came into view, shrinking all the while. Then the narrow Aleutian land bridge, then the western edge of the American continent.

Within a few more moments he could see the curvature of his home planet, with the crescent moon rising out of the east. A bright flash came from over his left shoulder. He turned to see the intense yellow ball of the sun, at first overpoweringly huge, then shrinking, shrinking. He turned back, but the earth was gone, replaced by a tiny blue ball which shrank to but a pinpoint of light. Very quickly the sun too shrank to a mere pinpoint, one of hundreds and then thousands more, twinkling against a black background.

He felt the slightest sense of movement, as though he was slowly turning. The star field moved from left to right, then stabilized. In the center of his view he could barely make out a bright dot, larger than the pinpoints of light which surrounded it. It gradually became larger, and then more quickly began to fill his field of view.

The object was circular, with hundreds of thin spikes protruding from its perimeter. Its center wavered, shimmered, looking like sunlight reflecting off the surface of a lake.

Within moments the object filled his view. The shimmering surface seemed to rush toward him. Soon the perimeter was out of his field of view.

He felt that he was falling, plunging downward toward that shimmering surface. The thought of falling into a lake filled him with dread. He started in near panic when he felt a mild tingling pass over his body. Leona was saying something. Her voice was soft and gentle, but he couldn't make out what she was saying. He was awestruck, overwhelmed by the visual and physical sensation that surrounded him.

As quickly as it had begun, the falling sensation stopped. The shimmering surface dissolved, replaced by a black background filled with more specks of light. In the center another speck was growing, taking on a shape different from what he had just seen. This object was long and slender. As it grew closer he began to make out shapes on its surface. They were angular, multifaceted, much like the crystals he had seen inside caves where his family had frequently taken shelter.

Just as had happened before, the object continued to grow until it filled his entire field of view, except it didn't seem to grow as rapidly.

Again he felt a slight sensation of movement as the object grew ever closer. Four blinking lights on the surface of the object came into view, this time from the right. The lights were in a diamond pattern.

Again the sensation of movement, as the diamond pattern rotated until it was a square. The top two lights were light blue in color. The bottom two were yellow. The lights came closer and closer, until suddenly a narrow line of white light appeared between the two flashing yellow lights. The line began to expand, growing wider from bottom to top, until it reached the level of the two blue lights. Just as it did so, the pulsing yellow lights turned a continuous green.

As the shuttle moved closer, Nahm could now see that the white light was actually an opening in the side of the huge object. The opening grew larger as the sphere moved slowly forward. Beyond the opening was an enclosure, like a well-lit cave, except the walls, ceiling and floor were flat, smooth.

A narrow yellow line appeared on the floor. The sphere was following the line, Nahm could tell, because all along the places where the walls met the floor, other objects were parked. Some of them were spheres like his. Others had strange, unfamiliar shapes. A few of them reminded him of birds in flight. His sphere was passing close by them as it followed the yellow line.

Nahm saw the line begin to flash, changing from yellow to green, then back again as the sphere continued moving forward. Ahead he could see the line ended. The sphere approached that end, then stopped. He felt the slightest jolt as the sphere settled in position. The light stopped flashing, this time staying green.

Directly in front of him he saw an opening appear in the wall. There were two people standing just beyond the opening. They took a few steps forward as a flat platform extended from the wall outward toward the sphere. One was male and the other female, he could see. They wore strange clothing, similar to what Leona wore.

Leona again tapped on her tablet. The walls of the sphere once again appeared, blocking Nahm's view. Immediately an opening appeared in the side of the sphere directly in line with the extended platform.

The taller person, the male, began walking forward, hands clasped behind his back. The female remained where she was. Nahm saw that she was smiling.

Nahm rose and moved closer to the opening, but stopped short, reluctant to step onto the platform. The tall man stopped at the end of the platform and extended a hand toward him.

"Hello, my new friend," the man said. "My name is Evander. Be welcome on board the *Brighid*. There are two of your friends here who will be very pleased to see you."

CHAPTER 70

"It amazes me that these people can restore youth!" said Ahmahn to his two closest friends.

Broc had emerged from the "regen" chamber only a few minutes ahead of Nahm. Both men still retained their grey hair and beards, but the wrinkles in their faces, which before had dominated their appearance were now much smaller, almost invisible. Both men stood more erect now than before the process had begun. Their general countenance seemed to be more youthful. Even their eyes seemed to be brighter.

Evander smiled as he stood to greet the two men. "It pleases me to see you looking so well! As many times as I've seen the process, I'm always amazed to see such remarkable transformations." He stepped forward and put his hands on each man's shoulder.

"As I said to you before, your youth has not been restored. It is your general health that has been improved."

"But I feel so much better! As when I was a young man!" Nahm smiled, stretching his arms out to his side, inhaling deeply. Turning to Ahmahn, he added. "I feel as good now as you look!" Then to Broc, "You too look better, even if you are still old."

The four men laughed good naturedly. Evander stepped backed from the three men.

"Come, my friends. Let me show you around the ship. Perhaps you would like to learn more about us and our culture." Evander led them out of the room and across the hall to a bank of doors. Evander pressed a button next to one of the doors, which opened to reveal a small room. As the men stepped into the small space, Nahm asked:

"I know that this ship, as you call it, is very large. How many people are here?"

"Many thousands are on board this ship. But we have some ships which are much smaller." Evander responded.

"You mean like the one which brought us here?"

"Yes. There are several like that one. But there are also some which are somewhat larger. The one you came here in can only accommodate six people at a time. Those are used exclusively for missions like the ones which brought us together. They are designed to operate primarily outside a planet's atmosphere."

"I don't understand this word 'atmosphere'", said Broc.

"Atmosphere is the air we breathe." The three men looked confused. Evander smiled reassuringly.

"I know much of what I say you don't understand. But be assured; as we explore this ship things will become much more clear. Come. Let's return to the flight deck, the place where you arrived on the *Brighid*. There I'll explain more completely about atmosphere."

The four men remained standing in the small space as Evander spoke. After only a minute the door opened again. They could see that they were now in a different location than the one they had just left. There in front of them, across a wide hallway was another door, this one of transparent glass, flanked on both sides by windows. The four stepped out into the hall.

"I remember this place." said Broc. "But how did we get here? I remember we walked along a hallway before. This time we went into that small room and then turned around, and now we're are here. How is this possible?"

"Before, you were new here." Evander began, "We thought it best that you become comfortable here before being introduced to our technology. That's why we had you do something familiar, like walking, to help you feel comfortable.

"The regen chamber that you both experienced is part of our technology which needs to be explained."

"Wait!" said Ahmahn. "Do you mean to say that your people do not need to walk? I don't understand."

"Certainly we all walk. But usually only for short distances. Do you remember the first room you entered when you arrived? That room is called the 'orientation' room. When you left that room, though you didn't notice, you were relocated to a place several hundred yards away.

"To you it seemed that you had only crossed the hall to the 'regen' waiting room. But in fact, you had travelled a much greater distance."

"This is not possible!" shouted Broc. "I did not walk such a distance as you describe!"

"And that is why you were allowed to walk when you first left the hangar deck . . . so that you would not be disoriented, as you are now. Come. Let's go back out onto the hangar deck. I'll explain more as we walk. First, and this is very important for each of you to remember. See that green line on the hangar deck floor?" Evander pointed to the line directly under the sphere that had brought Nahm to the *Brighid*.

"Yes," offered Nahm. "I remember seeing it change to green from yellow when Leona and I first arrived."

"Good!" said Evander. "There are a few other places on this ship where you'll see that green line. In those places, as well as the hangar deck, it is vital that you not attempt to enter if the line is yellow. It has to do with 'atmosphere', as I mentioned before.

"When the line is yellow it means that there is no air inside the room. Without air (or 'atmosphere') we cannot breathe. It's like being under water." The men nodded, still not completely understanding.

The door to the hangar deck opened as they approached. There before them sat the sphere that had brought Nahm just a few hours prior. Flanking it on both sides were other spheres. Flanking them and extending all along the walls were other craft varying in size and shape. The platform which had been there when the sphere arrived, had retracted back under the floor, revealing a short flight of six stairs. The four men descended and turned to the left at Evander's direction. As they walked slowly past the row of spheres, Evander continued his explanation.

"Ahmahn, you expressed concern about how we were able to move long distances on this ship without walking. What you observed is actually the most important part of our technology. We refer to it as 'teleporting,' or 'T.'

"The room we just left is called a 'T' chamber. When we step into such a room, we are moved to a different place on the ship. We say the name of the place we want to go and the chamber takes us there."

"How is this possible?" said Ahmahn. "I felt no movement."

"A good question, my friend. You see, much of what we perceive as movement has to do with our senses. For example, as you jump off a ledge or a high place toward the ground below, your body feels lighter, your skin feels the movement of air across it, and particularly, your eyes see that you're moving from one place to another. When you land on the ground, your body senses that you are no longer falling.

"However, if those senses are interrupted; if their sensitivity to movement is blocked, then you will not recognize that you are moving.

"When we enter into a "T" chamber, our senses are essentially blocked, so that we can move from one place to another without feeling the sensation of movement.

"Remember when you were on the shuttle on your way here? Remember the huge spiked object that you felt you were falling into? Had your eyes not seen its approach, you would never have known that you were moving."

"I remember that," said Nahm. "I felt like I was falling. My eyes told me this, but not my body. It was very strange. You are right. Had I not seen it, I would never have known."

"That huge object you saw is called a 'LINK.' It's a gigantic machine that has the capability to move us, in small shuttle craft or even whole ships like the *Brighid*, from one place in space to another place very far away, without us feeling that we have moved at all, or that much time has passed."

"How is this done?" asked Broc.

"It is a process we call 'Matrix Mapping and Transferral,' or MMT. The LINKS refer to it as 'Seeing,' and before you ask, there is little more I can explain . . . because I simply don't know. Long ago, when we first discovered the 'LINKS.' . . ."

"You mean you did not build that thing?"

"Oh, my . . . no. My people, as advanced as we think we are, cannot begin to do what the LINKS can do."

"There are more of those things?"

"Oh, yes. Many thousands. When you came here, you experienced just two of them. You entered one and exited from another."

The three men slowed to a stop, trying to digest all this new information. Evander noticed their distress and decided to change the subject.

"Your understanding will come soon enough. For now, let's take a short ride, shall we?"

Evander led the men toward one of the bird-like vehicles which had a short flight of stairs leading up into an opening in the side of the craft. To the right, as the men entered, was a long empty cylinder-shaped space large enough for a man to walk upright in. A row of web-like chairs lined each wall.

To the left was a short ladder attached to a platform. Evander gestured for them to climb the ladder, warning them to duck so they wouldn't bump their heads on the low ceiling. The platform they stepped onto was what Evander called the 'flight deck.' To the left were three chairs, two facing a row of windows, and the third slightly higher and centered behind them. A fourth chair was located to the right, facing away from the windows, toward a bank of dials and switches.

Evander squeezed into the left forward-facing chair and gestured that Ahmahn sit in the right one. Broc took the center seat and Nahm the one on the right. As soon as Nahm sat down the seat rotated to face forward.

Evander started pressing buttons and twisting knobs as he explained.

"This vehicle can do everything the spheres can do, but it can also do something which they cannot. Pretty soon you'll see what I mean. I think you'll enjoy it."

Through the bank of windows they could see out onto the hangar deck. People who just moments before had been working on and around the other craft, were now all moving toward exits spaced around the deck. The now familiar lines on the floor were pulsing from green to yellow.

Inside their craft they could hear a faint whirring sound which increased in pitch until it was more of a soft squeal.

As soon as the lines on the floor outside stopped pulsing and turned yellow, their craft lifted off the floor and began moving forward, again following a yellow line. The line ended at what looked like a wall, which soon began to raise. It was not a wall, but a door, the same one they had entered through before.

Evander drew their attention to a rectangular green light on the console in front of him. It was marked with the letters 'INS.'

"This little button is what makes this craft different from the spheres. You'll understand what I mean in just a few moments."

The craft moved forward and out through the hangar door. The brightness of the hangar deck was replaced by a field of pure black dotted with stars. Evander took hold of what looked like a small stick protruding vertically from the console immediately in front of him. He moved it slightly to the left, which caused the craft to bank in that direction as it moved outward, away from the *Brighid*.

Each of the men felt a slight increase in weight as the craft manoeuvred, pressing them lightly to the right. Then their weights returned to normal as the craft began moving in a straight line along the length of the giant mother ship.

"My friends, we're going to take a short trip to a world, a planet, that we're just beginning to explore, with thoughts to 'seeding' it, just as we did to your 'earth.'"

He moved the stick to the right, causing the craft to bank right. They felt themselves being pressed lightly to the left. Again the craft stopped banking, this time pointing away from the mother ship, toward what looked like a small bluish dot surrounded by tiny white specks of light, filling the view before them.

Evander pressed the stick slightly forward. This time they felt that they were being pressed back into their seats. The view before them didn't change. The light blue dot remained centered in their field of view. Evander pressed another button and the view disappeared, to be replaced by a view of the *Brighid*, shrinking in size as they watched.

"As you can see from this rear view, we're moving away from the *Brighid* at a fairly rapid rate. You can tell we're moving because you can see it, and feel it. Now, watch what happens when I press the green button."

The color of the light pulsed from green to yellow, and then remained yellow. Immediately the sensation of movement stopped. They once again felt their normal weight. They were no longer being pressed back into their seats. Evander pressed a button on top of the stick.

As they watched, almost instantly the *Brighid* shrank to just a point of light, indistinguishable from the others which filled the screen. The view switched back, facing the direction they were travelling.

This time the bluish dot was rapidly growing. Very quickly they began to see changes in the color of the dot as it grew. Brownish green swatches began taking shape in the darkening blue. Greyish white wisps, like smoke, became visible, partially covering many of the swatches.

"That is what I saw when I left our world! Have we returned?" Nahm exclaimed.

"No. This is another world, very similar to yours, but as yet there are no people there. Before we take orbit around this planet, let me explain a bit about this button.

"Remember when it was green, you could sense movement. The weight of your bodies seemed to shift slightly as the craft turned. Then, when the light turned yellow, the sensation of movement stopped."

"Yes. I remember those feelings when we were in the sphere. But they weren't so strong then." Ahmahn replied.

"That's because the system was operating in automatic mode. For purposes of demonstration, I operated the system manually so you could sense, so you could 'feel' the difference.

"That button controls what we call an "Inertia Nullification System,' or INS. It has another name, too, which I'll demonstrate when we descend into the planet's atmosphere.

"This ship uses some of the technology used by the 'LINKS.' It isn't designed to travel the great distances afforded to us by the 'LINKS.' But! This ship can do something which even the 'LINKS' can't do. It can maneuver through a planet's atmosphere without the need for Inertia Nullification.

"When the rectangular light turns back to green, a different system is in play. We also call it INS. But now, when the ship is in atmosphere, INS stands for Inertial Navigation System. It allows us to keep track of where we are, relative to a known point on the planet's surface, just like it did when we were moving around the outside of the *Brighid*.

"Once we were clear of the *Brighid*, we began to move away, at first at a relatively slow rate, which you could feel. But if we were to stay in 'green mode,' it would take us several days to travel from the *Brighid* to the planet. When we switched to 'yellow' mode, the ship could travel very much faster without us feeling the increase in speed."

"Then what is the difference between the two, what did you call them . . . 'systems'?" asked Ahmahn.

Evander was again pleasantly surprised to hear Ahmahn ask such a question. It was further confirmation that this man was indeed unique, significantly more intelligent than his peers. He smiled as he responded.

"It's all very complicated. Much of it I don't understand, myself. Let me just say that the 'LINKS' employ Inertia Nullification as well as MMT, or Matrix Mapping and Transferral, and probably other systems that are completely beyond our comprehension."

The craft had decelerated and was beginning to settle into the planet's atmosphere. They could feel buffeting as the wings of the craft began to bite into the air.

"We could still use Inertia Nullification here, if we wanted to. But then we wouldn't feel what it's like to fly like a bird. The 'wings' on this craft are similar in shape to those of birds. They allow us to manoeuvre in the atmosphere just as a bird does, except our wings don't flap They remain stationary. Instead of moving the wings, we use what we call thrusters which push against the air and allow us to speed up, slow down and turn."

Evander once again grasped the stick, this time in his left hand, as his right rested on the center console, index and middle fingers manipulating two small spherical controls.

Ahmahn sat quietly in his seat, closely observing all that Evander did and said. It was obvious that he was enjoying himself. His enthusiasm was affecting everyone. Broc and Nahm sat transfixed, wide-eyed, watching the spectacular view through the wind screen. Amon's attention focused on Evander's words. Here was a man who genuinely loved what he was doing.

"Sometimes we humans think we're smarter than we really are. But for all our knowledge, for all our advanced technology, for all our supposed sophistication, we are still unable to replicate the magnificent simplicity which is found in nature. Sometimes, though, we come close."

A wide smile came upon his face as he focused his attention through the window before him.

"Hold on my friends! Feel what it's like to *fly!*"

CHAPTER 71

The flight around the planet was short in duration, but long in excitement. The three friends marvelled as the sights flashed past. First, lush forests, then lofty mountain ranges, then barren deserts, finally, vast stretches of turquoise blue oceans.

After several minutes of aerobatic maneuvering, the three friends were feeling a bit queezy. Evander recognized the symptoms and so slowly ascended until the craft no longer responded to his stick manipulations.

Once again he punched the INS button as the craft rose out of the planet's atmosphere and its gravitational pull lessened. The view through the window quickly transformed from familiar sky-blue, to white-specked black.

The craft continued "rising" until in the far distance they could just make out the shape of the *Brighid*.

"We won't be moving quite so quickly this time, so you can get a better look at the *Brighid*. It is truly an amazing spacecraft. It's almost like a small world in itself."

Taking the craft through a few helical laps around the mother ship, Evander maneuvered back to a hangar bay, this time on the opposite side of the ship.

As they entered through the hangar door, several other craft were visible parked along the perimeter. These were different from the others they had seen on the other side.

"These craft are much more specialized than the ones you've seen. The smallest ones are for two people only. They're carried inside those larger craft parked on the far wall."

"The larger ones are designed to remain for extended periods of time on the worlds we visit. It doesn't happen often, but sometimes it becomes advantageous for us to remain on a planet for more time than is usual."

"Why would you want to do that?" asked Ahmahn. "Is it not your objective to allow races to grow on their own, without interference? It seems to me that this is a contradiction. Do you not increase the chance of being detected if you stay for a longer period of time?"

"Certainly that is true." responded Evander. "But our technology is such that we can avoid detection with a high degree of success. Just to cite one example, did you know that all the time your father was experimenting with weapons, he was being monitored? It's unlikely he would have told you this because it all happened before you came along."

"I knew nothing of this." said Ahmahn.

Evander brought the craft to a stop in one of the vacant parking stalls. Once the green 'all clear' signal came on, the four men exited the craft. Evander led them out of the hangar as the conversation continued.

"We also monitored the progress of you and Broc and Nahm and your clans, as well as many other clans, a few of which failed to thrive. Though it pained us to remain uninvolved, those other clans had made choices which took them in directions where failure was inevitable."

"Why then did you choose to intervene with us?" asked Nahm.

"We didn't actually intervene in the sense that we did things to influence your development. All we actually did was provide you with transceivers, so that if you chose to do so, you could contact us."

"Could you not have done so with the others, rather than allow them to perish?" asked Nahm.

"I know it might seem that in so doing, we were being cruel. But the truth is we cannot save all those whom we monitor. Our first priority must always be to allow people to make their own decisions. When we made contact with you, you had already demonstrated a willingness to stand for what you believed to be high moral standards, standards which we too uphold. You chose the right course of action. Had you not done so, we would not have made contact."

Broc was not satisfied with Evander's response. "Does that not beg the question: What is morally right? And who of us is qualified to make that decision?"

"Excellent question, my friend." Evander was pleased that the conversation had taken this direction. "All people are born with a conscience, that is, an ability to discern between right and wrong. There are, of course, many factors which influence the decisions we make. Sometimes we make bad decisions and must suffer the consequences of those decisions. If we are wise, we will not make similar mistakes again.

"All too frequently, people make decisions based on their own selfish desires, with little or no concern for the long-term consequences. If they repeat these bad habits enough, at some point it becomes almost impossible for them to redirect themselves back in a positive direction."

"That must be what happened to the Tal." said Broc. "They were beyond reason."

CHAPTER 72

Later that night the three 'brothers' lay quietly in their beds. The events of the day had been beyond description for each of them, and though they were tired, sleep eluded them. After a time Nahm spoke.

"These things Evander talks about; conscience . . . agency . . . freedom. They all make sense. They touch me deeply. I wonder why I never considered such things until he spoke of them."

"Maybe it's because you were so busy living them that you saw no need to give them description." said Broc.

"Ours is a new culture," Ahmahn added. "In our world we exist on a survival level, not like what we see here. Evander's culture is thousands of years older than ours. They no longer must concern themselves just with surviving from one day to the next. Their technology has afforded them the luxury of exploring other facets of their lives. They have a much better understanding of their relationships with one another. It seems that they have eliminated conflicts such as what happened with our brother Sef."

"My brother," said Nahm. "It has been forty years since you left us . . ."

"Yet in my time it has only been a few days," Ahmahn pointed out.

"This is true. Nevertheless, for us much time has passed. Many things have we learned in that time. Many conflicts have we confronted. There have been those in our clan who have vied for power and control; who have wanted to exercise dominion over others, to take away our rights to decide for ourselves. We have experienced frustration and anger under such conditions. Often conflicts have arisen which have divided us. On many occasions it has been those conflicts which have caused some families to leave the group, to form their own clans."

Broc sat up on the edge of his bed.

"And so it is, my brothers. Because we have been nomadic; because we have desired to explore our world; when such conflicts have arisen, rather than stay and resolve our differences, too frequently we have chosen to separate. We have learned to co-exist with those of like mind, but we have failed to appreciate and understand those with whom we disagree.

Ahmahn felt the need to interject, to find common ground between him and his two friends.

"Yet, for all this, still we think alike. How many times have each of us lain awake at night wondering at the marvels which surround us? How often have we puzzled over the reasons why events unfold as they do? How often have we rejoiced, only to be brought down in anguish? How often have we felt despair, loneliness, isolation, even while surrounded by our friends and families?"

Ahmahn's thoughts went back over the events of his life. The joys of his childhood, traveling with his mother and father; the discovery of Broc and his family; how they had been joined by Nahm and Sef and all the others. He remembered Nera, great with child; the day she died; how he had felt it near impossible to deal with his anguish; then later, how Mahrohm had chosen him as her mate, even though he had been reluctant after his loss of Nera; the similarities between those two women, and their differences; how he had loved them . . . how he still loved them, how he still mourned their loss.

"My brothers, my heart begins to grieve for not knowing the

fate of those I love." Ahmahn paused briefly, taking hold of his emotions, lest they overpower him. "I rejoice that you have come here. My heart swells with my love for each of you. And yet I see what the years have done to you. These machines which surround us may have restored some semblance of your youth; but still, time has taken its toll. I see it in your eyes."

"As do we also see this in you," said Broc.

"For us many years have passed, while for you it has been only days. Yet in your countenance can be seen the toll the events of your life have taken."

Reaching across the narrow space that separated their beds, he placed a hand on Ahmahn's knee.

"For each of us the decision to leave our people was most difficult. Yet as we studied it out in our minds and in our hearts, each of us saw the wisdom in allowing others to take up the challenge. Though we feared for their well-being, we knew that they must learn on their own terms; that they must stand or fall on their own merit. And now that we are separated, we wonder how they have fared."

Ahmahn stood slowly, stepped out from between the two beds and walked the short distance to the opposite wall. Turning back to face his friends, he hesitated, unsure of how to express what he was feeling. The dim light from overhead cast shadows across his face, rendering his expression indistinct. He hoped his friends would not see the tears in his eyes and the anguish that he felt in his heart.

"My brothers, I fear that I lack the tenacity which you possess. Those many years of experience you've acquired are as a void for me. Though I strive to understand, how can I if I have not walked a similar path?"

"The path for each of us has been different," said Broc. "We are brothers of the heart and of the spirit, but we are each separate and distinct. Each of us must learn in our own way. My dear friend

Ahmahn, neither I nor Nahm have lost a mate, or a child, or yet a second mate. Neither of us has felt such anguish."

Nahm started to stand, then hesitated and sat back down. Looking first to Ahmahn and then to Broc, he took a deep breath, then began.

"Our losses and our loves are unique to each of us. Though we strive to empathize one with another, in our hearts we know that we cannot completely do so. We are kindred spirits, yet we are separate. Perhaps it is that feeling of lonely separateness which draws us together."

Ahmahn clasped his hands in front of him and bowed his head. He was now beginning to feel confident that his friends would understand. . . .

"My brothers, do you not long to know what has become of your loved ones?"

"We do, assuredly." said Broc. "But we also know that our decision to come here has rendered that impossible. This we learned just as you did. Our bloodline may still continue, but those people with whom we associated have most likely gone the way of all life."

Ahmahn returned to his place and sat facing his friends.

"I wish to know what has become of my people, of my race. For me it has been but a few days, but still I wonder. Was I hasty in deciding to leave? Could I have done something differently? Also I wonder, is there something more I can do?"

"I feel the same," said Broc.

"As do I," said Nahm.

Ahmahn sighed in relief.

"Thank you, my brothers. I had feared you would think I wanted to abandon you after so short a time of our reunion.

"We don't know what to expect upon our return, but of this we can be certain. It will not be the same as it was."

CHAPTER 73

"Much has transpired since you chose to return to your world." Evander escorted the three men into the Com Center, where Zuri was waiting.

Ahmahn walked up to her and extended his hand. She did likewise and they stood quietly for a long moment before Ahmahn spoke. "It is my understanding that it was you who initiated my 'seeding.'"

Zuri felt embarrassed as she replied. "Actually, sir, all I did was follow Evander's instructions. It was the Bio-pod that did the actual implant."

"Nevertheless, it is my honor and pleasure to meet you."

Evander motioned that Ahmahn should join the others at the console. "As you know, because of time dilation it will not be possible for any of you to return to the familiarity of your own times. However, there is much that we can report from the records kept since your departure."

Evander pressed a few buttons on his tablet. In the center of the console a hologram began to form. A spherical grid-work quickly formed, then was overlayed with a neutral-colored texture. The sphere began to rotate. As it did so, the neutral color was replaced by shades of green and brown and blue.

"This represents your home world. The blue represents oceans which surround continents, the places where your people now reside."

A yellow spot appeared in the center of the African continent, and began to spread northward and southward. Yellow fingers began to sprout, moving outward to the east and west.

"The spot you just saw is your original homeland. As your people increased, you can see how they began to spread, until eventually they filled the whole of the continent."

Evander continued, tracing the yellow lines, explaining how the human population continued its growth. Pointing to the Sea of Marmara, north-east of the Mediterranean sea, he explained, "Nahm, Broc; this is the place where your tribes separated. This is also the place where Ahmahn made his departure."

One yellow line continued westward until it stopped in the British Isles. Another line proceeded eastward, branching out to fill the remainder of the Asian continent.

Pointing to the line that stopped in the British Isles, Evander continued. "Broc; this is the place where you confronted the Tal."

A red dot appeared where the green line stopped. A thin red line moved back slightly eastward, then turned south and followed the coastline to the Strait of Gibraltar, where it began fading and eventually disappeared.

"The Tal followed your migration northward out of your homeland. And while you tarried near the Sea of Marmara, they continued westward. Your progenitors eventually defeated them here." He pointed to the Rock of Gibraltar.

From the Sea of Marmara the yellow line continued eastward, eventually crossing a narrow strip of land which connected to another large continent.

"Nahm; your people have populated all of the eastern continent and have begun filling this one also." He pointed to North America.

Back on the African continent a blue spot appeared.

"Ahmahn, do you recall how some of your clan departed and went westward into the desert?"

"Yes. A few of them returned, but most did not. I've often wondered what became of them."

"Many perished in that harsh land," said Evander. "But some survived by staying close to the great inland sea. Over time they built large communities, especially in this lush region." He pointed to the Nile delta region.

"There they thrived and became engaged in building your world's first successful large civilization. But unfortunately corruption has begun to set in. The people have chosen unwisely. They have been seduced by promises of great riches and power, and have chosen as their leaders, people who value domination over cooperation."

"It is as I feared, then. Some of them have succumbed to their base desires and have corrupted those who follow them."

"Yes. Some. But not all. We fear that if these corrupt few continue to grow in power and influence, this new civilization may not survive."

"But what of the tribes of Broc and Nahm? Can they not help prevent this?"

"If it was that easy, then yes. But you must understand, those tribes are far away. And each of them will have their own challenges, similarly as Broc had to face with the Tal. Not necessarily with an aberrant race, but certainly with problems unique to each of them. It has always been the case. As the LINKS say: 'It has ever been so.' In time your brothers may see an opportunity to lend a hand with their own people."

"This is so, my brother," said Nahm. "Your brother and I will follow the proceedings of our people. In time we may see a need for us to render assistance. But now . . . you were the first. It is fitting that you be the one."

"Yes," added Broc. "In times past we have learned from you. Now, after all this time, we may learn from you again."

"I must go there, then." exclaimed Ahmahn.

AHMAHN THE UNSEEN

CHAPTER 74

There's a strange, almost transcendental change that occurs in the desert every morning just before the sun breaks the horizon. Strange as it may seem, the deadly heat of the day is completely replaced every night by a bone-chilling cold that can, and has killed many an unprepared creature caught in its frigid grasp.

Now, as the outlines of mountain tops in the east changed from black to gray, then to silver-edged brown, the all-encompassing cold was forced to shrink back into the sands. There it would wait until the cover of darkness when it could once again emerge to dominate.

The temperature change was abrupt. It always was this time of year. Trade winds coming off the Mediterranean Sea had not yet shifted northward, as they always did with the coming of summer solstice. The cool air they brought with them struggled for dominance over the on-rushing heat, forming dust devils which danced erratically across the shallow valleys between the dunes. As the sun broke the horizon, the last of them dissolved into nothingness, obliterated by the relentless heat.

The old man lay still in his bed. He had been awake now for several minutes, but remained, eyes closed, wrapped in that enchanting netherworld between slumber and wakefulness.

He felt the oppressive heat first on his cheek, even before the sun's rays touched the side of his tent.

Slowly and carefully he stretched, forcing the pain and stiffness out of his worn out old joints, forcing his mind to surface to the reality of the dawn.

"Today's the day!" That was his first thought as he felt the uncomfortable cold quickly replaced by heavy, suffocating heat. He had experienced this sensation almost every day of his live and had grown accustomed to the feeling. But today he was caught off guard, caught up in the realization that today was the culmination of a lifetimes work. He shuddered, with excitement as much as with the sudden change in temperature.

He was an old man, by most standards. For his near fifty years he had lived and worked here at the edge of the desert. He had taken two wives here. He had raised eight children here, all in the shadow of hundreds of magnificent stone monuments, a few of which he had hewn himself.

He was a master stone mason. He had worked all his life with stone. Though he would never admit it to another person, (least of all, either of his wives) stone was, and always would be, his one true love.

As a young man he had begun as a lowly hod carrier, lumbering up and down the steep, pebble-strewn trails leading into and out of the quarries. Across his back he slung stone slabs, some seeming more than his own weight. Up those narrow trails he had climbed, sometimes on all fours, sometimes slipping, only rarely falling . . . sweating and toiling day after day, for years seemingly without end.

His tenacity did not go un-noticed.

After years of dedicated service, he was promoted out of the quarries, left to earn his way as an apprentice to any craftsman who would have him. Some of his earliest memories were of watching with fascination as skilled craftsmen transformed rough stone into beautiful works of art. He dreamed of some day being able to do the same. And so his dream had been fulfilled.

He and his life's work had grown up together. From time to time he and his family had moved, but only to new job locations, and usually that had not been very far. This was his lifetime home, here at the edge of the desert.

He sat up slowly, scratching that special itch; the one on his right shoulder where the big callus was. His jaw popped gently as a yawn escaped, jarring his memory. He remembered how it had been so many years ago, when he was young and ambitious. He and his friends had anxiously awaited the time when they would be old enough to work in the quarry. That was the place where everyone got their start. All citizens were free to visit any time they wanted to observe the work being done there. But most people stayed away after seeing it for the first time.

It was hot there . . . hotter than most other places, primarily because it was below ground level. The winds which are so common in the desert, swirled right over the tops of the surrounding hills, pausing only long enough to deposit dust over everything below.

The old man stepped out of his tent and carefully stretched once again, being careful not to look directly into the rising sun. Now, as he had done thousands times before, he turned deliberately and slowly, looking back over the top of his tent at the magnificent structure he had helped create.

Sun rays crept over the tallest of the blooming date palms, casting hazy shadows into the dusty morning air. Hummingbirds buzzed and flitted about quietly, moving from one blossom to the next, gorging themselves on the sweet nectar.

The air was hot, sticky, oppressive, with only the slightest hint of a breeze barely jostling the palm leaves. Below them in the newly transplanted Baobabs, birds of all sizes and colors hopped from branch to branch, incessantly squawking their greetings to one another.

Then like an explosion, they all flew out of the trees at once. Not a voice could be heard above the mad flapping of feathers slapping the air, trying to escape the approaching commotion on the ground below.

The hod carriers were in an exceptionally good mood today. Walking in loose ranks, usually two abreast, they talked excitedly. Today they didn't have to carry any more stones. The day had finally come.

For just under a year they had carried bricks and stones of all sizes and shapes down this shallow hill from the quarry.

Now the construction was done. Now all that was left to do was the final clean-up. Then the celebration would begin.

The temple, the newest building to be commissioned for King Khufu, sat in a shallow depression, just to the south and east of the 'bent' pyramid, the tomb of the former Pharaoh, King Snefru.

Yellow-orange rays touched the top course of bricks, the last the hod carriers had had to labor under.

Creeping down the face of the wall, the rays fell upon a freshly painted yellow orb. The orb, six feet in diameter, rested on top of the head of a forty-five-foot-tall profile of a man. Both were carved in bas-relief into the stone. Where the head of a man should have been, the profile of a ram's head stared resolutely into the distance.

A nemes (headdress) sat atop the head, then cascaded stiffly downward, covering the broad shoulders of the carving. Thin shadows accentuated the smooth straight outline of the body. Far below at the statues feet, workers knelt, shoulders bent to the task of collecting remaining paint pots and reed brushes. Last minute touch-ups were finally complete.

This, the last of the many figures carved into the wall, stood head and shoulders above the others, equalled in height only by the figure which it faced. Its size and stature were commensurate with its importance. The new Pharaoh had decreed the new god Ahmahn-Ra to be chief among gods, and had commissioned that the new god's likeness be carved in magnificent splendor on the temple wall opposite his likeness. Each stood on opposite sides of the temple entrance, facing each other.

The entire building rested on a foundation eight feet above ground level. Extending across the entire front of the building, sixteen stone steps descended from the portico down to the plaza. At the bottom of the steps and flanking the entrance were two stone obelisks, each nearly 30 feet tall. The entire face of the temple was painted in beautiful bright colors.

The temple stood facing east at the head of a plaza over 200 yards long and 80 yards wide. High walls enclosed the north and south sides of the huge space. Each wall had a wide portal midway down its length. Guards flanked each opening, standing at relaxed attention, feet spaced at shoulder width, watching the hectic activity within. At the east end of the plaza sat two large statues of crouching lions, each facing back toward the temple. Beyond the statues a stone ramp descended to the street below.

Throughout the plaza, overseers strutted about authoritatively, shouting and pointing, berating the occasional unfortunate slow-moving worker. Other workers dashed about the courtyard collecting odds and ends left over from the construction. Some carried worn copper chisels and wooden mallets. Others, yolks on their calloused shoulders, labored under the weight of baskets filled with stone chips. Following behind, old women stooped over reed brooms, sweeping up the last evidence of months of labor. The workers chattered to one another in eager anticipation of the majestic ceremony which would soon begin.

As the last of the clean-up was completed, overseers shooed the remaining workers out of the plaza, then looked about intently, trying to find anything which might still be out of place. Just beyond the walls of the plaza the workers dropped their burdens, dusted themselves quickly, and then raced to stand in the queues which had been forming since dawn.

Most of the city had turned out. A murmur of excitement filled the air as the guards snapped to rigid attention, blocking access to the plaza. Those at the front of the queues jostled for a clear view of what was about to begin.

Far to the east the faint sound of drums beating cadence began. An electric silence fell over the crowd as everyone strained to see. There in the distance the first ranks of soldiers marched in columns rounded the corner. Twenty-score foot soldiers, followed by five-score drummers moved majestically up the street toward the Grand Plaza. On and on they marched, feet slapping the ground in time with the pounding drums.

Swarms of people lined the street, cheering and waving palm fronds as the army marched forward. The pace never slackened as rank after rank ascended the ramp and entered the plaza.

Separating into two columns, they continued, one turning to the left, the other to the right. At command, each column turned west, marching parallel, ten yards from the massive walls. They marched in perfect unison, the sounds of sandal-clad feet and pounding drums echoing off the high walls. When the first man in each column reached the foot of the temple steps, the command to halt was given. Another command and each column turned outward, facing the walls. Each soldier took a wide stance, shield and lance held at the ready. The drum corps then moved forward into the plaza where it split and moved along side the soldiers. Another command and the portal guards moved aside.

Throngs of excited citizens swarmed forward, separating left and right, jostling for the best viewpoint. Too quickly the space between the guards and the walls was filled. Portal guards once again blocked the entrances. The overflow ran east, quickly lining both sides of the street below.

In the distance a new procession could be faintly seen. Dust stirred up by marching feet still hung in the air.

The procession drew nearer. Up the ramp they came. Rank after rank of lesser bureaucrats entered between the two majestic stone lions. Waving and shouting, they moved forward to the base of the steps.

Behind them, honored guests moved forward. At the base of the steps guards separated everyone to the left and right, then formed themselves into a barrier, blocking access to the central plaza.

Next came the Elite, favored of the Pharaoh, ranking military and government officials. Progressing ever forward with aloof, feigned indifference, they ascended the stairs. Stopping just below the highest level, they moved outward, fanning away from the center.

The drumming stopped. The noise of the throng quickly abated to a whisper; then to complete silence. All eyes turned to the east.

At the far end of the plaza a phalanx of one hundred Elite Guard marched slowly, silently up the ramp, proceeding between the silent stone lions.

In the center of the phalanx, high above all others, the Pharaoh sat upon his litter-borne throne. Thirty-six bearers carried the litter at shoulder height (twelve on each side; six in front and six in back). Standing behind and to the Pharaoh's sides, three slaves stood holding palm fronds interlaced with ostrich feathers. These they held above the Pharaoh's head, shielding him from the sun. Behind each slave a guard stood at the ready, sword drawn.

Centered in front of the Pharaoh was a short lavishly decorated platform half the width of the litter. Upon the platform rested an ornately carved rectangular container covered in gold flake. Upon the containers lid was a carved and gilded likeness of a falcon, wings outstretched to its sides. Upon the falcons head a disc rested on edge, facing forward. It to was covered in gold. At the corners, midway down the sides, gold rings were attached, two in front, two in back. Two carved wooden poles, each six feet long, extended through the rings. Holding the end of each pole a bearer knelt, shaved head bowed, eyes closed.

As the phalanx approached, all citizens dropped to their knees and bowed their heads until the Pharaoh's litter passed.

The next litter was surrounded by a smaller phalanx of soldiers. This time the citizens remained standing as it passed. Upon the litter the Pharaoh's three wives sat abreast in elegant splendor. Behind each woman a slave stood, palm-frond shade in hand. Again, each slave had a guard.

The last litter in the procession was much smaller than the others and was not surrounded by soldiers. Eight litter-bearers, two on each corner, carried the litter at waist height, befitting the lesser status of the High Priest whom they carried. No slave shaded him. No guard watched over him.

The phalanx of soldiers surrounding the Pharaoh opened in front as his litter approached the stairs. The bearers ascended, keeping the litter level. At the top of the stairs they continued onto the portico. Slowly the litter was rotated until the Pharaoh's throne faced outward toward the plaza. After lowering the litter to the floor, the bearers bowed deeply and backed away.

The litter bearing his wives stopped at the foot of the stairs. The three then rose and walked to the edge of the litter. Majestically they stepped from the litter onto the bottom step. Upon reaching the top step, they moved to the Pharaoh's right, where they turned and faced the onlookers.

The litter bearing the High Priest stopped several feet short of the first step. Once the litter was lowered to the ground, the priest stepped forward and down onto the smooth stones. Dropping to his knees, he bowed down, touching hands and forehead to the ground. There he remained for several long seconds. Arising, hands clasped in front of him, head bowed in humility, he began to ascend the steps.

A quiet murmur began among the onlookers. This was the new High Priest. He alone, out of hundreds who had vied for this most coveted position, had been chosen by Pharaoh himself. This most lowly of priests, whom no one could recall ever seeing before this day, had now been elevated to a position of power and authority second only to Pharaoh himself.

At the top of the steps he paused. A nervous silence fell upon the crowd. Several moments passed.

The Elites knew that this was a moment of testing. They knew that what the priest chose to do next would forever influence his standing with them, the entrenched aristocracy. Should he choose to be viewed as their equal, they would find ways to undermine his authority. They would not willingly share their power and influence with anyone; let alone a relative stranger. They would discredit him at every opportunity. Plots would be set against him. His days as High Priest would be numbered.

More moments passed. Tensions continued to build. Those closest to the Pharaoh cast discrete glances to one another. Already, silent alliances were being formed.

At the top of the steps another priest watched in veiled disdain. Seshat-Sekhentiu had held his position as Chief Priest for many years. Even when the late pharaoh Snefru died, Seshat had managed to out-maneuver his competitors. When Khufu took over power, few dared question Seshat's right to remain. Several had tried. Two had not survived the attempt. Their 'loss' had been appropriately mourned within the circles of power. However, after the 'unfortunate' deaths happened, competition for his position had dwindled very quickly.

Now this upstart . . . this stranger had appeared out of no where and had gained immediate favor with Pharaoh. "How could that be?" the question plagued him. Yes, this newcomer was only High Priest of the new god (and there were so many high priests and so many gods). But he had not earned his position. He had not been appropriately appreciative of the status and influence of those who surrounded Pharaoh. For one person to wield such power so quickly was unheard of. If he could attain this much power this quickly, what more could he do?

Seshat watched as the newcomer skillfully manipulated the onlookers below. Such talent! Skills such as this in the hands of

the right person could be quite useful, if he could be persuaded.
. . . If not, well. . . . Much had to be considered.

CHAPTER 75

Raising his head, the priest looked up at the pharaoh. The slightest hint of a smile crossed the pharaoh's lip, then quickly vanished. In that brief moment, shared knowledge was again confirmed. The priest's eyebrows arched knowingly as he nodded ever so slightly. Then in one smooth motion the High Priest prostrated himself before Pharaoh.

The crowd roared its approval. This new priest, chosen by Pharaoh, to intercede between god and man, had humbled himself before their beloved leader. Their confidence and respect for this new high priest was assured by this single gesture.

Tensions began to dissipate. Cautious smiles broke upon faces of those who moments before had been plotting how to control or eliminate this newest threat. As one, they began to applaud, raising their voices in approval. For now, their positions were secure. But time would tell.

The priest rose to his feet, clasping his hands in front of him. Again making eye contact with the pharaoh, he bowed deeply. The crowds roar became deafening. Priest and pharaoh again locked eyes. At a slight, almost imperceptible nod from pharaoh, the High Priest turned to face the onlookers. Stepping forward to the edge of the portico, he raised his hands high. Silence fell upon the crowd.

"People of the chosen! Behold your Pharaoh!" he shouted.

As one, the drums began a resounding roll. All within the plaza faced the portico, dropped to their knees and bowed their heads to the ground.

"Arise . . . and be transfigured before the most high *Khufu!*" his voice carried across the crowd. A reverent silence fell over the onlookers.

"Son of the morning! Seed of the loins of Snefru! Favored of the womb of Hetepheres! King of the upper and lower kingdoms! He comes before us now in his beneficence! Behold . . . he brings unto us *revelation!*" The High Priest raised both arms, extending them in a beseeching manner. Once again the masses roared their approval.

From his throne, Pharaoh watched with veiled curiosity. What this stranger had told him was true. He was able to sway the masses. His public oratory was extremely effective, even though he had confessed to having no formal training in the art. When he had first appeared on the scene his display of humility had put even the most arrogant of the Elites off guard. How else would he have been able to persuade them to allow him an audience with the most powerful man in the world?

And the things he had said and done in private! The marvels he had described! The small demonstrations he had conducted seemed plausible, at least on the small scale. But could they possibly work on the gigantic scale he had described? Such feats of engineering had never existed. Would these concepts really work? If they did, science and engineering would take giant leaps forward. And Pharaoh would get the credit. Khufu's achievements would be admired above all those of his predecessors.

He, like all pharaohs before him, had been born of royal stock. Even with such advantages he had struggled. He had not been above engaging in any number of 'discrete' actions to gain and hold power. This newest of schemes ('discovering' a new god) had been nothing less than a manipulation to strengthen the peoples' support. He might be Pharaoh. He might be 'all powerful'; but without the support of the masses he would be more vulnerable.

The power struggle never ended. His father had taught him, and experience had proved, that politics was nothing more than war clothed in the garments of diplomacy. This new 'priest' could prove to be an asset if he was handled properly. But if he failed to produce . . . well, Pharaoh was not without his resources.

"Even as we gather here in this place," the priest gesticulated, focusing the crowds attention, "noble or common though we may be; yet we do not go unnoticed!" The cheering increased. Gesturing for calm, he continued, "Pure may be our intent; but alas, we are but imperfect mortals. The cares of our lives seem trivial in the eyes of some; yet we know that to us they are all important. Are the cares of the weak less than those of the strong?"

"No!" the crowd shouted.

"Behold our great Pharaoh; master of all he sees! Before him our foes wither! At his request, men toil with one accord! We gaze upon him in awe! And he, in turn, knows our plight!" The high priest stepped forward, feet apart slightly, arms outstretched, beckoning the onlookers to strain forward in anticipation.

"Who are we that we would pray unto an unknown god? We would as soon gaze upon the bright sun at mid-day and be henceforth overwhelmed by its majesty! Behold our great Pharaoh! His bowels are filled with compassion! In profound humility he has prayed in our behalf! And his prayers have been answered!" His voice increased in volume, stirring the crowd into near frenzy.

"Behold, he has seen a vision!" His voice raised in crescendo; his arms spread high above his head, fists clenched.

"Fall we then upon our knees, that we may worship the *unseen god*; full of majesty; even beyond the sun!" the priest turned, facing Pharaoh and the huge carving in the temple wall beyond. "Now sing we praises to the unseen god! *Ah-mahn-ra! Ah-mahn-ra! Ah-*

mahn-ra!" The drums and the people took up the cadence. After a few moments, the high priest turned back toward the throng.

"See our great Pharaoh! See him now offer in our behalf a gift! A golden gift . . . worthy of a god! Pray you now that our all-powerful god *Ah-mahn-ra,* the *unseen god* may accept this token of our adoration!

The High Priest turned and dropped to his knees as Pharaoh arose and stepped down from his throne, tokens of power held crossing his chest. Turning around slowly, he raised his arms, copying the High Priest, though he remained on his feet.

The four bearers on the litter arose, lifting the golden 'gift' above their heads. They stepped off the litter and moved to one side. Slaves rushed in and moved the litter out of the way.

Khufu walked forward toward the massive temple doors, in step with the cadence. The gift bearers fell into step behind him. Guards opened the doors wide, then held them in place as the procession approached. Pharaoh continued forward followed by the four priests. The High Priest arose and turned toward the chanting crowd.

"Hear ye, oh people of our pharaoh! He goes now to commune with our god! Bid him well!" The chanting intensified. "I go now to intercede in your behalf, that god and pharaoh may remember their love for you!"

Turning away from the crowd, he bowed his head, folded his arms in front of him, and walked slowly into the temple.

CHAPTER 76

Once inside the darkened interior, the bearers placed the 'gift' on the altar in the center of the room, then stepped back to await instructions.

"You may now depart. Close the doors as you leave." Dismissing the bearers, the High Priest followed as they turned and walked back toward the light. As the doors closed, he slid the massive bolt into place and turned to face the pharaoh.

Several feet behind the altar large curtains hung, ceiling to floor, wall to wall. The space beyond was the 'holy of holies.' No one but the pharaoh and the high priest were allowed within. In the gloomy darkness two divans sat separated by a low wooden table, upon which sat an incense bowl and an unlit oil lamp.

The pharaoh stepped around the altar and walked toward the curtain, motioning for the high priest to follow. The priest hurried forward and held the curtains open for his king. Stepping carefully into the semi-darkness, Pharaoh went to the table and lit the oil lamp. The light it provided cast faint shadows on the dark sandstone walls.

"And so, King Khufu, it is done." The high priest said as he closed the curtain and moved to sit on the other divan.

"And so it is!" Khufu spoke in a smug voice. "You have woven this web well. Careful that it does not ensnare you. Many there are in my kingdom who would sooner slash your throat than risk the threat your presence represents."

"I care nothing about them." the High Priest was quick with his response. "They are but vipers dressed in cloaks of respectability. Should you deem it expedient, you would crush their heads under your heel."

"So I would, should I see fit. But do not forget our last conversation. Even a pharaoh must sometimes be a slave. His power is as mud upon a river bank. Hold it gently and it remains. Squeeze it with your might, and it seeps between your fingers."

"I do not forget, King Khufu." the priest stood his ground. "I have watched as a fly upon a wall for generation upon generation. Many of your progenitors were wise beyond their years. Many great things did they accomplish. Yet in their time greed overcame them all. For that reason among others I withheld my gifts from them."

"Why then do you deem me 'worthy' of your generosity? Know you not that you may also be crushed under foot?" Khufu had engaged in this verbal sparing match many times before with this man. He sensed that the priest enjoyed such confrontations.

"It is as you say; but may I remind you . . ."

"True, I am of a beneficent nature." Khufu stopped the priest with a glance. "But I am not always free to do as I please. And you, with all your years and wisdom . . . you, with all your promised gifts . . . may per chance one day tread upon a serpent's tail."

"It is just such wisdom which draws me to you, my Pharaoh." The priest knew it was time to end this sparing match. The pharaoh was certainly in awe of what he had learned from him; but he was still the supreme ruler of the land. It wouldn't do to provoke him too much and chance ruining all that he had thus far accomplished.

"And thus it is, High Priest." Khufu rose from his seat and gestured toward the curtain. "Remain here for now if you wish. I must return to my people . . . and once again put on my yoke. Come to me when you are ready. Together we have taken this first step. Soon we must map the path we have chosen."

The priest held the curtain for his king and then moved ahead to open the bolt and push open the massive doors. He squinted as the light momentarily stung his eyes. He bowed deeply as the pharaoh walked majestically past him toward his waiting liter-bearers.

The priest arose and watched for many minutes as the entourage left the courtyard and proceeded back down the long street. The crowd quickly dissipated, leaving the courtyard once again empty.

The priest turned to face the room.

"I will remain here for a time," he said tersely to the two remaining guards. "See that I am not disturbed."

The guards bowed shallowly as he walked passed them, hands clasped in front of him, head held erect.

As the doors closed behind him, the room fell once again into a dreary semi-darkness. Torch light reflected off the smooth stone floor, cast strange erratic shapes on the ceiling high above. The priest turned and slid the bolt back into place. The sound of the huge wooden beam thudding into place reflected upward into the stone ceiling, and crescendoed back down into the darkened chamber.

CHAPTER 77

The high priest turned back and walked toward the altar, his footsteps barely audible above the concussive echo. As he placed his palm over the gilded hawk head he felt an immediate warm tingle radiate through his wrist and up through his arm. A quiet hiss escaped from the chest's cover as the seal was broken. Folding the lid back on its hinges, the priest gazed down into the interior. A faint red glow emanated from within, highlighting his cheeks while casting dark shadows around his deep-set eyes.

Pausing, hands still gripping the lids edge, he considered momentarily what he was going to say. Then, reaching down into the interior, he lifted the transceiver out and placed it on the altar. As soon as he let go, the red glow was replaced by a soft metallic-blue light. It seemed to fill the entire object, though none of its interior components could be seen.

The holographic image of a young woman formed, layer by layer, just above the device. Long, dark hair fell gracefully down around her shoulders. The image dissipated a few inches lower.

"Hello, Ahmahn. How did it go?"

"As well as can be expected, I suppose. Please try to remember to call me by my new name. Where's Ambia?" The high priest reverted immediately to his usual manner of speech.

"Sorry about that . . . 'Yunu.' Still sleeping. She told me to wake her as soon as you made contact." Celisa leaned forward to reach for something just out of view. As she did so, part of her holographic face disappeared. When she returned to an upright position, her image re-formed.

"Ah, don't bother her now. Let her sleep. I just wanted to call in and decompress a little. All this theatre has taken its toll." Ahmahn's shoulders slumped slightly as the tension decreased.

"Nice outfit. A little warm for this time of year, don't you think? Celisa said playfully.

"Yeh, don't I know it!" His white robe hung limply down to the floor, just touching his bare feet. A gold braided sash was tied loosely at his waist. A narrow strip of yellow cloth was wrapped once around his shaved head. Tied in back, its ends hung down almost to the floor.

"What else is on your agenda for today," she asked. "Any more ceremonies to attend?"

"Just one later tonight. It's not really a ceremony though. Khufu wants to get together and work on some layouts for the foundation. Says he needs to work them up so it looks like his idea. Needs to schmooze his chief engineer."

"Is he gonna do the sketches or are you?" Celisa leaned back in her chair when she did so, the back of her head disappeared.

"He will. Don't know how else it can be done without someone getting suspicious. Besides, he's a quick study. And he's no stranger to shoddy design. Remember the mess his father made? Khufu was there for the whole thing."

"Okay. But are you sure he can talk enough engineering to make it sound convincing?"

"I don't see why not. He can paraphrase the examples I've given him. Besides, structural engineering is still pretty primitive around here. No one really knows much about the subject, and that includes Khufu's man."

Celisa leaned slightly forward.

"Look; we all agree we're dealing with a pretty primitive culture here. But these people aren't stupid. What if the pharaoh lets slip where he got his information?"

Ahmahn knew where she was headed with this tack. She had always been a little paranoid about this scheme being exposed.

"Listen; we've discussed this a hundred times before. It may be "our" first mission; but we've proved ourselves up to the task. The Procurators chose us. Don't forget that."

Ahmahn took some of the edge out of his voice.

"Look; I of all people should understand the risk we're taking. You weren't raised in this culture. I was. You and Ambia and all the others were raised in an advanced culture. Your planet was well into space flight centuries before my parents climbed down out of the trees. And it hasn't been that long since that happened."

Celisa was noticeably shaken by his directness.

"Ahmahn please . . . I mean 'Yunu.' I'm not suggesting you can't do the job. It's just that . . . this is our first contact mission, and I don't want to see it get messed up because we forgot to cover all the bases."

"Okay. I'll concede the point." He knew full well what she was thinking, though she would never admit it. He wasn't one of "them." Therefore, how could he be as good as them? A pretty primitive ideology for someone from such an advanced race.

"Just remember . . . we're a team. We look out for each other. Plus, this isn't the first time intervention has taken place. It's just "your" first time. Like Andreo says, 'there's nothing new under the sun.'

Ahmahn knew little would be accomplished by pursing this subject. Prejudice wasn't anything new. He had experienced it in his own culture. He shouldn't be surprised to see it here, either.

"Well," he rubbed his hands together. "I guess it's time to take the next step, as Khufu likes to say. Thanks for helping me decompress."

"You're welcome, handsome. Good luck. Call me as soon as you can."

"I will. Bye."

What was with this girl anyway? She didn't trust him, but she wanted him to call? Sounded like she might have another agenda.

As he placed the transceiver gently back in its container, the blue light faded quickly to red. Carefully closing the lid, he stood quietly for another moment, his head bowed,his hands gently clasping the 'gift.' Puffs of air rushed outward through his fingers as the container decompressed. Tilting his head backward, eyes still closed, he exhaled deeply, letting the facade once again close over him.

CHAPTER 78

Ahmahn entered the pharaoh's palace through one of two entrances hidden from public view. The main entrance was for formal occasions the public was meant to see. But when Khufu wanted private meetings out of public view, he and members of his inner circle used the hidden ones.

Political intrigue had always abounded within the palace walls where no one but a select few could observe. It just wouldn't do for the public to see their supposedly omniscient king as he really was. Just another politician struggling to maintain his power.

As he walked past the guards, Ahmahn (Yunu) focused all his attention on getting back into character. This newest charade was more difficult than the others he had initiated. In the past, he had been able to blend in with the crowd by acting and dressing like one of them. By doing so, he was able to move about among the population freely.

Using a made-up name (Yunu), he got a job as a hod carrier and went to work on the job site that would eventually become the Great Pyramid.

But now, as the high priest to the new god Ahmahn-Ra, he could not blend in. Nor did he want to. His purpose was to stand out . . . to be noticed. And by doing so, to gain influence in the court of the Pharaoh, all without revealing his true identity and purpose.

As he neared the kings chambers, he could hear that an argument was in full swing.

"How dare you question the wisdom of your Pharaoh?" Queen mother Hetepheres lashed out at the hapless chief engineer, Kanufer.

"My lady," he pleaded. "I would never question my king. I only wish to express my concern regarding this new concept which he . . ."

"Silence!" She yelled as she slammed the tip of her staff down onto the marble floor.

"My lady, please," Shehat, the Chief Priest gestured toward the engineer. "I am sure he only wishes to point out that this concept is new and untried. His many years of experience and study surely must be taken into consideration here."

"Both of you, please!" Khufu motioned toward a steward standing off to the side. The steward rushed forward to refill the kings wine goblet, then backed away discretely.

"Mother," Khufu shifted his weight on the divan, gesturing toward the engineer with the goblet. Wine sloshed over the edge and fell to the floor. The steward rushed forward to wipe up the spill.

"Kanufer speaks from years of experience. I take no offence to his remarks."

"Thank you, my king." The engineer was noticeably relieved.

"Nevertheless . . . such remarks border on impudence." Hetepheres thrust a bony finger toward the engineer.

"Watch that you do not overstep your bounds." She sneered over her shoulder. The engineer nodded and lowered his eyes.

"My Pharaoh," Ahmahn stopped at the edge of the room and bowed deeply.

"Ah! Here is our new high priest! Come in! Come in!" The Pharaoh turned toward him and smiled. Two more stewards rushed forward carrying another divan. Ahmahn nodded to the stewards, then sat down, folding his hands in his lap. "Thank you, my king. I'm grateful to have received your invitation."

"Your chief priest and my engineer were just discussing the merits of my design for my tomb. Perhaps you might have something to contribute to the conversation."

"My king; no. I am but a lowly priest. I have no knowledge of such things." Amon was careful not to provide even a hint that he knew anything about the subject.

Seshat glanced warily toward him. Then in a condescending voice; "It is so, my king. We priests possess no knowledge of such matters."

"Why are the two of you here then?" Hetepheres glared at the two men.

"They are here at my invitation, mother. I value their perspective . . . also, their presence soothes me." Khufu knew there was friction between the two priests. Seshat guarded his position and standing jealously and had voiced his suspicion and dislike of the new priest from the day of his arrival. The king knew that if he did not smooth the way between them, Seshat would manage to discredit the new priest . . . or worse. His mother, on the other hand, was easier to deal with. She had been rude, terse and demanding even from his childhood. He knew that she was being protective, of him of course, but also of herself. He could handle her.

"But to continue," said Khufu. "The construction of my father's tomb was fraught with difficulties from the very beginning."

"My king, you were but a child when the foundation blocks were first put into place. How is it possible that you would remember such things?" Kanufer, now feeling renewed confidence, continued his argument.

"You are right, my friend. I don't have memories of those early days. It was many years later, as I approached manhood, that I noticed how the sands around the perimeter began to bulge outward and upward."

"That is so, my king. But it is only natural that such would be the case as the height of the tomb increased. It was our belief, based on much experience, that the sands would eventually settle."

"Ah, but that never happened, did it? And what experiences do you site?"

"We built many models, and each of them performed as we had anticipated."

"Models? How big were these models? How much did they weigh?" Khufu saw the engineer waiver and hesitate before responding.

"My king, our models were precise in every detail. Every stone was hewn precisely and was placed exactly as if it were the actual block to be used in the tomb."

"And was every block in the model tilted slightly so as to concentrated the total weight toward the center?"

"Yes, my king. As every model was completed, we saw that the sands around the perimeter stabilized."

"Why then do you suppose that when you were building the actual tomb that each successive layer began to shift from its designated position?"

"We were never able to understand that issue entirely. It was therefore decided to change the slope of the sides of the pyramid so that less weight would be carried by the blocks beneath. Once that was done, the lower courses of blocks settled into position and we were able to complete construction."

"Yes!" Khufu jumped to his feet, casting a quick sideways glance toward Ahmahn, the high priest. Then, pointing an accusing finger toward the engineer. "And what was the result? The tomb you built was less a monument to my father and more a reminder of your flawed design."

"My pharaoh, it was not my . . ." The engineer shifted uneasily in his seat, looking around the room for some indication of support. Seshat, the chief priest would not make eye contact. The queen mother, by contrast, glared at him so intently that he was instantly filled with dread. Lowering his eyes, Kanufer sat motionless and mortified before the truth of what the Pharaoh had said. Of all the royals, he feared the pharaoh's mother most. He had seen how she dealt with others who fell into her dis-favor in the past. He now feared less for his position and title and more for his life.

Khufu saw the opportunity he had been waiting for. He walked over and placed a hand on the engineers shoulder.

"Be not concerned, my friend. We all know that you were not always free to do as you pleased in service to Snefru my father." He glared at his mother and the chief priest. Many a time the two of them had connived and colluded to subvert the will of the former pharaoh. He was convinced it was through their collusion that the former chief engineer had been removed, only to be replaced by the pawn now sitting here under such severe scrutiny.

"What has happened in the past cannot be changed. All that can be done now is to ensure such mistakes do not happen again." He gave the engineers shoulder a gentle squeeze, then walked slowly toward the center of the room. He glared accusingly at his mother and the chief priest. Both looked toward the floor uneasily. Then, seeing an almost imperceptible nod from the high priest, he began.

"It is my belief that the design of my father's tomb was flawed from the beginning. First of all, the structure lacked a solid foundation."

Seshat raised his head in response. "My pharaoh, there was ample bedrock beneath the center of the structure where the most weight was concentrated."

"Undoubtedly this is true," Khufu responded. "But such support was lacking along the perimeter. This allowed the blocks of the outer structure to shift, thus rendering the whole structure unstable. Engineers attempted to compensate for this by tilting the blocks toward the center where there was more stability. This only made the problem worse. Now as each successive layer was added, more weight was concentrated on the inner edges of the blocks below. When the sand along the perimeter shifted under the increased weight, the pressure on the inner edges of the blocks forced them outward even further. Eventually the only recourse was to decrease the slope of succeeding courses. It compromised the overall height of the structure and ruined the symmetry and beauty of the structure. The resulting decrease in weight helped to stabilize the structure, but the aesthetics were beyond repair. Perhaps an illustration will help explain." The pharaoh motioned to two servants standing at each end of a low stone table covered with food items and cutlery.

"Clear that table and bring it here to the center of the room." Then he turned to his new high priest.

"Now that we are all together in this room, we will dispense with formality. I will call you by your name rather than your title."

"As you wish, my Pharaoh." the high priest bowed as he spoke.

"Yunu . . . that vessel there in the corner," he pointed toward a tall decorative urn. "Bring it here and place it in the center of this table."

"As you wish, my king." Yunu retrieved the urn, placed it on the table and then stepped back.

"You two," he pointed to the servants still standing at each end of the table. "Pick the table up. Be careful not to let the vessel fall." They did as they were told. It was obvious that they were struggling with the added weight.

"Now, Yunu, slide the vessel toward one end of the table."

"But my pharaoh, the servants already struggle . . ." Ahmahn feigned alarm.

"Do as you are told!" Khufu was enjoying playing out the act he and the high priest had rehearsed the night before.

As Yunu (Ahmahn) slid the urn toward the end of the table, everyone could see the servant struggling to maintain balance under the increasing weight. Finally the servant's grip failed, sending the table crashing to the floor. The servant holding the other end was forced backward and fell under the added weight.The urn shattered on the marble floor. Hetepheres jumped to her feet and was about to rebuke the servants when Khufu intervened, motioning her away.

"See then how, when the weight of the vessel is moved to one end, how it is impossible to hold it stable. But when it was placed in the center it did not fall." Khufu glanced first to the high priest and then turned toward the others. He could see how this dramatic act had had its desired effect.

"And thus it was with the stones of my father's tomb. The weight was not distributed evenly, which forced the sand underneath to be squeezed outward."

"What does this have to do with anything?" Hetepheres returned to her seat.

"I think I understand, my pharaoh." Yunu stepped back as the servants rushed to clean up the mess.

"The stone blocks of your father's tomb were stacked steeply so the structure could be taller. The increased weight forced the outer blocks to shift."

Khufu nodded with a smile.

"That is correct, high priest Yunu." He stepped around the laboring servants and returned to his divan.

"What can we do then, my pharaoh?" asked the engineer.

"My father was a great leader, well respected by all. It was fitting that he should have a magnificent memorial to his greatness. He wanted this memorial to reach high into the heavens as a reminder to all of his greatness. But he did have one failing. He did not understand the limitations of the materials used for his pyramid's construction."

Hetepheres and Seshat were taken aback that Khufu would speak so candidly. Such conversations were common among the inner circles of power. Khufu's brothers and sisters as well as Snefru's wives and concubines had all talked about him behind his back. But for such conversations to be held in front of lessers like these servants and Kanufer the engineer was unheard of.

"What you say borders on blasphemy, my son!" Only his mother would have the audacity to confront the pharaoh in such a manner.

"Mother, try to understand . . . this is not a political issue. This is about engineering. My father's perception of himself clouded his judgement. He was not skilled in the engineering arts. No one here should be surprised by that. All we have to do is look at the results of his interference in the construction of his tomb. We all know that a pharaoh's word is taken to be almost divine. To speak against royalty is to risk everything, including one's own life. Those few who found the courage to speak candidly suffered the consequences."

Hetepheres knew exactly what her son was referring to. Snefru had gone against the advise of his chief engineer in the design of his tomb. The design had failed. No one but the chief engineer himself had dared to confront the pharaoh, and for that he had lost his life. The records of his birth and life were erased. His family members (those who failed to escape) died when their homes mysteriously caught fire. The few who survived disappeared and were never heard from again.

Khufu looked toward the engineer, then cast a fleeting glance at the high priest.

"I will not make the same mistake. My power is absolute, but my knowledge is not. Many things I can learn from those close to me. Much I can learn through introspection. And much I can pass on to others."

"My pharaoh, your wisdom surpasses us all . . ." said Seshat, hoping once again to ingratiate himself with the pharaoh.

"Your patronage is duly noted, chief priest. But in this matter it is misplaced." Rising from his seat, he continued. "In the few short years I have been pharaoh I have accomplished much. Gods willing, I will do much more. The tomb which is to be erected in my honor will reflect those accomplishments. If it is flawed, it will not be due to my self-aggrandizement." Motioning toward Yunu, he added:

"Come high priest. Let us now return to the temple, that we may supplicate ourselves before our god and seek his will."

The Pharaoh walked toward the door, leaving the others sitting. The high priest fell into step behind Khufu as he walked out of the room.

CHAPTER 79

Once Khufu and the high priest were gone, Hetepheres stood and began pacing the floor.

"This new priest!" she exclaimed in an angry voice.

"My queen, if you please." Seshat warned as he gestured toward the servants.

"Of course," she acknowledged as she stopped to face the chief priest. Then in a shrill voice: "All of you! Out! Leave us immediately!"

The two servants began quickly gathering what they could of the mess left on the floor.

"Leave that! You may finish when you are called. Now, leave! Take the others with you!" The two servants scurried quickly toward the door. One of them dropped a shard from the broken vessel, but dared not stop to retrieve it. The remaining guards and servants followed in quick succession. Once the room was cleared, she continued pacing.

"This high priest! Yunu he calls himself! He ingratiates himself with the pharaoh!" She snarled the words, claw-like fingers clenching and unclenching as she paced. "He draws my son into secret combinations! Who knows what poisons he infects him with?!"

"My queen, I am aware of your concerns." Seshat rose and walked to the table at the edge of the room where he refilled his goblet. Then slowly returning to his seat, he continued. "This man comes to us seemingly out of nowhere. My informants tell me he was working as a hod carrier when the pharaoh came upon him during one of his visits to the construction site."

"And now he is a high priest," Hetepheres spat the words as a cobra spits venom. "who pays homage to a new god! Who so easily catches the ear of my son! What intrigue does he bring into this house?!"

"My queen, my informants tell me he came out of the south, from among the Nubians. Nothing is known of his family. He never says anything of them. The few people who know anything about him say all he speaks of is this new god Ahmahn. They say they believe him to be a prophet."

"A prophet indeed!" Hetepheres spun to face the chief priest, pointing an accusing finger. "We both know there is no such thing as a new god! This is nothing more than a passing whim my son has conjured up for his own amusement."

"That may be so, my queen. Even if it is, we are powerless. He and his 'god' have already won the hearts of the people. Even if we could persuade him otherwise, were he to recant now, the people would reject him."

"Reject a pharaoh? Impossible!"

"On the surface, of course you are right. No one would have the courage to do such a thing. But certainly the people would murmur among themselves. It is not beyond possibility that a revolt could begin to grow quietly."

"Revolt against a pharaoh? Never!" She was near apoplectic with rage.

"My queen, please! Stop to consider. This new priest has thus far done nothing which might be considered subterfuge."

"Subterfuge you say? What could he possibly do which would compromise the throne?"

"Because he comes from Nubia, it is possible he knows of our dealings with the tribal leaders in the region."

"That is impossible. They have too much to loose by exposing themselves. Particularly Kishkamin."

Seshat lifted the goblet to his lips, taking a long sip, gathering his thoughts before responding.

"Our bond with the Nubians is built not on trust, nor politics. It is built on treasure. That is where their loyalty lies. So long as they are paid, they will hold their tongues."

Hetepheres glared up at her accomplice.

"Pray, Chief Priest! Pray that this is so. Otherwise you may find your head upon a pike, like so many others who have underestimated those desert vermin."

CHAPTER 80

Under the cover of darkness the two men entered the temple through a concealed entry in the rear of the building. Now, sitting together in the dim candle light inside the 'holy of holies,' the Pharaoh was first to speak.

"It went well, don't you think?" Khufu leaned back in his chair, extending his bare feet in front of him.

"Remind me to have the cobbler replace this strap. It is beginning to chafe." He leaned down and picked up the sandal, inspecting it.

"As you wish, my pharaoh." Ahmahn observed carefully, looking for any hint of how the pharaoh would broach the subject. From childhood, Khufu had played an intimate part in the circles of power which surrounded the throne. It was difficult for him to adopt an air of humility in Ahman's presence. It was a tenuous wire upon which the two of them were dancing. Khufu was powerful. But the knowledge that he had gained from Ahmahn made him realize that his power was limited. He knew that he needed Ahmahn, or at least his knowledge, in order to prevail against the forces which were building against him. Hoping to provide Khufu an easy entrance into the subject, Ahmahn asked:

"What news from the Nubian emissary?"

"His information is worse than useless!" Khufu toyed with his sandal a moment more; then dropped it to the floor.

"The tribe he claims to represent is but a small group of nomads. If what he claims is correct, why haven't they capitalized on this before now?"

"My pharaoh, sometimes it is difficult for even a wealthy man to hold on to his treasure. This king, as he calls himself, rules over how many?"

"Only a small number, a few hundred at most."

"Perhaps he fears his treasure will be taken if he exposes it."

"What good is treasure if you can't spend it?"

A trite statement, thought Ahmahn, coming from a man with so much wealth that he paid it practically no heed.

"Perhaps he desires to spend it prudently." Ahmahn tried to manipulate the course of the conversation.

"Assuredly this is true." Khufu bent to put his sandals back on, favoring the tender spot on his heel.

"Why, then would he offer me his fortune without any guarantee whatsoever that I will do as he asks?

"He must surely be surrounded by other 'kings.' Perhaps he has been threatened and needs your backing so he can retain power."

"That is not at all uncommon among 'those' people." The pharaoh spat the words out distastefully.

"They have fought among themselves for generations. Even my father was unable to settle their disputes. They are a primitive people . . . and barbarous."

Ahmahn had been waiting for this moment to interject.

"Nevertheless, it may just be possible to win their confidence with a few well-timed overtures. Perhaps this 'king' may be the means through which you will unite the tribes."

Khufu stood and began slowly pacing the floor in front of the altar. He remembered how his father had struggled with the southern nomads. They, like the sands upon which they trod, had always just slipped away. His father had expended treasure and blood to win favor with those allusive tribes. But his efforts to control and organize them had always met with failure.

"Remember this!" Khufu spun to face the priest. "Remember this, 'Yunu,' if that is truly your name! My armies are sufficient to conquer any foe! I have but to speak it and that barbarian king and all who follow him will be wiped from the face of the earth."

"Most certainly this is true, my pharaoh."

Ahmahn had seen such outbursts before. The pharaoh speaking in such an emotional manner here and now, privately, without fear of consequence, had a miraculous way of showing how much Khufu, the man, trusted 'Yunu,' the stranger from the southern desert.

Ahmahn was certain the pharaoh felt safe in his presence. An occasional opportunity to vent was sometimes very hard for a man, especially a pharaoh, to find. It was in part this display of trust and understanding which he had offered Khufu from the very beginning that had allowed him to attain the position he was in now.

The pharaoh knew his power in military terms. But, young as he was, he was frequently uncertain of what he should do politically. He was surrounded and 'protected' on all sides by relatives and 'friends' of the family. He was certain not all of the advice they had given him had been without 'advantage' for them also.

Ahmahn provided an outlet, a place where Khufu could test his ideas in a protected environment, free from prying eyes and wagging tongues. Ahmahn was as close to a friend as the pharaoh had ever had. Amon knew this and valued the friendship. It was one of the reasons he was here.

The *Brighid* had kept records of the reign of Snefru, and Ahmahn had researched them thoroughly before returning to his home world.

He had studied Khufu from the time he was just a boy sitting on his mother's lap. Hetepheres had been beautiful back then. She was in her prime, sitting proudly at the side of her husband, King Snefru, Pharaoh.

He had seen the young Khufu passed from one servant to the next, to the next. There was always someone for him to play with, but that person was always an adult, a servant. Not a friend.

The only children the future pharaoh ever saw were his younger siblings. Even then they were separated much of the time. Each child had his own set of servants. Each servant had things that had to be coordinated with the other servants. Schedules had to be kept, bathing, washing, eating, playing. Everything was scheduled.

Khufu had grown up a lonely child. All his needs and desires had been filled . . . all but one. He had never had a close friend.

Ahmahn understood the isolation the pharaoh felt. He remembered his own early days, back in the forest. It was so hard being the center of everyone's attention. Family and friends were constantly badgering him with their problems. It seemed he never had time for himself. He never had anyone to confide in. The young, one-day pharaoh reminded him of himself. Ahmahn had grown close to the young boy. Now he was doing so with the man.

His mind had been wandering. He needed to get back in character.

"But would it not be more advantageous to gain the nomads as allies, my king, rather than defeat them and then have to feed them? After all, its nothing but desert where they live. Let them keep it. But let us form an alliance with a few of their more influential leaders, and we can rest secure from an invasion from the south, or the west. We will have friends in all the right places."

"If we've thought of this, then others have too." The pharaoh rose to his feet and stretched.

"This opportunity has not gone unnoticed by others close to my court. Of this I am reasonably certain. The Nubian question has been a topic of consternation for generations. Lately, though, I seem to be hearing more than usual."

Ahmahn saw this as an opportunity to infiltrate a little further into the inner circles surrounding the pharaoh.

"My king, I am not without my 'resources' from before the time of our meeting. Perhaps they can be of assistance in this matter. They will be discrete, I assure you."

"Your past perplexes me, high priest." The pharaoh turned to face him, hand pursing his lower lip.

"How is it that you have come to be who you are? My people tell me only that you came out of the southern desert, sole survivor of an attack by unknown assailants. How is it that without any formal schooling, you master such complex issues as mathematics and engineering?"

"And what of your age? You are but young, more so even than me. Yet you claim to possess the knowledge of generations."

"My king, such things can be learned, if one has keen eyes and ears and a willingness to expend the effort. It is, and ever has been my joy to see monuments raised to the greatness of mankind. I am fortunate that this knowledge has come as an added reward for my fascination with the subject. And I am grateful that you would entrust all this to my keeping."

"As usual you change the subject." Khufu snapped. "I want to know more about *you*, not what you think. You are a man such as I have never known before. You are sometimes devious, as I see from your response just now. But there is an air of honesty about you that I cannot fathom. Why is it that I am prone to trust you?" Khufu gazed at the floor momentarily, thinking.

"Beyond that, there is something you hold back. There is more to you than you will allow me to see." The pharaoh strode slowly up to Ahmahn, tapping him slowly on the chest. "What is it, Yunu? What will you not tell me?"

"My king, all that I am is here before you. I am but a man with a profound love for my people." Ahmahn raised a hand, gently grasping the pharaoh's arm.

"True, I carry with me secrets, as does every man. They are common among us. They may be secrets of shame, or guilt or remorse or regret." Ahmahn looked deeply into Khufu's eyes.

"But they are unique to me, just as yours are to you." They are personal, they are private. And, they are harmless." He smiled as he squeezed the pharaoh's arm reassuringly.

"I am here before you now as a friend more than anything else you may suspect. I have seen a side of you that not even the privileged have seen. You have opened yourself up to me in a way that I am sure you would not do with others. I appreciate and respect your trust in me, and will never do or say anything that would compromise that trust."

Placing his other hand on Khufu's shoulder, he continued:

"I am required by law to love the Pharaoh. But the man, my brother. Him I love willingly."

CHAPTER 81

Ahmahn had made numerous 'jumps' back and forth between Earth and the *Brighid* prior to his arrival in the advanced cultures of the Pharaohs. From his first departure from the Sea of Marmara so long ago (as measured in Earth time), his concern for his race had remained foremost in his mind. Therefore, his first 'return' had been to the deserts north of his homeland. There he learned the fate of those who had departed during his clan's initial trek northward.

Though many had perished in the harsh, unforgiving desert, so too, many had learned how to survive. They had remained, for the most part, wanderers, moving from oasis to oasis, living off what little they could find.

As would be expected in such a harsh environment, competition between tribes was fierce. A fertile oasis was a place to be prized and protected from intruders at all cost. Over time, communities sprouted up in these rare, coveted spaces. Frequent conflicts occurred, as would be expected from people competing on a survival level. Miniature monarchies ruled over them, enforcing peace among the inhabitants and driving off unwanted intruders.

Over time Ahmahn began to recognize a pattern to their behavior. Always there arose an individual who dominated and took control. Sometimes that individual was of a benevolent nature, concerned for the general welfare, willing to intermediate between disputing parties, striving to find common ground. Where such an individual came to power, the community was stable, well adapted to living peacefully together.

Other times, sadly much more frequently, such benevolent behavior was a rarity. Tyrannical leaders rose up, manipulating and subjugating the people for their own selfish desires.

In such cases communities became deliberately isolated, distrustful of one another, even openly hostile. Tribalism became common, often taken to extremes. Prejudiced ideologies grew out of these hostilities. Airs of imagined superiority became common. Unjust leaders took advantage of and even encouraged such behavior, manipulating it for their own selfish ends.

On rare occasions Ahmahn had briefly infiltrated these small communities, trying to better understand their inner workings.

He was in fact a stranger among them, not to be trusted, always watched by suspicious eyes. It was hard, and sometimes impossible, for him to gain acceptance.

He understood their trepidation. These people were vulnerable, not just to the harsh climate, but to strangers coming out of no where, killing, pillaging, taking what they wanted, draining the small communities dry, then leaving the survivors to fend for themselves.

He learned early on that the best way to gain acceptance was to arrive bearing gifts; fruits, nuts, wild grain, meats, anything of value, asking nothing in exchange except their acceptance of him in their midst.

He never stayed with one community very long. He would sometimes leave to explore or to investigate other communities which his transceiver had informed him about, and then return to pass the information on.

But most frequently he would not return at all, instead traveling between communities, observing, learning of their plight, studying how they survived, helping where he could without taking control or imposing his will.

Over time, word spread of him, this stranger bearing gifts, offering his help to those in need, then disappearing, not to be seen again for years or even decades.

Stories of his comings and goings became legend, mythological. To a people desperate for relief from their daily travails, the name Ahmahn became a symbol of hope, a figure of majesty.

Tales of his coming with the sun, bearing gifts and wisdom, then without notice disappearing once again, spread from one community to another, until finally the name Ahmahn became mythological.

In the hearts and minds of the primitive people of the Nubian deserts, he came to be known as *Ahmahn the Unseen*. The *Sun God*.

CHAPTER 82

Ahmahn had observed the evolution of civilization from its very beginning. He had literally, been there. He had experienced it first hand. He and his 'brothers' had been instrumental in its development. Now, so many centuries later, with the fate of that civilization hanging in the balance, he felt compelled to intervene.

The Egyptian Empire was the first self-sustaining large scale civilization on the planet. Several other smaller ones had survived for a short time. But inevitably they had failed, collapsing from within due to poor leadership.

Advances in technology had been influential in the success of the Egyptians. But, despite those advances, political intrigue had set in.

Power, avarice, greed, lust. All the worst characteristics of human-kind were threatening to impede, if not completely destroy the advancement of civilization. The decadence he had witnessed during the reign of Khufu's father Snefru, had continued unabated into this generation and now threatened to destroy the very fabric of morality.

Secret combinations among the Nubians had begun filtering northward, threatening to overwhelm the communities along the northern Nile valley and Mediterranean coastline, and by extension, the kingdom of the Pharaohs.

The reign of Snefru had been one of continuing confrontations with the dozens of small tribes to the south. It seemed that every community, every oasis, even every roaming caravan had its own despot, eager to exercise his power.

Ahmahn recognized early on that, though Snefru was a mighty pharaoh who commanded huge armies, he was a weak leader. He was easily manipulated by power-hungry individuals within his own organization. The added pressure of negotiating with the decadent Nubians might easily cause him to capitulate, allowing them to infiltrate and erode his already tenuous grip on power.

Ahmahn had seen the subterfuge develop, but was unable to prevent it. To have done so would have exposed him for who he really was.

Ironically, Snefru's death at the hand of his own Chief Priest had forestalled infiltration of the Nubians.

Snefru's own wife had colluded with the Chief Priest to fill the power void they saw the pharaoh as having created. There was no altruism in their motives. They wanted power for their own selfish ends, and were quite willing to do what ever was necessary to obtain it.

Ahmahn recognized this, and when the young Khufu was elevated to pharaoh status, he saw a chance to intervene, to place himself in a position where he could influence events for the benefit of the citizens without exposing himself.

What better way to do this than to pose as someone he was not; to take advantage of the mystique which had become associated with his name; to cloak himself in the robes of a priest; to ingratiate himself with royalty; and in so doing, to hide in plain sight.

CHAPTER 83

"Call the Moguls together. Instruct your runners to tell them we meet at Hakim's camp on the eve of the new moon. Go now!" Kushkamin motioned his man out of the tent. Shifting his huge weight on the pillows, he gently pushed a concubine aside. She immediately jumped to her hands and knees and backed quickly out.

"Tell the others there will be no need for them tonight." He belched a thin smile at her as he stretched his feet out in front of him and pulled his robe closed.

Across the enclosure from him, Jahfir, Kushkamin's trusted confidant did the same. The dark-skinned slave boy, his favorite of the day, smiled up at him nervously. Then he too backed out of the tent.

"The new moon? Why so soon? Why must we disrupt the people's monthly ritual? You know they won't be happy about this."

"They will just have to make do, my friend. We must conduct affairs which will soon effect even them. They are but Kahfir, I know." the warlord sneered to himself. "They are below our consideration. But this 'Chief Priest,' this Shehat; words do not impress him. *Numbers do*. He and that old hag he calls the queen mother; both of them know that their plan cannot succeed without a horde to back them."

"A horde, you say? Indeed! I would hardly call five hundred men a horde." Jahfir scratched his groin, then stood slowly, adjusting his clothing back into order. "Besides, how can you be sure all the tribes will unite behind this scheme? We only have ten who are leaning in our favor, and even *they* are not guaranteed."

Jahfir walked slowly across the space, careful not to ruffle the loose-woven carpets which kept the sandy desert floor at bay. The rotund Kushkamin rolled over on to all fours, then extended an arm toward his friend.

"Help me up, you fool," he grunted, standing slowly, leaning on the other man's lanky frame. "You know as well as I that the promise of gold will be more than enough to persuade them. And when our plan is put into motion, the Pharaoh and all his armies will not be able to stop us. Rest assured, when word leaks out, as we know it will, even the remote tribes will be begging us to let them in on the plunder."

"Your plan is well-conceived, my fat friend. Take a bribe from Shehat in return for feigned loyalty to him. Then, claiming it to be *your* treasure, offer it to Pharaoh as a token of your fealty to *him*. Take from the one to pay to the other, while deceiving them both in the bargain. What an ingenious ruse you have woven."

The two men walked slowly toward the exit, laughing and slapping each other on the back.

"But I have yet to see this 'mountain of gold' this priest promises. Only the sack full you brought back from your meeting."

"Be not concerned, you bony fool. That great structure they call a tomb is certainly filled with treasure. If he does not give it willingly as he promised, we will take it."

"Assuredly. But what if Pharaoh calls your bluff and demands payment in advance?"

"The Pharaoh is a young and trusting fool" spat Kushkamin. "He is so self-absorbed that he cannot see the conspiracy forming right under his nose. As you know, I am a persuasive man when the situation calls for it. When the time comes. When we descend upon him, he won't know what is happening until it is too late.

"And his armies? Will they just stand by and let this happen?"

Jahfir loosed his grip and turned to push open the door flap. A swirl of dust circled his bare feet.

"By the time that phase of the plan is in play, Pharaoh's armies will be chasing ghosts south into the wilderness." Kushkamin stepped back quickly. "Now go! Take a boy with you if you choose. I must rest. Tomorrow I must tell the people to prepare to leave. Hakim expects us there in three days. That is, if this cursed storm will allow it."

The two men embraced once more. When Jahfir was gone, Kushkamin turned back toward the room.

"The whores will be grateful for tonight's respite," he chucked to himself as he waddled back toward his bed.

CHAPTER 84

Hakim paced back and forth, kneading his hands constantly as he spoke.

"Your highness, I understand your uncertainty. We both have much to loose if the other tribes get wind of this plan. But be assured, my absence is not seen as unusual. I often leave, sometimes for days. My people think nothing of it."

"My concern is not that your absence will be noticed." Shehat said as he filled his goblet. "It is your demeanor. You wear your thoughts all over your face. Look at you! Pacing the floor like a ram in heat."

"Chief Priest please! Understand and be confident. The ten tribes are united behind *me*, not Kushkamin, though he believes otherwise."

Hakim stopped pacing. Turning his face full toward his conspirator, locking eyes with him, he continued.

"The lust for gold is not unlike the lust of the loins. A little now and then satisfies, but always it returns. Never is it enough.

"Kushkamin is a slave to his lust. He is like a hungry cur. Feed him a little and he will follow wherever you lead. As long as he believes he will continue to be fed, he will be loyal. In this respect he is no different than those who follow him."

"Nevertheless, Hakim, he is no fool. A dog thinks only in the moment. You may think of him as a dog, but Kushkamin is a man. And men plan ahead. Men conspire."

Hakim paused, smiling thinly. An eyebrow raised as he walked slowly back to the divan on which he had been sitting. Once again he composed himself.

"As it is with *us*, then!?" he said, again locking eyes with Shehat as he reached for his empty goblet.

"Assuredly so." Shehat picked up the wine flask, gesturing it toward Hakim. "But *our* 'conspiracy' is not for a chest full of gold or a few pleasurable spasms of the gut. Together we will overthrow a dynasty. Then all that we desire will be ours forever. Not just for a fleeting moment. It will fall into our hands like wine into this chalice, and we will drink of it at our leisure."

Shehat filled the goblet. The two men sat back and sipped, each absorbed in his own thoughts.

After a few quiet moments Hakim wiped his mouth before speaking.

"What then of the old hag?"

Shehat chuckled as he responded.

"The queen mother has no real power of her own. Only what she borrows from her son. When he is gone she will be left standing alone. All her gold, all her finery, all her screeching, will be of no benefit. She still believes she has influence over me as she once did when she was young and alluring, and her husband was still sucking wind. But her influence has diminished, as has her beauty. Now she can no longer cajole. She can only threaten. Be not concerned about her. She is but a bump in the road *we* now travel together."

CHAPTER 85

Khufu's great pyramid rose ever higher above the desert floor. Now, at just over 350 feet, it was well over two thirds complete.

Pharaoh and his high priest stood side by side, holding onto the thin railing of the chariot as it bounced roughly along. Khufu cracked his whip over the horses' heads, urging them forward up the steep earthen ramp which covered most of one side of the pyramid.

When the chariot slowed and stopped on the narrowing plateau, servants steadied it as the two men dismounted.

Khufu walked over to the edge farthest away from where another block was being settled into place. The laborers as well as their overseers smiled in his direction, never stopping their work. The Pharaoh acknowledged them with a smile.

"The view gets better every time I come up here. Already it surpasses my father's, and there is much yet to be added."

The high priest stayed two paces behind the pharaoh, as was customary to show respect. Yunu, hands clasped in front of him, leaned forward slightly as he responded.

"My king. The people love it when you walk among them. They love you all the more when you stand here for all to see."

"Yes. How often have I told you, high priest? Your insight and wisdom have been a boon to my reign. The old ways; the ways of my fathers are no more. My people love me, not because I put more food in their bellies. They love me because I have made them a part of me."

"It is so, my king. They sweat and toil enthusiastically not because you command them, but because you persuade them. They see the sweat on your brow, the dust on you sandals, the callouses in your palms and they feel you are one of them. That is why this magnificent structure has grown so rapidly."

Khufu turned toward his confidante, now speaking more quietly.

"This morning I walked in on my mother as she was conversing with the chief priest. I only heard a few words before she noticed me and abruptly stopped talking. She looked quickly down toward the floor and then began speaking again, as though nothing had happened."

"What was it she said?"

"Her words were, 'Tell him we will accept no more delays.' When I asked her about it, she brushed it off as nothing important, muttering something about a problem with the kitchens."

"Who else was she talking to? Was there anyone else in the room?"

The Pharaoh walked back toward the chariot, waving at the workers and smiling.

"No one except Shehat. What concerns would he have with the kitchens?" Moving closer to Yunu he whispered: "There is something not right about these two lately. My mother has always kept Shehat close, but of late they are thick as thieves."

Yunu too was aware of this issue. He had been watching them closely himself for several months. Cautiously he began:

"Khufu, my friend. Perhaps now is the time that I should confide more about myself to you. Can we perhaps take a ride together? Away from prying eyes and ears."

"So! My suspicions have been right all along!" said Khufu forcefully.

Yunu placed a hand on Khufu's arm, looking over the pharaoh's shoulder. Standing close to the chariot, holding the horses' reins, one of the servants looked self-consciously away, then quickly began grooming the nearest horse's mane.

"My Pharaoh . . ."

"Yes. I noticed." Then, more loudly: "Perhaps we should go to the temple to meditate for a while." More for the servants to hear than for the high priest.

"Excellent, my king." then to the servant: "The Pharaoh wishes to commune with *Ahmahn Ra*. We will go there immediately."

CHAPTER 86

They entered the temple through the main entrance so that everyone in the courtyard could see. The Pharaoh entered first, slow and majestic, followed closely by the high priest, arms folded, head bowed.

Once they were inside, sentries closed the two huge wooden doors behind them, then took stations in front, securing the entrance.

Once inside, the high priest bolted the door and then moved ahead of the Pharaoh, motioning for him to remain where he was.

"Why do you do this, high priest? You know no one may enter without either your or my permission."

The priest moved quickly forward, checking behind the thick curtain beyond the altar. Convinced that no one else was there, he walked back toward the Pharaoh.

"My king, one can never be too cautious. The rear entrance is guarded, but if my suspicions are correct, there may be those among us who cannot be trusted."

Khufu walked forward, approaching the curtain as usual. The high priest stopped him.

"My king, my friend. Come. Stand before the altar. There is something I must show you, and much that I must say."

Khufu did as he was asked. The high priest stood behind the altar and placed his hands close to the corners of the gilded box.

"My king. You were right from the very beginning. I am not who I claim to be."

The high priest placed his hands on the tabernacle.

The seams at the edges of the box began to separate with a slight hissing sound.

The high priest folded the lid back. As he did so the interior began to glow, red vapor rising slowly, spilling over the edge.

"My friend. I am not Yunu. My name is Ahmahn."

"You are the sun god?!" The Pharaoh staggered slightly, his mouth dropping open.

"No my Pharaoh. I am not a god. I am but a man. I am that man whom the desert people say 'came with the dawn,' whom they say brought gifts and treasures of knowledge. For my purposes I thought it wise to maintain the illusion . . ."

"But that legend is old! Hundreds of years old! This cannot be!" The Pharaoh was aghast . . . then filled with anger.

"You deceived me! You claimed my friendship! My trust! And all along you lied!"

"My Pharaoh. It is true that I did not tell you my real name, though you sensed something amiss from the start. It was you who chose to believe my words, even though you knew nothing about me.

"But *this* you must believe. *Never* have I misled you regarding my feelings for you, or for *our* people. Come. Step closer. There is something inside here I want you to see."

Ahmahn reached into the box and slowly withdrew the transceiver. As he did so it changed from a dull red to blue.

"Please, my king. Move the tabernacle to one side so that I may place this object on the altar."

As Ahmahn did so, the blue color faded from the transceiver, revealing a smooth metallic finish.

The Pharaoh stepped back as Ahmahn came around to the front of the altar.

"What is this thing?" Khufu was almost beyond words as his mind tried to sort out what he was experiencing.

"Perhaps we should retire to the inner chamber so we can sit as I tell you my story."

Turning back toward the transceiver, Ahmahn said: "Follow."

Khufu started, as the object rose slightly off the altar and hovered, motionless.

Ahmahn gently took the Pharaoh by the arm and led him through the curtain. The transceiver floated along behind them.

Once the two men were seated on divans facing each other, the transceiver moved to a point between them, then settled slowly onto the floor.

"My dear friend. I know you're stunned by what you have witnessed. Please remember and understand that, above all else, I am your friend, your confidante, and truly, your brother."

Khufu was now almost in a state of shock. Seeing this object float in space, move of its own accord, respond to the high priest's commands. It was almost more than he could absorb. He sat mute, hands clasped in his lap. His mouth hung partially open, lips moving slightly, trying in vain to find words for what he was experiencing.

Ahmahn recognized the stress his friend was under and leaned slightly forward, speaking softly.

"Let me begin by saying I'm here with you now because I fear for your life and the welfare of your kingdom.

"I was here when you were born. I was here when your father Snefru became Pharaoh. Before him Huni. Before him Khaba, then Sanakute, then Narmer who united the kingdoms; all the way back to Ptah, the first true leader of the kingdom."

"Ptah was not a pharaoh! He is a god!" Khufu exclaimed, having finally found his voice.

"It's true he is remembered as you say. But to me he was an excellent carpenter, and a good friend. He was the first to attempt unification of the kingdoms, but he was murdered in his sleep before his work could be completed."

"You cannot know these things! Only the elite . . . the royals have this knowledge. You are a deceiver!"

"My friend, my Pharaoh, nevertheless it is true. I tell you these things so that you may come to believe what I must reveal. Of all these men, of all who came before you, none of them have been faced with what will soon confront you."

"You presume to tell a Pharaoh what he must do?! You came to me out of nowhere. I will send you *back!*" The pharaoh was becoming desperate.

"Should you choose to do so, it is within your power. But before you decide, there is more I desire to tell you. You expressed your concern about your mother and the chief priest."

Khufu nodded, remembering the secretive manner in which they had responded to his unexpected intrusion.

"My Pharaoh, they conspire to dethrone you."

Khufu jumped to his feet, filled with rage at the thought.

"How can you know such a thing? She is my *mother!* She would never . . ."

He paused in mid-sentence as an old forgotten memory began to surface.

"Yes. You remember that day so long ago, when as a child you saw Hetepheres walking with Shehat in the garden. There was a child walking between them, each holding one of his hands."

"Yes. I remember. He was singing. His singing became quiet as they passed from my view."

"My friend, calm yourself. Please sit. What you think you re-member is not what actually happened."

Ahmahn walked over and sat beside him. Placing a hand gently on the pharaoh's knee, he continued:

"That boy you remember. He was your older brother."

There was a long uncomfortable pause. Neither man moved.

Then slowly the pharaoh turned toward Ahmahn, tears filling his eyes.

"Yes. . . . He was Tolneh. He was sick. . . . I remember now."

"You never saw him again, did you?"

Khufu shook his head slowly, then stared intently at the floor.

"This will be hard for you to hear, but I swear on our friendship that it is true. What you heard was not your brother singing. He was crying. He didn't want to go with them, but he had no choice.

When they were out of the garden they were out of sight of prying eyes. When she was sure no one could witness, your mother smothered the boy.

"Shehat dug a shallow grave next to a small statue of a hawk, and placed your brother's lifeless body in it. Then he moved the statue to cover the grave."

For a long moment Khufu paused, remembering.

"I know this statue. It is still there, just outside the inner court. But how can you know this? You said there was no one there to witness."

"It's true that there were no people there, but this device *was* there."

Ahmahn pointed to the transceiver and gave the 'activate' command. Immediately it rose a few inches off the floor and hovered.

"This is called a transceiver. Later I'll tell you more about it and how I came to possess it. But for now I'll only show how it was present outside the garden, but yet was unseen."

He gave the 'mask' command, where upon the device began to shimmer, becoming hazy, gradually matching the light intensity of the room and the floor coloring, until finally it was nearly invisible.

"How . . .?" whispered Khufu.

"Later, my friend. For now, let me continue."

"Your brother had a sickness called epilepsy, or 'falling sickness.' Most of the time he was normal. But sometimes, for no apparent reason, he would fall down. His eyes would roll back in his head and his body would begin to shake. Then after a time he would again be normal, not remembering anything about what had happened."

"Yes." Khufu nodded slowly. "I've seen this before in some of my people. They have become possessed by demons."

"No. They are not possessed. They are sick.

Your parents believed as you do, that Tolneh was possessed. They feared that when your older brother grew to adulthood and became Pharaoh, that the demon would possess him again and take control of the kingdom.

"They could not afford to let that happen while he was in power. They feared it would compromise *their* power, their access to the throne. So, to prevent this from coming to pass, they chose to put him down.

"To ensure that no one found out, they also had his wet nurse, his servants, and all who knew of his sickness, killed. This device, this transceiver witnessed it all."

Khufu had been just a toddler then. The memories he had of his brother seemed more like dreams than actual memories. Over time, as his life became filled with new experiences, the memory of his older brother faded.

"Had he lived, he would be Pharaoh, not I."

"This is true, my friend. But there is still more to this story. Your father came to be Pharaoh not through blood line, but through bloodshed.

"During those times, as now, power struggles were prevalent. Though the upper and lower kingdoms had become united, still there was dissension. Through military maneuverings and political compromise your father won control of the kingdom.

"Shehat became chief priest as a result of that compromise. His lineage is Nubian, not Egyptian. Factions from the two original kingdoms never could arrive at a compromise as to who would be the ultimate ruler.

"It was decided that a representative from a 'neutral' kingdom should act as arbiter, operating behind the scenes, thus preserving the image of the pharaoh.

"Your father, who by then had become pharaoh, knew of these long-held disputes. His spies identified the dissenters and brought them before him.

"Shehat was present at their trial. He was forced to witness their be-headings and was threatened with the same unless he would swear publically his loyalty to your father. Reluctantly, he did so.

"But Shehat had his own agenda. His plan was to eventually bring his Nubian bloodline into power. To do this he seduced your mother and planted his seed in her. Your older brother Tolneh was the offspring of that union."

"Then I *am* the rightful pharaoh!"

"Yes. Your father knew all of this, the indiscretion between your mother and the chief priest, the illegitimate child, everything. But he was powerless to do anything, for fear that the scandal would be made public and his position compromised.

"As it turned out, the death of your half-brother solved the problem for your father, and created a whole new problem for the chief priest, which brings us to this point. Shehat and your mother are conspiring with the Nubians to have you overthrown."

"But I am the rightful ruler. My people are loyal to me, *not* to my mother or Shehat. They would not let that happen!"

"Ordinarily I would agree. But there is still more to this story. The chief priest has been in contact with the Nubian leadership many times over the last few years. Together they have conspired to seize power under the guise of a staged invasion from the south."

"How can you know these things? Ah! The 'resources' you spoke about. Tell me. Who are they? How do they contact you? You never leave the city, and security is such that no stranger can enter."

Ahmahn smiled and pointed to the transceiver.

"This, my pharaoh, is my 'resource'; or more accurately, this and others like it."

"There are more?! How many? Where are they?"

Ahmahn was not prepared to reveal more about them, particularly their relationship to his friends aboard the *Brighid*. It would be difficult enough to explain how he had 'lived' as long as Khufu thought he had. But explaining extra-terrestrials, and time dilation? Perhaps there was another way.

"My friend, for all these years you have trusted me. Is this not correct?"

"Yes, but *this!*" Khufu swung his outstretched arm toward the device. "Did you make it? How did you make it? Where are the others? How many of them do you have?"

"In due time, friend. It is less important how I came to acquire them than it is to deal with the looming threat posed by Shehat."

"This. This . . . 'transceiver,' as you call it. It is beyond my comprehension! It rises in the air at your command! It follows you! It even disappears at your command! *Surely* it is supernatural . . ."

"My brother. In times not so long ago people who had never seen a chariot thought it had come from the gods. Even today in the lands far to the south, people who have been isolated for all their history would not comprehend even the clothing we wear. Yet we ourselves are not gods, though they would perceive us to be otherwise. For now, let us set this matter aside and decide how we will confront this most eminent threat."

Khufu sat quietly, mulling over all that had been said: His brother, whom his mother had killed! His father, who had concealed the act, even from *him!*

Shehat, who would kill a pharaoh for his own self-aggrandisement. And his mother! And the transceiver!

It was too much to absorb all at once. The Pharaoh took in a deep breath and then slowly stood to face the high priest.

"My friend Yunu . . . Ahmahn. . . . You once said something which I have never forgotten. It was here! Right here in this very place. 'I am required by law to love the Pharaoh. But the man, my brother. Him I love willingly.' From that day to this, those words have rung true to my soul in a manner which I cannot deny. The high priest Yunu, the illusion; Ahmahn, the man, my friend, my brother! The illusion, I will maintain. The man, my true brother. Him I will love willingly."

CHAPTER 87

Word had been passed to the ten tribes. All was in readiness.

Kushkamin paced confidently back and forth before his army. To the rear the mounted regiments stirred restlessly, anxious to advance. In the front, rank upon rank of infantry stood at rigid attention. Sweat rolled down their faces as the sun baked their helmets.

"A good day for a battle." Hakim rode up and jumped down from his mount. His stiff leather body armor slapped his thighs as he strode up to Kushkamin. The two men squared and faced each other.

"The armies of Khabir and Asad stand ready on the east flank. You have but to give the command and they will advance toward the city."

"Good! Excellent! Are your commanders clear on the tactics?"

"Yes. They will feign a charge, drawing Pharaoh's forces out. They will then retreat after a short engagement, drawing the enemy into our trap. "There are four tribes of Kushites hidden well to the south. When we have drawn out the enemy, spreading them thin in pursuit of our forces, the Kushites will advance and launch their attack.

"They are all excellent bowmen who will quickly decimate Pharaoh's mounted divisions. Khabir and Asad will then wheel to the

496

west, and then north to join your forces, while the Kushites close on what remains of Pharaoh's infantry."

Kushkamin laughed out loud, elated at finally being able to execute the plan he and the other tribal leaders had concocted and refined for so many months. The last minute addition of the Kushites, his distant relatives, had done much to swell his confidence.

"We almost really *do* have a horde!" He bellowed in excitement. "My eight tribes will sweep through the city like a storm in the winter! Khufu's puny elite guard will be as nothing before our advance. Who knows! It may be so easy that your flanking units will not be needed."

Hakim smiled, feigning agreement. What Kushkamin didn't know was that as soon as Pharaoh's mounted forces had been defeated, the tribes of Khabir and Asad would wheel around and execute a full-on charge into Kushkamin's right flank, effectively forcing them westward. In the mean time another force of Kushites, hidden in the western-most reaches of the Nubian stronghold, would advance on the left flank, further pressuring Kushkamin's army.

To the rear, the Kushite archers would launch salvos into the rear of the army, obliterating the mounted forces, effectively surrounding the army on three sides, squeezing it forward.

Pharaoh's infantry would not be deployed as Kushkamin had been led to believe. Instead it would be waiting, hidden in the central part of the city, per Shehat's instructions. It was instructed to hold its ground until the last minute, then to advance as a phalanx, creating an anvil upon which the remnants of Kushkamin's army would be pulverized.

CHAPTER 88

What none of the players in this gigantic chess game knew was that Ahmahn had been monitoring their plans from their inception. His 'resources' (transceivers) had recorded all the conversations between Kushkamin and Hakim, so by the time overtures were being made to the Kushites (the southern-most tribes, as Hakim had called them), they had already been recruited by the Pharaoh. There was a long-standing animosity on the part of the Kushites because Kushkamin had betrayed and abandoned them to join up with the Nubians. It took almost no negotiation to persuade their leaders to go along with the deception.

The battle began. The eastern flank advanced as planned, drawing Pharaoh's mounted forces southward. After a short engagement, the conspirators' plan began to crumble.

Instead of pursuing the fleeing Nubians, the horsemen turned west and attacked the eastern flank. Before they realized what had happened, the southbound Nubians ran head-on into a wall of Kushite archery. Within minutes that battle was over.

The remainder of the plan quickly fell apart. Within a short time Kushkamin realized what was happening.

The horsemen he had expected to charge through his infantry ranks and attack head-on into Pharaoh's city, never arrived. They had been slaughtered by more Kushite archers. Now the rearmost infantry ranks began falling under a fusillade of arrows from the

Kushites who had swung north toward their rear. To the west Kushkamin's forces were also under attack. All around him his men were dropping, one after another.

Kushkamin's men were running in all directions, panicked, dropping their weapons as they fled the bloodbath. He knew then that he had been betrayed.

Enraged, he began searching frantically, finally locating Hakim, surrounded by a wall of Kushites. He was standing mute, all the color drained from his face, his sword hanging limply at his side.

Kushkamin fought his way toward Hakim, but soon was himself surrounded. Though he swung his sword furiously, no one tried to kill him.

"Hakim, you worthless Kahfir! You have betrayed me!"

Hakim chuckled, shaking his head in realization.

"And so I have. But alas. All my conniving. All *our* conniving, has brought us naught. It would seem that the man I colluded with has, in fact, betrayed us both."

The two circles merged, forming one large circle around the two men. A dozen men fell on them, quickly disarming them.

From outside the circle they heard a single voice rise above the din.

"Open! I will see these two!"

The wall of warriors parted slightly. A small man came limping through the opening. He was clad in little more than rags. Numerous wounds on his arms and legs dripped blood. A gash across his forehead had congealed, but part of the skull was visible.

He walked slowly up to Kushkamin, stopping close, glaring up into his face.

"Remember me, Kuchie? Has it been so long since we last spoke? Do you not remember? How we spent hours on end running through the dunes as children, splashing in the tepid waters near our homes?"

A look of surprised recognition came upon Kushkamin's face.

"Yes. Now you remember. I'm your old friend Kazim. The boy

who you grew up with. The boy who shared your secrets, your dreams.

"Yes! Now you remember. The son of the man you betrayed and murdered so he would not tell how you abandoned me, and my family, and your own family too, then ran into the night, never to be seen again."

Kushkamin's shoulders began to tremble.

"How did you. . . .?"

"How did I know? And more! How did I escape? It's all very simple. When you ran into the darkness, I followed. But your legs were longer than mine. I couldn't keep up. When I gave up and stopped, I heard them. The assassins who came at your bidding, to murder them all. My family. *Your* family. All the others of our clan. I buried myself in the sand beside a baobab so they could not find me. The one we used to climb. Remember?

"When the dawn came the assassins were gone. All that remained were the headless corpses of our fathers and the other men. I found infants, floating face down in the water, spared from evisceration, but left to drown. Children and women, raped and beheaded. Even the animals were not spared.

"I left that place of death and wandered for days. Finally your uncle Hamal found be and took me in. I told him my story. I remember his face. It looked like it was made of stone.

"From that day until now I have dreamed of this. The day when I could avenge the deaths of my loved ones. But alas, I must forego my revenge.

"Instead I must fulfill the commitment I made to my Pharaoh. You and this other cur, together with all the other moguls who survived this battle, will be taken to the palace. There you will stand before our beloved Cheops who will take revenge in my place."

CHAPTER 89

Once again the temple plaza was filled with people. But this time the throng was silent.

For days before the battle, citizens had been making ready. Pharaoh's elite guard had gone from house to house, warning of the coming danger, encouraging people to prepare themselves.

They were naturally afraid, unsure whether or not their pharaoh would be able, or even willing to protect them. Historically, the reigns of pharaohs had been marked by greed, self-aggrandisement, abuse of power. Citizens were treated as slaves, forced to do the will of their "betters".

But this pharaoh was different. Early in his reign he had been as they expected; aloof, seemingly uncaring about their lives or their welfare. But as time went on they began to see a change.

Even before the construction began on his pyramid, he was frequently seen mixing with the citizens, bestowing gifts, helping the less fortunate. It was not uncommon for him to be seen toiling in the fields, helping with the harvest. Some said they had actually seen him down in the quarries, driving wedges into the stones which would eventually become part of his monument.

People started becoming comfortable in his presence. Their affection for him had grown, especially after his announcement that those who labored in his behalf would be better compensated.

Even lowly hod carriers, the lowest of the low, had begun to trust his word.

Then when the battle began, it was Pharaoh's elite guard who had taken the front lines of defense along the southern ramparts. Khufu was seen riding back and forth behind the lines, shouting orders, offering encouragement. His mere presence buoyed everyone's spirits.

When the battle was over, it was their Pharaoh who rode victorious, not at the head of the army, but in its midst, surrounded by battle-weary but joyous warriors, filled with elation that he and they had won the day.

Now, gathered here in the plaza, before the temple of Ahmahn-Ra, they waited and watched, anxious to see what their Pharaoh would do to the defeated survivors of the battle against their city.

Palace guards once again formed a perimeter around the inside wall, preventing citizens from advancing toward the center where the prisoners were being held.

At the top of the steps, the portico, usually filled with bureaucrats and other officials, was empty, save for three lone figures.

The Pharaoh once again sat on his throne at the top of the steps. Standing to his left, the high priest, hands clasped in front of him, head slightly bowed. To his right, Shehat stood rigidly still.

"I must remain calm. (Shehat's thoughts raced through his head in quiet desperation).

"No one must suspect! I must maintain my composure. I must prepare myself.

"I have done it! I have escaped detection. My plan has failed, but I have survived, so long as Hakim remains silent. But, should he speak against me, I have but to assert my authority and proclaim my undying loyalty to Pharaoh. I have left no trace of my dealings with this man. Who will believe the word of this Nubian traitor over *me*, the Chief Priest of the Pharaoh? Surely no one."

Shehat looked down at the clutch of prisoners. Very few had survived the battle, a hundred or so infantry and horsemen, a handful of low and mid-level commanders, and the two remaining moguls. All had been stripped naked but had been left unbound, except for the two figures kneeling in front.

Hakim's hands were bound behind him. His knees were bound close together, making it difficult for him to balance. To his left, Kushkamin was bound in like manner, but owing to his obesity, he had tipped over and was laying on his side.

For a brief moment Shehat and Hakim locked eyes. The silent confrontation ended abruptly when the chief priest looked away, a smug expression on his face. Still, Hakim glared at him.

There was not a sound, not even a murmur as Amon stepped forward to speak.

"Our beloved Pharaoh will address you!" he said, and backed away, head bowed. The Pharaoh stood, then stepped forward to the edge of the portico. All eyes locked on him. Was the Pharaoh really going to speak?

"Citizens!" Khufu bowed ever-so slightly.

The crowd was silent, stunned. Speak directly to his subjects? Humble himself before them? This had *never* been done in all the history of the kingdoms.

The Pharaoh stood and stepped forward to the edge of the portico.

"My people! Brothers in arms!" He took a few steps down and stopped.

Behind him, Ahmahn watched in gratified pleasure as his friend humbled himself before his people.

Shehat, on the other hand, was beyond shocked. This just was not done! A pharaoh lowering himself before the masses? This was blasphemous! How could he do such a thing?

Khufu continued.

"My dear people! My brothers *and* sisters! You have labored long and diligently in my behalf. You have sacrificed. You have given freely, for all this time, that this temple, and the magnificent monument rising beyond have come to be!

"Behold their beauty! Behold the wonder of the labor of *your* hands!

The throng stood in awed silence as their leader spoke.

"You have demonstrated your faith in me, your king. You have labored diligently, and fought bravely. For this and much more I am grateful.

"Many of you have lost loved ones, as have these few remaining warriors before you. At today's dawn there were many more of them than there are now. Their families will mourn tonight just as will we all.

"Through your bravery and sacrifice our city has been saved. You fought not so much for your Pharaoh, but for your families, for your wives and children, for your right to be free. For this and much more, I honor you."

The Pharaoh bowed again, this time more deeply.

A murmur began, faint at first, then grew, until it was a roar. Khufu raised his hands. Silence once again fell over the crowd.

"Now. To the task at hand."

He addressed the prisoners.

"You! Who have fought against us. You! Who have been vanquished! *Now* is the time of your reckoning."

The Pharaoh took a few more steps down. Pointing toward the two bound prisoners, he commanded:

"Remove these two from between us! I will speak with these defeated warriors!"

Guards immediately pulled Hakim to his feet and pulled him to the side. The fat Kushkamin they dragged bodily out of the way.

The Pharaoh descended to ground level and walked forward until he was within only a few yards of the prisoners.

"Yes! You *are* warriors. No man who takes up the sword should be called less. You have sacrificed. Many of you have died. And for what? For the vain flatterings of a misguided few? For the promised reward from evil men who would use you for their own selfish ends?

"For them, there will be no mercy, in this life or the next. They soon will receive their reward. They will go naked before the people. They will wear their shame like a crown for all to see. They will grovel before those whom they chose to destroy. They will remain captive within the city walls, where their deeds will be made known to all. Their lives will be spared, but their deeds will follow them always, until in despair they will lay themselves down."

The Pharaoh took another step forward.

"Know you of justice and mercy? The line is thin which separates the two, and it is a rare man who knows the difference. A man who rules others has power to mete out the one or the other."

Khufu turned ever so slightly to his left without looking back. Ahmahn saw the movement but didn't react. Pharaoh turned back toward the prisoners.

"I tell you what in your heart you already know. The men who ruled over you were malevolent. They allowed greed to overshadow their judgement, and so they purposely misled you. Perhaps you too felt that greed in some part. But you are not the same as them. *You* did not wilfully conspire. *You* did not order men to their death.

"With leadership comes responsibility. They turned their backs on that responsibility and now must live with the consequences. For you there is another way.

"As your Pharaoh I hold sway over your fate. I hold the power of life or death in my hand. And, I take responsibility for my decisions.

"You have fought bravely, even under the hand of tyrants. And for that you are not in need of mercy. Instead, I offer justice.

"If you will swear allegiance to the Pharaoh, and turn away from avarice, I will grant this boon. You will earn the right to citizenship in this kingdom by the sweat of your brow as recompense. You will not be treated as slaves, but as equals. You will receive wages commensurate with your diligence, sufficient to care for the needs of your families. Through your own effort you will earn respect, from me, from the people, and for yourselves.

"If you agree, raise a hand above you head."

As one, all the men did so.

Khufu turned and walked back up the steps. Upon reaching the portico, he glanced briefly at Ahmahn. Their eyes met, but no words were exchanged.

The Pharaoh turned to face the prisoners.

"Now, place that hand over your heart and repeat . . . 'I so swear'".

In unison, they all swore.

"Never forget this day! Today you are free men!"

As one, the throng erupted in a continuous cheer. Khufu raised his hands, but the cheering didn't diminish. A few began chanting his name.

"Khu-fu . . . Khu-fu . . . Khu-fu . . ." But soon another chant overpowered it.

"Che-ops . . . Che-ops . . . *Che-ops!*"

Ahmahn stepped closer to the Pharaoh, shouting above the din:

"*Cheops* they call you! Before this day they respected you. Now? *Now* they *love* you!"

CHAPTER 90

The three men retired to the Pharaoh's receiving hall, accompanied by a dozen armed guards, as was customary. Pharaoh was in the lead, while the chief priest and the high priest follow behind, abreast of each other.

Shehat was conspicuously silent, searching for something to say. The high priest paid no attention to him, instead focusing his attention on the Pharaoh's back.

"You will remain here." Khufu pointed to a place on the floor as he continued forward. He came to his throne and turned to face the two priests. Staring coldly at Shehat, he began:

"Summon the queen mother!" He commanded as he sat down, adjusting his robe to cover his feet. Never did his stare waver.

The guards had already stationed themselves at each entrance. They stood in mute silence, eyes focused on the two men in the center of the room. The silence was palpable.

Shehat was noticeably uncomfortable. Before, it had always been customary for the two priests to seat themselves on the divans close the throne. He knew then that something was wrong. Hesitantly he began:

"My Pharaoh . . ." Khufu raised his palm toward the man, who stopped speaking immediately. Shehat felt his palms becoming clammy. He swallowed, trying to bring moisture back into his mouth. It wasn't working.

Distantly he could hear the sound of footsteps, rhythmic, regular, the sound of soldiers marching. The cadence grew louder, until to his left he saw the queen mother under escort. This was not unusual. She always had an armed escort wherever she went.

The guards escorted Hetepheres to her customary position to the right of the throne. She turned, and was about to sit. Khufu broke eye contact with the chief priest, turning to his mother.

"You will remain standing, mother."

"What do you mean!? Remain standing *indeed!*" she rasped.

"You will be *silent!*" the Pharaoh yelled.

Khufu turned his attention away from her, again focusing on the two men before him. Hetepheres attempted to speak, but the Pharaoh stopped her with a penetrating glare.

"You *will* remain silent, or I will have you bound and gagged!"

Khufu motioned. The two guards moved closer to flank her. Hetepheres seemed to noticeably shrink where she stood.

"He knows!" The thought transfixed her.

"High Priest Yunu. You will come forward to take your customary place at my left.

Once again focusing his stare at the chief priest, Khufu pointed his sceptre at the man as he began speaking.

"Shehat. You are no longer chief priest. Remove your priestly attire now."

"But my Pharaoh, I can explain . . ."

"You will cease to speak *immediately*, lest I revert to that which tempts me at this moment. Guards! Remove this man's garb, all but his loincloth. Shackle his ankles. Shackle his wrists. Drive him to his knees!"

Ahmahn sat down slowly, watching the queen mother's reaction. She was noticeably pale. She looked to be trembling as she looked from her son to Shehat, then back again.

"There are no words either of you can utter which will disentangle you from the sinister web you have woven. Together you have conspired to overthrow me. And in so doing, openly oppose the principles for which I stand.

"For generations this kingdom has grown, in size, power and influence. We and the leaders before us have built a civilization, the first and only one of its kind in the world. As we have grown, we have become too accustomed to the luxuries we enjoy, so much so that they no longer satisfy us.

"Power. The ability to control, to manipulate, to force our will upon others. This has become the aphrodisiac which we crave above all else. It is all-consuming and is never sufficient.

"It is that which has corrupted us so much so that we are no longer concerned for those who are under our care. It has warped our thinking to the point we have forgotten if it weren't for *them*, we would have to do for ourselves."

The Pharaoh stood slowly, walking toward the now defrocked chief priest.

"*You*, ignoble 'priest'!" Khufu spat the words. You, who profess loyalty. You, who profess humility. You, who claim to intercede with the gods for the benefit of the people who place their trust in you."

Khufu stared fiercely into the eyes of the man now cowering before him. Raising his sceptre as though to strike, he hesitated, then turned toward his mother.

"And *you*, mother to a Pharaoh! You, who colluded with a priest. You, who spread your legs, and conceived a bastard child. You, who killed that child for your own selfish ends. Your treachery is beyond that of the man with whom you conspired."

Khufu turned away from his mother and walked slowly, deliberately, back toward his throne. There he stood rigidly unmoving, contemplating what he should do next. He looked across at Ahmahn. Their eyes met.

Ahmahn sensed his consternation. He knew the struggle his friend was experiencing. Whether to lash out, to take retribution, to be avenged of the wrong committed upon him. To do what he had been taught from birth. Or whether to exercise restraint.

The Pharaoh had the authority, the power to do with these two as he pleased. No one would dare question his decision.

But these new concepts which the high priest Yunu . . . the man Ahmahn, had introduced him to, had a profound impact on his thinking.

Khufu, like all the other pharaohs before him, had been raised in a community of privilege. From his birth, through his early formative years, into adulthood, he had been taught that he was superior, elite, and that all others were but there to serve him. This was his reality. He had never considered it to be otherwise.

But from the day that Yunu came into his life, Khufu's belief system had begun to change.

The concepts which the high priest introduced him to were foreign. Freedom. Cooperation. Responsibility. Compassion. These were abstract concepts which he understood on an intellectual, self-centered level, but had never felt the need to apply in his own life.

But over time, as he had continued conversing with the high priest, learning from him, he had come to be comfortable with these concepts. He had begun applying them in his life and had experienced the simple satisfaction derived from doing the right thing without expecting something in return. And in so doing he had received an unexpected reward . . . inner peace.

And now these two. His mother and his chief priest, conspiring to do away with him, to discard the values which he had so recently come to appreciate and hold as sacred. To once again subjugate the people who he had come to love and appreciate. Essentially to stifle the right of the individual to choose for himself.

The pharaoh broke eye contact with the high priest. Ahmahn saw resolve on the face of his friend.

"So. Now. What shall be your punishment?"

Khufu sat, then turned to face Hetepheres.

"Mother. Your treachery is deserving of the ultimate punishment. But alas, you *are* the Queen Mother. For all you've done, for all your scheming, your lying, your deception, yet you are still my mother and I cannot bring myself to meet out that which you deserve.

"Therefore it shall be your lot to live with the knowledge of your foul acts. To carry this burden throughout the remainder of your miserable life. To stand in silent support of the Pharaoh you and your lover chose to betray.

"Your treachery shall be made known to no one but those within this room. Your guards will know, but they will not speak of it, even among themselves. They will watch over you and protect you. But you will henceforth never leave their sight. Nor will you leave the confines of this palace.

"You will not speak unless spoken to. Your silence shall be your torment. And when at last you pass from this life, your body will be given full honor, commensurate with a person of your station. And I, as your Pharaoh and as your son, will mourn your passing."

A long moment passed before Khufu looked up from the floor. He looked up toward the ceiling, took a deep breath, and then settled his gaze on the defrocked priest.

"Shehat. I remember as a child seeing you walk these halls with my father. It seemed that you were always at his side. It just seemed natural that the two of you should be together. For so long I took that for granted. Never did it come to my mind that you would betray him.

"But indeed, betray him you did. Not with the cur Hakim, as you have done against me; but before that, even before my own birth, with my father's own *wife!*

"From the day of your arrival within these walls you have plotted and schemed, weaving your web of deception, even as you professed undying loyalty to my father, even as you luxuriated in the embrace of his wife.

"The lust of the loins, this I can comprehend, for it is of the natural man. Even the desire for power is comprehensible. But to deceive even those people most close to you; to smile, to cajole, to flatter, to lie, all for the sake of a lust for power. This I cannot fathom.

"You would destroy a nation. You would subvert a civilization, turn it back toward barbarism, all for the sake of what? Vanity? Greed? Power?

"This vain ambition is beyond comprehension. It is beyond justification. And, so far as my authority is concerned, it is beyond redemption."

The Pharaoh leaned his sceptre against the side of his throne, clasped his hands together and lowered his head in thought. Another long uncomfortable few moments passed.

Through all this, Ahmahn sat quietly, listening carefully to his friend's words, sensitive to the emotions barely being kept in check by a man trying to reconcile the training of his upbringing with the knowledge he had so recently acquired.

"My Pharaoh . . ." Shehat dared to utter.

Ahmahn spoke quietly, tersely:

"It is wisdom in me that you should hold your tongue."

Shehat opened his mouth to speak, but stopped short when the Pharaoh rose deliberately to his feet.

"This, then is my decision. You have disgraced this throne. You have disgraced this bloodline. You have defiled and disgraced a queen. And you have disgraced your progenitors. Therefore it is meet that your name shall no longer be known or remembered among this people.

"From this day forward until your work is finished, you shall be hidden from the sight of men. By night you shall go among the monuments wearing chains; mallet and chisel in hand. In all places where your name or likeness is inscribed, you shall cause them to be removed, destroyed, that they will no longer be seen or remembered among this or an other people, for ever more.

"Then, when your work here is complete, you shall be taken seven days ride into the wilderness. There your shackles will be loosed and you will be set free, with one half skin of water, one half loaf, and your loincloth. There, if you choose, you will commune with the gods you profess to adore. Perhaps they will show mercy."

CHAPTER 91

The temple walls were falling into shadow. The huge stone visage of Khufu, the peoples' beloved Cheops, peered through darkening orbs across the portico, past the massive temple doors, into the face of the 'unseen god,' Ahmahn-Ra.

The doors were open, swung fully back, exposing the dark interior. Conspicuously, on this night no guards stood in attendance.

The pharaoh stood alone at the edge of the portico, gazing out across the plaza. Not so long ago, it had been filled with joyous citizens, gathered to celebrate the completion of the Great Pyramid. But now it was quiet. Not a soul was present. The Pharaoh's Elite Guard had cleared the entire area around the temple and now stood watch, ensuring that no one came close.

Khufu's thoughts went back to that day long ago (How long had it been, he wondered), when the high priest had stood on this very spot, and had wooed the throng; the place where it had all begun.

To his rear, from inside the darkened enclosure, a faint blue glow appeared, then began slowly pulsating as it moved forward out of the darkness.

Ahmahn, clothed in his priestly white robes, walked slowly through the doorway. His head was bowed and his hands were clasped in front of him, as was usually the case when he performed before the public. This time though, there were no theatrics involved. He too was remembering. The day when the grand endeavour had begun.

To his left, the transceiver floated, keeping pace with his strides. The high priest stopped at the portico's edge, standing close to his Pharaoh. Together they stood quietly, each absorbed in thought. The transceiver's blue glow slowly faded to a metallic gray as it settled to the floor beside Ahmahn.

"We have come a long way, you and I." The Pharaoh mused quietly without turning his head.

"So we have, my friend. Do you think it was worth it?"

"Oh, my . . . yes! Most certainly! Together we have united the wayward tribes. Together we have exposed and defeated treachery and deceit. Together we have brought peace to a nation and a semblance of true freedom to its people. We have accomplished much, but there is yet much more to do."

Ahmahn looked at the man's profile, outlined against a fading orange/red almost cloudless twilight sky. The long straight nose, except for the slightest bump rear the brow line, the strong protruding chin, dominant even without the ceremonial beard which usually covered it.

Here is a truly great man, thought Ahmahn. Not so long ago he was haughty, aloof, even arrogant, at least outwardly. Inwardly he was uncertain, reluctant, insecure; surrounded by people who were envious of his power and position. People who plotted and schemed against him, all the while professing their loyalty.

But now Khufu had matured. He had faced adversity square on . . . and had prevailed. He had chosen virtue over vice, truth over deception. He had chosen the right, and he and his people had prospered because of that choice.

Ahmahn reflected on why he had come here in the first place. The pretence of building a structurally sound pyramid had been his "in." But his real purpose had always been to help construct a firm foundation upon which a rigid autocracy could be transformed into a fledgling democracy. In this he had been successful. Though he was still a monarch, Khufu understood the importance of the exercise of free will among his people. The transformation within the man had only taken a few years. The transformation of the government would take generations.

Ahmahn was confident that Cheops (the affectionate name given to their Pharaoh by an adoring and appreciative people) had the strength of character, as witnessed by his example, to plant seeds of virtue for coming generations.

"So, Ahmahn. Now we part." Turning toward the high priest, Khufu was smiling.

"I'm still surprised that you insist upon leaving. Don't you desire to stay a while, if only to witness the fruits of your labors?"

"There is a part of me that wishes to do so." Memories from his past flashed through Ahmahn's mind.

"How I would enjoy watching your children grow to maturity. How I would take pleasure watching you become a doting grandfather."

He took a step down and sat, resting his forearms on his knees. Khufu remained standing, looking up into the darkening heavens. Ahmahn sighed and continued.

"But my work here is done. Were I to stay longer, I would be tempted to interfere, to exert influence. That I should not do. You. You, my friend, my brother. You are the one who must carry this burden. And you will do well. You are a man of strength and integrity. A man of courage and conviction. Leadership is always a burden, and few there are who can carry that burden well. You are one of the few."

The Pharaoh walked slowly down a few steps until the two men were at eye level. A light cool breeze washed across him as he descended, sending a chill down his back. He folded his arms across his chest as he spoke.

"How will you know what becomes of us? Aren't you curious to know what the future holds?"

"Oh, my. Yes! One is always concerned about the ones he loves."

"Then you should stay, at least for a while."

"No, it's time for me to move on. But I will not loose track of your doings. I will be able to see the results of our time together."

Ahmahn looked over at the dormant transceiver, and then continued.

"Even as we speak, inside your tomb there are four devices similar to this one, only smaller. Two of them are boring slender shafts from the king's chamber through to the outside veneer . . ."

"Why? What is the purpose? You know my tomb must be secure from those who would desecrate it."

"Yes. I know. Be not concerned. Neither of them, nor the two in the queen's chamber can be accessed from the outside."

"My queen's chamber also? Why would you do such a thing?"

"My Pharaoh, the structure you have constructed is the most stable of any man-made object in the world. Its foundation is the bedrock of the planet. Here in this place the ground almost never moves, as it sometimes does in other places. This monument to King Khufu will remain standing long after most other monuments have collapsed and turned to dust.

"Once the shafts are completed, the devices will remain hidden within. The shafts have been located so as to align with certain constellations in the heavens, specifically on the first days of summer solstice. The two in the queen's chamber align with Ursa Minora, and Sirius. The two in your chamber align with Osiris, the god of the netherworld, and with Thuban the Immortal."

"But why? I don't understand!"

"Located in these four constellations are devices called LINKS. Among other things, their purpose is to monitor this world. From time to time the devices which bored the shafts will send invisible messages to these LINKS, letting them, and me in turn, know how this world is fairing."

The Pharaoh was beyond comprehending. He sat down next to the high priest and placed a hand on Ahmahn's shoulder.

"High Priest! You speak of things beyond my ken! First the

'transceivers,' then the borers! Now you speak of things far away among the stars which watch over this world! You tell me you are but a man. But the things you do and the things you say persuade me that you must indeed be a god!"

"No, my friend. I am as I have said, just a man. If I were to tell you all that I know, it would only serve to bewilder you, and defeat the purpose for which I came here in the beginning.

"Better that you and I should make a pact between just us two, that the things you learned during my time with you, and the devices you learned about here tonight remain a confidence between only us."

"I will swear such a pact to you, my brother. Your love and your trust I will never betray. But what will I say of the borers? How will I explain the transceivers?"

"Upon my departure this device," he placed a hand on the transceiver, "and others like it will mask themselves so that no man can see them. The borers will also hide themselves. You needn't be concerned . . ."

"But the shafts! They cannot be hidden!"

"Together you and I created a myth, about an unseen god who, for convenience, we gave my name. The people accepted this myth and will continue to do so. Let us then create another myth.

"Let it be told that the god Ahmahn-Ra created portals in your tomb so that your Ka, your spirit, could escape your body upon your death, and once again mingle with the gods as it did before your birth."

"Yes" Khufu nodded. "That will explain the shafts; and it will instill within the people hope for another life after this one. And thanks to you and your teachings, I will set an example for my people of how a just man should conduct himself."

Ahmahn stood just as the transceiver began to hum quietly, once again glowing a soft blue. Slowly it rose a few feet off the floor and hovered in place.

High up in the northern sky a faint whisper became audible.

As the sound came closer the darkening sky seemed to shimmer. The first stars of the night blinked off and then back on as the shimmering apparition passed.

The whisper soon gave way to a low-pitched hum. For only a split second as the last rays of the setting sun caught it, the apparition became a bright yellow orb, the same color as the one carved into the temple stone above the god Ahmahn-Ra. Then, as quickly as it had materialized, it was gone. The apparition settled at the base of the stairs, where it solidified into a metallic sphere, hovering a dozen feet above the surface.

"The time has come, my brother," said Ahmahn, arms outstretched toward the Pharaoh.

Khufu ascended the last few steps and moved into Ahmahn's embrace. For long moments the two friends held each other, not speaking. Tears came to each man's eyes as they backed away, arms outstretched, hands on each other's shoulders. There were no words uttered between them. None would be adequate. None were necessary.

Ahmahn was the first to move. Without speaking, he backed away just two steps. The two friends stood unmoving for just a few seconds, their eyes locked on one another. Then in unison, they both bowed deeply.

Ahmahn turned slowly and descended the steps. As he did so a disc descended from the humming sphere and hovered inches above the ground.

Ahmahn stepped onto the disc, then turned to face the Pharaoh.

Khufu stepped once again to the edge of the portico, and then bowed again, this time lower than before.

When the Pharaoh at last stood upright, the disc where his friend had been standing was gone.

The sphere once again began to shimmer, to loose definition as it slowly rose into the air.

Khufu watched its ascent until it was impossible to discern the shimmering from the darkened sky.

Remembering, he turned to look for the transceiver. It too had disappeared.

For what seemed like a long time, he stood there, unmoving, staring blankly at the floor. The tightness in his throat began to subside. Finally the tears stopped.

Slowly the Pharaoh turned to face the huge courtyard, barely making out the distant entrance flanked by two stone lions.

Coming to his full height the Pharaoh wiped the last of the tears from his face, turned, and walked slowly back toward the darkened temple entrance, past the two majestic stone statues.

Epilogue

"But son! I tell you I saw it! Right there in the courtyard! Right in front of the temple! It was *real*! It *is* real!"

"Now father. You know no one was allowed near the temple tonight. Pharaoh's guards made everyone leave after the ceremony."

"But son . . ."

"I know how much you love that place. How you made it your life's work to assist in its construction. I know how you love our dear Cheops and his sun god. Come, father. You are tired. Sit here next to the fire for a while. The day's excitement has worn you out. I'll fix you a warm drink to help you relax."

The son helped his father cross the room, relieving him of his worn old staff, holding him close so he wouldn't fall. Gently he lowered the old man into a calfskin tripod chair he had made just for him. Then he turned away toward the fire.

His father was incredibly old. Older than every person in the village. The son poured a small measure of mead into a bowl, then set it close to the fire so it would warm.

He remembered how he had sat at his fathers knee as a youth. How he had listened for seeming hours as his father told of his experiences in the quarry, how he had carried the huge stones up the steep slopes. How he had fashioned them into beautiful works of art. And how he had been filled with pride the day of the temple's dedication.

"I tell you it is true! I hid myself near the entrance to the plaza. I curled up under one of the stone lions so no one could see me. I carved those statues, you know. I hid under the belly. I knew there was room . . . because I made it with my own hands!"

"But father, how could you curl up so? It is all you can do to walk."

"Do not mock me, boy! I tell you I saw it! The sun god appeared to me! I saw him standing next to the Pharaoh. I saw them embrace. I saw my Cheops *bow* to him! I saw him ascend into the golden orb. I saw it rise into the air. I saw it disappear . . . become unseen!"

The old man's voice quieted as he continued.

"I saw him, I tell you. I saw Ahmahn-Ra . . . the *unseen god*."

"Yes, my father," the son said as he stirred the sweet-smelling liquid. "Here. Drink this. It will help you . . ."

The son turned to hand the bowl to his father. The old man's chin was resting on his sunken chest. His eyes were closed.

AWAKENING

CHAPTER 92

"From time to time one needs to just get away for a while."

Making deliveries in this part of the city was always risky, even during the day. But at night the chances of being mugged or robbed, or worse, went up exponentially.

That's why on this night the delivery man drove past his destination twice, looking for any signs that danger might be lurking close by. His co-worker had warned him about what to look out for in this neighborhood. He told stories about things that had happened. Rapes, robberies, murders were all too common these days.

Since the crash a decade ago, the economy had never recovered. The millions who had been living from paycheck to paycheck before the crash, were now all too frequently living without any form of income at all. Many thousands, if not millions, died struggling for survival.

When the stock market finally crashed, it took countless businesses down with it. Other than the few individuals who had seen it coming and had been prepared, the only "successful" survivors were the giant corporations, together with the government bureaucracies with whom they colluded.

Over night the percent of unemployed jumped to 30 percent. Within a month, as industries came to a halt and inventories dried up, that percentage had more than doubled.

At first the masses had protested, demanding that the government rescue them. But when government agencies themselves began to collapse for lack of funding, the population was left to its own devices.

As desperation set in, crime sky-rocketed. Police forces focused their shrunken resources on protecting what remained of the infrastructure: government buildings, corporate headquarters, high-end residential areas, and a few "commerce zones."

Within these zones, businesses were relatively safe from the crime that rampaged just outside the "protected" areas. In the mornings, those who lived "outside" made their way through the detritus to their assigned check points along the perimeter. There they were searched and their identities verified.

Once cleared and released, they made their way to their places of employment. There they spent their days in subdued desperation, constantly in competition with one another, ever striving to out-shine the other, hopefully ensuring against being "let go," cast out of the commerce zones, back into the chaos that was "outside."

Only a few months earlier the delivery driver had owned a small fast food franchise near the perimeter. The building it occupied had repeatedly been vandalized, owing to its proximity to "outside." The corporate overlords, fearful that continued vandalism would cut into their profit margin, had pressured him to increase security (of course without providing funding for the added expense).

There was no way he could afford to hire someone to guard the store at night, so he, his wife and their three children had been forced to move into the storeroom in the back of the building. That seemed to satisfy his overlords, if only temporarily. Not long afterwards, as the crime rate continued growing in the area, the corporate fathers decided to cut their losses and close down the franchise. Because the value of real estate in the area was near zero, they virtually abandoned the building. He was told his family could remain there, but he would no longer be in their employ.

Though he begged and pleaded, they refused to yield. Finally in desperation, he accepted the only offer they made, delivering part time for one of their other stores.

Satisfying himself that it was safe, the young man stopped his car in front of the building, then punched in the number on his phone. After three rings a voice answered.

"Who's this?"

"It's Jimmy from the Deli, sir. I have your order." The young man spoke rapidly as he scanned the area again.

"Where's Mike?" The voice was insistent, demanding. He could hear a noise in the background, maybe a TV or radio.

"He called in . . . said he was sick or something. I don't know for sure. The boss didn't say."

There was a pause, then a muffled thump, as though the phone had been dropped onto something soft, like a pillow or a padded seat cushion.

The young man sat tensely, waiting, listening, one hand gripping the steering wheel, the other pressing the phone against his ear. He hated coming to this part of town. The crime rate here was higher than anywhere else in the city. Since the firearms ban last summer, the only people who possessed guns were the bad guys and the cops. "Where's a cop when you need one?" had become literally true. In this part of the city rarely did you see a cop during daylight hours. Never did you see one at night.

When the boss called and asked him to work this night shift, he had almost quit on the spot. The boss had assured him it would only be for tonight; then he'd be back on days. Reluctantly he relented, fearing that to refuse might cost him his job.

His mouth was dry. He should have brought his soda, he thought as he glanced quickly to each side, making sure both doors were still locked.

"All right." The voice startled him. "I can see you down there. Come to the door and I'll buzz you in."

The young man dropped his phone, forgetting to turn it off.

With one hand he opened the car door. With the other he scooped up the cardboard box from the passenger seat. He scooted out and stood quickly, reaching to push the door closed behind him. Then remembering, he stopped. He had left the keys in the ignition. Shifting the box to his other hand he bent over to reach for the keys, bumping his head on the door jamb.

"Shit!" The man in the room heard from the phone now lying on the car floor. From his window high above he saw the man below slam the car door shut and hurry toward the building, his warm breath turning to vapor trailing behind him in the cold night air.

The building facade looked old, in disrepair. Most of the windows on the ground level were boarded up. The few which were still intact were covered in graffiti. Most of the businesses which had once occupied the rooms beyond had escaped to the suburbs long ago. The few which remained would most probably be gone soon too.

With his free hand the young man pulled his coat collar closed, shivering in the damp, cold air. He looked up, noticing light coming from only one window several stories up. The rest of the windows were dark. His toe caught the edge of the curb as he hurried forward. Stumbling to regain balance, he caught himself just before slamming into the steel mesh which protected the heavy metal-framed door.

He pulled at the cold metal handle, almost dropping the cardboard box. The door wouldn't open. He glanced around him frantically, thinking he'd just forget it all and run back to his car and get the hell out of there. Then a buzz, and the door came ajar. He yanked it open, then pulled it shut behind him. He heard a reassuring click as the door locked. He was now trapped between the outer door and the inner. He couldn't get further into the building, and he couldn't get out either. He was isolated in the dimly lit vestibule, safe from the darkness outside, but fearful of the darkness within.

"Put the box in the dumb waiter." A loud voice bounced off

the walls. A small door behind him creaked, startling him as it opened. He spun to face it, the contents within the box rattling as he turned. He pushed the box into the dark cavity, pushed the door closed and took a step back, clammy hands clasped in front of him. A faint whir came from behind the door, then faded to silence. Standing there feeling miserably exposed in the faint light, he realized he had to pee . . . bad.

"Everything seems to be here. Your tip is coming down." The intercom rattled loudly.

Shifting from one foot to another, the young man waited anxiously. He heard the whirring again, growing steadily louder. The small door creaked open again to reveal a few crumpled bills where the box had been. He snatched them up and stuffed them into his pocket as the outer door buzzer sounded. Without so much as a 'thank you,' he ran out, jumped into his car and sped off down the dark street.

"You're welcome." Aaron Brock (the pseudonym Ahmahn adopted for this latest "visit" to his home world) muttered to the window as he watched the car's tail lights shrinking into the darkness. Holding the cardboard box in both hands, he turned and shuffled slowly across the cluttered living room toward the kitchen.

The floor was strewn with discarded food wrappers, unread junk mail, dirty clothes, typical detritus kicked aside to form a narrow path between the rooms. Another similar path veered down the hallway, turning midway down and to the right into another darkened room. The hallway continued for several more feet. The pathway did not.

Using the box as a plough, Aaron pushed the clutter on the table to one side and slid into a chair, easing the dozing cat out of the way.

The fat orange tabby growled his displeasure at being so rudely awakened. Dropping quietly to the floor, he stretched, back arched, erect tail quivering. Then he traced a tight circle around the man's leg, purring, letting him know all was forgiven . . . if only he would give him just a small morsel.

Aaron reached down and scratched the cat between the ears, then ran his hand down its back. The tabby purred with pleasure, arching its back in encouragement. When the scratching ceased and no food was forthcoming, the cat sat down and stared up at the man, tail slowly twitching back and forth.

Scratching the stubble on his cheek, Aaron rummaged through the contents of the box. From it he withdrew a foil-wrapped corned beef sandwich, still warm from being 'nuked' at the deli. Next came a kosher dill in a sandwich bag, followed by a large styrofoam cup filled with burnt-smelling hours-old greasy coffee. The remaining contents were left unnoticed, later to be stashed in the 'fridge, box and all. Breakfast for tomorrow, or maybe lunch.

Aaron had taken to staying in his apartment almost full time now. There really wasn't any need to go out. His car had been totalled in the crash and he hadn't bothered to get another one. The deli would deliver any time, day or night, so why bother to go grocery shopping. The 'mini-mat' down the hall did well enough cleaning his clothes. He really didn't have any reason to go out at all. That suited him just fine.

The old woman who ran the 'mini-mat' was pleasant enough, even though they rarely spoke. She knew from experience what he wanted done with his clothes, so there wasn't much point in attempting to carry on a conversation.

She had been living in this building for thirty years now . . . longer than any of the other remaining tenants. She had seen dozens of couples come and go over the years, especially back in the days before 'the fall.'

Back then the city had been vibrant, alive with activity. The streets had always been crowded with vehicles, the side walks jammed with people, hurriedly going about their daily lives. A feeling of excitement always seemed to fill the air. That was New York City in its glory days. But no more.

As newlyweds, she and her husband had moved into the apartment across the hall from where the young man now lived. Of course back then he didn't live there. He was probably just three or four years old at the time and was probably still living with his parents somewhere else.

The old woman leaned back in her chair, sighing softly as she pulled the last cigarette from the pack. She fumbled absently in a sweater pocket, finally coming up with a packet of matches. The first match fizzled when she struck it, as did the second. She cursed under her breath as she tried again.

"I ought to quit these damn things," she thought as she lit up. "My poor Eddie never did, and look what it got him. A slow, ugly death as the cancer ate away at his vocal chords and throat. Maybe I'll be lucky and get hit by a bus. Except the buses don't run anymore." Memories of the early days came back to her as she sat there flicking ashes off the smoldering cigarette.

She and her husband had been on the waiting list for nearly a year. The apartments in this area had been in high demand in those days. The business district was only a few blocks away. Everyone wanted to live close to their work instead of commuting back and forth from the 'burbs.' With gasoline over thirty dollars a gallon, almost no one could afford to commute anyway. Light rail and bus lines had closed down long before, victims of the crime wave which eventually took over all but the most tenacious businesses. Commuters were regularly mugged, robbed, raped or killed by out-of-control gangs which ruled the streets.

Law enforcement had become a joke. Crime was so rampant that police had to patrol the streets in armored vehicles (squad cars were just too vulnerable to the massive firepower in the hands of the gangs). Gun control laws had only served to strengthen the hoodlums. They roamed the streets at will, the citizenry fleeing before them. Law abiding citizens were left with no means to protect themselves. Those few who still possessed firearms were regularly prosecuted if they used their weapons to defend themselves.

She always smiled when she saw him, even though he rarely acknowledged her. Sometimes he would mutter something unintelligible. But mostly he just handed her the bundle of dirty clothes, then turned and shuffled back down the hall, hands thrust deep into the pockets of his dingy robe.

"You ought to wash that thing pretty soon," she would sometimes say. All she ever heard from him in response was a muffled grunt.

"It's too sad," she thought to herself. He used to be such a friendly person, always smiling when she saw him, always chatting pleasantly whenever he came to deliver or pick up his laundry. And he was a good tipper, too. Better than most of the others.

But now, after the accident . . . how long ago had it been? She tried to remember. It must have been back in the winter sometime because she remembered the big wool overcoat and the petite lavender jacket he had asked her to dry clean. She had missed seeing him for several months, and now it was nearing October. She had reminded him about the dry-cleaning and all he had muttered was, "It's no rush."

It was such a shame about his wife. To drown, trapped in her own car. "And him coming out without even a scratch." She thought out-loud. And the way the police and reporters had hounded him. It was no surprise that he had retreated into himself, becoming practically a recluse. It was just a damn shame. And such a waste.

"Oh well," she sighed quietly, as she turned back to her work.

The tabby was finally giving up on getting a hand-out. After circling the man's legs once more and looking up at him expectantly, he padded quietly out of the kitchen, then turned and trotted down the hall. Stopping at the bathroom entrance, he glanced back toward the kitchen, giving the man one last chance. Finally, resolving that nothing was forthcoming, he walked in and gingerly stepped up into his litter box, sniffing his displeasure.

Staring blankly across the small room, Aaron chewed absently, the mere act itself a tasteless metaphor for his life. The corned beef was pasty and tasteless, offering sustenance, but little else worth savoring.

It wasn't so much that he was angry or resentful; he was just . . . numb. And tired. When you get constantly bombarded with all the crap the world lays on you, you finally just sort of shut down that segment of you brain which deals with it, and don't allow yourself to be bothered with it anymore.

There! That's it. That's the problem. What does "anymore" mean? Do you just not deal with the issue ever again? Or do you just file it away some place where you can get at it if and when you choose? But its far enough away from your "deliberate" attention that it doesn't offer much distraction and your conscience can rest comfortably, if not sometimes fitfully.

Raising the styrofoam cup to his lips, he took a habitually careful sip of what he knew, in some part of his mind, would be a cold, bitter-tasting liquid. Disappointed that there was not even the slightest hint of any warmth left, he took in one big gulp and resolutely washed down what was left of the pulpy bite.

Seemingly in a trance, he sat there motionless, except for the nervous twittering of his hands. They fumbled absently with the sandwich bag until the kosher dill fell out onto the table. The pungent smell of the limp, grey-green object assaulted his nostrils, causing him to wince as his jaw muscles tightened reflexively.

The thought of eating more made his stomach turn. Disgustedly he picked up the pickle and laid it beside the half-eaten sandwich, then wrapped them both up in the wrinkled foil. He had no interest in eating. The pleasure he had once derived from it now was replaced by bored disinterest. He now only ate to avoid dying.

Pushing the chair out from the table, wadded foil in hand, he walked the three steps to the trash can and dropped the thing onto the growing pile within. It hadn't started smelling yet, so he could wait to empty it. Maybe another day or two, if he was lucky.

Turning back toward the living room, he switched the kitchen light off, leaving the cardboard box, the sandwich bag and the puddle of pickle juice there on the cluttered table. By morning the juice would have run under the cardboard box, where it would dry into a sticky, smelly mess, effectively welding the box to the table.

The thought raced through his head that he should go back and clean up the mess now, while it was easy to deal with, rather than put if off until later, when it would require a lot more effort and inconvenience. He didn't loose a stride as the thought departed, leaving nothing more than a slight bad taste in his mouth.

Plopping heavily into the overstuffed recliner, he continued the seemingly unending struggle with the memories that had been plaguing him for so many months. No matter what he tried, his thoughts returned to that night. The night when his life had been turned upside down.

He remembered being jolted awake, feeling light-headed in the darkness. Absently he thought he heard a scream, but he was still groggy and couldn't be sure. He felt distant, detached for what seemed an eternity. Then he felt the hard slap of the air bag as the car impacted the water. He heard and felt the splintering thud as the windshield imploded, shredding the air bags. He remembered the chalky irritating smell of the gas exploding into his nostrils. Instinctively he tried to exhale. He remembered fumbling to push the air bag out of his face, then looking to his left. There, still strapped in the driver's seat, was Sharon, eyes wide in panic, a scream bubbling out of her mouth. The bubbles floated up and back, disbursing and disappearing into her long swirling hair. Her pale face was framed in darkness, highlighted only by the faint blue light from the dashboard. Then the light flickered and went out as water shorted out the electrical system.

He remembered again awakening, this time to a glaring bright light shining in his eyes. Distantly he thought he heard someone yelling.

"He's awake! BP normal! No injuries that I can see!"

Then the light moved away and soothing darkness began to engulf him once again. As he faded from consciousness, he thought he heard the distant, bubbling scream of a siren.

The next thing he remembered was the hospital emergency room. It all seemed to be a distorted blur; the bright lights; the uncomfortable squeeze of the blood pressure cuff around his arm; the sting as an I.V. needle was jammed into his other arm; people hovering around him, asking him questions.

"What is your name, sir? Do you know what day this is? Can you tell me what happened?"

There was so much noise! It made him feel uneasy. Then everything began to fade as the darkness returned.

He awoke again, this time in a different room. The lights were dim. The room was quiet. It smelled of alcohol and urine. His head was spinning. Something didn't feel right. He couldn't seem to think straight. He felt isolated, like he didn't belong.

Memories popped in and out of his head: A woman's face, her hair swirling about her head in slow motion; a man's bloodied face, eyes wide in panic. The man was screaming: "Where is she?! Where's Nera?!"

"Who's Nera?" he wondered. As soon as he focused on the image, it disappeared, to be replaced by another, this time of another room.

It smelled clean, antiseptic. A man was there, pacing back and forth, hands clasped behind his back. He was saying something, but no sound came out of his mouth.

Aaron sensed that what the man was saying was important. No matter how hard he tried, he couldn't make out what was being said. He struggled to let the man know he couldn't hear him. The man just ignored him, continuing to pace.

Aaron felt near panic. Nothing was making sense."You need to snap out of it." he told himself in a quiet, deliberately controlled tone. "You need to get hold of yourself. It's time!"

The flash of images stopped abruptly. Suddenly he was back in his room. To his left there was another bed. The safety rails on both sides were down. The sheets and blanket were stretched flat and smooth in military fashion. The cord for a call button lay coiled neatly on the pillow. For some reason it reminded him of a serpent, preparing to strike.

Above the foot of his bed a TV hung suspended from the ceiling. On the screen he recognized an old black and white episode of the Lone Ranger. The man in the mask and his Indian companion were talking, though Aaron couldn't make out what they were saying. He looked for the remote so he could turn up the volume. There it was, sitting on a table, next to a box of tissues. He tried to sit up so he could reach them, but couldn't. A wide strap was stretched across his chest, pinning him to the bed. He couldn't figure out why the strap was there. His mind was reeling. Nothing was making sense.

"Can someone please help me?" His voice was weak, barely more than a whisper. He tried shifting position, trying to free himself, but he couldn't move. Another strap was stretched across his legs. He tried raising his arms but both wrists were bound to the side railings with padded leather straps.

To his right there was a curtain, extending from the ceiling down to within a foot or so of the floor. Beyond it he could see the lower part of a closed door. Under it shadows moved back and forth erratically. He could hear voices, but couldn't make out what they were saying. He was about to try calling out again when one of the shadows stopped just outside the door.

Aaron heard the lock disengage and the door creak open on its hinges. The curtain still blocked his view. All he could see were pant cuffs and scuffed brown shoes as they came into the room.

"Mister Brock?" The curtain was pulled back abruptly. A tall lanky man clad in a wrinkled white lab coat smiled down at him. Around his neck was a stethoscope. In one hand he held a clipboard; in the other a pen.

"So, Mister Brock. How're we feeling today?" the man said, staring down at the clipboard, pen poised to take notes.

"Who are you and why am I being restrained?!" Aaron retorted. The man in the coat wrote something down and then looked up at Aaron.

"My apologies, Mister Brock. My name is Mike. I'll be your nurse-assistant for this shift. Is there anything I can get for you? Some water perhaps, or something to eat?"

"I'm not interested in food! Get me out of these restraints!"

"I'm sorry, sir. I'm not allowed to . . ."

"I don't give a damn what you're not allowed!" Aaron raised his head as far as he could. The man went back to writing.

"It's obvious that you are not in charge here! Get someone in here who is!"

"I'll be happy to do that sir, if you'll just give me a few moments to ask a few questions."

"I'll do nothing of the sort! Get someone in here who's in charge!"

"Just as soon as you answer some questions." He looked back to his clipboard. "Why do you think you came out of the accident unscathed?"

Aaron realized he wouldn't get anywhere with this man. Helpless to do anything else, he lowered his head to the pillow and remained silent. After a long wait, the man looked up again.

"I'm sorry Mister Brock. Didn't you understand the question?"

Aaron said nothing, just stared at the ceiling.

"Listen. Mister Brock, you need to realize something. You were brought in here tonight as the only survivor of a devastating car crash."

"Only survivor? You mean . . . Sharon is . . . dead?" Aaron blurted. The last few pieces of the puzzle crashed into place. It wasn't a dream, as he had hoped in his confused and bewildered mind. It was real! His wife was dead . . . and he was still alive! How could this be? He hadn't even received a scratch!

"You know that, sir. That's why we had to restrain you. You were thrashing about all over the place, screaming that you had to get away. We couldn't reason with you. You were out of control. We had to sedate you." The man moved closer to Aaron's bed.

"Actually, sir, I'm not a nurse assistant. I'm a behavioral psychologist. I was asked to come in and evaluate your mental state. Everyone here hoped that someone non-threatening, like a nurse aide would be less intimidating; That you might be more receptive to someone like that instead of some authority figure." He moved to the edge of the bed. "May I sit?" Aaron nodded.

"Well, I volunteered to wear that guise. We all saw how you were when they brought you in last night. The police thought you might become suicidal, so they had the E.R. doctor sedate you. You do realize, don't you, that your walking away unscathed from a crash like that is unheard of."

"What do you mean, 'unheard of'?"

"Sir, your car was headed west on the Brooklyn Bridge when it was struck head-on by an on-coming semi. Witnesses say your car flipped once in mid-air and then crashed through the guard rail and plunged over two hundred feet into the bay. It just barely missed an outbound container ship. Someone on board saw the car hit the water. He said it sounded like a bomb had just gone off."

Aaron lay there stunned, unable even to speak. His wife was gone.

CHAPTER 93

For a few days after he was released from the hospital, he was the center of attention on all the news programs. Talking heads endlessly discussed how miraculous it was that he had escaped uninjured while his wife had been mangled and trapped in the twisted mess that had once been their car.

Reporters shoved microphones in his face, asking asinine questions: "How do you feel about loosing your wife?" "What are your plans now that you're alone?" "Do you think you'll be remarrying any time soon?" Instinctively he wanted to lash out, to scream "Leave me alone!" But the absurdity of the questions and the profundity of his loss compelled him to ignore them and just turn away . . . to turn inward.

After a few days the sensationalism of the accident wore thin. The media lost interest and moved on to more "newsworthy" events, like the fire on the east side where a family of four was asphyxiated and then burned to death while they were sleeping. Or the "gang related" shooting that had occurred last night just a few blocks from here.

Finally, Aaron was left alone to work through his grief. He went from day to day mechanically, becoming accustomed to feelings of numbed detachment.

Religious leaders and a few close friends sought to comfort him with explanations of how he had experienced some sort of miraculous event. In an effort to placate them so they'd leave him alone, he went along with whatever they suggested. But deep in his heart he knew that they were wrong. There was more to it than that.

This wasn't at all an unfamiliar state of mind for him. Loss of a loved one was always painful. It was, just by its very nature, right? It always brought the bereaved into full confrontation with their own mortality. It was the natural order of things. Certainly!

But why was it then, that he wasn't "overcome with grief" over the loss of his beautiful wife? The question plagued him as much as, if not more than, did the loss itself.

Was he such a cad that he felt only mild remorse over loosing her? The more he thought about it the more he began to believe that death, although abrupt, was not the end. It was only a stepping stone. He had seen it so many times. . . .

What was he saying!? "So many times!" The only direct experience he had with death was when his parents died. He didn't even remember that clearly. He was only four or five when it happened.

Memories of his childhood and upbringing had always been somewhat confused . . . unclear. They seemed more like movies than actual memories. Try though he might, he could never seem to focus on any particular event. The few photos he had of his childhood did provide evidence he had actually been places and done things. But somehow they seemed unreal, like they had happened in another life or had happened to someone else.

Aaron was raised as an only child and was orphaned around age five. At least that was what he could piece together. He didn't know his exact age since all the family records were destroyed when the house caught fire. His mother and father were both killed in the fire. Authorities found him, a young boy some time later, wandering down a street not far from the still-burning house.

All he had with him was a cigar box filled with a few prized possessions, and the pajamas he was wearing.

In that cigar box he had a few pictures of himself taken on camping trips and one of him riding his new bike. He had only two pictures of himself taken with his parents. An old wrinkled black-and-white showed him at about age three. He was standing between his parents, holding their hands. It was a close-up, so mother and father's faces were out of the frame.

The other one, an old faded Polariod showed him with his father in a swimming pool. He looked to be a year or so older in this one. He was standing chest-deep in the water wearing goggles. He had a snorkel in his mouth. His father was standing next to him. The water only came up to the top of his father's trunks. He was wearing sunglasses and had some white stuff smeared all over his nose. He had his arm around him. He was smiling.

CHAPTER 94

It seemed that he was spending most of every waking hour in a fog. On one level he knew that he needed to get on with his life. But on a different level he felt that it just wasn't important. He had lost the love of his life. What point was there to continue living?

Who could he share his feelings with? Did he even want to? Who would be there for him on those rare occasions when he felt vulnerable and needed a shoulder to cry on or a knowing pat on the back?

He found himself wandering from room to room, gazing blankly at the artefacts of a shattered existence. The coffee mug she had left half empty on the kitchen counter next to the picture of the two of them and her parents. It had been taken on their wedding day; the scent of hair spray and perfume in her bathroom; the towel draped over the shower door; the pile of shoes and stockings which always seemed to accumulated on the floor next to her side of the bed. His heart felt like it was being shredded. But somehow it didn't seem to matter.

One day he found himself in his office, sitting at the computer, hands poised at the keyboard. Absently he checked his E-mail, staring habitually at the screen. He read the words, then deleted them without really remembering what he had read. the words were gone forever. He didn't care.

Then somewhere in the depths of his gray funk, a thought slowly materialized. *It's time.*

The thought momentarily startled him. For some time now he had known that he couldn't continue this way. He knew that at some point he'd have to quit feeling sorry for himself and get back to living his life. But he had always managed to push the thought aside and retreat once again into his protective cocoon. There, surrounded by distant and clouded memories, he felt a small measure of comfort.

Sitting there staring absently at the screen saver, he gradually came back to reality. Two words began to form in his mind. *It's time.* For some unknown reason these words startled him. *It's time.* What did that mean? Why had those two words triggered such a response? He shuddered as a thought came to him.

His stomach knotted as he tapped the space bar to bring the computer screen back up. He pulled up the browser and typed in the two words. When he hit enter, the screen immediately went blank.

To his left he heard the computer stop. Then, as though it had begun a restart, it whirred back to life. Faster than had ever happened before, the screen flashed on. There on the screen staring back at him, was *him!* Breath caught in his throat as he heard and saw himself say:

"Take a deep breath. You are not going crazy. Relax. Calm yourself. This is going to take a while." His mouth went dry as he watched and listened.

"A sequence of recent events has triggered a subliminal prompt in your brain. That's why the words *It's time* came to mind. I . . . you . . . selected this sequence some time ago. The sequence or the events themselves weren't really the trigger. Rather, it was your emotional response. What I'm about to tell you will be startling. But you'll recognize its truthfulness as my explanation progresses. Here comes the hard part.

"You are not who you think you are. Remember how vague and unreal your past life seems to you? That's because it never really happened. You made it all up so that you'd have an explanation for why you are here . . . there. . . . Whatever! Any way, the point is this. At the time you recorded this message you were approximately 50,000 years old, as measured in Earth time. Still with me? Remember . . . breathe."

To have been told this by any other means would not have been successful. It all had to do with rhythm. Who would know better than himself how to time his remarks so that they would have the expected impact at just the right moment. More simply, believability.

He was surprised, but not awe-struck. The implications of this discovery were numerous, the most predominant being: Ageing. How would one go about overcoming the physical distress such a long life would endure. He knew the answer to this question would be forthcoming. The image on the screen continued speaking, so he froze the thought and stored it away.

"Yes. We'll get to the whole pile of implications later on. For now just sit back and enjoy the experience . . . again."

Aaron sat quietly in front of that screen, listening and watching so intently that he was sure he could feel the heavy veil of depression lift from his shoulders.

Finally! This was something that filled in the blank! The emotional component of his life had recently been on overload. That must have been the trigger! Not the death, but his emotional response to it. Watching another companion age before his eyes was always so difficult, but there were ways of adapting, of gradually getting used to the idea. But an abrupt, unexpected death had a whole new set of issues associated with it, not the least of which was the emotional response.

Emotion had a way of clouding issues from time to time. There was no getting around that. But, after all, it was always about attitude in the long run. It had everything to do with perception, and absolutely nothing to do with logic, at least on the surface. The average person would be so wrapped up in his own life that he really wouldn't pay close attention to the goings-on of another.

There were, of course, exceptions, such as family or another intimately close person or group. The question remained. How would one cope with the emotional baggage of 50,000 years worth of living?

"No, you are not immortal." His attention snapped back to the present. "At least your body isn't. Anyway, that's another story. So here's what has happened. Roughly 50,000 years ago you were born to a couple of highly advanced simians. They were without language. I don't know their names. I'm not sure they even had names. What I do know is that they were 'seeded' simians. Your parents.

"Your ancestry goes back to the beginning, when intelligent life first came to this planet.

"I don't know how long your parents were around before they had you (me). All I know about their history before I came along is what I learned from them. They were my (our) "parents," but they weren't our genetic ancestors. This much I do know. Ours was the first generation of humans on this planet.

"Our parents did have the ability to reason (on a rudimentary level). It's just that they had not evolved sufficiently so that their vocal cords were physically capable of producing actual speech.

"Let me explain. Modification, as I call it, isn't really physical in this context. It is a physical process, but it has to happen as a result of a change in the genetic code . . . not as a result of any surgical procedure.

"As you know, not all gene sequences are activated in the same way. An example is, say, blue eyes versus brown. Or blond hair versus black. It's all a matter of what proteins are present at a particular time during conception and gestation. Geneticists in your time understand this concept, though on a very elementary level.

"But back to the point. Just prior to the time when your parents "got together" and you came along; they were visited (in their sleep) by what we call Seeders. No point in going into much explanation about Seeders now. Just don't get excited! Think back to your studies in extraterrestrial life. It only takes a small stretch of intellect to understand what I'm telling you. Besides; as your memory continues to come back, this will all fall into place.

"Using a technology we don't really have a clue about, they "upgraded" your parents so they would be able to conceive and raise a human. This amounted to a genetic modification to their reproductive systems, in addition to an enhancement in their reasoning abilities.

"Earth has been around for millions and millions of years (Duh!! Pardon me for patronizing). During the course of this planet's evolution a lot of things have happened. None of them is unique. They happen all over the galaxy (and the universe too, for that matter). They may not be unique, but the exact time they will happen is somewhat unpredictable.

"Just a word or two about the Seeder job description. Their primary job is to introduce "intelligence" to worlds that have evolved to a certain level. In order to be effective at this job, they need to monitor evolutionary development.

Then, when the time is right, they introduce humans into the ecosystem, by way of the 'seeding' process.

"Now, as to why you're just now finding this out. I think it's fair to assume that everyone fears death (some more than others for various reasons). Most people would love to live forever . . . at least until they stop to think what living forever would entail.

Imagine the stress of outliving everyone you know. Imagine what it would be like to be able to 'predict' with astonishing accuracy the outcome of any particular incident, simply because you've been through it many, many, many times before.

Imagine how difficult it would be to see someone you care deeply about heading in a direction that you know would only end in disaster, but being unable to redirect them.

Now, think about not being able to tell anyone about what you know. Talk about stress!

"Well, that's part of the deal. You're not allowed to tell anyone. You can't interfere. Your job is to observe and report . . . *only!* Maybe a discrete nudge once in a while; but no overt interference in the 'natural' course of events.

How you deal with the emotional ramifications is another issue altogether, as you've found out.

"Fortunately, the Seeders have been there and done that. They've provided a mechanism whereby you can opt out . . . at least temporarily. It's like a sophisticated pressure relief valve or computer virus that only you have control over.

"Whenever you become saturated with too much information and you think you'll pop if you don't get some relief, you have an 'easy button' you can press. Then all your memories get put away in an encrypted file that only you can access. And in their place is a fabricated history, which you can use to fill in the hole created by the missing file. Only you have the password. But you can't use it because you don't remember it. It's been filed away too.

"Well, it's not really a password in the strict sense. It's more like a set of guidelines that have been preprogrammed into you brain. The criteria are somewhat generalized, but the level of intensity in which they occur is actually the trigger.

Apparently you've recently tripped your trigger, to use a crude euphemism. Whatever has happened has caused a few inactive circuits in your head to be re-energized. The circumstances were just right. The intensity level was just so. The switch was thrown, and here you are.

"As you read through the following pages, things will become more and more clear. To bombard you with everything all at once would be self-defeating. The idea is to expose you gradually. Otherwise you'll just pop again. And that's what we're trying to avoid, right?

"It's pointless for me to continue this narrative. You'll get it all figured out soon enough. Just let me caution you. This information is for your eyes only! Don't tell anyone anything about this . . . ever! You already understand why. Right?

"The part of your computer that contains this information isn't really part of your computer. (What, you say?!) Yes, you heard me right. When you type in the key words, there is something that links you to an encrypted database that isn't part of the computer. (Don't ask. I don't know). You can access this information from any computer anywhere in the world. No one else. Just you. (Again, don't ask.)

"Once you're in this program everything you type bypasses the computer completely. Whatever you type and whatever comes up on the screen immediately disappears when you walk away. The only way anyone else can see what is happening is if they are standing right next to you or looking over your shoulder when you're active in the system.

"If anyone but you tries typing anything, the link breaks. If they try copying, the link breaks. Even you can't copy anything from this program. Pretty high-tech stuff, huh!?

"This message will go away as soon as you exit and will never be brought back. Instead, the next time you type in your access, another screen will pop up with a prompt. You'll then have full access to the database the Seeders provided. If you're at the regular browser screen and you type in any other words but yours, the computer will function normally. Man! What a security system!

"Okay! You got a handle on all this? Just take your time and absorb as much as you think you can handle in one sitting. Remember . . . you've been here before. . . . Bye!"

CHAPTER 95

The screen went blank; then the browser screen came back up.

Aaron sat there, trying to sort out all the information he had just been bombarded with. All of what he had just heard made perfect sense. What surprised him most was that he was taking it so well. Restoring a memory, (a complete memory!) was an enormous undertaking . . . wasn't it? Well, there was nothing for it. He was dealing with it pretty well, he thought.

He typed in the two words, and there it was . . . a dark blue screen with the prompt he had just told himself about. (?!) When he clicked 'exit,' the browser screen came back again. Just to experiment, he typed the word 'music.' Up popped the familiar list of sites anyone would see. He backed out to the browser and typed IT'S TIME. There was the blue screen again. This time when he typed MUSIC, two prompts came up:

Listen
Exit

He clicked 'Listen' and was suddenly awash in the most beautiful sounds he had ever heard. Almost immediately he felt as though he was floating, careless, in a place foreign but vaguely familiar. He closed his eyes, letting the feeling carry him away. Too soon this beautiful music began to fade. When it was finally completely gone, he opened his eyes, feeling refreshed and relaxed. The room was dark. He was slumped in his chair, one arm dangling at his side. His cat was curled up in his lap. Apparently he had been "out" for some time.

Feeling refreshed and invigorated, he straightened up in his chair and looked at the screen. The browser had replaced the blue screen. He typed IT'S TIME, and again the blue one reappeared. He typed 'music' again. But this time he kept his eyes open, watching the screen. Another set of prompts appeared as the first two faded out. No music followed.

Recall
Add New
Exit

He clicked Recall. A list of unfamiliar titles appeared, filling the page with four columns. He scrolled down through what seemed to be an endless list, finally coming to the last page, which was only partially filled. The last entry was just a line with no title. When he clicked it a blank document appeared. Out of curiosity, he typed, "What's going on" and clicked the 'transmit' button in the top left corner of the tool bar. Almost immediately, the cursor disappeared and a female face appeared.

"Welcome back! Are you feeling better? It's been a long time."

Startled, Aaron typed, "Who are you?"

"I'm Asha. You're not fully yourself yet, are you?"

"I don't understand. What's going on?" He said aloud. Then remembering, he began typing. Before he had made two keystrokes, the face on the screen responded.

"You can type if you wish, but it isn't really necessary. The program recognizes your voice patterns. Maybe you ought to spend some more time reading in your archives. They'll help you get back up to speed. Then when you feel up to it, give me a call. Okay?"

The face on the screen disappeared and the four columns reappeared, just as he had left them. He clicked on the blank line and said, "Are you there?" No response. He tried typing instead,

"I'm ready now." No response. He tried again. Again, no response. Just the blue screen.

Sitting there in confused silence, he tried to absorb what had just happened. He felt overwhelmed and somewhat frightened. Then an idea popped into his head. He checked his watch, and then said aloud, 'music.'

Immediately his mind was filled with those beautiful sounds. He leaned back in his chair and closed his eyes, letting the music wash over him. When he felt like he had become more relaxed, he opened his eyes. There were the three prompts.

Recall
Add New
Exit

He clicked Exit, and then checked his watch. Only a few minutes had passed. So, he did have control! He wasn't totally at the mercy of the program. The music had been mesmerizing the first time he accessed it, and he had allowed it to carry him away. Apparently there was some sort of power present that had influence over him if he chose to allow it. But if he chose not to, somehow the program knew it, and closed.

"Who's this Asha person?" He said to myself as he sat there motionless in front of the screen. "And what was this about an archive?" Then it dawned on him; that's where he was now! He was back at the blank document. "Anybody there?" He said aloud. The words appeared there on the line.

He waited for some sort of response, but nothing came. The toolbar at the top of the screen read ARCHIVE—NEW DOCUMENT. Of course there wouldn't be a response. He was at the wrong place in the computer. He closed the document without saving and returned to the blue screen. He said "anybody there" again. The face of this Asha person reappeared.

"That was quick. What's on your mind?" she said.

"I don't understand. What's going on? And who are you?"

"Look, Ahmahn"

"That's not my name! What's going on?" Aaron demanded.

"Okay. Settle down for a second. It's obvious you're not up to speed yet. It'd be easier for both of us if you'd just go to your archives and read the last few entries. Since you wrote them, they'd make more sense to you than if I tried to explain what you're going through right now."

"Why didn't you answer the last time I called?"

"There's a sub-routine in the program that won't allow it. If you or anyone else tries to exit the program and then re-enter within a specified amount of time, it locks you out. It's a sort of fail-safe routine that you created.

"I created?"

"Yes. You really need to do some review. I can tell you're really distraught right now. Just go to your archive and read for a while. That'll do you a world of good."

"Okay. But first . . ."

"Look. You're only getting yourself all worked up, and it isn't helping. Please trust me on this. You've been through this many times before. If you'll just review what you've read, it'll really make you feel better. I'm going to leave you alone for a while so you can work this out on your own. Okay? Talk to you later."

Her face disappeared and the ARCHIVE screen reappeared. Aaron tried several more times to reconnect, but nothing happened. Finally giving in, he pulled up the archive screen, scrolled down to the last page, and clicked on the last archive entry:

CHAPTER 96

This is what appeared on the screen:

Reference Data
Initial Orientation for 23rd C.

In the latter part of the twenty-third century national governments were in the process of re-evaluating their positions and policies regarding interaction with one another. It had become evident over the last few decades that traditional diplomatic policies, adopted and instituted among governments around the world, were failing to fulfill expectations of those engaged in the diplomatic process.

It wasn't so much a problem of misinterpretation between languages, as much as it was a failure on the part of the participants to either recognize or compensate for shifts in priorities within individual countries.

It shouldn't have come as a surprise to the individual citizen to realize that his government wasn't performing in a way he thought appropriate. It was becoming apparent that politicians were more interested in attaining and retaining power than they were in doing the will of their constituencies. For most politicians, word parsing and obfuscation had become the order of the day.

Few people really took the time or expended the effort necessary to stay well informed on the affairs of government. Complexities of day-to-day living made it easier to let 'someone else' keep track of national and international affairs. Frequently even local governing agencies were left to their own devices. It seemed that people were too busy living their lives to appreciate the extent to which they had relinquished control of their governments. Consequently, governments became more self-serving and less responsive to the people.

What the individual had believed were "rights" (based on his experience and up-bringing) had increasingly become referred to as "benefits." Governments continued to promise more and produce less (growing in size and cost in the process), even as the average citizen looked on in "shocked" disbelief (from the comfort of his recliner).

Life had become so comfortable and routine that individual initiative had been replaced by a media-induced apathy. Only when the individual was directly affected did he put forth any significant amount of effort in behalf of any particular ideology. In other words, he assumed he had rights, and only complained when he realized that they could be (or had been) taken away. By then, of course, it was usually too late to do anything about it.

Effectively, through an immature and corrupted education system, people were taught what to believe. Values and morals, having been traditionally taught in the home, were increasingly being taught in the schools and in the media.

Anyone with a PCD (Personal Communication Device) had easy access to more information than he otherwise would have been able to acquire through traditional (and laborious) personal research. Sadly, most people never availed themselves of the information, opting for entertainment rather than enlightenment.

The government-sponsored educational institutions theoretically broadened individual horizons. But was the information the individual was being taught correct? Was it true? Was it right? Was it designed to enlighten . . . or to manipulate? More importantly, was the individual willing to expend the effort necessary to verify that what he was being taught was correct? For the majority of the citizenry, sadly, the answer was no.

Communication implies an exchange of ideas. In other words, one person puts forth an idea and the other puts forth a response. Concepts of all sorts take shape, are scrutinized, evaluated, poked and prodded until a consensus is reached and/or a direction is chosen. The individual learns how to function within the group.

Order is created and maintained through effective communication. This is how an "enlightened" society ought to function. But, for many reasons, including those described above, this had not become the case.

Global communication had in fact become a double-edged sword. While making it increasingly easy for governments to communicate one with another, this global communication network had also made it far too easy for misguided or poorly organized ideas to be transmitted between countries.

International diplomatic communications had become so commonplace that, rather than being viewed by the general population as important events, they had become all but ignored by a majority of the citizenry. The population had become "comfortably numbed."

The citizenry in general, paid little attention to what went on within government. Busily engaged in day-to-day affairs, the average citizen paid less and less attention. Consequently, government bureaucrats and politicians became increasingly free to do as they pleased, without fear of being scrutinized and/or criticized by 'the masses,' as they preferred to call those under their influence and control.

As would be expected from such an immature race, greed and subterfuge have gained a greater hold within government until ultimately it is now on the verge of destruction. The citizenry has essentially ignored what has happened and is oblivious to anything beyond the here and now."

CHAPTER 97

Reference Data

Background

"The process thus described repeated itself frequently over the course of the life of my race upon this planet. A few highlights of its history as I knew it will serve to illustrate and contextualize how I fit into this puzzle. Examples I cite will be primarily from memory with references included as they are pertinent.

My archives remain hidden by choice. Much of what I wrote during times in the past reflects biases or prejudices I had at the time of my writing, and are, therefore, not particularly objective. My wish is to convey an objective, if not apologetic appraisal of the proceedings of my race upon this planet, in the context of my own personal experiences.

I know not how many individuals have taken the course I have chosen, other than my friends Broc and Nahm. Undoubtedly, since our culture is but one of countless others, certainly there have been other individuals who have felt the need to do as I have done.

I don't consider myself to be anything other than an ordinary human being. I am, however, fortunate to have been endowed with a deep concern for the welfare of my race, coupled with a level of curiosity which I seldom saw exhibited by most of my peers.

I am certain it was curiosity and concern which lent me the

courage to take the steps that eventually led to this place and time. My only regret is that I didn't do this much earlier.

I am fortunate to have been associated with individuals who had a firm foundation of knowledge and experience from which I could draw. Evander, my mentor (and now my friend also) contributed greatly to my intellectual and moral development.

The philosophical concepts they taught me laid the foundation upon which I was able to build throughout the early decades of my life. Though we have been separated for so long, his love and encouragement have not been forgotten.

From the time I left until this moment, I've been engaged in developing a greater understanding of, and appreciation for my fellow beings; their hardships and their challenges.

I reserve the right to speculate and offer my own perspectives as I observe these challenges. Though not all pieces of this "puzzle" presently fit together, many of my observations are correlating easily. To the extent that I am able to separate myself emotionally from the turmoil that surrounds me, I'm delighted, but not awed by my new-found understanding."

As he continued reading, the events began unfolding in his mind almost effortlessly. At first they lacked clarity or continuity. But as he continued awakening memories, he began to realize just how fundamentally uncomplicated, how utterly simplistic they really were.

These were *his* experiences! He knew it now because the threshold had been crossed. His fear of the unknown had been replaced by a familiar, comfortable understanding of the present, and how he fit into it.

If he continued reading older and older entries, a more complete picture would eventually present itself.

Randomly he began scrolling through the pages and pages of columns.

One date caught his attention. He thought he remembered.

But it would be fun to go back and read it again, if only to help settle himself.

CHAPTER 98

January, '53.

"The situation here has continued to deteriorate. As I told Evander at our last meeting onboard the *Brighid*, I've tried everything I can think of to defuse the situation. But Stalin insists that I explain my repeated absences. How can I possibly do that without compromising everything we've worked to achieve? The man is totally paranoid. He doesn't trust anyone, even his closest advisors.

"Nikita came up to my flat last night with some terrible news. Apparently Joe called him on the carpet and accused him of collusion with Malenkov. How ridiculous can that be? Those two have been at each others throats since before Lenin died.

"It's probably safe to say Stalin doesn't have any idea Nikita and I have been working up plans to discredit Malenkov at the next council meeting. I think Georgy (Malenkov) suspects something, and he may have even dropped a few hints around Stalin's staff. But I think he's too much of a paranoid in his own right to press the issue directly. Too many skeletons in his own closet, so to speak. He wants Stalin's job as much as Khrushchev does. And I'm certain he'd do anything to get it, short of assassination. (He'd probably do that too if he could get close enough to pull it off without being found out.)

"Nikita, on the other hand, is a prudent politician. I think that's why I've been able to work with him so effectively. He's willing to look at the big picture. Sure, he's conducted a few 'purges' in his time. But he's never made a move without Joe approving it in advance. Even his actions against the Germans in Leningrad didn't happen until they were Okay'd by Moscow. His plan of attrition came at a huge cost in man power, but it worked.

"Malenkov, unlike Nikita, wanted a full frontal assault against what was at the time a very strong German front. Had we succeeded in breaking through that front, we would still have had to protect our flanks. If we'd have had reserve forces, maybe it would have worked. But without the needed reserves, that would have been impossible. I think Nikita understood this and was able to persuade Joe to accept his plan.

"Now, so many years later, I still see the two of them sparring with one another. Malenkov still wants the top job. But I don't think he would know what to do with it if he had it, short of killing off all his rivals. Then he wouldn't be much different than what we have with Stalin.

"It wouldn't necessarily be a bad thing, letting them kill each other off. It might help to clean things up a little sooner that way.But that sort of thing tended to get out of control unexpectedly. Better to exert some influence where I can to keep things headed in a generally positive direction.

"Khrushchev, on the other hand, sees how powerful the West has become since the end of the war. I've tried to make it clear to him that collectivism can only work with the approval and support of the general population. That's why the United States was able to win a war on two fronts. The government had the support of the people. I think Khrushchev understands this and knows that the Soviet Union cannot stand unless its citizens are in support. Nonetheless, he still has Stalin and his minions to contend with. How he'll be able to protect himself from them will be interesting to see. It's not unheard of for Stalin's guests to die mysteriously on the way home from one of his late night meetings.

"Nikita's secretary just called. They just rushed Stalin to the hospital. We've been instructed to go there immediately. It's decision time."

What? He knew Khrushchev? He knew Stalin? Of course he did. He remembered. But for him to have been there then, he would have to be at least 250 years old now! He didn't look much older than fifty or so. There was still a blank spot there in his mind. Maybe several. His memory still had many holes.

He didn't have time to be concerned about that just now. That would come in its own due time. For now . . . why hadn't he continued the narrative? It must have been pretty hectic back then. It was uncharacteristic of him to leave a story incomplete. Something must have happened.

"Well, enough of that." Aaron said to the screen. "Let's get back into it! Let's see what it was like back in the beginning." He auto-scrolled back to the top. The four-column format was still in play. But the titles were numeric now. He highlighted the "1" and clicked.

CHAPTER 99

1.

"Pa died last night. When I came in last night, he was already in his nest so I was careful not to awaken him. This morning when I arose, it looked like he was still asleep. After a while I went in to check on him. I spoke his name many times but he did not answer.

Aaron's eyes teared up as he read. His heart felt like it was about to break. The anxiety he had felt had receded. The confusion was gone. Now all he felt was profound sorrow, mixed with all-consuming happiness.

The memories began to flow. The swaying of the nest. The gentle warm caresses. The musky scent of thick fur. The satisfying taste of warm breast milk.

Then he knew. These were *his* memories. These were his feelings. They were as much a part of him as the all-consuming apprehension had been only moments before. He continued to read:

Fur? Breast milk? How far back had he gone? The file had no date attached to it, so there was no way of knowing when it had been written. He did recognize how different the writing style was. It seemed to be something that had been written by a child. The words were direct, to the point. The sentence was simplistic, as though the person who wrote it had a very limited vocabulary.

"Was that person really me?" Aaron said to himself, and to the cat nestled on his lap. More questions. Not enough answers. He closed the file and opened the next one.

2.

Leaving

"We have traveled six days now. Nahm came back this morning. He says there is food and water for many days ahead. He is tired from his journey, so we will stop for him to rest. Tomorrow Eff, his son, will go in his place. Nera and Sara will care for his new baby girl Payah.

"The others say not to go more, and I think we must rest for a time. I'm not sure what to do next. I asked Asha. She did not give an answer. She says come with her for a short time. I will go with her tonight when everyone is asleep. I will hide this thing in the ground before I go."

The next file showed a marked change in writing style.

3.

"I've been back now for a few days. I was with Asha and the others for many days. But When I returned here, nothing had changed. My family was still sleeping. The machine was still buried where I left it. Asha explained that this would happen, but I don't understand at all. How is it possible to leave for many days and yet return at the same time I left. It seems that the more I learn, the more there is that I don't understand.

"While I was there I learned many more new things about how to speak and write, but Asha says I must be careful not to show my new skills to anyone here. She says that my people must evolve naturally, that I should not interfere. But how is this possible if I remain among them? I am not strong enough to hide myself from them forever.

"Asha says I will not go with her again for a very long time, but that I can speak with her using this machine which she calls a 'transceiver.' I understand.

"When I speak into this box, marks come on it. When I stop speaking, they stop coming. Sometimes Asha answers. I can see her face, but not her really. She says it is called an 'image.' Sometimes it doesn't work. I don't understand.

"Tomorrow will be the same except for me. I know more now. I must learn how to lead without pushing, to encourage others to the fore. If I must lead, it must be with great care. This is my challenge. This is my joy. This is my sorrow. This is my life.

CHAPTER 100

Aaron leaned back in his chair to absorb what he had just read. The process of reawakening was sometimes difficult. Sometimes the memories came back in inconvenient order. Sometimes that made it harder. But not this time. The images cast up by the record he had just seen awoke within him all that had gone before.

Aaron had now approached a level of self-awareness that he had lacked for several years now. His memories were no longer surprises to him. They were filled with experiences which had largely unfolded quite naturally, if only for an occasional tweak here and there.

Now he recalled why it had taken such a drastic measure to force him into interacting once again. It was that the most recent loss of a loved one would more likely hold sway over his selfish instincts. This was, after all, his home, the place where his progenitors had been seeded. Though he had found more to life than that normally available to most members of this world, he nonetheless felt an obligation to see it through to its end. It was time to reactivate the character and re-enter the flow.

He could still have some influence from his present position, but it would have to be totally clandestine. Strictly editorial. But it couldn't last long. He must first establish an actual face-to-face meeting with someone within the current power structure, and then move in behind the scenes to get a feel for what was going on. It wasn't his first time, after all.

For the last several years, archival retrieval had done the job he would normally have had to do in person. The program was accurate, responsive on an incredibly subtle scale. Sometimes it was hard to tell who the 'real' Aaron was anymore. That's what made the program so great! It could imitate, to a very high degree of accuracy, his own personality traits. It was a perfect disguise for those times when he needed to be alone for a while . . . get his head sorted out.

But now it was time to drop the disguise. It was time to get back into this life and get a good feel for which way the energy was flowing. He flipped to the correct screen and typed "Asha . . . this is Ahmahn."

CHAPTER 101

"Hey, buddy! You're back, huh?" Her hair was shorter than the last time. She seemed to be in a good mood. Perhaps a bit forward, but nonetheless, pleasant.

"Yes, thank you." He smiled to himself. "I believe it is time for the four to meet. Will you set it up, please?" He spoke in his usual low-key manner, being assertive without being rude.

"Sir, I'm not sure they're anywhere close by." Asha was surprised he had recovered so quickly, but his forceful, authoritative voice left no doubt. She also noticed the subtle change in its presence. This time it was more low-key. More persuasive, less demanding.

"Please make the arrangements immediately. Let me know when we're ready to link."

"Yes, sir. Any preference?"

"Make it twenty-four hours, if possible. I'll try to be flexible."

Asha hadn't seen this side of Ahmahn in a long time. The loss of his wife had affected him deeply. Before, he was more harsh. Gentle . . . but harsh. Now? Not so much. But every indication was that he was back up to speed and ready to move forward. The loss of a wife, or a child, or even a close friend was always difficult. And he'd experienced it how many times? She couldn't imagine. She was in her mid twenties. And he was what, thousands of years older by Earth standards? That was just so far out of her league that she just couldn't grasp it. She had better let Ambia know, she thought to herself. As she turned to punch up her number, Ambia walked into the room.

"What character did he call in?" Ambia was somewhat upset at not being called immediately. Then seeing Ahman's profile diminish and go out of sight on the O.O.D. console where Asha was now seated, she realized that 'immediately' was now!

"Never mind. I saw." Ambia padded across the polished floor, sleeve-covered hands clutching a mug of steaming chocolate close to her chest. Carefully, she slid into the seat next to Asha.

"How'd he sound?" Ambia offered the hot drink to her friend.

"Up to speed as far as I can tell. Not as snotty, though." She took the proffered gift, brought it close to her lips and gently blew away the steam rising over the edge. Carefully, she took a sip. Sweetness seared into her jaw muscles, keeping her from speaking immediately.

"He didn't have that much to say, I take it." Ambia reached across the small table and gently took the drink out of Asha's hands.

"Only that he wants to call a meeting of the four. But that's nothing out of the ordinary."

"Did he say how soon?"

"Twenty-four hours. That's all he said."

"Did he say where he was going?"

Asha shrugged.

CHAPTER 102

Ahmahn knew how bad the situation was in the cities. It wasn't safe to be out alone at night throughout most of the city, under anything other than emergency circumstances. He had been fortunate to have purchased the lease on his apartment well back in the '30s when security systems were built tough and came built-in, as part of the lease. Not the cheap plastic battery-operated sensors that passed for home security these days. Sharon had told him what a good deal it would be to . . .

He hesitated only for a moment, remembering. . . .

"All right, Leo!" (that was the cats name)

"Let's get with it!" He walked resolutely down the hall and into the bathroom.

"Outa here, cat!" He thumped the litter box with his toe. "I gotta take a shower!"

A few minutes later he was at the computer. He typed "IT'S TIME" and began typing before the screen came up.

"Thank you, Ahmahn. I am now in voice mode. How may I be of assistance?

"Thank you, Hal." Ahmahn had named his computer after the one in the Space Odyssey vid he had loved so long ago.

"Where are the three, Hal."

The screen immediately came to life, showing a globe. As each name was spoken, the globe rotated and zoomed to the appropriate location.

"Nahm is in the Central Asian System. Broc is still in South Africa, and Haden last reported in at the Hague. This was yesterday morning."

"Hal, please. A brief political overview."

"As you wish, sir." The globe zoomed in to a tight shot of the Hague Center from satellite. View resolution was good down to about a foot.

"Haden reports the situation there hasn't changed much. He can't do a vid for security reasons, but here is a shot of the residence where he's staying."

The view resolution immediately went almost crystal clear as the view moved in to show the word DANZIG carved into the dark, stone facade over the front entry. The view slowly began backing out, as thought a camera was being lifted up, out above the empty streets.

Finally the view steadied high above the surrounding structures, high enough to see the flat, gravel covered roofs.

"He says he will probably be able to break free tomorrow late evening."

"Please tell him to call when he is ready. I'll make myself available from seven our time on."

"Very well, sir. Broc is currently in a small town called Lenasia. It's about forty klicks south-east of the Johannesburg ruins. He reports looting still continues, but on a sporadic basis. Most of the population has begun moving south, toward the Suikerbosrand Nature Preserve.

Politically, the war lords still retain power, what little there is. Most of the population is dead or in hiding. Soon the tribal leaders will be fighting among themselves. Essentially, they are down to small arms and machetes. They pose no threat to any plans you have currently in place."

"I assume Cairo is aware of this."

"Yes. Sultanih is there now, but nothing much has happened. There's talk of another summit in a few months, this time in Alexandria. Shall I notify his highness Al-Atrasha of your return?"

"Yes. Please inform him that I am recovering nicely from my recent loss, and look forward to seeing him at his earliest convenience. Hopefully in just a few days."

"Security forces have already been placed on standby in the Med." The computer continued. "We have several assets assigned to the casino and hotel in Alexandria. They report only minor activity. Cleaning crews and supply trucks, mostly."

"Looks like that's gonna be the place. Let me know when they start shipping in vegetables. Then we'll know it's gonna be soon."

"Nahm reports the Chinese are getting pretty antsy again. The plague in Thailand has stopped spreading, but disease control is getting out of hand."

"Even the 'Mongol hordes' can't keep up with it, huh? Sounds to me like they're learning a little late how expensive communism can be."

"Apparently so, sir. They've had to commandeer a small container hauler fleet to help move the bodies. Their resources are stretched to the breaking point."

"Have Sultanih call as soon as possible. I need to get up to speed locally."

"He reports that a unit of Forward Air Controllers have been deployed along the West Bank. They haven't set anything up yet. They're just waiting."

"That sounds like an advance security detachment to me. Alexandria may be sooner than we think."

"There is a high likelihood that this might indeed be the case, sir." Hal's voice matrix was a crude re-engineering of the original 'Hal' voice, taken from one of the mass-produced discs that were in common use during the time the original was created. Background noise sometimes filtered through, giving the track an almost sandy, hissing sound.

"Please inform the three we must link immediately."

"As we speak, sir."

"Thank you, Hal. I'll be in the study."

"Thank you, sir."

CHAPTER 103

Haden sat quietly in an over-stuffed chair, looking out into the night. His tenth floor corner suite faced Westward, providing a panoramic view of the ocean only a few blocks distant.

Just below the darkened horizon he could make out distant lights, winking on and off erratically. Since electronic communications had been compromised during last nights assault on the Binnenhof complex (the Netherlands' government center), all secure communications had been by courier, rather than radio or electronic means. The flashing lights were most likely coded messages being sent between ships of the protective naval blockade.

He was a diplomatic envoy for the North American Alliance. He had been taken totally off guard by the attack.

So far there had been no confirmation as to where the attack had originated. Many in the conference were convinced it was the Western Alliance that had initiated the assault as a reprisal for the United Nations pulling out of New York City and relocating to the Netherlands.

Haden was convinced that he knew otherwise. Arthur Walenberg (U.S. military attache and Haden's close friend), had been with him when the attack started. Walenberg was just as surprised as he when it all began.

Why, Haden reasoned, would the U.S. risk killing its own diplomats? It had too much to loose on the international scene if that happened.

Since the collapse of the Dollar two decades earlier, the United States had been desperate to avoid foreclosure. Thus the 'Western Alliance' had come into existence. The U.S. had to maintain some leverage, some semblance of credibility on the world market, so it declared nationwide martial law and took total control of the economy. It sold off all businesses located in countries where the U.S. owed money, in exchange for relief from the debt it owed.

The only remaining leverage it had was its military. It was still the most powerful in the world, but without a vibrant economy to support it, it couldn't last without outside support.

That was why Haden and Walenberg had been sent to this conference; to persuade the world that a "military for hire" was indeed a valuable asset for any nation to possess.

Though there was only minor damage to a few surrounding buildings close to the conference center, it had been decided to evacuate the whole complex rather than risk being caught by another attack.

Haden and Walenberg had decided to room together in a suite of rooms above the Danzig, a once popular pub just northwest of the Hague complex.

Haden's thoughts were interrupted by the sound of a door opening. He turned to see Walenberg, pipe clenched between his teeth, clad in a bathrobe and slippers, shuffling toward the mini-bar.

"I don't give a damn what the Europeans say, I miss having fluoride in my bath water. This crap smells like a sewer."

"Yeh. And it doesn't taste much better. Grab me a bottle of that sparkling water, will you?" Haden stood and stretched, then walked over to join Art at the bar.

"Here's to you, Bro." Art screwed the top off a mini-bottle of vodka and raised it in a toast.

"Nostrovia," said Haden as he took the top off his bottle and raised it.

"What does that mean, anyway? Are you part Ruskie or something?"

"Don't have a clue. Think I heard it once in an old Russian movie or something."

The two friends clicked bottles. Art downed his vodka in a single long gulp, then dropped the tiny bottle into a trash can beside the bar.

They turned back toward their seats at the window. Art lit his pipe as they walked. Haden sat down, careful not to spill his water. Art flopped into his chair. A few sparks erupted from his pipe, falling onto his robe. He brushed them away casually as he spoke.

"So, Bro. You've had some time now. What do you think's going on?"

Haden sat the bottle down beside his chair and rubbed his hands together slowly.

"Well, first off; why only the one attack? Tracking shows only two planes were involved. They came in at tree-top level from inland somewhere and exited almost due West. Nothing vital to the infrastructure was hit, just a couple of buildings close to the Binnenhof. Minimal casualties. I don't think even one person was killed. They could just as easily have hit the main complex, but they didn't. And only one pass per aircraft."

"Low-order explosives, too." Art took a puff from his pipe as he responded. "I think this wasn't an attack. I think it was a message."

"Agreed! But the question is, a message from who? Who had something to gain from this?"

Walenberg rose and went back to the bar, returning with two more mini-vodkas. Screwing the tops off the bottles, he handed one to his friend.

"Come on. Take one. It'll help you think."

Haden took it, but didn't drink. Instead, he gestured with the tiny bottle for emphasis.

"Consider this. They came from inland, but they left heading West. Maybe that means that they were low on fuel and had to take a direct route back to their base. That suggests our guys were involved. The satellite lost track just minutes after their departure, and we haven't heard anything since."

Walenberg took a short swig and winced as he spoke.

"Looks like we may have been in one of those rare blind spots at the time of the attack. Otherwise we should have seen them coming."

"Fair enough. But where did they go?" Haden slumped back in his seat. "Still no communications from the satellite. How could it have been knocked out without us detecting?"

"A low-yield tactical nuke, maybe. Launched straight up at the satellite, with no active homing Doppler for the sat to detect and track. Just a speck on the lens, as far as the satellite is concerned. No need for a direct hit, either. Just get close. EMP takes the sat's electrical out before it knows it's under attack."

"Makes sense, I suppose." Haden brought the bottle to his lips, then hesitated. "This is all academic anyway. Why should we be concerned with the 'how'? Let the analysts work that out. We need to know the 'who.'"

"And the why." Art finished his drink and reached out toward Felix.

"Gimme that thing. You're gonna spill it if you're not careful."

"You sure you want to do this? This'll make three, you know."

"Actually, Mr. Haden, it'll make six. Two shots per bottle, jus' in case ya didn't know." His words were beginning to slur.

Haden sat forward, shaking his head, then rested his elbows on his knees.

"What ever you say, boss. So. . . . Who has the most to gain from this? The U.S. has all its cards on the table, face-up. All they . . . we . . . have is muscle."

"Maybe our bosses think a little show of strength will sweeten the pot a mite."

Art was slow to comment.

"I suppose that's a possibility. But it's never a good idea to bite the hand that feeds you. Besides, it's hard to bluff without a hole card."

"Hmmm. You're quite the poker player! Well, I suppose that puts us in the clear."

Arthur Walenberg, the United States Military Attache, started to get up, thought better of it, and slumped back into his chair. He fumbled for the lever on the side of the chair and pulled it back roughly. The leg support flew up, throwing both his feet into the air. One slipper came off and landed between his legs. Ignoring it, he pushed against the arm rests until he was almost horizontal.

"Let me know if ya come up with any more ideas. For now, I think I'll jus' sleep on it."

Within less than a minute Walenberg was out cold. He'd been active throughout the day, coordinating the evacuation, and had been sipping from his hip flask all along. His physical activity kept him alert and the effects of the alcohol had been minimal. But now, in the warmth and quiet of their suite, the alcohol was taking its toll.

Haden knew that his friend would sleep the night through without even a stir. He rose quietly from his chair and walked toward his bedroom, turning the lights off as he left.

CHAPTER 104

Haden opened his laptop and sat it on the night stand beside his bed. He typed in his code words and then sat down on the bed. Within only a few seconds Ahmahn's face appeared on the screen.

"Good to see you, my brother," Ahmahn's image said. "Apparently things have begun to stabilize."

"A bit, yes. All the representatives arrived as scheduled, but we hit a bit of a snag before much could be accomplished. We've been attacked from the air. . . . Before you get excited, let me assure you it wasn't much of an attack. Only two aircraft were involved and damage was minor. No significant casualties that I'm aware of."

"I had no idea," Ahmahn responded. "Hal reported some security issues, but said nothing about an attack."

"It only happened a few hours ago and was quite brief. We've moved everyone out of the Binnenhof and distributed them in facilities outside the complex. We've shut down all electronics until we're sure they're secure."

"Do you know where the attack originated?"

"No. That's why I called. We need to know who's behind this."

"Okay. give me a second." Ahmahn's image flickered and disappeared, to be replaced by a smaller version of himself, with Evander's image beside it. Evander was the first to speak.

"We detected the explosions but were waiting for the all-clear from you."

Haden responded: "We need to know where the planes came from and where they went."

"Hold one," said Evander. His image flickered and partially disappeared, then quickly re-stabilized.

"We show the sortie originated from a small private airstrip to the southwest of Cairo. The aircraft were two obsolete F-18's, based on their engine output signatures. No radio communications from either of them. Both planes ditched in the sea about two hundred miles off shore. No ship traffic in the area, so either the pilots were picked up by a sub or they went down with their planes."

"Cairo, huh?" said Ahmahn. "I've been out of the loop for a while. Someone want to fill me in? Anyone heard from Sultanih? (Salim Sultanih was their eyes and ears inside the Mid-eastern Alliance's military. A year previous, he had been caught in the act of trying to infiltrate Walenberg's organization, and had been 'turned.' Now, in exchange for keeping his identity as a double agent secret from the Alliance, he provided "intel" on the inner workings of their military machine.)

"Our last contact was a little over a week ago." Evander continued. "Broc was confident enough in the accuracy of Sultanih's report that he elected to head south to Johannesburg so he could monitor the tribal unrest going on down there."

"Say what you will about Broc." Haden was becoming impatient. "You've all known him much longer than I have, and my fear is that that familiarity may have clouded your judgement about him. Consider for a moment the severity of the situation we now face. In the broadest sense, the so-called 'western alliance' is little more than a bunch of political wind bags trying in vain to keep some measure of credibility on the world stage. Yes, their military is the largest in the world and could probably crush any opposition from a single nation. But if several countries united against them, the best the Americans could hope for is a stalemate. Without sponsorship they lack the resources for any prolonged military engagement. The middle-east powers know this, and though they continue to fight among themselves, should the necessity arise, they would unite to defeat the West if they perceived it to be a serious threat. Ahmahn should be here keeping contact with Abdullah, making sure that such an alliance doesn't happen."

Evander had been listening intently to Haden's remarks and had noticed a flaw in his argument.

"May I remind you, friend Haden, that of all of you, Ahmahn has been the one person most closely attuned to the goings on in this part of the world. He knows the mind-set of these people best because he is one of them. He has associated with them from before the dawn of civilization.

"But more importantly you of all people should be attuned to the Western political/military/industrial mind-set. You have courted their military attache as your close friend for how many years now? You have rubbed shoulders with the best and brightest of their leaders. Surely during that time you have recognized their inherent lack of a unified political will".

"This may appear to be so now." replied Haden. "But their traditional ties to the independent states throughout the world remain strong, in spite of their political remarks to the contrary. Should the situation warrant, I'm certain the West would rise to their defense."

Ahmahn felt he must interject.

"My fiend Haden; you have only just recently joined us. And though I do not doubt your motives or your integrity, I fear that your perspective is somewhat clouded. It was late in the twentieth century when you elected to join us, and from your comments it becomes clear that you brought with you much of the popular thinking of that era. During your time with us aboard the *Brighid*, over two hundred Earth years have transpired. During that time many things have changed, including the virtual disintegration of most of the remaining independent states. The high moral values that the 'West' once held dear have since diminished, to be replaced by hedonistic attitudes.

"Beyond that, when you elected to return to Earth, you chose to 'infiltrate' the political elite where you believed you would have the most influence. And you *have* made positive inroads, as witnessed by the relationship you have developed with your friend Walenberg.

But if you will look at that relationship objectively, you will recognize the inner conflict which plagues the man. He wishes the words you speak about the patriotism of his people were true. But he also knows that if he were to repeat them to his superiors, they would, at best, fall on deaf ears, and he would surely loose credibility in the process.

"Sadly, as evidenced by the apparent apathy on the part of the general population during generations of subtle subjugation, Walenberg exemplifies the rule, rather than the exception."

"That might be the case on the surface," Haden responded. "But I still believe there is within those people a 'silent majority' which still holds traditional values as sacred."

Evander once again interjected.

"Brother Haden, I applaud your faith in the human species. I am certain that to some degree your faith is justified. But may I remind you that your contact has been exclusively with the upper echelons of Western society, not with the general population. The elites are a closed 'society within a society,' disconnected and separate from the common man, concerned only with their own agenda. They speak in lofty terms when pontificating before the 'masses.' Their words are woven to deceive, to mislead, to manipulate. Their only real concern is the preservation of their power and status among their peers. They will say and do whatever is necessary to do so.

"And the common people, so caught up in the ordeals of every day living, the distractions, the misdirections, have chosen to capitulate, to not swallow the bitter pill, to not take responsibility for their actions. They have given little thought for the future, thinking only of their short term comfort. It is precisely that 'silent majority' which has allowed this corruption to gain dominance.

"Ahmahn has understood this for a very long time. He has, just as you have, tried to persuade your people to do what is right, rather than what is expedient."

"That is why each of us is engaged in this noble cause." Everyone was startled to hear the voice of Broc. "I logged in to the discussion only minutes ago, and would now add my thoughts.

"Each of us sees our people falling prey to apathy. We see they have grown accustomed to a life practically devoid of discomfort. Their every need is provided for. They have but to reach out and it will be handed to them. They no longer appreciate or even comprehend what it took for their comforts to be made available. And in so doing they have lost their integrity. They have lost their moral compass. They are without direction. They are without purpose.

"That is why I chose to return to my homeland. Of all the nations of the Earth, mine was the first. Ahmahn and Nahm were both there at the beginning. They can attest to the struggles we endured. And they also can attest to the irony that, of all the nations which have come into being, of all the advances our species has achieved, still in our hearts we are as primitive and self-serving as those in Johannesburg who hack each other to pieces with spears and knives."

Evander now felt a need to speak candidly.

"My friends, my brothers. Each of us feels much alike in these matters. I must confess that in the matters of your world, I have perhaps become more involved than I should have. Your world is not the first I have observed, but yours is the first in a very long time that I have taken such an interest in. Certainly it is partially because of the relationships we share. But that cannot be the only reason. There have been dozens, if not thousands who have come before you. Though it may dishearten you to hear me say this, your world is not unique among all the others. The difficulties you have faced are unique to you, but they are common among the other worlds. And to be quite honest, few have succeeded in rising above their own pettiness. Perhaps it is because I see such potential on this world that I have taken such an interest. I sense that events on Earth are rapidly approaching a point of no return."

"This is what we sense too, Evander. That's why we are speaking now." Haden shifted uncomfortably on his bed.

"We still haven't heard from Nahm, but it's probably safe to assume the Russians and Chinese are still at it."

"All indications are that they've reached an impasse," reported Evander. "Our local transceivers all reported a marked decrease in military activity over the last few days. Perhaps their pandemic in Thailand has gotten the best of them."

"Pandemic or not, they still represent a significant threat to the region. I'm worried that Nahm hasn't reported in. Evander, I know it's against protocol, but would you try to contact him?

"Only if you all agree it is necessary," said Evander. "Already I fear that I may have gone too far."

"My dear friend," said Ahmahn. "I'm sure we all agree that the severity of the situation warrants a higher degree of participation on the part of the *Brighid*."

"Very well, then," said Evander. "I'll alert a unit to locate him and make contact."

"As for this conclave here at the Hague," Haden continued. "It seems pretty obvious that it's not the big secret we all thought it was."

"Perhaps that is why we have not heard from Sultanih. Perhaps he has been discovered," Ahmahn interjected. "That would explain your recent air attack."

"Very possible," said Haden. "Evander?"

"Yes, of course. I'll re-task a unit immediately. The one assigned to him appears not to be activated."

"I see now it is prudent that I return to Abdullah," said Ahmahn.

"Regardless of Sultanih's situation, it is imperative that we know the situation with the caliphs. Is he still in Bodrum?"

"Our last track indicated so," said Evander. "The Turkish consulate still shows a suite of rooms reserved in his name. Shall I dispatch a shuttle to pick you up?"

"Thank you, yes," said Ahmahn. "When I've re-established with Abdullah I will contact you all so that we may plan our next move."

THE ONSET OF REALITY

CHAPTER 105

Watching the sunrise from this altitude was always fascinating. Ahmahn never seemed to get used to it, even though he had been flying for many years. The air was always clearer up here, high above the clouds. From time to time a break in the clouds would reveal a miniaturized hazy view of the landscape flowing past him in slow motion far below. The Sicilian coastline, still dotted with man-made light, would soon emerge from the nights darkness to be greeted by a grey overcast morning. The forecast called for extensive rain all along the south-eastern coastline, accompanied by high seas as the remnants of a storm played themselves out against the rugged shoreline. People living along the coast would still be enduring the buffeting from the storm which had hit in the middle of the night.

Up here, at forty thousand feet, the ride was smooth. Had he not been looking out the window, he wouldn't have noticed the sensation of any movement at all. Aside from the hiss of air rushing past the fuselage and the muffled roar of the engines, there was virtually no sound inside the cabin. It was as though he was alone here, high above, isolated, as the world crept past far below.

The two passengers who accompanied him would soon be awakened as the aircraft began its descent. But for now he felt very much alone in the quiet darkness . . . alone with his thoughts . . . and his fears.

Since his most recent 'awakening', he hadn't seen any really significant change in the world situation. Nations continued quarrelling and politicians continued making promises. Meanwhile the threat continued to grow.

He knew he would soon have to decide. Either remain here and try to help avert disaster, or return to the *Brighid* and watch helplessly as his world destroyed itself.

The luxury ten-seater aircraft began a slow circular descent through thin clouds. Though the sun had not yet broken the horizon, there was enough light to make out the featureless view below. Ahmahn watched through the small circular portal as the wispy clouds disappeared, revealing nothing but a smooth sea below, stretching from horizon to horizon. Where could the land be, he wondered.

As the aircraft made one last turn, setting up for final approach, he could just make out a thin sliver of land, certainly not more than a mile long and significantly less in width. To the right of the runway he could make out a row of maybe a dozen small buildings. Other than that, the island appeared to be barren.

"You look so concerned, my friend," came a familiar voice to his right.

"Indeed, your Highness," Ahmahn said without turning. "I can see nothing but a few small buildings. Did I miss something as we approached? I saw no evidence of watercraft or docking facilities. Are we to wait here until a ship arrives?"

"Be not concerned, my friend," the voice continued. "Much is not as it would seem."

The aircraft continued its descent, touched down gently, then quickly decelerated to a slow taxi. As it turned right off the runway, Ahmahn could see more clearly just how small the few buildings were. The center building (the one they were now approaching) was the only one which showed any activity. Only a fuel truck, a towing tractor and a few men could be seen. The rest of the parking ramp was empty.

The plane came to a gentle stop, still in the middle of the ramp. Immediately, the two vehicles sprang into action, heading straight for the small three-engine plane.

"Come now, my friend. By the time we retrieve our bags and reach the terminal, my men will have begun re-fueling and preparing the plane for departure. As for how we are to depart this place, you will see soon enough."

The sting of salt air and jet fuel assaulted his nostrils as the plane's door dropped open. Two men, clothed in black turbines and military uniforms scurried up the steps.

"Your Highness, welcome," said one of the men as he hurried down the narrow isle toward them.

"Your vessel is prepared and awaits your arrival." The man bowed deeply and took the bags that were offered him.

"When can we depart? I am anxious that we get under way as soon as possible."

"Immediately, your Highness. Your quarters are prepared and a meal awaits, if it be your desire to partake."

"Very well," said the King. "Let your commander know that we will leave immediately."

The man bowed again quickly, then he and the other hurried back down the stairs, arms fully laden with baggage.

King Abdullah was first to descend to the tarmac. Ahmahn was next, followed closely by the one remaining passenger, Sultanih.

The two soldiers ran ahead with the baggage and hurried toward the building.

"See to it that places are set for myself and my assistant. You may begin refueling immediately thereafter." Abdullah spoke to one of the soldiers. "As you wish, my King." The soldiers rushed ahead and propped the double doors open, then hurried into the room carrying the baggage.

"Colonel Sultanih, you will return to the plane immediately. Your bags are still onboard. You will return to base immediately after the aircraft is fueled. There you will await further instructions from me. You will contact no one. You will accept no other assignments until you hear from me or my assistant."

"As you wish, my King." The colonel gave Ahmahn a quick glance, then turned back toward the plane.

The doors remained open behind them as they entered. Abdullah glanced over his shoulder to ensure his instructions had been followed.

The room was dimly lit by a single low-wattage light bulb suspended by its wiring a foot or so below the ceiling. The space was completely empty, except for a short ramp leading up to a narrow platform on the opposite side of the room. The two soldiers were nowhere in sight.

Unusual, thought Ahmahn. Only two men on the tarmac. No one to greet the King, other than those two. No evidence of any activity anywhere except at the terminal building itself. No one here inside the terminal either. No furnishings. Inadequate lighting. He assumed the facility must still be under construction.

"Now, my friend!" Abdullah smiled and motioned for him to come closer. "Now your curiosity will be quelled." The king pulled him close, placing a reassuring hand on his shoulder. "Indeed, all is not as it seems." The two ascended the ramp. Ahmahn saw that the platform too was empty, except for what looked like a three foot circular hole in the floor immediately in front of them.

As Ahmahn closed the distance, he could see that it was indeed a hole. Standing at its edge he peered down at a circular hatch, leaning slightly backward. Inside the hole he saw a ladder leading down into what looked like the conning tower of a submarine.

"Now you see!" said Abdullah. "Nothing is ever as it seems."

The two descended into the conning tower. Immediately the submarine submerged. After less than two minutes, they heard a muffled explosion.

"That, my friend is the end of yet another illusion. The 'island' we landed on was not an island at all. It was but a ship, made large enough to accommodate my aircraft. It and the aircraft are now settling to the bottom of the sea."

"But what of the crew? What of colonel Sultanih?" he asked, alarmed.

"Those? They are nothing. They are Kafir. They are sub-human. They have served their purpose, and are no more. I will tell you more once we are alone, away from prying ears.

"As for the world . . . they will be told that our aircraft crashed into the sea and that there were no survivors. We are now free to do as we choose. Only a select few know any of this. And soon we will join them in Alexandria. This is the meeting that will decide the fate of the middle-east for decades to come. And you—*you*, my friend—will be part of it."

The two men descended through another hatch into the sub's control center. The ship's captain bowed deeply and escorted them to his cabin. There in the cramped space a small table had been set with the meal the King had ordered.

"Thank you, Captain." said the King condescendingly. "That will be all for now."

The meal was sparse, two sliced up sautéed squid, some kind of leafy vegetable and a piece of dry bread. Ahmahn washed the last tasteless bite down with a gulp of water.

Abdullah pushed himself back from the table and belched quietly before continuing.

"So you see, once we verified Sultanih was the mole, it was a simple matter to track his movements. We didn't need to 'turn' him. He was already 'our man,' even though he was working both sides of the fence, so to speak. We already knew of the Chinese' plan to bomb the Hague, but I saw no practical advantage to eliminating the Western Alliance from the equation. They are only a tool, a military force. In the game of world politics they no longer have any credibility. They have 'sold their soul for filthy lucre,' as the religious say. They are only a whore, to be paid for service and then discarded.

"The Triumvirate has always desired to eliminate Israel. However, to me Israel is but an inconvenience, a mere irritation, never a real threat. Sometimes it can even be useful, much like the Americans. It is easy to use their mere existence as a tool to organize their would-be enemies. There are, however, many who would disagree, even within my own realm.

"The other two members of the Triumvirate, the Chinese and the Russians, are somewhat myopic. They want to eliminate *all* opposition, including Israel *and* America. But what they fail to realize is that without any opposition to fight against, they will be forced to actually produce the utopian society they claim to advocate. Even *they* know it is an impossibility, though they profess otherwise to their people. If the masses were to discover this, they would rebel. And then where would the leadership be? Therefore they maintain their facade.

"Ask yourself; if they are so in favor of creating a utopian society, something their individual governments both advocate, why then have they not joined forces and actually done it? Truth be known, they are in no way altruistic. Rather, they crave power and dominion over others."

"But my King. If you will pardon my saying, do you not also advocate the same thing?"

Abdullah chucked.

"Alas. You again ask the right question, even knowing that in doing so you risk much, if not all. This, my friend, is among other things, the reason why I admire you. You possess the courage of a bull and the cunning of a tiger. Very well then. I will reveal myself to you.

"The Russians and the Chinese, they are bulls; full of courage and bravado. Me? I am the tiger. The bulls will charge forward, confident in their strength.

"The tiger too possesses strength. But he also possesses cunning.

He will manipulate the herds where the bulls reign. He will show himself, but only long enough to distract, to disrupt. He will be selective. He will watch. He will wait. He will search out a weakness. Then, when he is sure of his success, he will pounce. And then, as suddenly as he has appeared, he will seize his prize and once again disappear into the background, leaving the bulls to snort and stomp the ground and shake their heads in wonderment."

Ahmahn nodded understandingly. This man, this King, truly understood the inner workings of a corrupt human psyche. He was thoughtful, and subtle and cunning in his dealings with others. No wonder he had become such a power in the middle east.

"Now, my friend, let us return to the subject of the Americans, and their so-called Western Alliance. Their leadership reminds me of 'upperclassmen' in a university. They surround themselves with lesser powers, the Brazilians, the Mexicans, the Canadians and Brits, much like the seniors in university who surround themselves with sophomores . . . 'wise fools.' Though they are relatively new on the scene, still they see themselves as more knowledgeable than their lessers, and thus more deserving of praise. The adulation they receive persuades them that they are right, and they expound ad nauseam on the virtues of their cause. They pontificate about free enterprise, individualism, the right to choose, all noble virtues, while behind the scenes they amass wealth and power and influence, invariably at the expense of those to whom they preach. The titans of industry and commerce use their wealth for their own self-aggrandisement. They collude with their political counterparts to perpetuate the status-quo of the masses, while continuing to amass more wealth and power.

"In a very real sense they are no different than the 'progressives' and 'socialists' they claim to despise. They and their so-called 'enemies' are but wolves, each wearing a different disguise so as not to alarm the sheep."

"Now, as for the attack in the Netherlands; the Chinese, being the bulls that they are, wanted simply to eliminate the competition. Their culture was hundreds of years old when the American 'upstarts' came to power, and their animosity toward them has simmered and boiled ever since. They knew they would never persuade them to take their side, so they decided to take them out of the equation. They saw the attack on the Hague summit as an opportunity to put the Americans in their place, to deprive them of leadership, rendering them impotent, at least temporarily, until their next electoral sham. In doing so, the Chinese hoped to 'level the playing field' between themselves, Russia, and the Arab Emirate, as they call the coalition which I have formed.

"My sources discovered the plot when they found out about Sultanih. As a matter of fact, they discovered that he was actually a *triple* agent, working with the Chinese to undermine both the Americans and my organization.

"We back-tracked his movements and located the planes the Chinese had purchased from an old Syrian regime. The remnants of the regime were holed up south-east of Damascus and were selling off their inventory to the highest bidder. Sultanih was the middle-man who arranged the transaction. He co-opted two pilots from *my* air force to fly the planes to Cairo.

"The planes arrived fully armed with sufficient weaponry to completely destroy the Binnenhof where the 'summit' was to be held. We successfully tracked them to an abandoned airstrip, and once Sultanih and the pilots departed, my troops infiltrated the facility, downloaded the munitions and replaced them with less powerful ones which were identical in appearance. The new munitions were programmed to impact a smaller building adjacent to the Binnenhof, thus sparing the delegates.

"The mission proceeded as they had planned. The pilots ditched their planes in the sea, were picked up by helicopter and flown to Scicli on the Sicilian coast. From there they walked the few miles to the strip where my jet was parked. So far as they knew, everything had gone as planned. They reported as scheduled to pilot us to the 'island,' and you know the rest.

"The Hague summit will go on, though a bit delayed. The Chinese will be surprised to learn their little scheme has been foiled. While they are off balance, the Russians will undoubtedly try to take advantage. And, while they spar with each other, I will persuade the Americans to do my bidding."

"And what would that bidding be, by King? Would you have them attack Israel themselves?"

"Oh my! Never would I do such a thing. After all, Israel is only an irritation, not a threat. They are content to keep to themselves. The only time they become aggressive is when they feel threatened. After all, they are a very small nation with their backs to the sea. They are surrounded by aggressors. They have a right to defend themselves, a right which I do not dispute, so long as they behave themselves.

"No, I will persuade the Americans to remain neutral regarding Israel. I will provide them with the petroleum they need, at a price that they can just barely afford. And in return they will participate in the distraction. I will, with their help, cause dissension among the tribes within my kingdom; enough to keep the warlords distracted and controlled, but not enough to be a serious threat to me.

"What then is your objective, my King? Israel represents the only serious threat to your dominion."

"This is true, Ahmahn. But there is something about my people which you need to understand. They are for the most part ignorant people. They have little or no formal education. They are desert-dwellers who are in constant competition with one another for survival. Couple their ignorance with destitution and the result can be desperation. These people are, and have been for centuries, in a state of desperation. Desperate people will all too often do desperate things. And that is what I try to prevent.

"Don't you have the power to bring your people out of their ignorant state?"

"Could I bring them together and speak to them as one, perhaps. But their leadership would then see me as a threat."

"Could you not remove those leaders from power?"

"Once again, perhaps. Even in the smallest tribes there are factions within factions, within factions, each with its own agenda. To win the hearts of the masses I must first win the support of the appropriate faction so that I may gain access to the people."

"They are ruled by despotic war lords who keep them in a perpetual state of ignorance. They are told they must cling to the old ways, which they do willingly because they know no other way.

"The war lords see the bounty being produced by Israel and they want it. But they also know that by themselves they cannot get it. They know they must have the cooperation and support of the masses.

"Even if the tribes were to unite and defeat Israel, what would they do then? They know nothing but conflict. They have not the wherewithal to take advantage of their bounty. When it is gone they will once again revert to fighting among themselves.

"To most, I am seen as a powerful man, and I strive to encourage that perception. But the truth is I only retain the illusion of power so long as I have the war lords on my side. Should I cease my cajoling and go directly to the people, I would be eliminated.

"The reality is I am as a juggler in a carnival. So long as I keep the balls in motion, I am in control. The moment I mishandle one, they all come crashing down and the fragile alliance I have concocted will disintegrate."

CHAPTER 106

Alone in his berth, Ahmahn pondered this most recent unfolding of events. He felt conflicted. He had been reluctant to insert himself into this seemingly useless exercise. His intellect told him that his civilization had reached its zenith, and that decline was inevitable. Even Abdullah, for all his efforts to prevent a confrontation, was in fact unknowingly facilitating escalation. His efforts to keep the Arab tribes un-organized had only encouraged the war lords to become more unpredictable. The thwarted attack by the Chinese would only encourage them to escalate. The military forces controlled by the Western Alliance were his to command only so long as his war lords continued to supply them with petroleum. The Russians would continue to compete with the Chinese and would take advantage of any opportunity they saw. The failed attack in the Netherlands would surely been seen as just such an opportunity.

In his heart he could not honestly believe that his race would allow this to happen. During his life on Earth, and during his visits with space-faring races he had witnessed first hand the inherent goodness of his species. In the face of adversity they had always managed to rise above selfishness and pettiness. They had managed to transform deficits like self-doubt and fear into assets such as confidence and resolve. It was these attributes which persuaded him that he must not, himself, give in to his frustrations.

Evander had warned him this would be a difficult decision to make. Not all parties involved would be willing to participate in such an overt show of hands. It was for this reason that he had relented to return one last time to try and bridge the gap that had separated so many of his race for so long.

Until now he had always played a 'behind the scenes' roll. It had always been difficult for him to hold back in the face of such obvious folly, but over the centuries he had learned that restraint usually yielded better results than more overt methods. People were pragmatists when faced with tough decisions. They tended to band together, to gain strength from one another, to strive for consensus. This was, after all, how communities and even nations were built. Unity, self-sacrifice, patriotism, all were looked upon as virtues, especially in the face of less than desirable alternatives.

He had also learned that politics is the bedfellow of pragmatism, and that both are blood sports. Practically speaking, when one's neck is nearing the noose, one's politics takes on a more personal importance.

Civilization was becoming more uncivilized. World leaders knew it, and no individual or group had been able to do much to prevent it.

More importantly, many had seen the unravelling coming and had turned it to their personal advantage, profiting from it at the expense of the population as a whole.

Many others (the so-called "moral majority") had also seen the change coming, but had been unwilling to do much, if anything, to stop it. That was what he had been afraid of. He had spent his whole life trying to help his world progress. But of late he had become increasingly fearful that, despite his efforts, things were continuing to deteriorate.

It seemed that the world had been turned upside down. Moral standards which had served mankind so well for millennia had now become subject to negotiation. Honorable men and women were increasingly subjected to undo scrutiny and ridicule. Rather than stand up for the right, they had opted to remain silent, hoping to avoid criticism. It seemed that the world as a whole had become timid and complacent, bending to the dictates of a vocal minority for the sake of "getting along."

Politics had become defined as the "art of compromise." Instead of taking the moral high ground and standing firm, politicians had opted to secure their own station and standing, living to fight another day, so to speak, essentially giving in without outwardly seeming to do so. That attitude was inherently flawed because compromise meant taking a step backward.

CHAPTER 107

Egypt had attained hegemony over Africa, India and most of the Mediterranean coastline. Russia had regained power over many of her satellite countries, and was once again a major world player. She and her few allies were locked in a land war with China in the former Pakistani Republic. No matter who won the conflict, Pakistan would soon cease to exit as an independent nation.

Western Europe was in economic meltdown. The union they had formed so long ago had become stagnant. Standardization of currencies had initially stabilized most national economies. But government interventions (such as commodity price controls and regulations) had essentially eliminated incentives for efficiency or product improvement. If a manufacturer developed improvements to existing products, government regulations prevented him from charging more for those improvements. Also, if a manufacturer developed a new product, the government established what was considered a fair price for it. What had ostensibly been an effort to level the playing field for all competitors, ended up stifling competition. Rather than producing quality, the focus changed to producing quantity. Markets became flooded, and when this happened, demand plummeted.

When product sales decreased, so did employment. As unemployment increased, so did the costs of government programs that provided for the needs of the unemployed. Since government was unable to generate revenue on its own, the growing burden was being carried by fewer producers. Eventually the tax burden on the working citizenry became so great that it became easier for them to live off the government than to provide for their own needs. Western Europe was essentially caught in a self-consuming cancer of its own design.

Despots continued to come and go, each leaching as much as he could from the system before being removed from office, only to be replaced by another who possessed an identical agenda hidden behind a different rhetoric.

The "Western" powers (now only North and South America) had become totally Socialized. The citizenry provided a meager economic base for what had essentially become a military police-force-for-hire. From a political standpoint they were "anyone's dog who'd hunt with them."

The Japanese, Thais and all other remaining countries in the region played little part in world politics. Their populations were small, and their resources were in short supply. They were essentially at the mercy of the Chinese.

The Israelis had managed to hold on to their narrow strip of sea coast on the Med. Over the decades their politicians continued to curry favor with the West. But now that the U.S. "Republic" was finally being drained dry, the atmosphere in Jerusalem was grim. It was still politically correct around much of the world to tolerate the Jews. But with the decline of western political influence, many citizens of this garden by the sea feared for the life of their nation.

Ahmahn awoke to the blaring of a klaxon, followed by . . .

"Prepare to surface, prepare to surface," then a loud thump on his door and a muffled voice. "We've arrived sir. Make ready to depart the ship."

CHAPTER 108

The twenty-story hotel wasn't the tallest in the area, but it was the nicest and most elaborate in Alexandria. The building stood at the back of a huge cul-de-sac that extended out into the bay. A narrow tree-lined boulevard connected the cul-de-sac to the mainland.

The hotel was flanked on the left by a casino, and on the right by a marina. Directly in front of the hotel a heliport accommodated up to a dozen helicopters. Oddly, not a car or limo could be seen anywhere.

When the facility was completed two years earlier, the public was invited to come and participate in the grand opening. News media from around the world came to record the event. The boulevard was filled bumper-to-bumper with vehicles carrying the general citizenry, eager to see the magnificent new complex.

Tours were organized. Guides lead groups of people through the beautiful facility. At the marina they could witness VIPs arriving on their private yachts. Across the tarmac, helicopters arrived every few minutes. Kings, shahs, and potentates from around the Med took this occasion to come and be seen by the public.

The inside of the hotel was a magnificent structure in its own right. Twenty-foot tall columns lined the perimeter of the grand lobby. Huge tapestries hung on thick hand-carved granite walls. High above, crystal chandeliers hung from the domed ceiling, giving light to the huge windowless room.

Tourists were herded through the grand entrance and across inlaid marble floors, past the reception center, to a bank of six elevators on the opposite side of the room. Each one was large enough to hold as many as two-dozen people.

Each of the guest rooms was actually a suite of rooms. As few as three and as many as a dozen rooms were each individually and lavishly furnished. Guests marvelled at the luxury and attention to detail exhibited in each one. As was customary in this land of opulence, no expense had been spared.

The elevators only went up to the fifteenth floor. The top five floors were accessed from three elevators located in a concealed room behind the main lobby. One was a service elevator. The other two were for 'special' guests only. They only went up to the nineteenth floor. The top floor could only be accessed by the service elevator.

Only a select few had access to the top floor. In addition to the elevator lifting systems, it also housed the entire cul-de-sac's security and defense systems. This fact, of course was not known by the general public.

After a quick walk-through of a few guest suites, the gawking tourists were ushered back into the elevators where they were whisked back down to the ground floor.

The tour ended in the casino, where guests were allowed to spend a few minutes lounging, gambling or visiting before being shepherded back outside to waiting limos.

For months after its opening, the hotel enjoyed full booking. The media proclaimed it to be the new Riviera of the Mediterranean. Celebrities and the wealthy of the world came to see and be seen.

Now two years later, the limos were gone. The parking lots and marina slips were vacant. Aside from a minimal staff, the hotel itself was empty. The boulevard which provided access had mysteriously 'washed out' several months earlier, and little effort had been made to repair it.

CHAPTER 109

Ahmahn had arrived with the entourage of King Abdullah of Tunisia just after sunrise. Only a select few knew of their arrival. There was a small dock behind the hotel that was used for off-loading freight and other supplies. It wasn't easily seen from the casino or the marina. It was, after all, a service dock. It just wouldn't do for anyone to see the mundane day-to-day operations of the facility. Even if someone were able to observe, they wouldn't see what lay eighty feet beneath the dock.

The land on which the buildings stood was actually a man-made island. Before the island was created, a deep under-water trench had been dug and lined with concrete. The superstructure of the hotel was then built right over the top of it. The trench was wide and deep enough to accommodate two small tactical submarines. The subs could 'surface' enough to expose their conning towers inside the expanse under the hotel.

Ahmahn was the first to exit the sub. Seeing that all was clear, he stepped aside and held the door as a majestic-looking man stepped out. Then, one step behind, he followed the man up the short ramp to the dock. Cuffed to his right wrist, he carried a thin attache' case. Inside were passports, letters of introduction, a small hand-held radio, and a nine-millimeter semi-automatic pistol.

"Welcome, your Highness." The concierge bowed as he spoke. The king nodded in acknowledgement. "Your excellency, your suite has been made ready; if you will please follow me. Accommodations for your staff are still being inspected and will be ready quite soon. My assistant will take them to their rooms when they are ready." He bowed again, as did the young and obviously nervous young man at his side.

"Thank you." The king nodded toward Ahmahn. "My secretary will accompany me." He gestured for the concierge to lead the way.

"Your Highness, you are among the first to arrive. Her majesty, the Duchess of York asks that you be informed her husband, the Duke will not be in attendance. He has been delayed in Huanong and informs us that his wife the Duchess will speak in his behalf. President Grismon of the American Alliance arrived only hours ago and sends his regards. He requests that you receive him as soon as you are settled in your rooms."

"Please inform the president that I am quite fatigued after my long voyage and wish to rest. I look forward to meeting with him in the morning when the conference begins."

"Very well, sir . . . er . . . your Highness, the man said nervously. "Will you please follow me?" The three men moved off toward the elevator, leaving the remaining entourage behind with the assistant.

The king's suite was on the nineteenth floor, indicative of his standing among the delegates who were to attend the conference. Two guards standing at the entrance saluted and opened the doors at his approach.

"Please inform the Director we have our own security. They will arrive in moments to replace your men." Ahmahn spoke sternly, freezing the hapless man with an icy stare.

"But mister secretary, our security is . . ."

"Thank you. That will be all for now." The king interjected condescendingly. Nodding for Ahmahn to lead the way, he turned his back to the man.

"As you wish, your Highness. I will send a maid to prepare your bed immediately."

606

"That will not be necessary," Ahmahn said dryly as he closed the two heavy doors.

The concierge remained motionless for another moment, standing alone there in the hall, facing the door which had just been closed in his face. His jaw muscles tensed. His hands clenched into fists at his sides. Anger at being reproached vied with fear of what his employer would do when he found out his orders had been over-ridden.

Ahmahn slid the locking bolts into place, pausing for only a moment to gather his thoughts. He felt badly that he had treated the servant with such rudeness. His actions with the concierge were typical of the duties he was expected to perform as the kings "man." He had spent much of the last year insinuating himself into the good graces of this, the most powerful remaining monarch on the planet. To step out of character at any time would almost certainly bring disaster.

Ahmahn was by nature a gentle person. Over his many years he had learned that a soothing word went much further toward maintaining good relations than did harshness. His natural inclination when confronting the concierge was to speak kindly, but persuasively. But he knew he must not let his guard down. He must remain in character continually so that the king's suspicions would be allayed. Though Abdullah pretended not to notice, Ahmahn knew his every move was being watched. His strong words with the hapless servant had been for the king to see.

As for the king himself; It was imperative, at this late date, that he be guided slowly and carefully. He was, by general agreement, one of the most influential people on the planet. Ahmahn must be careful how he influenced the chain of events that was about to unfold.

Abdullah watched with thinly veiled amusement as his "man" closed the door in the servants face. He liked to watch power being wielded, especially when it was he who was doing the wielding. But he also enjoyed watching others wield it in his behalf. He and they both knew that he could take away that power at any moment. It gave him a feeling of perverse pleasure to watch as people came to the stark realization that they were powerless in his presence.

Still, there was something not quite right about this man Ahmahn. He couldn't put his finger on it. It was only a minor concern really. In the year that he had been at his side, he had never given the king reason to doubt him. His words and actions had always been consistent. Even when Amon left to go to the Johannesburg ruins, he had requested a contingent of Abdullah's elite guard accompany him, not so much for his own security, but rather to assure the King that he was loyal and could be trusted.

What was it then that made Abdullah feel so uneasy? His mind pondered these things as he watched Ahmahn dismiss the concierge.

CHAPTER 110

"Your Highness, I am still very much concerned that the American delegate may have been compromised. His request for an audience only lends weight to my suspicions." Ahmahn spoke to the door, then turned to face the dark-skinned Arab, now seated comfortably on one of several devans spaced in a rough circle in the center of the room.

He walked toward the circle slowly, head slightly lowered, browns furrowed in thought. He paused at the perimeter of the circle, and stood unmoving for many moments.

The king scrutinized every movement he made.

"Come! Sit, my friend! You can relax now. No one will see you if you let your hair down for a moment." Ahmahn looked to be nervous for some reason. Still he just stood there, his eyes seemingly glazed over, his focus so intense. He didn't seem to have heard what was said.

The king felt strangely uneasy, noticing Ahmahn's lack of response. He had always appeared to be intently tuned in to what was going on around him. It wasn't like him to show hesitation over anything, for any reason.

"Very well then. Suit yourself." The king grunted as he leaned forward in his chair. Gripping the arm of the divan for support, he stood slowly and carefully. The rush of relief his legs had felt when he first sat down, now trickled back in as he strained to lift the great bulk of his body. He turned and gripped the divan arm with both hands, carefully kicking off the shoes he was wearing.

"Your majesty! Please. I can get a servant here to help you undress." Ahmahn broke from his concentration and took a step toward the king.

"Nonsense! Please. Allow me to indulge myself. It is so seldom I'm actually alone. There is always someone within earshot, if not actually visible around me twenty-four hours a day. I can't even relieve myself without someone hearing the water splash."

He chuckled to himself, shuffling slowly toward the bed in the adjoining room. When he turned to continue speaking, there was Ahmahn, standing only an arms length away. Startled, he barked.

"God . . .!," then sucked in his breath reflexively. Composing himself, he let it out slowly. "Allah be praised that you are so stealthy." He smiled at the tall figure, then continued walking toward the bed.

Sighing as he sat down on the edge of the bed, Abdullah pulled the heavy cloak from around his shoulders. He loosened the sash around his waist and let it slip quietly to the floor. Then he reached up to begin untying his turban.

"May I assist you, my king?" Ahmahn said, but did not move closer. He knew what the response would be.

"No, no. I've been doing this since I was a child." His finger fumbled for and found the end of the finely woven black silk. Pulling it out of its fold, he slowly unwound the material.

His long gray hair fell nearly to his waist. He was past his prime by many decades. Noticing Ahmahn's stare, Abdullah said: "Ah, so you see from my hair! I am Sikh, not Muslim. I wear my Turban as a Muslim would, but only for show. After all, my people are mostly Muslim. It just wouldn't do to let them see that I am not of their faith."

"It is not for me to judge, my King."

"Ah well," said Abdullah. "The turban is for the Muslims to see.

The hair is for the Sikhs. As for me, neither is of any consequence. I bear allegiance to no particular god. Besides, I like my hair long."

Ahmahn watched in respectful silence. When Abdullah let down his façade, the strain of leadership was easy to see in his demeanor. The furrowed brow, the crows feet at the corners of his eyes, the drooping eyelids. There was a deep-seated fatigue there behind those eyes. He could sense it. He had seen the signs so many times before.

Maybe that was why he had chosen this man instead of one of the two other members of the Triumvirate. The others were both men of stature. Each had risen to power much as had king Abdullah. Each had commanded respect around the world.

But when Ahmahn had gotten close to each of them in turn, he had sensed something wrong, virulent. Each wore the same facade as Abdullah . . . an air of detached indifference so typical among those of the ruling class. But upon closer inspection, he saw them for who they really were. These men were . . . amoral. They seemed to take perverse pleasure in forcing their will on others.

King Abdullah was different, but only in subtle ways. He lusted for power, just as did the other two. And his public demeanor was almost identical to the others, detached, aloof. But upon closer inspection, Ahmahn saw in him an air of quiet confidence which was lacking in the other two. Privately his humor was frequently self-deprecating, never at the expense of someone else. He seemed to see himself in others, and was not above placing himself at their level, at least philosophically, if not physically.

When dealing with others he was attentive and focused, never condescending or arrogant. He was assertive without being harsh. He was persuasive without being pushy. On rare occasions when someone found the courage to be critical of him, he strove to remain calm and objective, endeavoring to see himself from their perspective. Though he was not a religious man, he strove to be moral and ethical in his dealings.

He had recognized these traits early in their relationship. He had watched carefully for these many months and was confident that Abdullah was a man who could be trusted and respected.

Ahmahn stepped closer and knelt before him. He removed the king's socks and began massaging his feet.

"Bless you, my trusted friend," Abdullah sighed as the tension in his feet and calves melted away. "Now. As for this issue you bring up . . . what you say may be true, but we cannot yet be sure. The 'west' has lost so much status of late. It may well be that this new leader (Grismon is his name?) has been instructed to gain as much support as he can before the council convenes. If I were him, that's what I would do."

Ahmahn nodded in agreement as he finished the massage, then washed and dried the kings feet before responding.

"Grismon is an opportunist. He is here only as window dressing. He doesn't have the delegates to have any serious influence. I think he knows this and is doing all he can to swing things in his favor."

"How can you say that?" The king was surprised at Ahmahn's response. "He represents the most powerful army in existence. He knows that no major world policy can be implemented without the support of the military."

"That is true, but only on the face of it. It is commonly known among those who matter that he will align himself with whichever group is most likely to succeed politically. That way he can use his military to 'win friends and influence people.'"

"An interesting turn of phrase, young man. Interesting that you would use it in this context. And I trust you are not suggesting that what I say is of no consequence."

He sensed a slight uneasiness in the king's response, suggesting that the question he posed was more probing than might at first be suspected. He believed he knew the king well enough that he could possibly ignore the comment, thus dismissing it as nothing more than a subtle challenge. To do so would strengthen the king's resolve that he had made a good choice taking this man into his confidence, while knowing very little, if anything firm, about his background.

"My king, the plan you described seems well thought out. The Americans are truly as you describe them. They will sell their wares to the highest bidder."

CHAPTER 111

"Your Highness, may I please remind you of your appointment this afternoon with the Ministry Production Council? We are within the two-hour window which you proscribed for us."

Ahmadih, personal aide to Crown Prince Mujah of Syria was a very meticulous and punctual man. His responsibilities included scheduling all appointments for the prince and/or any member of his immediate family.

It seemed that everyone had a problem that they believed only the prince could handle. Every morning there would be a que of people waiting outside his office. Ahmadih managed to sort through the crowd quite efficiently without ruffling too many feathers. It was for this reason that he found such favor with the prince. He was able to maintain good relations with the prince's subjects without causing much disruption of his finely tuned schedule. His loyalty to the prince and the royal family in general was without blemish.

He was still young for this kind of work. At twenty-eight, he had spent all of his adult life in service to the royal family. His father, who had died in service to the king only two weeks earlier, had been the example he had grow up with. He admired and strived to emulate him completely.

Ahmadih's father had led him and the rest of his family through some very hard times during the days before the 'Alliance.' Whenever anyone in the family had voiced complaint, he had always been quick to remind them that staying close to the royal family would always be the most secure route for them to follow. It had been that way for Ahmadih's grandfather, and great grandfather before him, so why should he believe anything should change?

Everyone in his immediate family was in service to the royals in one way or another, and loyalty ran high. Three generations of the Syrian aristocracy had received their education in Great Britain, and consequently many aspects of Social Democracy had become adopted by the Benevolent Dictatorship in the country. By and large, the citizenry was content.

The Syrian royals were descendants of nomadic chiefdoms, where everyone depended on having shrewd leadership and a strong army in order for a community to survive. For many generations these individual clans had struggled one with another. Many lives were lost and vendettas sworn before the majority of the tribes gave up on killing and opted for a cease-fire.

Ahmadih knew his county's history well and had no interest in returning to those bad old days. However, when Abdullah came to power and began consolidating the countries of the middle east, pressure began to bear on the Syrians to join. The Syrian king had expressed his displeasure with the proposed alliance on many occasions. Consequently political pressure from Syria's neighbors began to mount.

As the scheduled meeting of the Triumvirate drew nearer, rumors began to circulate that the king of Syria would abdicate rather than submit to the dictates of the Middle-Eastern Alliance.

Within only a few hours of that announcement, a raid was staged against his private residence. Ahmadih's father and the king were in the process of composing his letter of abdication when the raid began. In the confusion, an unidentified suicide bomber, disguised as a servant, slipped into the room and detonated. Immediately after the explosion the raiding party withdrew and disappeared. No one had recognized who they were or where they came from.

A state funeral was held five days later. The following day Prince Mujah announced that Syria would be joining the Alliance.

CHAPTER 112

The first day of the conference went pretty much as Ahmahn expected. Each group of the Triumvirate branches consisted of a president (or premier, in China's case) and three staff members, all of whom sat at a three-cornered table at the head of the room.

President Grismon was the sole representative for the Western Alliance. He brought only one guest: Arthur Walenberg; U.S. Military Attache. Both men were given a place in the audience along with representatives from each country within the Triumvirate.

"Why are these two here?" Ahmahn wondered to himself. "Did the Hague conference not go well for the West? Or are they here just shopping for a better deal? Ah, well. We will find out more when 'the four' meet tonight."

The opening ceremonies had been brief, with little fanfare. Brief mention was made of the 'tragic' death of the King of Syria. All expressed their regrets and condolences to the family and to Prince Mujah, who was seated in the place reserved for his father.

A few select members of the press were allowed to take pictures of the dignitaries, and conduct brief interviews a few minutes before the conference got under way. After the interviews were finished, all present then stood as President Georgy Abramov of the Russia delegation read the Declaration of Resolve which had been adopted at the previous meeting a year earlier:

We, the members of the Middle-Eastern Alliance do hereby

affirm our unity with and fealty to, The Triumvirate, that we may, through unwavering diligence, attain that for which we strive: Universal Equality among all men and all nations.

The meeting agenda was then read by Mr. Ju Jinping, Chairman of the People's Congress of the Peoples Republic of China.

Each item on the agenda was discussed at length. Dissenters were given time to state their cases. Minor changes were included or excluded, and then the participants signified approval by show of hands.

Prince Mujah then asked for the floor.

"Fellow delegates. As you know, I am not accustomed to participating in such proceedings. It was always my father who did such things. Nevertheless, now that he is gone, I must do my duty, to honor his memory, and to fulfill my obligation to my country.

"As you all know, my father had numerous issues with the Middle-Eastern Alliance which were never fully resolved. That being said, it is my belief that progress was being made, and eventually a compromise would have been reached were it not for his untimely death.

"My country has stood alone these many years, striving to maintain sovereignty in the face of concerted opposition."

"It was my father's belief that a united Syria is a strong Syria. He was right. And, if it is true for my country, it must also be true for this new Alliance. Soon I will be honored to take my father's place as supreme ruler of my country. It is my intention to continue his good work, and to take it to its logical conclusion. Syria is proud and honored to be counted among the sovereign states which form this Alliance."

It sounded to Ahmahn that the Prince was speaking out of both sides of his mouth, trying at once to sound statesman-like for his people, while at the same time trying to placate the members of the Triumvirate.

Ahmahn watched closely when the Prince concluded his speech.

Every member of the Triumvirate stood in applause. He could detect no adverse reaction from any of the delegates.

Prince Mujah had been careful not to mention the circumstances of his father's death. That fact, coupled with a lack of response from the other delegates was a source of consternation.

Syria had been leaning ever closer toward democracy, and was realistically the only remaining friend of Israel in the region, if not the entire world. The death of this sympathetic monarch did not bode well.

Who could have been behind this assassination? And what motive would they have? Perhaps it was a dissident within the Syrian monarchy. Maybe one of Abdullah's operatives. The Chinese? The Russians? Every one he thought of could have had some motivation. Perhaps the Prince himself. After all, his speech before the assembly did not rule out such a possibility. After all, it wouldn't be the first time a ruler had been 'removed' from power by one of his offspring.

CHAPTER 113

The tomb of Tutankhamun had been abandoned now for at least a decade. After the destruction of the Aswan Dam, the Nile had flooded well past Luxor. Almost all of the ancient relics had been destroyed or looted, including all of those in the valley of the kings.

The tomb still smelled musty, though it had been dry for a very long time. The ancient wall murals were all but completely gone, crumbling into piles on the floor.

A transceiver sat on the floor, glowing a light blue. Above it, Evander's hologram hovered silently, listening to the conversation.

The four 'brothers' stood in a circle around the device, their bodies casting eerie shadows on the crumbling walls.

"Grismon represents a military force larger by far than anything anyone else could possibly muster." said Haden. "But that's all. He's a 'representative,' a figurehead. He has no real, personal power. He can't tell his armies what to do. He can only tell them who they're going to be working for.

"He knows his military can't move without fuel. His country's resources petered out decades ago, back when the United States was still trying to become 'energy independent.' But when that became too cost prohibitive, the population rebelled and Grismon and his crew were forced to go back and make nice with the middle east again. Earlier, when the U. S. quit buying oil from them, it hurt a lot of people in high places. And they haven't forgotten."

"Yes. I recall." said Ahmahn. "Tell us more of what transpired at the Hague."

"Unfortunately there's not much to tell. A lot of the people with those long memories were there at the conference. The Brits, the Danes, the Germans, no one was in a mood to discuss arms deals, and Grismon was hiding in his room claiming he was not feeling well. I'm convinced he was just plain paranoid. He was afraid to show his face. Since no one knew who set up the attack, no one trusted anyone. Grismon was high on everyone's list as the probable culprit.

"Walenberg returned from the last meeting totally frustrated; told me he and his boss were heading to Alexandria to try and cut some sort of deal, and Grismon wasn't going to be too picky."

"Ahmahn tells me it was the Chinese," said Nahm.

"Yes. It was their plan to 'eliminate' everyone, but Abdullah caught wind of the scheme and turned it to his advantage." Ahmahn turned toward the hologram.

"Evander, is there anything you can add to the conversation?"

"As a matter of fact, yes. One of our high-altitude units recorded a small contingent of American 'special forces' northwest of Damascus the day before the assassination of the Syrian king. Reports indicate that the Prince had a 'rendezvous' with a lady friend close by."

"Hmmm," Broc said. "The Americans to the north, the Chinese to the south and the Syrian leadership right in the middle. Seems like this Prince fellow was pretty busy."

"It does seem that he has his own agenda, doesn't it?" said Ahmahn. "But would he be prepared to have his own father killed?"

Evander offered another perspective.

"It seems to me that there were two stabilizing forces within this triangle; the Syrian king, and Abdullah. Traditionally it has been the Arabs who have fomented unrest. But ironically it has been two Arabs who have endeavoured to keep the peace.

"Here's a possibility worth consideration. Prince Mujah sees his country becoming more and more isolated. He believes that at some point either he or his father will have to confront their opposition. Their only 'ally,' Israel, is already isolated and being threatened with annihilation. He doesn't want that to happen to him, so if he's more of a pragmatist than a patriot, he'll see the advantage in siding with the majority, moral/ethical stance be damned."

"Precisely!" said Haden. "What better way to demonstrate his loyalty to the Triumvirate than to undermine the Western Alliance."

Broc stepped frward a single step. "There are just so many possibilities to consider. Diplomacy; politics; echonomics . . . even theology could have an influence on decisions. There may even be other factors involved of which we are completely unaware."

Evander was the last to speak.

"It's clear we are all stating the obvious. We just don't know how events will unfold. Our archival studies consistently record that most cultures have been unable to advance beyond the situation that Earth now faces. Perhaps it would be best for us to return to our posts and continue monitoring. It is possible that we may discover something previously overlooked. Let us pray that this is so.

CHAPTER 114

By the fifth and final day of the conference the delegates had worked themselves up considerably.

Behind the scenes the Russians and Chinese had still not settled their differences. The battle for Afghanistan still continued. Neither side really cared much about the so-called 'insurgents.' They were more interested in intimidating the other than they were in defeating the Afghans.

Publicly they focused their rhetoric on uniting to defeat the 'forces of imperialism,' blaming 'the west' for all the world's perceived ills.

The Arabs were becoming more difficult for Abdullah to control. Though none of the Arab states was really disappointed that the Syrian king had been assassinated, many were using the incident to bolster their claim that Abdullah had not been persuasive enough to bring the Syrians 'into the fold,' and had therefore elected to 'eliminate' the obstacle.

From the sidelines Ahmadih watched all these days as his Prince began gradually to reveal himself to his father's enemies. For days Mujah walked among them, currying their favor. At night he met with them, out of sight and out of earshot, always returning a bit more detached, a bit more condescending.

"How dare he prostrate himself before these vermin?!" Ahmadih thought to himself. "My king is not yet cold in his grave and already his son sullies his name! I have sworn loyalty to a coward who lacks the conviction to stand for his beliefs."

The conflict grew within him as moment by moment he saw his beliefs, his very moral fabric being demeaned, shredded by the man he had sworn fealty to. It grated him to hold his tongue, to continue serving someone he no longer respected.

Still the conflict raged. Gone was the young prince he had respected in his childhood. Gone was the man he had learned to love . . . replaced by a vile, self-serving ingrate with no self-respect; who was only interested in his own gratification.

Gone also was Ahmadih's father, whom he had loved and respected and admired, who had devoted his life to serving a just master, only to be cut down by that master's reprobate off-spring.

"Where is his loyalty? Where is the honor which he owes to his father and to his people? And now he becomes so brazen as to curry favor with Abdullah, that serpent who weaves this evil within the people of my world. This cannot stand!"

CHAPTER 115

Toward the end of the last day of the conference, King Abdullah stepped onto the podium and faced the audience.

He and Ahmahn had discussed at length the moves which must be made to stabilize the assemblage, to back them carefully away from the precipice. Too many had openly advocated a show of force against the west, particularly since Grismon had still not been willing to reveal with whom he would align.

Still others had said now was the time to strike against Israel, since it was obvious they now stood completely alone. They were convinced the Europeans were impotent without Grismon's backing, and would offer no resistance.

Now, with Syria entering the fold, the aggressive ones would be more emboldened.

The time was now ripe, thought Abdullah, to take this young Prince Mujah in hand, to force him to publically take a stand in favor of non-aggression. Though the prince had begun to develop alliances, particularly with the Chinese, he was still un-tested in the political realm. The fact that the Hague attack had not brought the desired results had called his credibility into question. And because of that perceived weakness, he was vulnerable to political pressure, something Abdullah was adept at applying.

Ahmahn, sitting to the rear of Abdullah's seat, was reviewing the notes he would speak from shortly after the king finished his public manipulation of the prince. He watched intently as Abdullah called Mujah to come forward to stand at his side.

Ahmahn noticed a stirring off to the right of the podium where the servants were seated. A young man, (wasn't it Mujah's aide?) had risen from his chair, moved to the end of the row and was standing with arms folded, close to the curtain which hid the servants from the rest of the audience.

As the young prince approached the podium, the servant took a few short steps forward. He could see the tension in his body as he shifted his weight from one foot to the other. Ahmahn unlatched his briefcase and carefully slid his hand inside.

Prince Mujah had no sooner arrived at Abdullah's side when the servant lunged forward, yelling "Traitor! Murderer!" as he pulled a handgun from under his jacket and began firing erratically.

Ahmahn was prepared. He stood abruptly, nine-millimeter in hand. Quickly he took aim for center mass and squeezed the trigger twice. The servant dropped like a wet rag. None of the servant's shots had found their mark.

The room erupted in pandemonium. Everyone hit the floor as security personnel swarmed toward the podium. The prince was crouched behind the king's robes, quaking with fear. Abdullah had not moved, only turning his head when he saw the assailant's approach.

Ahmahn dropped his gun and raised his hands. Seeing that he was unarmed, security surrounded him and the two others and rushed them off the stage.

After a few minutes calm was restored. The servant's lifeless body was carried away and everyone resumed their seats. The two dignitaries again approached the podium. Mujah was simply too shaken to stand, so he was escorted back to his seat.

Ahmahn and Abdullah conferred briefly before the king addressed the audience.

"In light of what has just happened, I have decided not to speak at this moment, but will have my assistant speak in my stead. Listen carefully to his words as though they were mine.

Ahmahn approached the podium, but left his notes sitting on the chair. Abdullah knew what was about to happen.

He stood motionless and silent before the microphone. He looked intently across the room, at the dignitaries, at the audience, even at the servants. Then, after several more long moments he began.

"I will not speak about the proceedings of this conference. That rhetoric and repetition has been endured long enough. I will not speak about lofty ideals or vain accusations. They serve no purpose other than to stir emotion rather than stimulate intelligent discourse.

"Instead, I will speak truth unvarnished and direct. You *will not* like what you hear. It will make you uneasy. It will make you angry. But, if you are wise, it *will* make you think.

"In this room I sense no humility. Instead, I sense arrogance, vanity, self-aggrandisement."

The crowd stirred but he continued.

"The fact that you still consider yourselves to be somehow, morally superior, in spite of everything which has come to pass right here, before your very eyes, leaves me gasping in disbelief. How can you be so self-engrossed as not to recognize the presence of malevolence all around you? Are you blindingly naive, or are you all willing participants? I think the latter . . ."

The room seemed to decompress as everyone gasped in astonishment at his statement. Everyone began at once, shouting indignantly and gesticulating madly. Premier Lin spoke first, though his remarks were barely heard above the din.

"How dare this, this 'assistant' be so brash as to interfere in these proceedings?!" His normally composed expression was fracturing under the tension.

"I demand that this person be removed from these proceedings immediately! His credentials identify him as only a special assistant to King Abdulah. As such, he has no standing to address this . . ."

Abdullah rose slowly from his seat to the right of the podium. Seemingly taking no notice of the eyes that were now all locked on him, he took great care to insure all his robes were in proper order. With one hand he straightened a small wrinkle in the opposite sleeve, taking care to brush it smooth. Adjusting his sleeves to cover his wrists, he clasped his hands and turned toward the podium.

The commotion in the room began to subside immediately as the king walked forward. Premier Lin stopped in mid-sentence, his jaw frozen in place just as was the rest of his body.

Total silence fell upon the room when the king stopped a few steps short of the podium, then bowed ever so slightly toward Ahmahn, who was still standing at the microphone. Breathing seemed to stop. The King of Tunisia! The most powerful man in the world . . . bowing to this man?

All eyes saw the king's gesture. Who was this man, this "assistant," who drew such respect from such a powerful man? All were stricken to see Ahmahn acknowledge the king only with a slight nod of the head.

The silence was complete. No one knew what to say. What could they do? Compared to King Abdullah, no man was his equal in stature among the citizens of the world. The king moved to the microphone.

"My fellow delegates." He paused and smiled at Ahmahn before continuing.

"My friends . . . my enemies." He looked around the room. Some eyes smiled back at him. Many averted.

"Oh, my!" he laughed. "Does it surprise you that I speak so boldly? It shouldn't, you know. I have done so in the past, as many of you will recall. This time I speak boldly again . . . maybe for the last time."

What could he mean . . . 'last time'?

Once again bowing ever so slightly toward the onlookers, he continued.

"Let us be candid with each other, if only for a few moments." He looked around the room slowly, seeming to make eye contact with everyone at once.

"We have known each other for a very long time, some of us. Others, not so long." He glanced at Prince Mujah, sitting there in his father's chair, clammy hands groping each other nervously.

"Yes!" he thought to himself. "My suspicions about him are true. Soon all these delegates will understand why I have responded to him the way that I have. 'Keep your friends close, and your enemies closer.' Such words have served me well in the past. They will, very soon, do so again. Soon the world will know what many have suspected for lo these many years, that the Prince conspires with whomever he can to bring his evil plans to fruition. But for now I will hold him close, building his confidence, letting him believe that I'm unaware of his plans to overthrow me, just as he did his father."

Focusing once again on the issue at hand, he continued:

"Within this room reside all the major powers of the planet. I am not embarrassed to acknowledge that I am considered by most to be first among equals. Please, take no offense to what I say. I do not say this to arouse anger or suspicion. The time for such pettiness is past. I remind you of my stature here among you only for one reason. Perhaps when you consider what I say in light of what you have come to know about me, you will weigh my words more carefully.

"A few of you I have known for many years. Some of you, all my life. I do not give my trust easily. Those who know me well know this to be true. Whether you have been an ally, or an adversary, you all know me to be a just man. Though many of you will not willingly admit it, I am deserving of your respect."

There was a stirring in the room as people shifted their positions, clearing their throats, whispering secretively.

"And I give as good as I get." Abdullah gripped the sides of the podium with both hands, leaning forward for emphasis.

"Many in this room have earned my respect. Some have yet to do so. I do not give it lightly. Nor do I offer condemnation of those with whom I disagree."

"What I say here and now before this assembly is vital for your understanding of my position, and by extension, the positions of the other members of the Triumvirate."

He motioned toward Premier Lin and President Abramov. Both men sat stoically, unmoving.

Abdullah suspected that, given an opportunity, the Chinese and the Russians would combine forces and move against him in support of aggression toward their foes. Their alliance, even between themselves, had been tenuous at best, but after defeating the 'Arab Alliance,' they would most certainly turn on each other.

At some point, when the looser felt desperate enough, restraints would be discarded, hell would be unleashed, and . . . no one would be the winner.

Abdullah looked directly at the man sitting across from him. Mujah felt his piercing stare. In their private conversations, Abdullah had been reticent regarding what should be done about Israel, and by extension, the western powers. The prince knew now that, no matter what had been said previously, Abdullah had taken a firm position regarding Israel and the Western Alliance, and was now going to make it public.

King Abdullah continued:

"This man," he gestured toward Ahmahn. "has earned my respect, and my complete trust. Never before in all my dealings with the most powerful people around the world have I heard such direct and blatantly honest commentary."

Premier Lin could be seen whispering to his assistant, who

quickly rose from his seat and hurried out of the room. Ever so discretely Lin and Mujah exchanged glances.

Abdullah saw the exchange, but continued.

"Does it make you uncomfortable that I say these things? Well it should. For how many generations have we bickered and negotiated, and sometimes fought and died, and all for what? Power? Prestige? Wealth? And what have we gained in the process but more bickering and negotiating, and death? And as we do so, the people of our world struggle for survival, while we, the 'elite' sit in our high places congratulating ourselves for our 'accomplishments.'

Abdullah looked directly at Premier Lin, who stared coldly back at him.

"This 'assistant' as you call him, possesses more knowledge and insight regarding our present dilemma than do any of us here." He could hear gasps here and there as he paused. Premier Lyn broke eye contact long enough to whisper something to a nearby aide, then stared back coldly.

Abdullah knew that what he was about to say would forever alter his position and standing, in this group, and throughout the world. By voluntarily taking a subordinate position to Ahmahn, he was risking everything, most particularly his power. All he could do was trust that his reputation and influence would carry the day. He stood there for several more seconds, forcing back that fleeting moment of doubt. He cleared his throat, waiting for the murmur in the room to cease.

"This man has gained my confidence in such a way that I find it difficult to explain. And even if I could explain, you would not believe me.

"His insights, even his very presence causes one to know the truth which he brings forth in any setting, in any context. He possesses the wisdom of one of 'ancient days.'

"In the past I foolishly thought of myself as wise beyond my years. Yes, I had been raised in privilege. But I chose to spend most of my formative years among the masses . . . out in the barren deserts, or on the sweltering shorelines of rivers and seas.

"I saw first hand the disparity between the struggling, and the privileged. I vowed then, and I reaffirm now, that my people and I are one. We each share the one most precious commodity. Life! And so do all of you.

"And so I ask you now, to search within yourselves. Can you find even the smallest recess wherein honesty resides? If you can find such a place, then I beseech you to listen to the words of this man and let them fill that void. I have done so, and I have learned. Listen then, and learn for yourselves."

The king stepped aside so the 'man of ancient days' could continue.

Ahmahn stepped forward again and stood still, hands folded on the lectern. The air in the room felt heavy, even oppressive as the 'ancient of days' looked around the room gathering his thoughts. The words he was about to deliver must penetrate all within the room, ripping through their façades, drilling into their consciences, stripping each of them bare before the truth they could not deny.

"Are you so comfortable,here in your insulated, sterile protective shells that you cannot, or will not, see how your world is decaying, falling apart even as we speak? Why is it that instead of seeking genuine cures for the ills of your world, you spend your time maneuvering for your own personal gain? What possible more advantage could you ask for than that which you now possess? You hold the fate of your world in you hands, and here you sit, filled with contempt for any and everyone who chooses to disagree with you. Your arrogance is outweighed only by your naivete. Know you not that you are no greater or better than any other here at this confluence?

"Yes. A confluence. This time and this place are the loci for a confluence of powers, of peoples, of ideologies. Though many there are who would argue against it, this is the time of reckoning which all previous generations have regarded with dread and awe.

These are truly the last days. Not years, months, or even weeks. What will be decided here, this day, will forever set the course this planet will follow.

"Know you not that there are worlds beyond number, all of whom strive for recognition among the vast reaches of the universe? All of them have struggled with the same issues you now face. You are not unique in this regard. Nor are your feeble rationalizations which you call solutions. If you are to survive as a race . . . a human race, you must accept one another . . . or do away with civilization.

"How others have dealt with these issues has determined whether or not their race has survived long enough and grown mature enough to warrant the recognition they so fervently desire.

"Many there are in the universe who strive for recognition. Few there are who possess the strength of character necessary to achieve it.

"Know this then. When you endeavour to serve those beneath you, you perform service unto yourselves and to the world. When you choose to subjugate, to dominate, the burden of that choice is yours alone to bear. Your actions reveal your true character, and you *will* be held accountable. When you speak disparagingly of others, your words are as barbs which turn back on you. And when all your words have become fading echoes; when all your vanity has turned to despair, still you must decide. Choose the right. Or perish. Above all else remember this. Stasis will not abide."

The room was silent. Ahmahn turned away from the podium. A shot rang out. The crowd gasped. Abdullah lay crumpled on the floor.

OMEGA

CHAPTER 116

Ahmahn awoke to the sound of a baby crying. The infant mewed quietly for a few minutes and then fell silent. He wondered how the the poor little thing was doing.

The infant and her parents had arrived two days ago. Apparently the last of the survivors, they had escaped the latest of a series of assaults on what was left of Cairo. They had managed to remain undetected as they made their way out of the city.

The city itself was little more than a pile of rubble. Desperate people had gone on a rampage, taking everything of value and setting fire to what was left.

Since the EMP wars a year earlier, social order had collapsed globally. The 'pulses' had literally destroyed everything electronic. Even the planes that dropped the bombs crashed when their shielding failed. No one had anticipated what the effects of multiple EMP blasts would do. Supposedly hardened against radiation, even the most sophisticated weapon systems in the world were rendered useless as the bombs set off a world-wide chain reaction.

Ironically, it was the ozone layer high above, that facilitated the earth's electronic doom. For centuries activists had insisted that the layer was being depleted. They cited as evidence, the so-called 'hole' above the south pole. Fear mongers as they were, they insisted that the hole was growing, and that when it was gone, the earth would be cooked in the sun's radiation. The hole continued to grow and shrink over the decades. When it shrank, the activists were quiet. When it grew, so did their noise and feigned concern.

Just as the layer acted to filter most of the sun's harmful radiation from reaching the earth, so its under surface became an invisible barrier, reflecting the EMP waves back toward the surface.

Within minutes everything electronic was rendered useless. Planes fell from the sky. Motored vehicles simply rolled to a stop, never to start again.

The EMP's affected everything electronic, from home appliances and computers to international banking systems. Data bases were corrupted to the point that they were useless. Chaos ensued. Governments failed. Law enforcement was overwhelmed. People, desperate for food but unable to purchase it, stole it. Violence in all forms prevailed. Entire social systems completely fell apart. Civilization had effectively crumbled. Practically over night, twenty-third century society had degenerated to almost prehistoric conditions.

The young father awoke to his daughter's crying. His young wife still slept fitfully, holding the baby close in her emaciated embrace.

When he saw Ahmahn watching, he crawled the short distance along the sloped wall of the culvert, being careful not to awaken any of the other refugees.

"How's she doing this morning?" He asked when the father had settled beside him.

"Okay, I guess. Sarah's milk has almost dried up. When that's gone . . ."

"I'm sorry." was all Ahmahn could think to say.

"Look. I know none of this is your fault. You did what you could." The father wiped his nose on his tattered sleeve. "Sarah says not to worry. It's all in God's hands now. But it's killing me that I can't find food for her. I see her slipping further every day. She's giving all she has for our baby girl.

"She's almost two months now. Nice fat cheeks, chummy little arms, fat belly." The young father cast his gaze about abjectly. Ahmahn could tell he was trying not to cry.

"Listen. Ahmahn. I know you don't want to do it, but when the time comes . . ."

"Ed, my brother. I'm only going to be here for a short time. Probably not as long as. . . . Look. It's just not right that I should take her with me."

Ed placed a hand on Ahmahn's arm, looking pleadingly into his eyes.

"Please understand. It kills me to even think about loosing either of them. I'm even tempted to take her young life myself if it will mean Sarah stays with me for a little while longer. That's why I haven't given her a name. I don't dare get too close. But Sarah! She's the only woman I've ever loved. And she's giving her life for our child . . . one suckle at a time." He broke down into quiet sops.

Ahmahn remembered so, so long ago. He remembered his parents, snuggled close to him in their nest; looking into his mother's eyes as he nursed, seeing the concern and love, feeling the warmth of her caress.

He remembered Nera; putting his hand on her swollen belly; feeling their child moving inside her. He remembered the joy. Even now, so many centuriesw later, the memory made his heart ache.

He remembered Mahrom. The gentleness of her caress. Her penetrating, gentle smile. The earthquake. *No.* He would *not* remember that.

"Ed, don't you see I. . . . Listen. Let me think about it. I just. . . . Please. Let me think about it, just for a while." Ed smiled weakly up at him, then turned his face away, toward the place where his wife and child lay.

Ahmahn patted him on the shoulder and then crawled out into the cold night air.

He walked the short distance to the place where the transceiver was hidden. Ensuring no one was watching, he sat down beside it and placed a hand on it. The familiar blue glow started, followed close by the building hologram of his friend.

"Ahmahn." Evander said quietly.

"Any news?"

"No. Nothing yet. My brother, it's been a long time now. I think if they were going to report in, it would have happened by now."

"Haden, maybe." said Ahmahn. "But Broc? Nahm?. I won't believe it 'till I see the evidence."

"We're still looking. But there's a high probability that their transceivers have been damaged or destroyed. Their 'pingers' (black boxes) aren't transmitting, even though we've been sending out broadband prompts. Under these conditions there just isn't much we can do. Our technology may be advanced, but it does have its limitations. I'm sorry, but that's the truth."

Ahmahn sat quietly for some time.

Evander also was quiet. He thought back over the years, the centuries, they had been together. From the beginning he had been drawn to Ahmahn, yet he had never, until recently, been willing to reveal himself.

"Ahmahn, my dear friend. There is something I should tell you."

"Is it about my brothers?"

"No, my friend. It is about you and me.

"You have shared your entire life with me. You have confided, you have questioned, you have sought council, and have given it. And through all this time I have held back. Not because I had something to hide, but rather because I didn't want to taint our relationship.

"Ahmahn, my dearest friend. You and I are more alike than you realize. As your world crumbles around you, you are filled with despair. You question yourself, your motives, your decisions. You search within yourself, wondering if there was something you could have done differently which would have changed this outcome.

"But I tell you there is nothing you could have done, short of depriving your people of their right to choose for themselves what course they would take. You never attempted this, though I'm sure at times you longed to do so. I know this because I too have felt the same temptation.

"I too am the product of a failed culture. No one aboard the *Brighid* or any of the other ships knows this. I am one of a select few who have undergone trials such as those you have undergone.

"Remember Ardghal? How impressed you were with his insight, his compassion, his understanding? He too is like me, and like you. He has endured the collapse of his world. He has felt the anguish which you now feel. And out of that anguish has come a resolve. A resolve to be of help to others, that they might not have to endure the same."

"More than that. It was his seed which was implanted in my surrogate father. I am the fruit of his loins. Ardghal is my true father."

Ahmahn turned to look at the hologram. There was peace in his heart, as though some invisible burden had at last been lifted. Instinctively he had known all along that there was a connection between him and this man that went beyond the obvious, that transcended any relationship he had ever experienced.

"And I am your true son."

TERMINUM

"Father, there is one thing I would ask before we depart."

"What is that, my son?"

"There is a child, an infant. Her parents will not survive much longer. Her father asks that I take her away from this, this ending. Yes. He knows who I am. He knows of my beginning. He knows that I will soon depart. Never has he asked me to spare him or his wife. His thoughts are only for the welfare of his baby daughter."

"What will you do with her?"

"She must not know that I am to become a Procurator, like you, and like my grandfather, and his father before him.

"She will go to a couple who will raise her in love, in compassion, in the ways of truth."

"What will you call this child?"

"I will call her . . . *Dawn*."

REPORT FROM THE SITE
Axis: 72.625°
Radial Offset: +1.5° LINK: 625 x 1012
Optics Settings: 3-D (Infra-red optional secondary)
Phase Modulation: Standard Bandwidth: .001°
Compression Ratio: Maximum
Transmission follows:
(Viewer pans around and over, right to left; front to back.)
(Image data is compiled, compressed and transmitted via LINK.)

"Found in the rubble of an ancient stone structure. Adjacent to it is another object much degraded compared to the first. Both objects are identical in shape: roughly twelve inches wide, deep and long, and are a crystalline material."

(View tightens for close-up of inscriptions printed on each surface.)

"These glyphs show what appears to be a concise and repeated symbol structure indicative of a race that had become well advanced in the use of two-dimensional communication devices. The groupings, together with repeated use of specific symbols, as can be observed from scan analysis, will greatly aid our translation efforts.

"Planetary conditions remain stable, though no atmosphere is present to shield against meteor showers which have been prevalent. Risk levels associated with the most recent meteor bombardment have decreased sufficiently to allow for actual manned exploration, should it be deemed beneficial. The planet's orbit, though still decaying, has taken it out of the densest part of the debris field.

Archived records, though incomplete, suggest the debris field to be all that remains of the planet's moon.

"Though the condition of both artifacts is, by relative approximation, equal; the symbols seen on the nearer of the two retain a higher level of clarity. This may enhance our ability to determine the extent to which the now extinct race developed its communication skills beyond the standard three-dimensional process.

"Relative intelligence of this race was apparently well into abstract cognition with some attention to social organization, as is indicated by the close proximity of these objects to others found nearby. More data must be analyzed before any further definitive postulations can be brought forth.

"Elsewhere, work continues on analysis of the objects found inside several of these crystalline structures.

(View switches)

"It appears from initial inspection that the techniques used in the insertion process were relatively primitive, utilizing mechanical rather than molecular manipulation. The inhabitants of this planet apparently did not possess technology necessary to do otherwise.

"It is reasonable to assume, therefore, that the disc-shaped objects identified within the crystals may not retain their original structural integrity, owing to multi-environmental degradation caused by introduction of the aforementioned fractures. Physical reconfiguration, based upon material similarity and proximity at this level will not likely yield significant data. It is believed that these objects had shifted from their original positions sometime before the planet's seismic activity ceased. Additionally, the risk is great that physical repositioning of these artifacts may result in further degradation.

"Following is an holographic representation of the glyphs visible on the surface of the lesser degraded disc. Note: The power settings on the penetration scanners was set at lowest, so as not to further degrade the artifact."

----sperion. Conc----rations are still at criti---- -evels.

Hade- left this mor------ to search f--- survi---rs. Nahm ha- -ot been seen sinc- ---- d---- ago. I fear - will not la--- -he nigh-. Hope so---on- finds this. G---- bye. Bro-.

"Ground-penetration scans in the vicinity have revealed several rectilinear objects which appear to be in much better condition than the smaller ones shown in this transmission. Each object's dimensions appear to be consistent, approximately two by three by seven feet. Apparently they had been linearly aligned and buried some time before seismic activity ceased. Preliminary scans show no evidence of degradation of the exteriors to be present, as can be seen in the surface artifacts. However, owing to the depth at which the objects were found, the accuracy of our scans has yielded less than optimum data. Remote analysis of the container's interiors indicates decayed organic matter, which suggests these may be burial containers.

"The surface artifacts are crystallized, very similar to other objects found within the two-hundred-foot search area. We have identified numerous other sites similar to this one, scattered across much of the planet surface. Their circular patterns suggest that low altitude, high-order thermonuclear explosions caused the crystallizations.

"Wide-angle scans of the surface near by seem to indicate the one-time presence of several large pyramid-shaped structures located in relatively close proximity to each other. Their construction appears to have been composed of large cube-shaped stones fitted closely together and stacked one upon another. Numerous stones of similar shape have been found in the vicinity, suggesting a random but powerful redistribution prior to or during the planet's seismic period. However, since only the bottom three courses still remain in place, little can be determined regarding their original size or purpose. Similar structures have been located on the opposite side of the planet, though they are fewer in number and much smaller in size.

"Several burial plots have also been located a short distance from this research site. However, owing to the high degree of degradation, they have not yielded information significantly different from that obtained in other systems. Our most promising artifacts are those described in this report.

"Preliminary findings suggest that the inhabitants of this planet had made significantly greater technological advances than those of nearby systems, as evidenced by the quality of the artifacts thus-far discovered.

(See written and photo documentation attached)

"We are aware that previous missions here have yielded similar findings. Nonetheless, it is our recommendation, based on the quantity and quality of the artifacts thus far located, that an excavation team be dispatched to the surface to more effectively evaluate our findings.

"Orbits of the two inner-most planets remain relatively stable even though the star itself has recently entered the first stages of collapse. Data suggests that this planet's orbit will remain stable at least until the inner-most planet's orbit begins to decay.

"The exertion placed upon our scanning mechanisms continues to be a challenge, owing to our extreme distance from the planet, and its unstable magnetic field. Our technicians continue searching for more effective ways of gathering and processing data from the surface.

"Improvements in image quality continue to be a high priority for this mission. Should it be deemed of value, placement of a LINK closer to this system would likely improve the quality of our transmissions as well as provide more reliable data from our drones.

"The Cygnus Sector LINK appears to be beyond our reach. Numerous stars in its vicinity are nearing collapse. Their resulting electromagnetic instability degrades the LINK's ability to use them as positional locators. The risk/cost associated with resetting the LINK's program may outweigh its value in any salvage operation.

"However, if it becomes feasible to restore adequate control of this LINK, it may be possible to relocate it to the Orion arm long enough to facilitate collection of some representative artifacts.

"We await your decision."

Transmission Ends

www.ingramcontent.com/pod-product-compliance
Lightning Source LLC
Chambersburg PA
CBHW030133060726
47499CB00014B/22